From THE Wings

A NOVEL OF WOMEN AT WAR

D1366694

Also by Jeri Fitzgerald Board:

The Bed She Was Born In (2006)

Praise for The Bed She Was Born In:

"Jeri Fitzgerald Board has written a sweeping, important book which illuminates the lives of Southern women, black and white, as they struggle with the harsh realities of sex, race, class, and history. Yet this novel brims with life and love on every page. The Bed She Was Born In is a remarkable achievement—and a great read!"

—Lee Smith, Author of Fair and Tender Ladies and Family Linen

"Over the last few years, a new writing genre known as 'historical consciousness' has emerged, and Southern women have seized the baton in this arena. In The Bed She Was Born In, Jeri Fitzgerald Board gives us a tale of courage and endurance, but with a wry sense of humor, and a writing style so stripped of the superfluous that she moves action along as fast as Hemingway—and then clobbers you with a completely unexpected turn of events. This novel could be the companion piece to W.H. Auden's Any Girl, but it could also be the story of your wife, mother, sister, lover. It is not to be missed."

—John H. Roper, Historian, and Author of
Repairing the March of Mars:
The Civil War Diaries of a Steward in the Stonewall Brigade

"This is a book you could live in. This means even after you know how the story turns out, you'll want to read it again and again. Get a copy of The Bed She Was Born In. Read it. This is a book to live in."

—Schuyler Kaufman, Book Nook

Nominated for the Pulitzer Prize for Fiction, and for the PEN/Faulkner Award for Fiction; Finalist for the Southern Independent Booksellers Alliance Award for Fiction; and, the 2007 winner of the President's Award of the North Carolina Society of Historians.

The Bed She Was Born In is available on AMAZON.com

From THE Wings

A NOVEL OF WOMEN AT WAR

Jeri Fitzgerald Board

ISBN-13: 978-1986277396

Printed by CreateSpace

Book design by Aaron Burleson, Spokesmedia

This book is dedicated to London native,

Sybil Chirgwin
(1919-2012)

and to the millions of women like her world-wide,
who risked their lives to protect others during
history's greatest conflict.

While this work contains many references
to actual people and events, the stories and
characters herein are entirely the product of the
author's imagination.

From the Wings would not have been possible
without the excellent editing skills of Dawn
Shamp; the creative designs of Aaron Burleson,
Spokesmedia; and, the insightful suggestions
and support of Kathleen Wright, Frances Flynn,
Connie Clark, and Warren Board.

CONTENTS

From THE Wings

A NOVEL OF WOMEN AT WAR

CHAPTER 1

Amid the Ruins

London, England • December 4, 1941

I'm not sure when this story began. Perhaps it started when I moved to New York and made a name for myself on Broadway. Maybe it started with the emerald and diamond ring and dreams of life in a vine-covered cottage far from the city. Regardless of its bright beginnings, it took a sharp turn in the summer of 1940 when the Nazis marched down the Champs-Élysées. It wasn't long before I found myself shivering in a compartment on the boat train from Southampton to London. Inside the dim interior of that cold black-curtained cubicle, I hoisted my suitcase onto the rack above my seat and settled down across from the proverbial *handsome stranger*. A circumstance, a setting, a companion I could not have imagined just one week before.

The man sitting across from me was deeply engrossed in a stack of papers. His wavy dark hair, graying slightly at the temples, was brushed back from a pink flush that crowned well-defined cheeks. Even at a glance I knew he'd been blessed with what my mother called boyish good looks.

After a moment, he looked up and thrust a slender, manicured hand across the aisle. "Please pardon me for not getting up," he said, giving me a friendly smile. "Stoney Beeton-Howard. You're American, aren't you?"

I smiled back and extended my hand, leaning forward to grasp his. "Evelyn Sanderson. Why do you think I'm American?"

"Those beautiful white teeth, for one thing, and your new shoes. None of your clothes appear mended. I'd say you're very well turned out." He pointed to his own shoes. Although they showed good care, the heels were worn and the toes scuffed. "New shoes are all but impossible to get in England these days. I hope you've brought several pairs. You were on the *Althone,* weren't you? Is this your first visit?"

I removed my hand, reluctant to be done with the warmth of his fingers and wishing I could put them around my freezing ankles. "Yes, I was on the *Althone,* but this isn't my first visit. My mother and sister and I came here several years ago and our cousin, who was living in Surry at the time, took us on a wonderful train trip all over. Seeing your country is like looking at a series of beautiful postcards."

"You're from the South, aren't you? I would venture somewhere near the coast by your accent."

"Oh, my. You have a good ear, Mr. Beeton-Howard. I've lived and worked in New York for the past eleven years, but I grew up on the coastal plain of North Carolina in a little town called Baker. My mother lives there still. Have you been to America?"

"Yes," he answered as he pulled open the black attaché at his feet and stuffed the stack of papers into it. "I've crossed the Atlantic several times for business meetings in New York and Washington. I don't mean to appear rude, Miss Sanderson, but London is in ruins. Why would you choose to come here now?"

"To join the Red Cross. I want to lend a hand if I can."

Mr. Beeton-Howard looked at me as if I'd lost my mind. He was quiet for a moment and when he spoke again his voice was hardly more than a whisper. "An idealist. How refreshing. If only there were more of you in this world. We need you ever so badly these days, Miss Sanderson. I cannot tell you how much I appreciate the fact that you've come all this way to help us. It won't be easy, you know."

"I've led a fairly comfortable life and had the support of a loving family. Plenty to eat, warm clothing, that sort of thing. It's time for me to give something in return. And I decided this is the place because I really enjoyed being here so much when I was young. I haven't forgotten the people I met and how kind they were to me."

"Well, you've had a long night, so you might want to rest up before we reach London. Once you arrive, we'll put you to work 'round the clock and your kind intentions will be swallowed up by long hours on the job. I don't think people realize how much work there is to do here." He bent to pull a brown envelope from his attaché. "I promise to be quiet now and tend to my business." Pushing the cuff of his sleeve back, he glanced at a thin, silver watch. "Maybe you can manage forty winks before we reach the station."

I removed the wool hat I was wearing, leaned back against my seat, and while I tried to picture myself in a Red Cross uniform, the *clack, clack, clack* of the train's wheels played a soothing rhythm that put me to sleep.

I awoke to find Mr. Beeton-Howard kneeling on the floor in front of me, his hand on my shoulder. "You were crying in your sleep," he said. "When you began kicking, I decided to wake you. You must have had a bad dream."

Yes, I thought, a horrible dream. The tall man in the white suit pointing a gun, coming closer and closer . . . the same man who'd frightened me so badly when I'd happened upon him in the hold of the *Althone.* Squeezing my eyes shut, I forced that dreadful image from my mind, blurted a quick *thank you* to Mr. Beeton-Howard, and sat up. My fingers shook as I grabbed at the tail of my skirt and tried to straighten it while he continued staring at me. "You're awfully pale," he concluded before he rose from the floor and returned to his seat.

I wanted to say something, wanted to tell him how scared I'd been by what I'd witnessed in the ship's hold. Talk about being in the wrong place at the wrong time! I wanted to let this stranger know how much I'd appreciated his kindness there on the train. But all I'd managed was a weak *thank you* as we rumbled beneath the glass dome of Paddington Station.

There was a knock on the door of the compartment and a conductor opened it just slightly to tell us that, due to wartime exigencies, there would be a slight delay disembarking. I pulled back the dark curtains beside me and stared through the glass at a bleak concrete landscape where hundreds of servicemen stood in line behind a half dozen metal gates. Long and tall, short and squat, fair and dark, all were waiting—some for trains and others for coffee and doughnuts at a nearby Red Cross canteen. That's what I'll be doing, I thought, as I leaned toward the glass to get a better look. I'll be on duty in one of those Red Cross boxes morning, noon, and night.

I turned back to find Stoney Beeton-Howard smiling at me. Not a big smile, but a knowing one. His brown eyes, the color of rich brandy, seemed brighter, the perfect shade to complement his dark hair. He held my gaze for a moment longer, straightened the sheaf of papers on his lap, and stuffed them back into his case. Then he stood up, pulled on his coat, and said, "I pray Merry Olde England will be everything you expect, Miss Sanderson. I'm afraid you won't find it very merry these days. But, by Jove, you'll certainly have the opportunity to help. Just look at those poor boys out there, ready to board this train and take what might well be the last ride of their young lives."

I turned to the window again and focused on a small group of soldiers who were laughing and poking at one another, their carefree gestures testimony to innocent youth. "God help them," I whispered.

The door to the compartment opened again and the conductor made a slight bow to Mr. Beeton-Howard. "You may depart now, sir."

"First things first," my companion said. Before I could get up, he reached above my head and brought down my suitcase.

When he opened the outside door, a rush of frigid damp air swooped under my skirt.

"Thank goodness I brought these fur-lined gloves," I said, jerking them on. I bent to grab the handle of my suitcase, but Mr. Beeton-Howard insisted on taking it. I followed him down the platform steps onto a gritty floor where the air reeked of cheap hair tonic, engine oil, and its kissing cousin, coal dust. Laid over all was the unmistakable stench of creeping anxiety.

Soon we were struggling through a throng of servicemen and teary-eyed women. Mr. Beeton-Howard politely made his way among them and I followed behind, my eyes furtively searching the khaki-clad group for the tall man in the white suit.

A gate opened just ahead and a uniformed chauffeur came toward us. "Good morning, my lord," he said, touching a fingertip to the edge of his elegant cap. I stumbled to a stop and my mouth dropped open as *my lord* turned to me. "May I offer you a lift, Miss Sanderson? I'm afraid you'll not get a cab this time of night."

"That's . . . that's very kind of you," I stammered. "Thank you, but I'm being met by someone." I looked beyond my lord's maroon Bentley to a maze of trucks, vans, and cars. "At least, I think I am."

"We shall wait here, Rutledge," he told the chauffeur. "I want to be sure Miss Sanderson has a ride. It's just too dangerous, otherwise." He glanced back at me again. "Won't you at least sit in my car where you'll be warm?"

"I think I'd better stay here near the gates in case someone comes. I'll just look at my instructions one more time. I'm sure they said that someone from the London office would meet me here at Paddington."

I fumbled with my bulging purse and removed the letter I'd read a dozen times. My lord's chauffeur was immediately at my side holding a small flashlight. I opened the airmail envelope, now worn at the corners and smudged with my fingerprints, and scanned the letter written on cream-colored stationery with a red cross at the top.

Dear Miss Sanderson: It is my pleasure to inform you that you've been accepted in the Red Cross. Although your application and resume have not yet arrived (mail from abroad arrives very slowly these days), we feel confident that your comprehensive letter of inquiry has provided us with ample information to allow you to serve.

You are to report to our main offices on Grosvenor Square between the hours of 8:00 and 10:00 a.m. as soon as convenient. You have been assigned duty with the London Hospitality Unit.

It is our understanding that you will disembark **HMS Althone** *at Southampton the afternoon of December 3 and take the boat train to London. A member of our staff will meet you at Paddington Station. We are pleased to have you as part of our organization.*

Sincerely,
Theodore Lowe, Director

I folded the letter and, as I slipped it back inside my purse, Lord Beeton-Howard asked, "Is there anything I can do to help? I fear it will begin sleeting any moment and I wouldn't want you to be stuck here tonight in this freezing old tomb."

"I think I should wait until someone comes from the Red Cross because I don't know where I'm supposed to go. They didn't tell me anything beyond the fact that someone would meet me here at Paddington. They thought I would be here this afternoon, but we were so late arriving I'm sure they must have given up on me."

"Well, I have an idea of where you're to be billeted for the night and Rutledge and I will take you there. It's an old warehouse that's been converted to an overnight station for new recruits. Come along and rest assured that all is well."

At that point, Rutledge stepped up and took my suitcase from Lord Beeton-Howard. "What about my trunk?" I asked. "Shouldn't we take it?"

While Rutledge put my suitcase in the boot of the car, Lord Beeton Howard opened the back door and ushered me in. "Your trunk will be collected by RC staff and delivered to whatever boardinghouse you're assigned. No need to worry. You'll get it."

We made our way out of the parking lot and crept through the darkened streets skirting numerous wooden barricades, jogging in and out of head-high piles of broken stone, smashed window frames, and discarded furnishings at every turn. Uniformed men, whom I assumed were Defence (spelled with a "c" here) Wardens, stood holding flashlights amid the ruins. As we approached, they threw a thin beam into the back of the car, nodded to Lord Beeton-Howard, and waved us on.

I stared out the window and my heart sank when I saw an open horizon where elegant multi-storied buildings had once stood. Now they were nothing but endless piles of rubble. As we slowly drove past the burnt-out shell of St Paul's Cathedral, tears sprang to my eyes and I quickly settled back against the seat determined to look straight ahead. What horrors Londoners must have faced during the Blitz, I thought . . . bombs raining down, ear-piercing screams from fighter planes, monstrous fires racing from one building to another, killing thousands. As images of this roiling Hell began to take shape in my mind, I realized how little I knew of what the British had been up against night after night while I'd slept peacefully in my comfortable bed safe in New York.

I turned to Lord Beeton-Howard. "I don't think people back home know just how bad things are here. I certainly didn't. I guess it just isn't possible to convey this kind of incredible destruction on an ordinary newsreel."

My companion cleared his throat before he spoke. "Most Americans don't understand. But we really cannot blame them. They've no experience with this sort of thing, at least not since your Civil War. But we're very fortunate to have thousands of Americans here serving in our military and auxiliary forces, as I'm sure you know. Tell me, Miss Sanderson, what does your family do in Baker?"

"Well, my father was a banker, but he lost the bank back in '33. Then he lost the textile mill he owned, too. He died two weeks ago, quite suddenly, just before Thanksgiving. His younger brother, my Uncle Robert, has somehow managed to hold onto the only remaining family business, a general store. My Uncle Robert and his wife, Aunt Hephzibah, are very dear to me. My mother, Anna Sanderson, still lives in the house where I was born. She's trying desperately to hold on to it. Just before I left New York, she told me she'd rented my old bedroom to a nurse who'd come to town to take a job and had nowhere to live. I'm very relieved that someone will be there with my mother at night. She and Maddie, her housekeeper and cook, are starting a lunch business for local merchants in our dining room. Maddie is married to Fletcher . . . Fletcher Sanders. He runs Sand Hill . . . that's our farm. It's out in the country about two miles from Baker. My mother is sixty years old and what she's had to deal with over the last few years would have sacked most people her age, but she's indomitable. Both she and Maddie are great cooks and Fletcher grows all sorts of wonderful vegetables at the farm, so I'm sure their lunch trade will be a success." I paused, afraid my companion might be bored by my chatter. But he kept looking at me, so I went on.

"I have an older sister, Claire, who lives in Huntington Beach, California where she works for Consolidated Aircraft. She used to teach school, but she makes more money now building airplanes. She and her husband have two young boys, ages eleven and thirteen."

I was just about to ask Lord Beeton-Howard if he had any children, but before I could, Rutledge made a sharp turn into an alley alongside an old brick building. Everything was dark as pitch and there was no evidence of life save comforting plumes of smoke rising from matching chimneys on either end. Lord Beeton-Howard helped me out of the car, and as we started up the steps, the door in front of us opened and a woman wearing a belted overcoat and fur-trimmed boots stuck her head out.

"I'm terribly sorry to be so late," I began.

She didn't bother to look at me, but focused her attention on Rutledge who was standing in the drive beside the Bentley. Then she spotted the man behind me. "Oh, my goodness," she exclaimed. "Lord Beeton-Howard! What in the world . . ."

"Good evening, Miss Reynolds," he said, removing his hat. "Allow me to present Miss Evelyn Sanderson of Baker, North Carolina, a new Red Cross volunteer. The boat train from Southampton was very late and Miss Sanderson wasn't sure where to go. So I brought her here knowing you'd take good care of her. This is the place, isn't it?"

"Yes, it is. Thank you, sir. We sent someone to Paddington this afternoon, but they were told the train would not arrive until tomorrow morning." She shook her head and began to laugh. "I suppose it *is* tomorrow morning, isn't it?"

She gave me a quick glance and said, "I'm Marjorie Reynolds, your supervisor. Then she lifted her hand and waved good-bye to my companion. "Thank you ever so much, Lord Beeton-Howard, for your kind assistance. I'll see that Miss Sanderson is comfortably situated for the night."

She closed the door behind us, and I followed her down a dark hallway to a large room where hundreds of women were sleeping on cots spaced about two feet apart. "The only bath is right outside the door we just came in," she said. "Here's a torch in case you lose your way." She thrust a flashlight into the pocket of my coat. "Try to get some sleep, Miss

Sanderson. I know you must be weary from your journey. Breakfast, such as it is, is at seven o'clock. But these women," she swept an arm from one side of the room to the other, "will be up long before that. There are only four sinks and four toilets available for all of us, you see."

"That one is yours," she whispered, pointing to an empty cot at the end of a row. "As soon as you get settled in the morning, we'll take a little walk around the neighborhood so you can get your bearings before you report to HQ. By the way, your papers have not yet arrived, but I don't think that will be a problem," she mused, giving me a quick nod. Then she tiptoed her way back to the hall, leaving me on my own.

There were no sheets on the cot, but I found a lumpy pillow and a shabby comforter. I stooped to open my suitcase and hunted around in the bottom until I located a pair of wool socks that I put on as soon as I'd removed my shoes. Grabbing the sides of my hat, I jerked it down over my ears. Then I lay down on a narrow stretch of canvas that stank of mildew and old tobacco and hauled the thread-bare covering over me.

As I huddled there shivering in that godforsaken place, my mind raced through a jumble of regret. Why had I done such a foolhardy thing as coming to England in December? What had possessed me to abandon my career. . . forsake my lover. . . desert my family? My brain kept jumping back to the days just before I'd left New York, to a phone conversation I'd had with my mother when she'd begged me not to go, begged me to reconsider, begged me to come home to Baker for Christmas. But I hadn't listened to her because I'd desperately wanted to put some space between me and my recent past. Well, you've certainly done that, I thought, drawing myself into a tight little ball against the cold. Here you are in the dead of night surrounded by women you don't know, longing for the women you love. I pictured my mother and Maddie at home shelling pecans in front of a cozy fire as they talked about the dishes they'd be making for the holidays. How I longed to be there with them, to hear their gentle voices, to feel the warmth of the fire, and know that all would be well. I balled up my fist and punched the poor excuse for a pillow before I gave in to an overwhelming exhaustion. But the moment I closed my eyes the tall man in the white suit appeared, and the fear I'd felt as I'd crouched in the *Althone's* hold grabbed my gut. I knew I was in for another sleepless night.

CHAPTER 2

RC Skirts

London, England • December 8, 1941

Dearest Mama,

Pearl Harbor? What's Pearl Harbor? That's the question I've been asked by my Red Cross colleagues over and over, and I had to find a map of the Pacific to see for myself just where those godforsaken ships were anchored. I had no idea that our Pacific fleet was in the Hawaiian Islands and was just as surprised as everyone here to learn that the Japanese had attacked us at a place called Pearl Harbor. Red Cross personnel were told to report to headquarters at eight o'clock tonight, and when we arrived we learned that we'd been called together to hear the BBC's broadcast of President Roosevelt's address to Congress. As soon as FDR asked for a declaration of war against Japan, the room around me burst into applause. Everyone was so thrilled by this news they started laughing and dancing around slapping each other on the back. I've not been here long, Mama, but I've seen enough of what London looks like to understand their reaction. Afterward, we heard that Japanese planes had attacked US ships only a hundred miles west of San Francisco Bay. I'm sure Claire and Charles, and everybody living in California, must be wondering are we next?

I hope you got the brief letter I wrote to you from the HMS Althone. I finally arrived in London very early in the morning on December 4 and have been so busy with my new job that this is the first opportunity I've had to sit down and write a _real_ letter to you. I'm settled into what may be my permanent quarters, where I share a second-floor room in a boardinghouse that is the front half of what used to be an elegant Georgian manse. Thanks to the Luftwaffe, the back half no longer exists and all the windows on that side are covered with boards. There are black-out curtains over all the windows and I wonder if I will ever become accustomed to the gloom. Fortunately, it's located on a quiet street in the southwest section of Bloomsbury with a tube station nearby and I plan to walk to Red Cross HQ (about three quarters of a mile) when the weather allows. My landlady, Mrs. Denora Sutcliffe (whom everyone calls "Ma Denny") worked for the Red Cross during the last war, so she knows the ropes and has been very kind helping me get situated.

I know you must be wondering about the crossing, and I want to assure you that all went well even though I did not sail on the SS Stockholm as planned. Just after I talked with you the Tuesday morning before Thanksgiving, a woman called from the Red Cross office in NYC and told me a single cabin had become available on the HMS Althone, a transport ship that sometimes carries new RC recruits at a rate much less expensive than the Stockholm. I intended to write to you from the ship to explain all of this, but the first morning at sea I awoke with a sore throat and low-grade fever, which I blamed on all the stress surrounding Daddy's sudden passing, the funeral, etc., and the fact that you were left high and dry with not a penny to see you through. Thank goodness the ship's stewards, and several other RC recruits who were aboard, checked on me and brought me warm drinks and extra blankets. After a few days, I was right as rain. I think I just needed some rest.

Despite rough seas, things went well schedule-wise until we reached the harbor at Southampton. There, everything was chaos! You've never seen such crowds—thousands of soldiers milling about. A steward told me that they were waiting to board two destroyers hidden in coves at the mouth of the River Hamble, and that the boarding could not begin until it was dark. So those of us who'd been aboard the Althone had to wait almost two hours to board the boat train. It was midnight when we finally reached London and I was very disappointed that I did not get to see the countryside on the way in. I shared a compartment with a nice man, Lord Beeton-Howard.

I've been assigned duty with the London RC Hospitality Unit. (My papers have not yet arrived and _I've deliberately not told anyone here that I trained as a nurse._ I just don't feel comfortable doing that, Mama, as I have so little experience.). With my job, I'll help organize and host all the holiday events planned for the troops, and will be delivering coffee and doughnuts to them from the back of a van a couple days a week, and also visiting servicemen in local hospitals where I'll write letters for them, read aloud, shave them, etc. My uniform is brown with beige trim. Over the blouse, we wear a blue knit "jumper," (sort of like a pullover vest) that has a big red cross on the bust. We were given a set of dog tags just like the soldiers wear, and a gas mask in a little square cardboard box with a string handle. The soldiers and sailors call us "RC skirts."

It was gray and blustery this morning, but not snowing, so I walked to work with several colleagues from the boardinghouse. This was my first opportunity to be out and about in the city. Never have I seen so many uniforms. I just hope I can remember what uniform goes with what organization!

Lorries were everywhere, most of them military, and jeeps, cars, and a few cabs moving about. All of the red double-decker buses have been painted gray! The most popular mode of transportation seems to be the bicycle, as petrol is rationed so severely. We encountered thousands of people on their way to work in the War Offices at Whitehall, or the city offices further up, or factories and shops . . . all of us ducking around piles of sand bags everywhere. Most everyone here is thin and rather pale, as you would expect. God help them, they have been through so much. All along our route women were lined up waiting at the butcher's, the green grocer's, etc. You've got to be out early to try to get what you need because there won't be anything left by ten o'clock. I saw bins of potatoes, onions, turnips, and Brussels sprouts, but hardly any meat, and what little I saw was full of bones and gristle.

The only populace that seems to be thriving here is the rats! They're big and furry thanks to an unlimited supply of refuse—and very bold. One especially large monster skittered across the floor in front of me last night as I was returning from the kitchen.

London is a changed city, Mama, and I don't think either of us has seen a newsreel at home that conveyed the incredible damage done here. Rubble, rubble, rubble piled as high as the roof of a house! And sandbags by the millions, all stacked up to the top of the first floor of every building that's still standing. Remember all the lights at Piccadilly Circus and the fun we had there? Well, they are no more. There are no lights anywhere! Everything is as *dark as a tomb! Headlights on cars are taped to allow just a tiny half-inch beam. There is a strict curfew in place and no one is allowed to be on the streets at night except air raid wardens and emergency personnel.*

RC headquarters occupies a beautiful three-story stone building with a commanding façade. Larger-than-life ornamental lions sit on either side of a sweeping set of marble stairs that lead up to a double-door entry. (It reminds me of the New York Public Library.) When I arrived at reception, I was met by my supervisor, Marjorie Reynolds, who gave me a tour of the building that included the location of all the staff loos (restrooms), the general offices, the supply room from which we stock our vans, the kitchen, and the mess (cafeteria). Then, Marjorie took me around the neighborhood and showed me how to get to the nearest tube (subway) station, a nice little dispensary (grocery store), the chemist's (drugstore), and a newsstand where I can pick up the local version of fish-and-chips in a paper cone, and a copy of the New York Times or the Herald-Tribune.

We went back to HQ and immediately down to the supply room where she put me to work making eight, four-gallon urns of coffee. While it was brewing, I helped my partner, Grace Walton, load the van. There are built-in shelves in back that hold boxes of cups, as well as lots of bags of sugar and dry milk, cartons of cigarettes and gum, and all those doughnuts. You've never seen so many doughnuts! Grace told me that I was given the best shift, as they like to break in new recruits on a regular daytime schedule. She said that at the end of the week I'll be put on twenty-four-hour duty and will have to be ready to go at all hours, including the 4:00 a.m. shift (Ugh!), because the ships that bring the poor boys back from the front come in at all hours, day and night.

As soon as we finished loading the van, we set out and arrived at the docks in time to take over from an earlier RC crew. The wounded are always brought down the gangway first, put into ambulances, and taken to various hospitals. Then the ambulatory soldiers disembark. Those I saw this morning were covered with mud and stank to high heaven of greasy smoke. They told us they had been very near a large fuel explosion where many had been horribly burned . . . very sobering. Grace and I had planned to play some Glenn Miller as we served the doughnuts and coffee, but we changed our minds when we saw those poor burned boys. One youngster from Yorkshire told me that his best friend had been killed in the explosion, and another from somewhere in Wales said that his buddy had had his leg blown off. But they ate like wolves, having not had anything to eat for the past sixteen hours, and nothing before that except cold C rations. All were anxious to get back to camp, get cleaned up, and find a hot meal and a cot. They were exhausted, poor darlings.

My roommate at the boardinghouse is from a little town in southern New Jersey. Her name is Ida and her family raises vegetables for markets in New York, Newark, and Philadelphia. She's about twenty-two, is a second-generation Italian-American, and cute as a button. She works in the cafeteria at HQ. Ours is the biggest bedroom in the house and each of us has a twin bed and a dresser to ourselves. We share a wardrobe that has a mirror on the door and a washstand with a bowl and pitcher. There is a little gas heater with a coin slot on top. The bathroom is at the end of the hall and there are four other women here who share it with us. We are allowed only one bath per week. Ma Denny served us a bowl of porridge this morning. No milk or cream, but we each got a spoonful of honey on a piece of bread with a mug of what passes for coffee here. The girls call it roast chicory, but it might as well have been warmed over dishwater . . . just awful!

As promised, I brought along six large composition notebooks and have already begun to fill them. I wrote nine pages last night! You were right, Mama, to remind me to do this. Years from now, I'm sure I'll be glad I did, so that I can recall the details of my life and work here, not to mention the people I'll want to remember.

I must close now and get my once-a-week bath, (there's a green line painted in the tub to remind us not to exceed the regulation five inches of water), wash my hair, (every place I go someone compliments me on my "beautiful auburn hair") and do my nails because I won't have time to do these things next week while I'm on duty. Our unit is hosting a big Christmas bash this Wednesday, December 10 for anyone in uniform stationed in London, be they Brits, Americans, Czechs, Poles, Australians, etc. Thousands of foreigners, as you know, are serving here. Because I'm new, I've been assigned the task of "official hostess" that evening (along with nine other greenhorns) so we can meet as many people as possible. They say the band that's playing is terrific, so you know I'm looking forward to that.

Mama, I've never been "called" to anything before in my life. I've always jumped headlong into things that I thought would be fun. But I feel that I've truly been called to this work. Remember how I used to play dress-up in your RC uniform? You've always been my inspiration and you know full well that I've tried to be like you. I intend to do my best so you'll be proud of me.

I know you're staying as busy as possible to help keep your mind off all that has happened during the last few weeks. While Daddy could be a very demanding and unreasonable man, you and he had a long, successful marriage and I'm sure here at Christmas you're feeling his absence more keenly. And my being so far away isn't helping. When you go to Sand Hill to visit his grave, say a little prayer for him from me.

Please give my love and warmest Christmas wishes to Aunt Hepsi and Uncle Robert, to Maddie and Fletcher, and to Claire and all her family. I'll try to get a letter off to her before this week is out. I miss all of you so much and can't wait to hear from you. I know you are praying for peace, Mama, as I am every single day. I just hope my work here will help make it come sooner rather than later.

All my love to you,
Evelyn

CHAPTER 3

Keeping Up Morale

London, England • December 10, 1941

A tall, pretty brunette, who looked as if she'd been poured into the orchid-colored sheath she was wearing, was warming up at the mike when my roommate, Ida, and I walked into the large reception room at Red Cross headquarters on Grosvenor's Square. Garlands of fresh juniper and big red bows had been hung on the four mantles of that huge room which was redolent with the smells of Christmas I remembered so well—new-cut cedar and fresh baked cookies.

Someone handed us name tags decorated with a red cross in the left corner and a green star on the right to indicate our freshman status. Marjorie Reynolds appeared from nowhere and led us right back out the front door. "You girls stay here," she said, "and shake the hand of every man and woman who shows up. And give each of them a big smile. We want our guests to feel welcomed. I'll be back in a little while to relieve you. Have fun!"

Dozens of uniformed men and women started up the steps. Soon, there were hundreds—Army, Navy, Wrens, RAF, ATS, military nurses—all smiling at the prospect of a fun-filled evening. I kept scanning the crowd looking for the tall man in the white suit wondering if I'd recognize him if he showed up in khaki or dark blue instead of white. In the background, I could hear the opening notes of "Don't Sit Under the Apple Tree" and the girl in the orchid gown began crooning, her alto with a style that reminded me of

Jo Stafford. I began to hum along and soon the image of the man in the white suit faded.

About an hour later, Marjorie finally returned and brought two other recruits to take over our jobs. Ida and I stopped for a cup of punch on our way into the ballroom but didn't get to drink it. Two RAF officers presented themselves and quickly spouted their names, rank and unit. Without further introductions, they whirled us onto the floor. The singer blew a wooden whistle and shouted, "Pardon me, boy!" and we were off on a trip on the "Chattanooga Choo-Choo." Not a word was spoken, not a single foot was still, until the band slowed things down with "Moonlight Becomes You." That's when Marjorie Reynolds came over and interrupted my partner and me.

"You simply cannot monopolize the major," she said as she took me by the hand and pulled me away. "He's such a good dancer. Now, give the other girls a chance, Miss Sanderson." I reluctantly followed her out of the room into a hallway where she turned and said, "Sorry. I did that on purpose. There are some people who want to meet you."

She took me to a comfortable back room where four officers were seated around a gaming table drinking highballs and playing cards. All were on their feet the moment we walked in. Medals and ribbons gleamed from their tunics, and I knew immediately that they were older than the boys on the dance floor. Marjorie pushed me forward. "This is one of our new hospitality recruits," she said. "Gentlemen, meet Evelyn Sanderson."

Each shook my hand and politely said hello. Two were British, one was Australian, and one American. Marjorie motioned me toward an empty chair and went around to the other side of the table where she sat down between the two British officers. "Well, Colonel Morgan," she said, one eyebrow lifted toward the American, "is she who you think she is?"

The American officer, who was sitting on my right, turned and gave me a sheepish grin. "Aren't you Eve Sands,

21

the Broadway actress? I saw you onstage two or three years ago. I'm sorry to be so . . . so forward, Miss Sands. But I told Miss Reynolds that when I saw you at the entrance tonight, I was sure it was you. Am I right?"

I nodded and quickly looked down at my lap so they wouldn't see disappointment on my face. I'd come to England hoping to be a stranger in a strange land. I'd hoped to live the life of a regular kind of gal doing her duty for the troops. I'd hoped no one would recognize me.

Colonel Morgan cleared his throat. "Forgive me, Miss Sands," he said. "This is my fault. You see, I asked Miss Reynolds who you were, and if you were from North Carolina. She told me you were Evelyn Sanderson from Baker, so I asked her to invite you back here for a few minutes. I'm from a little town called Horse Bluff in the hills of Virginia. It's near Staunton, but I doubt you've ever heard of it."

"No, I haven't. But I can tell by your accent that you're not from New York."

Everyone at the table laughed at my little joke, including Colonel Morgan. "I'm afraid my motives for wanting to meet you, Miss Sands, are not based solely on our shared Southern roots. I had something else in mind. You see, the five of us," he raised his right hand and motioned toward his companions, "along with one other gentleman, make up the entertainment committee for the London office of the Red Cross. We're always looking for talented people to help keep up morale. And when I saw you at the door tonight, I recognized you instantly. You're just wonderful onstage, Miss Sands . . . so dynamic and engaging. Won't you please consider doing something, a song-and-dance routine maybe, for one of our upcoming events? We'd be ever so grateful, and the troops will adore you, just like the audiences at home."

Before I could answer, I heard a door open behind me, then softly close. Colonel Morgan turned around. "Well, here's our errant committee member now," he said. I looked over my shoulder and saw Lord Beeton-Howard coming toward the table. I was caught completely off guard, as he'd said nothing to me about his having any association with the Red Cross.

My lord gave us a bow and took a moment to remove the heavy wool cape he was wearing over formal evening clothes. I glanced at my watch and saw that it was a quarter of eleven and assumed he'd had an earlier commitment. The men at the table rose in unison and I followed. "I'm so sorry to be late," he said, shaking hands with each of them. He bent over the back of my hand, kissed it, and said, "What a pleasure it is to see you again, Miss Sands."

We all sat down again and Colonel Morgan told Lord Beeton-Howard how he'd recognized me when he'd arrived at HQ and that he'd asked me if I would consider singing at a future Red Cross event. Lord Beeton-Howard nodded. "Capital, capital," he said. "That's a smashing idea!"

Lord Beeton-Howard hadn't been present during our earlier conversation, but it was obvious he'd known what had been said. Why else would he have called me Miss Sands? I glanced at him as he spoke again to Colonel Morgan. "Perhaps we should have an article in the *Times* announcing this wonderful news."

I leaned into the table and addressed Colonel Morgan. "Please don't," I begged. "Please don't put anything in the newspaper. I'm here to do a job and I want to be known as a good worker, not an entertainer."

Colonel Morgan nodded at me and rose from the table. "Thank you, Miss Sands, for considering our request. I'm sure we'll all look forward to whatever you decide to do. It's late and I must go. Duty calls." The other gentlemen said good night and followed the colonel out the door. Marjorie accompanied them.

Lord Beeton-Howard turned to me. "Might I have a dance before you go, Miss Sands? It seems such a shame to waste all that wonderful music." We entered the ballroom just as the musicians began "I'll Never Smile Again." Lord

Beeton-Howard was a fine dancer, smooth and graceful, and I asked him where he'd learned.

"In school," he replied. "Ballroom dancing was a required course of study when I was at Harrow. And you, where did you learn, Miss Sands?"

"Please call me Evelyn, sir. My mother taught me. She's a marvelous dancer, and she and my father always looked the perfect pair on the dance floor."

The band broke into the jive rhythm of "Beat Me Daddy, Eight to the Bar" and my lord flung me into a spin and brought me crashing back into his arms, all but taking the breath out of me. We whirled and swirled across the floor for a couple of minutes, both of us sporting goofy grins while we worked up enough of a sweat to ruin my lord's fancy dress shirt. I could see he was enjoying himself, so I took the lead and started truckin' back and forth, my right hand making circling motions high above my head. Lord Beeton-Howard followed suit, and soon the couples who'd been sharing the floor with us moved back to form a circle. They clapped and hooted encouragement as we put on a show. When the music finally came to an end, I was pretty much done in.

We sat out the next one at a table, talking quietly over cups of punch. Things were winding down and soon everyone would go home to a cold flat, or perhaps to night duty or the graveyard shift in a hospital. I looked at the man I'd met on the train and said, "I've enjoyed seeing you again, Lord Beeton-Howard. Thank you for asking me to dance."

"The pleasure was mine, Miss Sands. My friends call me Stoney and I'd appreciate it if you'd consider me a friend. And I'd appreciate it even more if you'd have lunch with me tomorrow. Are you assigned a specific time for lunch at work?"

"I rarely get to eat lunch at work, Stoney. We're much too busy in the middle of the day to eat. But tomorrow is my first day off and while I've a million errands, I could meet you somewhere if you'd like."

CHAPTER 4

Dark L Syndrome

London, England • December 11, 1941

I dressed with care the next morning to be sure I'd stay warm. The weather had taken a turn for the worse, so I wore an old, but cozy, green cashmere sweater and wool skirt to lunch. A fine snow was falling as I hurried toward the tube station in my thick-soled boots, felt hat, and fur-lined gloves. When I arrived in the lobby of the Savoy Grille, I was surprised to see Stoney standing near the entrance talking with a man I thought I recognized. When I realized who the man was and where I'd seen him, my heart skipped a beat, and I slipped behind the corner of the coat station and stayed out of sight until he'd gone. Then I eased out into the passageway, handed my coat to the attendant, and followed the headwaiter to the table where Stoney was waiting.

While I was being seated, he rose from his chair and asked if I minded if he ordered for us. I smiled and told him I'd be delighted. The special of the day was steak and kidney pie, a kind of stew in a pastry, served with a salad of escarole and fresh mushrooms, all of it quite delicious and a far cry from the stale doughnuts and lukewarm coffee I usually bolted at work.

"C'est si bon," I said, wiping the last vestige of rich gravy from my lips before I settled back into my chair. "Merci, monsieur."

Stoney smiled and asked if I spoke French. I told him that I did.

"Well, well," he replied, "vous etes un trésor, mademoiselle."

He motioned to the waiter and ordered apple crumb and coffee for us. Even though there were strict regulations regarding food coupons and reasonable pricing in restaurants that served the working-class English, one could get almost anything in the high-end establishments if one had money. After finishing my dessert, I took a sip of *real* coffee before turning to Stoney to ask, "Who was the man you were talking to when I arrived?"

"I didn't see you, Evelyn, when you came in. It was as if you just suddenly appeared here at the table. The only person I've spoken to other than staff was Johann Claus. He works in the Belgian Embassy as an assistant to the ambassador. He's not the Assistant Ambassador, just an assistant. Why do you ask?"

"Because I thought I recognized him. But I must have been wrong. The man I thought I saw with you is named Heinrich."

Stoney gave me a puzzled look. "Why would you think you knew Claus? Have you met him somewhere here in London?"

"No. But I'm sure he's the same man I saw on the ship."

"The *Althone?*"

"Yes. This may seem rather strange, but I'm pretty sure I heard another man call the man you know as Claus by the name Heinrich." I was hardly aware of it, but at that moment my fingers began to clench.

Stoney downed the last of his coffee and returned the empty cup to its saucer. "I beg your pardon, Miss Sanderson," he said, his tone rather stiff. "But that's not possible. You see I've known Johann Claus for several years. In fact, I rented a cottage to him when he and his new bride came here from Bruges in 1938. During the months they lived there, I saw them often. I'm afraid you're wrong about Claus."

"I hope I am. But my gut tells me I'm not. If you don't mind, I'd like to tell you what happened." I glanced quickly back at him trying to gauge his reaction before I began. "The week before I left New York was hard," I began. "When I called my mother to tell her I'd joined the Red Cross and was leaving for England, she begged me not to go. She and I are close, so I was feeling pretty low about going so far away from her. And, on top of that, I was already upset about something unpleasant I'd had to deal with in New York." I looked down at the third finger of my left hand, at the naked place where the emerald and diamond ring had been. "Coming here was a very difficult decision, but once I'd made up my mind, I went on with my plans and boarded the *Althone* as scheduled. That evening the captain hosted a reception for Red Cross recruits. I went, but didn't stay but a few minutes because I didn't feel well. The next morning I awoke with a sore throat and low-grade fever so I stayed in my cabin for the next few days. On the fifth day out, my fever broke and I felt well enough to shower and dress. We'd docked in Lisbon that morning to take on a cargo of fresh fruit for the military bases here in England. It was sunny and warm, and I dropped onto a deck chair for a nap. The captain's steward woke me and told me the captain had asked that I join him that night at his table. But this presented a problem because I had nothing in my cabin suitable to wear. So the steward offered to help.

"We went down three flights of stairs to the luggage area deep in the hold and as soon as I'd located my trunk, he left me to get what I needed and told me he'd be back in a few minutes.

"I started searching in my trunk for a particular cocktail suit I had in mind. Then I heard voices coming through an opening in a wall to my right. I couldn't make out what was being said, but I thought I heard two men having a conversation in French. And that made me curious. I'd not encountered any French people on the ship, but I hadn't been out much.

27

I'm always looking for someone with whom I can practice, so I decided to have a look in case I recognized them. I stepped up on a crate that was sitting under the opening. It was an air vent, I guess, that had been covered with a screen of wire mesh. Through it, I saw two men standing in a storeroom lined with shelves of canned goods. One man was standing near a closed door on the far side, and the other, who was taller and wearing a white suit, had his back to me. The man over by the door removed his hat and I saw that he was bald—bald like Johann Claus. But here's the thing." I paused and leaned closer to Stoney. "Unlike today, he was wearing gold-rimmed glasses and had a mustache. I'm sure it was the same man with whom you were talking earlier. Anyway, the other man—the tall man in the white suit—called the shorter man Heinrich. He kept addressing him as *my dear Heinrich.*

"The smaller man, the man you know as Claus, seemed nervous. He kept running the tip of his index finger back and forth across his mustache. Then the tall man in the white suit said, "My dear Heinrich, this is the schedule you're to follow to meet your contacts in London." He handed a piece of paper to Heinrich and waited while Heinrich read it. Then he said, "Please note the locations . . . the Brass Bull, the Knight and Knave, the Rose and Crown.

"Then the man in the white suit repeated the information again . . . the names of the places and the names of the contacts. It was as if he thought Heinrich had not understood his instructions. But it was obvious to me that Heinrich understood very well because he kept looking down at his feet, shaking his head, as if he had no intention of doing what the man in the white suit wanted him to. Then Heinrich looked up and mumbled a string of words in rapid succession and I heard the word *ambassade.* At that, the man in the white suit grabbed him around his upper arm and spewed a stream of insults right in his face. Heinrich looked down again and the man in the white suit said something about *North Africa* and *char.* I think that's the French word for tank . . . right?

Stoney nodded and I went on. "And I wondered why they were talking about North Africa. But I soon figured that out because the man in the white suit continued to bear down on Heinrich with words he pronounced very distinctly. Heinrich was the pigeon being set up to meet certain contacts in London to relay information about the locations and future movements of British tank battalions in North Africa.

At that point, Stoney uncrossed his legs and shifted his weight from one side of his chair to the other. And while he seemed a bit uncomfortable, he said nothing. So I kept going. "I watched as Heinrich's florid face lost all its color. He began repeating *no, no* in this desperate little voice. That must have set the man in the white suit off because he jerked a pistol out of his pocket—a black pistol with a gray silencer attached to the barrel—and he told Heinrich that if he didn't do as he was told, he'd never see his wife and baby again. When he jammed the end of the silencer up under Heinrich's chin, Heinrich rose up on his tiptoes and kept going higher and higher until he lost his balance and fell back into the shelves behind him . . . which frightened me so badly that my mouth flew open and I let out a chirp. The tall man must have heard it because he made a slight pivot toward the wall behind him and I ducked. I huddled there for at least five minutes before I heard a click that sounded like a door had been opened. There were shuffling noises like footsteps and another click as if a door had been closed. Then the ship's engines fired up with a great rumbling, shaking the hold so badly that I all but lost my footing. As soon as I'd regained myself, I jumped down and threw my suit inside the trunk and slammed it shut. I thought I'd never get up all those stairs on the way to my cabin. After I got inside, I locked the dead bolt and forced the back of a chair up under the knob. I just knew the man in the white suit was out in the corridor searching for me."

As the memory of those terrifying moments flooded my brain, my heart began to pound and my hands closed around each other so tightly that my fingers swelled. Finally, I looked up at Stoney and said, "I didn't leave my cabin again until after the boat had docked the next day in Southampton."

Stoney stared at me from across the table for what seemed a long time, his face a mix of bewilderment and awe. "Oh, God, Evelyn," he whispered. "Are you sure? Are you absolutely sure?"

"Yes," I replied. "The tall man, the one who was standing nearest me, was slender and dark with very black hair slicked down with pomade. He looked like he might be Spanish or perhaps Portuguese. He told Heinrich that every Thursday night during the month of December he was to go to a certain pub at nine o'clock to meet a specific contact. I remember that on December fourth the contact's name was Alfred Cranbrook. And Heinrich was supposed to meet him at the Brass Bull. Tonight, Heinrich's supposed to meet a man named John Blackstoke at the Rose and Crown."

Stoney shook his head and said, "But how do you know the man you saw on the ship isn't someone who looks like Johann Claus?"

"Because the man I know as Heinrich had a speech impediment. And the man who was talking with you today when I came in has that same impediment."

Stoney's black eyes narrowed and the corners of his mouth dropped. "What in heaven's name are you talking about?" he snapped. "Claus doesn't have a speech impediment."

"Yes, he does. It's very subtle, but it's there. When I was in high school, my mother taught voice. And she had a student named Lucy Pollock who had the same problem as Heinrich. My mom called it "Lazy L," but speech therapists refer to it as "dark L syndrome" because people who suffer with it cannot roll their Ls the way normal people do. Double Ls are especially difficult for them because the letters become heavy on their tongues and they have a hard time moving them forward to the front of their mouths. It takes them just a moment longer to execute words containing Ls."

Stoney looked down as if he were suddenly fascinated by the napkin folded across his lap. He remained perfectly still for about ten seconds. Then he looked up and said, "If you're right, Evelyn, this could have serious implications. After all, Claus has access to all kinds of top secret and classified documents flowing through the embassy, including information about tank movements. You say he's to meet his contact tonight at the Rose and Crown?"

"Yes. I'm sure that's what I heard. I have no idea where it is, but Heinrich is supposed to meet a man named John Blackstoke there at nine."

"Well, I know where it is and I think we ought to be there to see what we can see, don't you? I'll pick you up at your boardinghouse at seven-thirty and we'll go to the Rose and Crown for a bite to eat. Why don't you wear your Red Cross uniform and I'll wear mine. That way we'll meld into the crowd. We wouldn't want him to see you and flee."

"I don't think Heinrich ever saw me, Stoney. When the *Althone* docked in Southampton, I didn't come out until the steward announced the last call for passengers to disembark. Remember the wool hat I was wearing when we met on the train? I wore that hat on purpose that day so I could pull it down to cover my hair. And I stood on the deck in that hat, with my coat collar turned up around my face, hoping they wouldn't see me. I watched Heinrich trudge down the gangway with his bags and get into the back seat of a waiting car. I went down the ramp as quickly as I could. And I was so afraid the tall man in the white suit might be lying in wait for me that I went straight to the Ladies Room inside the station and stayed there until it was time to board the train."

"Ah," Stoney whispered as he reached across the table and took my hand. "The dream . . . the nightmare you had on the train. It was the man in the white suit, wasn't it?" He gave my hand a squeeze. "Why didn't you tell me?"

"Because I felt I couldn't. We'd just met and I thought you'd think I was some kind of nut. But last night when you gave me a ride home from the dance, I decided that I'd tell you the next time I saw you."

Stoney rose from his chair and came around to help me with mine. "Thank you for confiding in me, Evelyn," he said, his face filled with the gravity of what I'd shared. "I'll see what I can do to try to get to the bottom of . . . whatever this is. I'm so sorry you've had such an awful scare."

He accompanied me to the coat station where he tipped the attendant. "I'll see you tonight at seven-thirty," he said as he opened the door to the cold.

* * *

I wasn't about to take a chance on being recognized by Heinrich that night, so I rolled my hair into a chignon, pinned it at the back of my neck, and pulled a black snood over it. My RC cap came down just above my ears and I felt confident that my hair would probably not be seen in the dim light of the pub.

Stoney picked me up as planned. When we arrived at the Rose and Crown, he slipped a half crown to the waiter and asked for a table with a good view to the bar. Over dinner, Stoney told me that he'd gone to Scotland Yard that afternoon to see his old friend, Inspector Ogilvie-Jones, and that the inspector and several of his men were among the bustling crowd in the pub. Two were posted outside and all were dressed in plains clothes. "See that man over near the cigarette machine, the one in the black pea jacket?" he said. "That's Ogilvie-Jones." I'd never seen a more unassuming officer of the law. Ogilvie-Jones was short, thin, and rather unhealthy looking.

About two minutes after nine, the man I knew as Heinrich walked in, removed his hat to reveal his bald head, and went straight to the far end of the bar. Through a haze of smoke, we watched as he spoke to the broad-shouldered dark-haired man already sitting there. Then Heinrich climbed up on a stool next to the man and ordered a pint. The two of them talked for a few minutes nodding now and then as if they were making polite conversation. A few minutes later, the bartender looked at the dark-haired man and said, "Want another, Blackstoke?" Blackstoke shook his head. He stood up, put on his hat, and addressed the bartender. "Time to go," he said.

I thought I'd made a mistake. That I'd been wrong about Heinrich, wrong about the meeting place, wrong about everything. A moment passed while Blackstoke fished a cigarette, and a small silver lighter, from inside his jacket. He leaned into the bar, put the cigarette between his lips, and flipped back the top on the lighter. His hand was steady as he held the flame to the end of the cigarette, steady as he slowly closed the lid. Then, in one quick motion, he plunked the lighter down on the bar, turned, and walked out the door. As soon as he'd gone, Heinrich grabbed the lighter and dropped it in his coat pocket.

Just then, a dozen airmen flooded the bar and Heinrich disappeared into a sea of dark uniforms. The fly boys began ordering drinks and Stoney leapt from his seat. "Come on, Evelyn," he said, grabbing me by the hand, "our chicken's about to fly the coop."

Outside a heavy snow was falling, and even though the blackout was in full effect, we could see that Inspector Ogilvie-Jones had the situation well in hand. We stood quietly watching as Blackstoke and Heinrich were handcuffed and put into the back of a gray van.

Stoney waited until the van drove off before he spoke. Taking my arm in his, he said, "Do you have any idea what a rare gift of observation you have, Evelyn? Wait until the prime minister hears about this. He'll recruit you for MI5!"

"MI5? What are you talking about? I'll have you know I'm very happy with my job at the Red Cross."

"I fear you underestimate yourself, old thing. Just think about the hundreds—maybe thousands—of lives you may have saved tonight. Perhaps you . . ." Stoney's voice trailed off, and as we started walking, he said, "Shall we go back into the pub and celebrate?"

Over brandies we continued to talk about how quietly, and efficiently, the inspector had handled the arrest of Claus and Blackstoke. "The chaps from Scotland Yard are ever so keen," Stoney said, "and they have a nose for situations like this. Now that they have Heinrich and Blackstoke, perhaps it won't be long before they apprehend the man in the white suit. But I don't want to upset you by talking about that. Please tell me more about *you*. You said you had a sister. Was it just the two of you growing up at home in Baker?" His voice had taken on a cheerful tone and when he looked down at me, his eyes were bright with curiosity.

"No. Claire and I had a brother. But he died." I paused recalling the bitterly cold day when my brother, McLean, had breathed his last.

Stoney eyes narrowed. "How awful. Was he older or younger than you?"

"He was older, but he didn't live to be very old. I was only seven when he died and I've never really gotten over it. You see McLean . . . McLean had no use of his arms or legs."

"What a heartbreak that must have been for your poor parents, and for you and your sister. How did that happen? Was McLean born that way?"

"My mother never revealed how it happened. She always told Claire and me that McLean was just like us and we were to treat him as such. Even though he lived only a few short years, he had a profound effect on my life . . . and still does. He was probably the real reason I went to nursing school."

"You're a nurse? Why did you sign up to work in the Hospitality Unit at the Red Cross if you're a nurse?"

"I've never practiced nursing, Stoney. I don't feel I have enough experience to be a good nurse. What I really wanted to do when I came to London was work in Hospitality and that's what I requested on my application and in my letter to the director. I'd like to keep on working there doing the things I'm doing now. So, I'd be grateful if you wouldn't mention my being a registered nurse to anyone."

Stoney raised his right palm. "On my honor," he said, "it will never pass my lips. But I'd like to know more about that if you don't mind. Why did you go to school for nurses' training if you didn't intend to become a nurse?"

"When I finished high school, all I wanted to do was sing and dance onstage. But my mother wanted me to further my education in a field that had practical application, like nursing. She's a wise old bird, and in the end, she made me a deal. If I'd complete a course of study in nursing, she'd let me to go to New York to follow my dream."

CHAPTER 5

A Wise Old Bird

Baker, North Carolina • June 4, 1929

I grew up in a house my father built for a woman who was not my mother. But I didn't know this until I was twelve and one of my older cousins spilled the beans. It seems my father was engaged to a woman who invited a friend home from school for the weekend. That friend became my mother. It was she who stole my father's heart and took him away from his fiancée. The house my father built for the other woman in the small town of Baker was a large two-story affair with four columns across the front in a style known as Colonial Revival. It sat in a row of similar houses set back about five hundred feet from the railroad tracks, the main route through town. My father was anxious to live in it, but he and my mother had to wait because of the birth of my big brother, McLean.

McLean, a quadriplegic, was destined to live out his short life of thirteen years in a wheelchair. His condition naturally affected not only me, but all the family. McLean could not walk, of course, nor could he hold a spoon, a pencil, or a washcloth. And even though he could not speak, he was very bright. He caught on fast and would moan deep down in his throat to let us know he understood. Our mother never allowed my older sister, Claire, or me to leave McLean out of anything we did, so the only time he was not with us was when we went on long trips. He simply could not travel by train. But he often went with us on short trips in the car where our mother rigged up a special seat for him right in front beside her.

McLean delighted in our childhood games. During the summer months Claire and I caught lightning bugs and butterflies, even frogs, which we put into jars that had holes in the lids so they could breathe. When we put these treasures on his lap, McLean would smile his crooked smile and coo. He loved to watch Claire and me as we danced the dance of the fairies. And when we sang our silly made-up songs, he'd howl along with us like Quasimodo chained to the battlements. And he always cried, softly and quietly, when our parents called us in for the night.

At some point, Claire, who seemingly transformed overnight into a full-figured teenager, outgrew that kind of foolishness and went off to be with her friends. That was when I came up with the idea of playing nurse. I constantly begged my mother to let me wear her Red Cross uniform. Each time I begged, she'd pat me on the head and tell me it was much too big. But she'd attach her Red Cross pin to the collar of whatever blouse I was wearing and brush my wild auburn tresses into a neat braid so she could pin her beautiful Red Cross cap to the back of my head. She gave me rags from the linen cupboard to use for bandages and old sheets to drape over McLean's chair so the wheels wouldn't show. I'd cover his hair with one of her colorful scarves, put rouge on his cheeks, and slip a pair of garden gloves over his useless hands. We pretended that he was a patient expecting a baby. I'd tell him about the kind of miracle that was going to take place just like the story of Baby Jesus. Then I'd swaddle one of my baby dolls in a blanket and put it on his lap while I sang "Away in a Manger." McLean would croon along in a syncopated cadence that somehow blended with mine. Like a faithful retriever, he loved the attention and never showed the slightest aversion to any getup I made him wear or any fantasy nursing procedure he had to endure.

Sometimes McLean would get really sick, especially during winter, and I would sit at his bedside for hours reading to him while he battled a cough, a fever, or worse. Mama would come and go, bringing warm broth and hot mustard plasters to put on his lily-white chest. When we removed his pajama top, you could see his ribs poking out like spindles on the back of a chair. Mama would stay up with McLean all night when he was sick, but Daddy slept through everything.

McLean died of influenza just before Christmas in 1918, the year I was seven. Our father was away on business when McLean succumbed, so Mama took care of the arrangements. Neither Claire nor I was allowed to look at McLean in his coffin, but I gave Mama his favorite toy, a stuffed monkey from which he'd managed to tear off the arms and legs, to put in with him. He was buried on Christmas Eve in the cemetery at Sand Hill.

That spring, one of my classmates contracted tuberculosis and was sent to a sanitarium. I wanted badly to do something for her, so Mama took me to the drugstore and gave me enough money to buy a candy bar for my friend, and one for each of the other children confined to her ward. Then we made a trip to the sanitarium to take the candy. Being in that hospital at such a young age had a profound effect on me. I was fascinated by the instruments laid out on rolling carts and watched carefully as the doctors used the shiny stethoscopes and little hammers with rubber tips. After that inspiring visit, I played hospital with my dolls, bandaged Mama in old rags every chance I got, and bragged to friends and family that when I grew up I was going to be a nurse.

But two years later, I forgot all about that idea when I saw my first Broadway show. In 1920, the musical *Sally* was getting rave reviews on the Great White Way, and Daddy took Mama, Claire, and me to see Marilyn Miller in the lead role. When Miss Miller sang "Look for the Silver Lining," the house was on its feet for a three-minute ovation. I loved hearing the orchestra warm up, loved seeing the lights go down, loved the excitement of so many people smiling and nodding to us even though we were perfect strangers. After we got back home, I sang "Look for the Silver Lining" morning, noon, and night. Mama bought the sheet music for Claire so she could play it for me, and we entertained Mama's book club, women's club, and church auxiliary. In September, Mama took me to Goldsboro to enroll me at Lady Ashworth's Academy of Dance where I took tap, ballroom, and ballet for the next six years.

Daddy went to New York on business at least once a year and I begged him to take us again. In 1925, when Claire was away in college, my parents allowed me to accompany them on a trip to celebrate their twentieth anniversary. The big show that year was *Lady, Be Good!* starring Fred and Adele Astaire—another hit that convinced me that dancing and singing onstage was the best possible way to spend my life. On the train ride home, I told Mama I had no intention of going to college as Claire had, but would leave for New York the day after I'd graduated from Baker High School. Even at fourteen, I knew my destiny was tied to the black grosgrain bows on my tap shoes.

The summer I turned fifteen, Mama, Claire, and I went to England to spend six weeks with our cousin, Peter Forbes, who lived in Surrey and worked in London. While there, we traveled extensively by rail to the Lake District, Cornwall, the Cotswolds, and the hauntingly beautiful Yorkshire countryside. The night before we sailed home, Peter took us to the London Pavilion to see Noël Coward's *On With the Dance* and I became more determined than ever to live out my dream.

One evening just a month before I was to graduate from high school, my father called me into his study and told me he had something he wanted to discuss with me. The study had always been the place where he'd "laid down the law" as he called it, regarding the things I'd be allowed to do—or not. As soon as I sat down, he reminded me that I was only sixteen. "And that's too young to go to New York on your own," he said.

I began my protest with, "But Mama went to live in *Italy* when she was sixteen. That's a lot further away than New York."

My father settled into a chair across from me. "Your mother went to Italy to continue her education. And she did not go alone. She lived with a chaperone and several classmates. It's not the same as your striking out on your own with this wild idea of performing onstage. No daughter of mine is ever going to parade around half naked in front of an audience like those Ziegfeld floosies! You're my little girl, Evelyn, and I would never allow you to do such a thing."

I could feel my face getting hot, but I didn't care. "I'm not a little girl, Daddy! I'm grown. And I know what I want to do with my life."

My father stood up and I saw tears in his eyes. "You will always be *my* little girl," he said, in a voice as soft as velvet. "And I will always want what's best for you. Why don't you do what Claire did and enroll at Peace Institute and get a teaching certificate? Then you can teach until you meet a nice industrious young man and get married. I'll give you the biggest, fanciest wedding this town has ever seen."

In the past when things had gone awry between us, my father had always tried to placate me with expensive gifts or promises he never kept. But I'd outgrown that kind of childish pacification. "I don't want to be a teacher!" I all but shouted. "And I don't care about a big fancy wedding! I don't want anything from you."

I sprang out of my chair and started toward the door. "I'm old enough to take care of myself, Daddy. And as soon as I graduate, I'll get a job and buy my train ticket to New York!" I stomped out and raced up the stairs to my room where I continued to fume until my mother came up to tell me about the party she was planning for my graduation.

* * *

A week later, Mama took me to Goldsboro to buy a new dress for the party. On the way home, she told me that my father was threatening to send me away to school if I didn't give up on the idea of going to New York. "He wants to send you to Sweetbriar in Virginia," she said, "and he thinks you should go immediately after graduation and attend summer school. I know you're hoping to get on a train as soon as possible, Evelyn, and get away from here. But your father isn't going to let you go to New York."

As we turned into the driveway at home, she made me an offer. If I would complete a course of study at Ruxton Hospital School of Nursing in Raleigh, she would buy my train ticket to New York and provide me with a small monthly allowance to help with food and rent. I didn't want anything to interfere with my plans to get to Broadway as soon as possible, so I bit the bullet and the next day, completed an application to Ruxton so I could put it behind me.

Ruxton Hospital offered a regular two-year course of study for an RN. But it also offered a rigorous one-year program that was a carryover from the years when there was a desperate need for nurses during what historians called *The Great War*. This program required an additional course per quarter as well as classes on two full Saturdays a month. While it was demanding and a bit more expensive, that was what I chose.

I spent the entire summer struggling with a course load that included physiology, organic chemistry, anatomy, and general psychology. I had had only one course in chemistry in high school and I knew right off the Bunsen burner that I was not prepared. The rigors of constant study, and the demands of the instructors, were almost more than I could handle. On the two Saturdays a month when I was not in class, I took the train home to Baker so Daddy and Claire could tutor me. No student was allowed to move ahead to the next level of study without a grade of at least B, and I would never have made it without the help of my father and sister.

Thanksgiving and Christmas that year remain a bit of a blur. I went home, but spent those holidays up in my room studying. That September, Claire had married her long-standing beau, Charles Kirby, and they were expecting their first baby. My father disliked Charles intensely, so Mama had to keep the peace when Charles and Claire were with us at home. I just tried to avoid the tension and keep my nose to the grindstone. Mama gave me a new cashmere coat and fur-lined gloves for Christmas in anticipation of my upcoming move to New York.

My family hosted our traditional New Year's Eve party, so 1929 began on a happy note. My father's younger brother, Uncle Robert and his wife, Aunt Hephzibah, were the first to arrive. The manager and bookkeeper from Daddy's mill, and their wives, were there along with the three male employees of the bank and their wives. After an elaborate dinner, Mama played several classical pieces on the piano. Then Claire played and I sang. At midnight, we rang in the New Year with champagne toasts. Daddy surprised us by ascending the stairs in a sleeveless undershirt, baby diapers he'd made from a sheet, a top hat, and a banner across his chest that said "Happy New Year 1929" in silver glitter. At midnight, we rang in the New Year with champagne toasts, and the next morning I caught the 8:15 to Raleigh to give myself an extra day to study for exams.

The courses I took between Christmas and Easter proved to be the most difficult of all. I'd been longing for the time when we would begin studying what was known as "the nursing arts," thinking that I would excel in that area. But it was far more complex than I'd ever imagined. The first week we did nothing but morning care for patients, which meant emptying bedpans, giving a patient a bath from a washbasin, etc. The next week we spent every single day in the wards changing sheets and making beds. I couldn't believe we were going to spend an entire week on beds and sheets, but I was unaware of the kind of perfection required. Each of us was expected to make a hospital corner to an exact forty-five-degree angle with a precise twelve inches of overlap. We were given twenty seconds to do this and were not allowed to measure anything. Next, we were required to tuck the top sheet so tight that, when thrown by the examining nurse, a quarter would bounce off it. That took some doing, but I finally got the hang of it.

Then we moved on to instruments, equipment, and sterilization. I had to judge the body temperatures of a group of six patients with nothing but the back of my hand held to each of their foreheads. I had to carefully move a man who weighed about two-hundred pounds around on the bed, without causing him pain or letting any part of his body touch the exposed mattress, while I removed his dirty sheets and put on clean. I had to insert a catheter into a woman who was hours away from delivering a baby. My hands were shaking so badly I thought I'd never be able to do it. But eventually it slid in and the poor woman kissed my hand and murmured "thank you" while she peed a full quart into the bottle attached to the end of the tube.

Every student was required to sterilize dozens of instruments and present them in correct order on a sterilized tray to the examining doctor. I got back on my feet with that one, getting the highest marks in my group. Next were the hypodermics. We had to know the size of the gauge on every needle and the slants on every bevel, plus the various syringes that would accommodate them. After we'd learned what medicines were administered from which hypodermic and in what amounts, we started giving shots to oranges. I'd heard nurses talk about doing this but thought it was a joke. It wasn't. Our supervisor taught us how to pinch the skin on the arm of a patient to make the process easier. We practiced administering shots to each other for several days. Finally, we tackled intravenous techniques and the special equipment needed for that very tedious job. As a child, I'd been taught to embroider and crochet by my mother. I had not liked it, but I was grateful as it made this delicate work much easier for me.

I went home for Easter knowing I'd done well on my courses. And I was eager to begin the internship at the hospital when I returned. Only eight weeks to go and I'd be home-free and leaving for New York. I couldn't wait to live on my own and make a living doing what I loved—singing and dancing onstage. No more bedpans for me!

Claire and Charles came over on Good Friday, but Claire's baby was due in June, so she and Charles went home soon after dinner. After they'd gone, my father retreated to his study and my mother invited me to join her for a few minutes in her sitting room.

"I have something important to discuss with you," she said. "I'm so very proud of all that you've accomplished in nursing school, Evelyn. None of this surprises me because I've always known you had it in you. And you wanted to be a nurse for a long time. Until we took you to see your first musical in New York, you were set on nursing. In a few short weeks, you'll graduate. And you'll have your training to fall back on if you need it . . . *and* the letters RN behind your name for the rest of your life."

My mother was thoughtful and even-tempered, but I could tell by the tone in her voice that she was going to air her concerns once more, and perhaps add more stringent conditions to my leaving for New York. She started by reminding me that she'd visited her sister, my Aunt Bethany, at her home in Raleigh the week before. After a moment, she said, "Do you remember your Uncle Bryson's cousin, Winifred Trask? You met her at Emily's wedding the spring you were in the eighth grade. Remember?"

I pictured a small brunette woman in a flowered dress with a big straw hat and an outgoing personality. I nodded. "Yes, Mama, I remember Winifred."

"Well, do you recall that Winifred lives in New York?" I shook my head and Mama continued. "She lives right in the heart of Manhattan in an apartment at Carnegie Hall." My mother did not stop for my reaction. "Winifred is a young widow, about thirty-eight or thirty-nine, and she works as a secretary. Her husband was killed in France. Your Aunt Bethany reminded me of Winifred last month when I spent the day with her."

I felt a flush rise from my throat as I knew what was coming. My plans to live at the new Barbizon Hotel for Women, with its beautiful indoor pool, were about to go down the drain.

Mama looked over at me, put her hand gently under my chin, and turned my face toward hers. "You are too young, Evelyn, to live alone in New York . . . or in any city for that matter. And you won't be twenty-one for three years. I telephoned Winifred a couple of days ago and she's offered to take you in and provide a home for you for a while. She has a studio apartment with a daybed in the living area where you can sleep. It's convenient to the theatre district and to a number of office buildings where perhaps you can find a part-time job. You know you're going to have to get a part-time job until you get established, don't you?"

I just sat there floundering in disappointment and disbelief. I could hardly believe my mother had done this without first telling me.

"I know you think I don't trust you," she said. "But this isn't a matter of trust, Evelyn. It's a matter of safety." She removed her hand from under my chin and put her arm around me. "There is no one on this earth more precious to me than you, dear girl, and I love you more than life itself. I cannot let you go without knowing that you're living with someone who knows her way around, who'll introduce you to nice people and provide a home for you. Winifred is not our blood kin, but she is our in-law kin."

"Your father and I have talked this over and he's agreed to let you try it. I don't think he would have ever let you go otherwise, and you know that until you are twenty-one, he will have the ultimate say in what you do and where you go . . . period. Unless you marry. Then, he'll be content to let your husband make those decisions.

"Your father is an old-fashioned, rules-oriented kind of man. And he simply would not have allowed you to go unless I'd found someplace suitable for you to live. He was very specific about your living with an *older woman*. So there it is. If you're wise, you will not say one word to him, as he is in an especially foul mood. I'm sure you sensed that at dinner. Something's going on at the bank, but I don't know what. All you have to do now, honey, is complete your internship in the hospital and graduate, and you'll have kept your end of our bargain. Then I'll keep my end by letting you go to Gotham-on-the-Hudson the day after they stick that gold pin on your collar."

She stood up, straightened her skirt, and smiled. "Please, take my advice, dear Evelyn. Keep all of this to yourself and try to enjoy the weekend. Come June, we won't be seeing each other much and I'm going to miss you." She leaned down, kissed me on the forehead and said, "Bon soir, mon cheri" before leaving the room.

* * *

The last eight weeks of training comprised an internship at Ruxton Hospital. After consulting with our nurse supervisors, we were allowed to select four different areas where we would spend two weeks observing, and two weeks applying our new skills. I chose emergency and general surgery, and obstetrics and gynecology, which counted as two areas. Several of our young women patients, who were in labor, were about my age and their travail was a completely new experience for me. I'd seen calves and foals born at Sand Hill, had even watched as a calf was pulled from inside the mother. But I knew nothing about human birth. It had looked so simple on the farm. I'd never known an animal to labor more than a couple of hours, so I was in for a rude awakening when one of our patients was in labor for eighteen hours and the baby was stillborn.

I happened to be on duty standing beside the doctor as he finally took the baby with forceps and the mother passed out in the process. When the doctor handed me the dead baby, a bloody blue thing no larger than a plucked chicken, I went rigid and thrust the little body away from me as if it were a boa constrictor. The supervising nurse raced to my side and sank her fingernails deep in my upper arm. "Go," she hissed under her breath as she handed me a towel. "Wrap it up and take it down stairs." Resting the lifeless bundle against my chest, I sniffed back tears as I fled the delivery room and hurried down the steps that led to the morgue. I just knew I'd failed and they would send me back home. But the incident was never mentioned again.

Two weeks later, I went to surgery where I thanked God every day that I was not a surgeon. The first week was filled with usual cases like removing gallbladders, appendices, and tonsils. But the second week was different. Early Monday morning, Emergency admitted a man about twenty-eight who'd broken his shin when he'd fallen down an embankment on the Neuse River hitting the rocks below. He was brought to Surgery from Emergency when personnel learned that the accident had occurred almost a week before when his wife had set the leg in a bark splint and had sewn flaps of broken skin over it.

The man and his wife explained to the surgeon on call, Dr. Randall, that when the accident happened, their truck was broken down and they'd had no way to get to town. The wife was visibly upset and cried off and on while the doctor and I cleaned the oozing pus from the area where the skin had begun knitting back together. The doctor sent the wife to the waiting room and called for an orderly to move the man to the operating theatre. He summoned his assistant, an intern named Briggs, and told him to prepare the ether. The surgical nurse who normally helped him was away, so he turned to me and said, "Get the instruments ready, nurse." I gulped, backed away from the operating table and fled to the cupboard on the far side of the room. I wasn't sure what he might need specifically, so I chose one of every instrument and hurried off to the sterilizer.

Soon the patient was deep in the arms of Morpheus, and Dr. Randall was making a long cut from his knee down through the infected area. Dr. Briggs stood close by swabbing the pus and blood from the opening. Fortunately, Dr. Randall was kind enough to call for each instrument as he needed it. I could see quite clearly where the bone had been broken. It was out of line and healing at an angle that would have caused the poor man to limp for the rest of his life. Dr. Randall commented that he saw no evidence of osteomyelitis, an infection of the bone marrow, and that he felt the man could make a good recovery in spite of the problems that had ensued. When the incision was large enough to allow him to do so, Dr. Randall put his thumbs inside it and moved the broken bone, aligning it correctly while the cast was being prepared by Briggs. I helped Dr. Randall secure the wrapping around the man's leg and assisted the orderly who took the patient to the recovery area. I did not eat lunch in the cafeteria that day, but went straight to my room and took a nap. I was exhausted.

The State Boards were administered during the first week of May. Three weeks later I learned that I'd passed. Whew! I called home as soon as I got the news so my mother could brag about it to her friends in Baker. On Memorial Day I decided to forgo the parade downtown and the festivities planned for patients on the lawn. I needed to sort my books, materials, and clothes and begin packing for the move back home, and subsequently, to New York.

Mama and Daddy, and Aunt Bethany and Uncle Bryson, were coming to my graduation ceremony at eleven o'clock on Thursday morning. My mother had planned a luncheon celebration after at the Sir Walter Hotel, and I wanted to have everything packed and ready to go as soon as it was over. I spent the afternoon and evening putting things in boxes, bags, and suitcases, and was in bed by nine.

My roommate shook me awake about four o'clock Wednesday morning. "Dr. Randall wants you in surgery," she said. "ASAP! He sent an orderly over from Emergency to tell you not to worry about putting on your uniform, just come as fast as you can."

"What's the matter?" I mumbled, half asleep. "Why does he want me?"

"Just go!" she shouted. "He needs you."

I grabbed the only thing handy—the dress I was going to wear under my graduation robe. And I did not take time to put on a camisole or slip beneath it. I ran my fingers through my hair, pulled it back with combs, slipped into some pumps, and flew down the stairs.

I ran as fast as I could across the damp lawn to the back door of the hospital and went straight up the stairs to the surgery. I found Dr. Randall hovered over a dark-haired girl about my age who was bathed in blood from her waist down. She was conscious, but just barely. I knew I shouldn't, but I took her hand. She looked so small and helpless lying there, her blue-black hair a mass of damp curls arrayed against the sterile white pillow, her dark eyes wide with fear.

"Prepare for a blood transfusion, Nurse Sanderson," Dr. Randall said, gently removing my hand from hers. "And get the tray ready." His assistant rushed in, wearing a striped pajama top over his trousers and a pair of bedroom slippers. Dr. Randall picked up a pair of scissors and held them out to him. "Cut off her clothes, Dr. Briggs, and bring the ether! We've no time to lose. She'll die in a matter of minutes if we don't hurry."

The heels on my pumps sounded like taps as I hurried across the floor to collect the instruments. With shaking hands I took several from the cupboard and turned to the sterilizer. It was supposed to be kept boiling hot night and day, but it was cold. I was too scared to tell Dr. Randall, so I turned it on and began sorting instruments. The faster I moved, the more I dropped. The sterilizer finally reached a boil and I put the instruments in, a few at a time, as quickly as I could, burning my fingers more than once. Then I arranged everything on the tray, crossed the room, and put it on a cart beside the operating table.

The girl was completely nude now, her legs wide apart, and Dr. Randall was trying frantically to stop the flow of blood pouring from between them. He leaned toward me so that I could wipe the sweat that dripped from his forehead. "Botched abortion," he said through his mask, "probably self-induced. Now, as soon as she is out, Nurse Sanderson, I want you to clean her up with Isoral and have the suction tube ready. I'm going to make a small incision just above the pubic area. We haven't time to shave her." He looked up at Dr. Briggs and said, "Try to keep the blood away from my fingers and the instruments while I search for the artery she ruptured with her knitting needle . . . or whatever the hell she used." He looked up at me and said, "Ready?"

For almost an hour we did everything in our power to save her. But our efforts were useless. Dr. Randall walked away, pulled off his gloves, and buried his face in his hands. "So young," he murmured, "so young."

Oh, God, I thought, how could this happen? I stood beside the table wondering who she was, where she'd come from, how she'd gotten herself in such a fix. I couldn't stop looking at her tortured face, now waxy smooth and pale as alabaster. Clumps of drying blood lay clotted on her stomach, inside her thighs, and all around her lower torso— a sacrificial lamb on a desecrated altar.

Patients died at Ruxton Hospital every day. Old people who had broken a hip and succumbed to the inevitable pneumonia; the middle aged who'd suffered massive heart attacks or lost a battle to cancer; even young children and babies, whose small bodies were powerless against monsters like diphtheria and spinal meningitis. Occasionally, we had to deal with the mangled chests and crushed skulls of people of all ages who were victims of automobile accidents. But teenagers rarely ended up in our morgue.

Dr. Briggs removed the bloody sheets and towels from under the girl's body and pulled a clean one over it before he called for an orderly to take her down. Then he went to call the police. We knew nothing about her except she'd been brought to Emergency by a young man who'd left her there lying on a sofa in the waiting room.

After Dr. Briggs left, Dr. Randall came over to me and took my hand and said, "I called for you this morning on purpose, Miss Sanderson. You have so much promise and such a good strong intuitive feel for nursing, which is rare in someone so young. You're going to make a fine nurse and I hope you'll consider surgery. Thank you for all you did to try to save that poor girl." Then he turned and walked away.

With feet as heavy as stones, I trudged back up the hill to my room. Dr. Randall's words played in my head and I felt guilty that I'd not been honest with him. I should have told him about my plans to go to New York, my dreams of Broadway. But I kept my mouth shut because I was afraid he'd be disappointed in me. I finally reached my darkened room where I stripped off my blood-stained dress, dropped it in the trash can, and fell onto the bed. My roommate woke me at noon to go to lunch with her, but I had no appetite. I could not get that poor dead girl's frightened eyes out of my mind. Later I got up, took a shower, and put on clean clothes and comfortable shoes. I spent the whole afternoon walking, all the way downtown and back, without stopping. I hoped to wear myself out so that I might forget her face.

The next day I tried to smile and act cheerful when I walked across the platform to receive a rolled piece of parchment tied with blue ribbon and a circular gold pin with RN engraved in its center. I ate almost nothing of the elaborate lunch we were served at the Sir Walter, and Mama made excuses, blaming my lack of appetite on excitement. I breathed a sigh of relief when we finally hugged my aunt and uncle good-bye at the hotel and climbed into Daddy's Cord.

On Saturday afternoon, Mama and I went to Goldsboro to buy some last-minute items. I saw a champagne-colored sheath in the window at Weil's and told Mama that I needed a new party dress. An hour later I left the store with the dress, some new lipstick, a pair of sandals, and a box of stockings. Sunday was my last day in Baker. Mama and Claire hosted a lemonade-on-the-porch party that afternoon to celebrate my going away and invited about two dozen family friends. That night, I wrapped the cocktail dress in tissue and placed it carefully on top of the clothes I'd already packed in my largest suitcase. I was still so tired from the emotional roller coaster I'd ridden for the last week that I was in bed by nine.

Early Monday morning, my parents took me to the station where Mama and I struggled through a long, but tearless, farewell. Daddy gave me a quick peck on the cheek. I boarded the train, found my seat, and blew kisses to them from the window until they were out of sight. Then I broke down and sobbed all the way to Richmond.

CHAPTER 6

Secret Sister

London, England • December 25, 1941

Dearest Mama,

*Merry Christmas! I've been thinking about you all day
and picturing your beautiful cedar wreath with the bright
red bow hanging on the front door, the crèche you bought
in Italy arrayed on top of the piano, and the luscious smell
of your Lane Cake baking in the oven.*

*I never dreamed I'd eat roast goose, but that is
the Christmas tradition in Merry Olde England. My
housemates Ida, Ruby, Desdemona (called Mona), Juliette
(called Jules), and I pooled our poultry ration stamps and
gave them to Ma Denny so she could prepare this special
treat for us. It was delicious and our feast included fried
potatoes, creamed peas and onions, Junket with canned
pineapple, and rolls made with hard-to-find white flour,
served with the inevitable margarine. For dessert, we had
the ever-popular plum pudding and I felt just like Tiny
Tim! Ma Denny complained that this one contained fewer
raisins and figs than usual, as they are so difficult to get
now. It was quite lovely when she lit it, the blue flame
rising above the holly leaves she'd stuck in the crown, and I
thought it quite good. She served it with a dollop of carefully
hoarded whipped cream, just as I'm sure you served your*

brandy-laced fruitcake, along with bowls of your wonderful ambrosia. Oh, Mama, how I missed your ambrosia.

We did not have a tree, but put cedar boughs on all the mantels and hung them over the picture frames in the lounge (living room) and dining room and had several candles burning in both rooms all day. My housemates and I chipped in and bought a nice bottle of hand lotion and a box of Blue Sky dusting powder for Ma Denny. She told us that hand lotion is beginning to disappear from the shops because lanolin is used in materials for lubricating war machines, so she was pleased to have a new bottle. Each of us girls wrapped an inexpensive "secret sister" gift and put a number on the back of it. Then we made a set of corresponding numbers and drew them out of a hat to decide who got what. I ended up with a box of Pears soaps. Then we sang carols just before dinner. Everyone begged to hear something "really American" (Please sing us a Yank song, Eve-leen!), so I sang "Over the River and Through the Woods," and substituted Christmas Day for Thanksgiving Day throughout.

Thank you, thank you for the gorgeous pink cashmere sweater! You shouldn't have, as I know it cost a fortune. And thank you for the silk stockings and flannel camisoles. What a godsend they will be in this miserable climate. I cried when I opened Maddie's box of fudge. Butter and sugar in such quantities are simply not available here. I shared it all around and still have a few pieces left. Please tell her I'm sending her a big hug! The box of oranges and sweet potatoes was just as welcome and will, hopefully, last longer. You can't imagine what a wonderful change they'll be. Oh, Mama, what a windfall all your lovely gifts were.

I have a feeling Christmas dinner here was more somber than usual, as two of the other women have a brother, and one a husband, who are on ships in the North Atlantic. Plus, everyone is still reeling from the recent sinking of the HMS Repulse and the Prince of Wales by the Japanese in the South China Sea. But they tried to make the best of it, and when I came down to the dining room a couple of the girls put a crown on me like the ones they were wearing, which were made of thin paper in bright colors. Before we began our meal, Ma Denny said the blessing and each of us made a little toast with our one glass of sherry. Then we pulled "crackers"—paper tubes that make a cracking noise when you pull them apart. The Brits say Happy Christmas, not Merry Christmas. Maybe I'll get the hang of it by next Christmas!

We had a caroling party for RC staff at HQ last night. About 200 showed up, along with members of our district board. It started at eight and ended in time for everyone to get to a late Christmas Eve service (or midnight mass). A woman named Frances Flynn, who works in Accounting, opened the festivities with "O Holy Night." What a gorgeous mezzo soprano! It made me weep. After, we gathered 'round a large tree we'd decorated with crocheted snowflakes and red bows. Beneath it was a gift for everyone—a box of razor blades for the men and a card of Kirby Grips (bobby pins) for the women. We had hot cider and cocoa (hot chocolate) and all sorts of biscuits (cookies), most made with lots of oatmeal. I confess that I stood at the refreshment table and dreamed of your luscious stuffed dates. Lord Beeton-Howard, the man who shared my compartment on the train from Southampton, was there as he is a member of the RC board. He greeted me with "Joyeux Noel" and we conversed in French for several minutes.

My partner, Grace, and I took the early shift this morning, which meant we were up at four o'clock and had our old "chugger" packed and ready to roll by four thirty. It was bitterly cold when we arrived at the docks where a battleship was departing for Iceland at six thirty. The men were in good spirits in spite of having to spend Christmas Day riding winter swells on the North Sea. There were Free French, Poles, Czechs, Aussies, and Norwegians mixed in with the Brits, so I learned to say Merry Christmas in several languages while handing out cups of coffee and hundreds and hundreds of doughnuts. Grace and I had set up the little record player in the back of the van so we could play Bing Crosby and Dinah Shore. I stood there smiling at those boys and shaking their hands, saying Merry Christmas and Bon Voyage over and over. But I couldn't help wondering how many of them will survive to see another Christmas. I did not cry, thank goodness, that is a no-no. No crying, no frowning, no tears! Keep smiling for the boys!

Our work will be much harder tomorrow evening when Grace and I are scheduled to meet a ship returning from Tunisia. I especially dread seeing the boys brought down the gangplank on stretchers, their bodies broken and covered with burns, the look in their eyes nothing but a vapid stare. But I stand there and smile as much as I can, and try to squeeze the hand of those who are conscious. "Steady on, old girl" as the Brits say.

As you can tell my work and my social life keep me very busy with hardly a moment to call my own. But when I get a few minutes to myself, my head swims with thoughts of this horrific war and the toll it's taking in so many places and so many ways. There was a big article in the London Times yesterday reporting details of the Japanese attacks on Manila, Hong Kong, Wake, Guam, and Midway. I know I shouldn't write this in a letter, Mama, but the incredible destruction and loss of life at Pearl, and of those other targets in the Pacific, is simply not comparable to what has happened here in London over the last seventeen months. This old city, with its ancient buildings and thousand-year history, has been reduced to a pile of sticks and stones. I know now that the newsreels we've been shown in movie theatres at home, the newspapers we've read, even the live reports we've heard from Ed Murrow on the BBC, cannot capture the extent of the destruction here, nor its aftermath. That comment is for you and you alone, as I know it would not play well in Baker or anywhere in the USA. I doubt seriously that the censors will allow it to remain in this letter.

When I arrived here, all of Britain was standing at a precipice staring down into an endless void. Now, they have our food and factories and brave young men for their fight against the Germans. And I am beginning to understand just how desperate that fight is and why we must prevail. We're much stronger together than either of us would be alone.

Before I go to bed tonight I'll double-check my store of ration stamps to be sure I have enough to get some toothpaste and mouthwash. Hard to believe I've been here long enough to have used up what I brought. I suppose you'll be rationing soon and know how much you dread that. Have you and Maddie made your black-out curtains yet? Are you collecting grease and scrap metal like the women here? Please write and tell me what you've heard from Claire, and all about your Christmas, and everything that is going on there. Give my love to Uncle Robert and Aunt Hephzibah, to Maddie and Fletcher, and to all our friends. I miss you terribly and love you more than words can say. And thanks to all of you for such wonderful gifts.

Ever faithful in England,
Your Evelyn

PS: The London Times reported yesterday that 381
British infantry, 212 Navy personnel, and 116 RAF
airmen have been killed so far this month.

CHAPTER 7

The Jig Is Up

London, England • February 9, 1942

"How could you, Miss Sanderson? How could you have done such a thing?" A red-faced Marjorie Reynolds stood behind her desk waving a battered brown envelope at me, an envelope addressed in my own hand. My application and resume had finally arrived at RCHQ and my supervisor was furious.

"A registered nurse!" she shouted. "An insignificant little piece of information you failed to mention in your letter when you requested admission. And we accepted you here at our London Office on the basis of that letter, never suspecting that your qualifications were other than what you'd written. How could you?"

While she continued to glare at me, I played for time by slowly removing the gloves I was wearing and lowering my shoulder bag to the floor.

Several painful moments passed before she told me to sit down and I gratefully sank into a chair in front of her desk. "I deliberately withheld that information," I said in a small voice, "because I've never actually practiced nursing and I don't feel qualified."

Marjorie shook her head. "I don't understand, Evelyn. Why didn't you just tell us you were a nurse when you arrived? Why would you withhold such important information?"

I could feel a lump rising in my throat but swallowed it before I spoke. "I wanted to be a Red Cross hostess," I mumbled. "I wanted to do the things regular RC workers do because I thought I'd be comfortable doing those things."

"But you've been working with the Red Cross for almost two months. And during that time, you've seen thousands of horribly wounded men being carried off ships. Surely you, of all people, must know how desperate London hospitals are for qualified nurses. Don't you realize that it's your duty to make yourself available to them?" She waited for my answer and when I didn't respond, she opened a file on her desk and flipped through it. "I think St Mary's would be a good fit for you and I'm going to ring them right now."

She picked up the phone, dialed a number, and asked to speak to the nursing supervisor. I listened as she had a brief conversation relating my qualifications. The receiver was hardly back in the stand before she told me to report to Matron-in-Chief Phyllis Young at St Mary's the next morning at eight sharp.

I left Marjorie's office in tears, upset with myself for not speaking up. Why had I no say about this? How could they just move me around like a pawn on a chessboard? Perhaps I should just go home, I thought, as I savagely kicked at piles of gray snow along the edges of the sidewalk. But I knew that wasn't possible. Now that we were at war with not only Japan, but also Germany and Italy, civilian travel was out of the question. What was I to do?

When I reached the boardinghouse, Ma Denny was sitting on the sofa in the lounge with a pot of tea and two cups on the table in front of her. "Come sit down," she said as I took off my coat. "I've just had a call from Miss Reynolds and I know you've had a bit of an upset."

I collapsed onto the sofa and blurted, "I don't understand how this could happen, Ma Denny. Why would they do this to someone who doesn't have any nursing experience?"

Ma Denny put her boney hand on my arm. "You'll understand, dearie, when you get to Saint Mary's. You'll see right away why your being there is so critical." She poured tea into the cups and handed one to me. As I began to sip from it, she lowered her voice to a whisper and said, "Almost anyone can make a pot of coffee and serve doughnuts. Almost anyone can read aloud to wounded men and write letters for them. And lots of people can drive a van. But you're different, Evelyn. You've had the privilege of an education . . . and not just any education. You're highly qualified, young lady, and whether you've had years of experience or not, we need you ever so badly in our hospital."

Ma Denny had always seemed such a quietly reserved woman that this surprised me, and her tone, and the things she'd said, forced me to look at her in a new light. It was clear that in this situation, I hadn't the foresight or understanding of either Marjorie or Ma Denny. The word *duty* came to mind and oh, do the Brits make use of that little word. I simply had to accept the fact that it was my *duty* to do what I could where I was needed most. The deal I'd made with my mother when I'd finished high school—her insisting that I complete a course of study in nursing before I moved to New York—proved to be insightful. But I'd never expected anything like this to happen and I was still perplexed by it. I turned to Ma Denny and asked, "But where will I stay? What about my things?"

"You're to stay right here with me," she answered. "Miss Reynolds called right after you left her office to ask me if you could possibly live here for a few more weeks. She said it might take as long as a month to find another place for you. I told her I'd be delighted to have you."

She stood up and took the empty cup from me. "Why don't you go on up to your room now and try to get a little nap before dinner. You've had a wringer of a day."

* * *

I awoke the next morning shivering from a bad dream. The tall man in the white suit had been standing at the foot of my bed talking to me. Words kept coming out of his mouth, but I couldn't hear them. He kept coming closer and closer and as he reached out to grab me, I saw that he had no teeth. I'd awakened in the dark with no light in the room save the face of the Big Ben sitting on my bedside table. It was 5:45. I knew I wouldn't go back to sleep so I put on my robe and went down to the kitchen where Ma Denny was supervising the girl who helped her with breakfast. The sight of the two of them bustling about in the warm kitchen soothed me and soon I was enjoying a cup of tea, weak but hot, and laughing at Ma Denny as she described what she would do if she were invited to have breakfast at Buckingham Palace with their majesties. Thoughts of the man in the white suit disappeared and soon I was hurrying back up to my room to dress for my appointment at St Mary's.

I liked Matron-in-Chief Phyllis Young the moment I met her. Tall and gracious, she welcomed me with a warm smile. I began our conversation by telling her that while I'd completed a degree in nursing at Ruxton Hospital, I'd never actually done any nursing and felt I was not qualified for a regular nursing position in a hospital the size of St Mary's. She was completely nonplussed and asked that I complete an application on the spot.

As soon as I'd finished the necessary paperwork, she invited me to accompany her on a tour. She took me first to the pediatric wing; then to the observatory balcony above the surgery theatres where we watched a team of doctors and nurses at work; to the lab; to the massive north wing which contained three stories of wards (filled with hundreds of wounded servicemen); to the cafeteria; and finally, to a lounge reserved for hospital staff. From a closet, Matron-in-Chief Young withdrew a gray uniform trimmed in burgundy braid and a white cambric apron. "Size six," she said, handing it to me. "That's what Miss Reynolds told me you would need. Please change into it now and report to Matron Gill at the third floor nurses' station in the north wing. She'll be your immediate supervisor. When you arrived at my office this morning at eight, you were on the clock, and you'll be working the seven-to-seven shift from now on. Welcome to St Mary's, Nurse Sanderson." She made a little bow as she left the room.

I did as I was told and reported to Matron Gill's office where I found a heavy-set gray-haired woman muttering to herself as she dug around in a file cabinet. She slammed a stack of papers on her desk and looked up to see me standing in the doorway. "So, you're the new girl," she said, giving me the once-over. "Well, sit down and let's get you started."

On that first day, Matron Gill had seemed brusque and demanding, but I soon came to know that deep down inside she is kind-hearted and completely devoted to her (our) profession. She gave me a thorough orientation and has been understanding, patient, and kind while I've stumbled along trying to find my way through situations that are vastly different from any in my limited experience. Much of this has had to do with vocabulary. For instance, the Brits say "elastoplast" instead of Band-Aid; cotton padding is called "cotton wool"; a beaker is a "mug"; the cast around a broken bone is a "plaster"; and the sterilizer is the "autoclave." While the fundamentals of practice are much the same, I have so much to learn!

Yesterday, Matron Gill called me into her office and promoted me—after only two weeks on the job—to a supervisor's position overseeing four wards of sixteen beds each. She did not wait for a response from me, but took me by the arm and led me to a tiny closet off a third-floor hallway where the door was open and a woman about forty sat behind a small desk. "This will be your office, Nurse Sanderson," Matron Gill said, "and Nurse Brack here will be your assistant." She left me with Nurse Brack and hurried away.

Constance Brack stubbed out the cigarette she'd been smoking and put out her hand. "Welcome," she said in a husky voice. While her smile seemed genuine, her eyes were cold and I wondered why. Perhaps she'd wanted the position I'd been given. Perhaps she resented the fact that I was an American. Maybe she coveted that little office. I thanked her for her welcome and went on to say that I'd been working for the Red Cross, but didn't say in what capacity. I decided on the spot not to tell Nurse Brack how little nursing experience I'd had because Matron Gill had told me earlier that Connie Brack had twenty years as a "general floor nurse" under her belt. While she was not an RN, she had me beat in spades when it came to practical application—something that was apparent from my first day on the job.

Connie Brack has been extremely helpful to me, and while she continues to carry a bit of a chip on her shoulder, she is forthcoming with her opinions and I don't know what I would do without her. I asked her to supervise our six nursing interns who are truly a gift from God. While they're very young, sixteen and seventeen, they perform well in the most trying circumstances and make every effort to maintain a professional stance. I didn't want to do this job, but I have to confess that things have not been as bad as I thought they'd be.

Ambulances filled with wounded arrive at St Mary's hour after hour, day after day, from various battlefronts. The weather has been particularly bitter, causing considerable hardship, and our patients have suffered terrible frostbite, not only to their fingers and toes, but also their noses. Dreaded gangrene has set in and dozens have ghastly raw stubs on their hands and feet where their rotting flesh was gnawed by rats. I was called in yesterday afternoon to assist Dr. Brompton as he removed bone from the ends of gnawed fingers and toes, and sewed the skin over to form a kind of stump. Most of these soldiers are so young, barely beyond boyhood. I find myself thinking about their poor mothers at home who must be wondering where their sons are and how they are and if they are getting enough to eat, with no idea of how much they're suffering—or even if they're still alive!

I had a big surprise last Friday afternoon when Marjorie Reynolds showed up at my office and told me that Britain's nightingale, Vera Lynn, had agreed to sing for thirty minutes at the Valentine's Dance at Red Cross Headquarters on the fourteenth. But she'd developed a bad case of strep throat and Marjorie wondered if I would please take her place? I flatly refused, but Miss Reynolds is a battalion on her own and I finally gave in. She found a beautiful pale pink chiffon gown for me, and, when he heard that I was performing, Stoney sent a huge corsage of gardenias. I was a hit with "Roses of Picardy" and saw tears in the eyes of some of the audience when I sang "For Sentimental Reasons." The weather was abominable—approaching blizzard conditions. But hundreds braved the elements and the dance floor was crowded throughout the night. I did a lot of dancing, met a lot of nice young men, danced with Stoney several times, and finally got back to Ma Denny's about two, and was on duty at St Mary's at seven.

When my shift ended this afternoon, I hurried down the stairs eager to get home. I had a dinner date with a naval officer I'd met at the dance and wanted to get a bath before I dressed. Just as I stepped onto the landing above the main floor, I came face to face with a small slender woman who smiled up at me and said, "Hey" as I sped by.

I turned, walked back up two steps to where she was standing, and put out my hand. "I don't think I've had the pleasure," I said, taking in a neatly arranged chignon of wheat-colored hair, large hazel eyes, and a scattering of impish freckles across a turned-up nose.

"Oh, I know all about *you*," she assured me as the two of us continued down the stairs to the lobby. "I know you grew up in North Carolina and came here to work for the Red Cross."

I moved closer. "And you are . . ." I looked at the badge on her collar. "Matron . . . ?"

"I'm Miriam," she replied. "Miriam Broadhurst. I work in surgery downstairs. I've been hoping to meet you so I could tell you how happy I am to have a colleague from the States."

"Thank you for this nice welcome," I exclaimed. "Where are you from, Miriam?"

"I grew up in Atlanta. You know, the place that's just a few miles from where Scarlett O'Hara grew up at Tara." Miriam and I shared a little laugh and I apologized for having to bring our conversation to an end. "Let's go to lunch," I suggested, and Miriam gave me a nod just before I stepped out into a whirlwind of snow.

CHAPTER 8

A Fast Learner

London, England • March 6, 1942

Another unusual day at St Mary's, and I'm beginning to think that "unusual" is the norm as nothing seems *usual* these days. When I arrived this morning, I found a hastily scrawled note from Dr. Brompton telling me to arrange for the immediate discharge of at least two dozen men in my care, and to add an additional four beds to each of my wards. He'd received word that two incoming battleships had reached the docks at Plymouth and more than three hundred of their wounded were being brought to St Mary's. Thank goodness Doctor B and I have developed a system, a routine for discharging patients that makes this task run smoothly. I gathered my staff to explain the situation and asked Nurse Brack to take care of the paperwork for the men who were being discharged.

The nursing interns and I spent the next two hours moving IVs, tubes and bottles, with the soldiers still attached to them and they still in their beds. What a blessing it is to have everything in the ward on rollers. At least half the men in my care are burn victims and all of them need an early morning dose of morphine to help them get through the day. So I quickly prepared and administered a tray of hypodermics. Dozens wore dressings that needed changing badly, but they simply had to wait. One poor boy had tiny bits of shrapnel in his rectum and penis. They were beginning to fester and I was so worried about him that I spent the better part of an hour removing them and getting him cleaned up, changed, and moved to a new bed. But none of my poor boys got a shave or a bath until after lunch today.

I don't know what Connie Brack and I would do without our fine group of nursing interns who spend hours washing and rewashing the badly soiled uniforms of the soldiers that are caked with blood and oil, and with animal waste or their own. Every day, the interns scrub everything in the ward with vinegar water—the beds, cabinets, and equipment. As soon as they had put the new beds in place this afternoon, I called them together and thanked them for doing such a good job. Then I gobbled down a Spam roll and a cup of tea and hurried off to find Matron Gill who'd left word that she wanted to see me as soon as possible.

I found her in the hallway conferring with a doctor making rounds. When they finished talking, she turned and pointed to her office, and I followed her in. She smiled as she motioned to the little chair in front of her desk. As I sat down she said, "I have some news for you, Nurse Sanderson. You're being transferred to the Emergency Surgery Unit on the ground floor." She paused to give me a moment before continuing. "You see, I wired Ruxton Hospital and asked for a complete set of your records—including the marks you received in each course. That's how I learned you were trained in surgical procedures." Her kind gray eyes looked directly into mine. "While your training was not extensive, it will be sufficient to get you started. You're a fast learner, Nurse Sanderson, and you've done a fine job supervising your wards. There's no doubt in my mind that you will make a good surgical nurse."

I opened my mouth, but she raised her hand and stopped me. "St Mary's is short of nurses with surgical experience, Evelyn. Desperately short. Do you realize how many wounded men brought off those ships from the North Atlantic this morning were taken directly to emergency surgery? Hundreds! This happens every day. And we simply do not have enough surgical facilities or qualified staff in the city to deal with a crisis of this magnitude."

"So, this evening when your shift ends, please clean out your locker upstairs and move your belongings down to the surgery unit. I know that you and Matron Broadhurst have met. She's one of the most capable nurses I've ever known, and I'm sure that you and she will get along well. She knows you'll be joining her staff and is very pleased. Now run along, my dear. Both of us have so much to do." With that, Matron Gill turned to the file cabinet beside her desk and began sorting papers into it.

I got up slowly, the burden of her words weighing on me. Surgery! Dear God, why did it have to be surgery? I started back down the hall, but ducked into the nearest WC and closeted myself inside a stall. Knots tightened in my stomach as an image formed in my mind . . . a slender, naked body, young and supple, covered in blood . . . a beautiful face, as pale as alabaster, ringlets of lustrous black hair . . . a ghastly death that remained my most vivid memory of Ruxton Hospital.

I took a deep breath, emerged from the loo, and started toward the stairs. Then I changed my mind, turned around, and headed back toward Matron Gill's office. I won't do it, I thought. They can't make me, can they? Somewhere nearby a bell started ringing, the warning bell alerting the hospital staff that wounded soldiers were being brought in . . . a soft *bleep, bleep, bleep* that meant everyone must clear the hallways. I flattened myself against the wall just as the first gurney came around the corner. On it lay a mass of bloody bandages wrapped in bloody sheets. I never saw a face as it went sailing past, but I could see that the left leg was missing, along with the left hand. Another gurney followed carrying a soldier with injuries to his chest. I rushed toward the stretcher and looked down into the face of a beautiful young boy with golden hair and pink cheeks. Surely he was no more than twelve. When I grabbed his hand, his bright eyes focused on mine, and I ran alongside him saying, "You're going to be fine. Everything's going to be okay. Just hold on . . . hold on." His eyes widened at the sound of my voice and his fingers clutched mine. By the time we reached the double doors to the surgery theatre my heart was racing, but I had to let go. Shame-faced, I turned and rested my forehead against the wall. How could you have been so selfish, so insensitive? I asked myself. How could you have even thought of saying *No* to Matron Gill?

This evening while the nurse's aides distributed dinner trays in the ward, I cleaned out my locker. I met the night staff coming in, umbrellas dripping, as I started down the stairs to Emergency Surgery. The ground floor of St Mary's contained three major areas that are vital to the function of any city hospital: the kitchen, the morgue, and the emergency surgery unit. Since it was dinnertime, scores of used dinner trays were stacked on rolling carts outside the huge scullery behind the cafeteria. I knew they might yet contain a little food, perhaps a spoonful of Bird's Custard or a bit of cold boiled potato, but it would be eaten before the night was over. No food was ever thrown away because too many people were hungry.

Around me dozens of women and men rushed about, moving equipment from place to place, yelling at one another above the din of crashing pots and pans. I smiled and waved as I went by and turned into the hallway that led to the surgery unit. Here the walls were lined with stretchers of bodies packed in linen bags waiting to be identified, to be claimed by loved ones, to be buried in the city's graveyards where centuries-old churches no longer stood. I hurried past them, trying not to think about who they were, or the life they'd led, or the horrible circumstances in which they'd died. I did not have to see their faces to know that most of them were very young, so young that they'd never know what it felt like to fall in love, get married, become a father. I shuddered as I thought of my own nephews, Wally and Cliff, and how I would feel if they were among this lot. I could hardly conceive that they, like the poor boys laid out in bags on these stretchers, would be so quickly gone from this earth, from this life, before they even knew what it was about.

I entered the double doors marked Emergency Surgery, walked past the two operating theatres where I would begin working the next morning, and headed to the offices at the back. I asked for the matron and was told that she was working in the supply room just ahead.

"Hey, North Carolina!" Miriam called as I walked in. She raised her arm and made a sweeping motion toward the floor-to-ceiling shelves behind her. "Welcome to my world!" she exclaimed from high atop a ladder. "This is what I do most evenings when my shift is over. Hand me that box of cotton bandages, will you?"

I reached down into a large crate stamped **LEND LEASE**, took out the remaining box, and handed it to her.

"Last one," she said, placing it on a shelf above her head. She came down the ladder, took my hand, and led me to her spacious, well-appointed office. No hand-me-downs here, I thought, as she moved a cushioned chair up near her desk. "I have a pot on for tea," she said, opening a drawer and bringing out two heavy white mugs and a round metal tin. "Let's celebrate! I can't tell you how pleased I am that you're joining our staff, Evelyn. Do you realize how nice it will be for me to not only *see*, but be able to talk with an American every day? I can't believe my luck!"

While she rinsed the teapot with boiling water, I told her that I was happy to see her, too, but I still had grave reservations about working in surgery.

"Here," she said, handing me a steaming mug. "This is what I do every evening when I have to face the elements. Oh, Lord, that sleety fog! That freezing rain! I brace myself with a nice hot cuppa before I start home. Since this is a special occasion, I have a special treat."

She looked at me, her gold-flecked eyes dancing as she pulled the lid from atop the tin and set it down between us.

As soon as the rich scent of butter and brown sugar reached my nostrils, I knew what it was. Inside, layered in wax paper, were a dozen pralines. "Where in the world did you ever get these?" I asked. "They must have crossed the Atlantic on angel's wings."

"Almost," she said. "No one in this whole hospital but *you* would even know what they are, Evelyn. Have one . . . and savor a bite of home." I took the smallest of the lot and bit into the sweet crumbly candy.

"I haven't had pralines in years," I exclaimed, trying not to smack my lips. "Where ever did you find them?"

Miriam took a piece of candy from the tin and sat down behind her desk. "I didn't," she said. "My brother, Simon, lives in Charleston with his wife and kids. He works at the shipyard there. They sent me these at Christmas and I've been saving them for a special occasion like this. I'm really looking forward to our working together, Evelyn. Do you realize that you're the only person in this hospital who understands what it's like to be not only an American, but an American from the South?"

I laughed. "Yes, I know exactly what you mean. I think I'll scream if someone calls me Yank again. I just can't seem to get used to it. How long have you been here, Miriam?"

"Since the spring of '38. Almost four years longer than you have. And I'm sure my adjustment was just as worrisome as yours has been, given where I started from. I wasn't always a nurse, you know. I spent the first thirteen years of my life on a cotton farm. My daddy was a tenant farmer and my mother worked just as hard as he did to keep the place going. And so did my big brother, Simon. Our dad died the spring I turned thirteen. And Simon finished high school a month later and joined the navy. My mom and I moved to Atlanta to live with her sister, my Aunt Delma, who has a drapery and upholstery business she runs out of her little house just south of Five Points. She moved her work into the basement so Mama and I could have the second bedroom upstairs. That fall, Mama got a job waitressing in a café about a mile from where we lived and I started high school in the big city."

I nodded as I took another bite of praline. "So, did you go to nursing school in Atlanta?"

"Yes. My high school chemistry teacher had a cousin who was a nursing instructor at Wesley Memorial Hospital School of Nursing. Her name was Clothilde Grady, and when my teacher told her I was the best student she'd ever had, Miss Grady encouraged me to apply for a scholarship to Wesley Memorial. She took me under her wing and guided me through the application process and helped me write a letter to the director. And when I was awarded the scholarship, she got me a job cleaning the hospital labs after classes. I could never have gone to school otherwise. By the time I finished my RN in 1936, I'd saved enough money to pay the tuition for an advanced certificate in surgical nursing, so I kept going to school. Then I married."

"Matron Gill told me about your husband, Elgin . . . about what a nice man he was and how he was killed during the Blitz. I'm so sorry, Miriam. Had you been married long?"

"Two years," Miriam said, her voice little more than a whisper. She looked down at her lap and I could tell she was uncomfortable, so I changed the subject. "Why did you decide to come to London?" I asked.

Miriam took another sip of tea, set the cup down on her desk, and wrapped her fingers around it. She looked away from me for a moment as if she were thinking about what she wanted to say. "I came because of Elgin. He grew up here in London, and after he'd completed training at King's College, he was hired at St Mary's. Elgin was twelve years older than I, and by the time we met, he'd made a name for himself as a surgeon. He was mechanically inclined and had all these ideas about ways to improve surgical instruments to make them easier to handle and more efficient. And he'd had a number of articles published in medical journals on the topic. The spring I finished my advanced certificate, the Atlanta

Medical Society sponsored a weekend symposium at Emory University. That Friday after classes, I decided to mosey over there and see what it was all about. I slipped into a room without knowing anything beyond the title of the session and the speaker's name, which was Dr. Elgin Broadhurst. Anyway, when the session was over everyone was invited to the back of the room for punch and cookies and a chance to meet Dr. Broadhurst. I found him very open and friendly and we stood and talked with one another until I knew I was going to miss my bus if I didn't excuse myself and leave. That's when Elgin asked me if I'd have dinner with him at his hotel's dining room. So, I called Mama and told her I'd be late, and Elgin flagged down a cab and we went uptown to the Peachtree Hotel. We had a wonderful meal, but neither of us paid much attention to our food. We talked about our work and our hopes for the future and the kinds of books we liked to read. When we left the dining room, I felt as if I'd known Elgin for years.

"As he put me in a cab to go home, he told me that he had to conduct another session in the morning, but asked if I would meet him at noon and show him around town. So, I took him to this Italian place for lunch, and afterward, we went to the High Museum. That night we had dinner at a steak house out on McDonough Road. On Sunday morning, Elgin joined Mama and Aunt Delma and me for church, and that afternoon, we treated him to a picnic in Piedmont Park. I made a seven-layer cake with fudge icing, and Mama and Aunt Delma fried a chicken and made potato salad and deviled eggs. We went all out for Elgin and he loved it!

"The next morning he caught a train for Charleston and I all but fell apart. The most wonderful man had walked into my life, and turned around and walked out of it. It was as if I'd had this fantastic dream and suddenly it had turned into a nightmare."

"Oh, my goodness," I said, licking the last vestiges of brown sugar from my lips. "What did you do?"

"I was just three days away from completing my advanced certificate. And on that very morning, I had a difficult lab to get through that was a major component of my final examinations. So I girded my loins, as they say, and headed to campus. As soon as the instructor let us go for lunch, I headed downstairs to the lobby to buy a sandwich and there stood Elgin talking with the receptionist. When I heard him ask her how to find me, I burst into tears. He turned around and saw me and went down on his knees right there on that cold stone floor and asked me to marry him. All these people were hustling back and forth beside us, but they stopped and listened while Elgin proposed. And when I said *yes*, they clapped and clapped. I was a little embarrassed, but so happy I began to cry again.

"That afternoon Elgin called the British Embassy in Washington and arranged for them to wire a temporary visa for me so I could travel back to England as the wife of a British citizen. Then he went to a jewelry store and bought a pair of matching wedding bands."

Miriam paused to show me the wide gold band on her finger. "I was a nervous wreck for the next three days trying to get through exams, trying to find time to shop for some new underwear and a nice nightgown, trying to pack. I didn't own a suitcase, but Aunt Delma came to the rescue and gave me one as a going-away present. And all the while Elgin was waiting patiently for me. On Thursday morning, I had my final three-hour oral exam and Elgin sat outside the door of the classroom and read so that he could take me to lunch when I finished. Mama and Aunt Delma gave a little party for us that evening and invited some of our neighbors and friends to meet Elgin. They'd been working like crazy refurbishing my only suit with a new lace collar and cuffs so I'd have something pretty to get married in. That Friday morning, May 12, 1938, Elgin and I took the train to Charleston, and late that afternoon we boarded a huge British liner, the RMS *Alcantara*. At ten minutes past midnight, the ship crossed into international waters and the captain married us. We had a glorious honeymoon aboard that beautiful ship and arrived here in London on May 17, 1938."

"Oh, Miriam," I blurted, "talk about a whirlwind romance. What a story!"

Miriam got up from her desk and removed a wool cloak from a hook on the wall behind her. "Yes, it was quite daring now that I think about it. One week. Elgin and I had known each other *one week* when we married." She pulled the cloak around her shoulders and picked up a purse from the side of her desk.

"You're staying at Ma Denny's boardinghouse, aren't you?" she asked, pulling on a pair of gloves. "I live in a flat just a block further *up the street* as we say in the South. Get your coat on, honey, and I'll walk you home."

CHAPTER 9

The Beech Tree Group

Hampshire, England • March 25, 1942

The past few days have been so busy at St Mary's that Miriam and I haven't had a minute to speak to one another outside the surgery. But yesterday I pulled her into her office and reminded her that I'd be off the next three days. At that time, I'd had no idea just what lay ahead and was content knowing I'd have some time to myself. But on that score, I was wrong.

Early the next morning, Stoney's chauffeur, Rutledge, picked me up in the Bentley and I was taken, along with two other people, to a farm in Hampshire—a journey of almost two hours. When Stoney called the week before and invited me for an outing in the country, he'd told me nothing about where I'd be going, only that I'd be joining him and some friends for lunch.

One of my traveling companions was a woman in her twenties, Sylvia Kendall, a native of Warwickshire, who moved to London at age fifteen to finish her education. She taught school for several years, but told me she currently transcribes documents at Whitehall. She's of medium height and very slender with thick dark hair, which she'd wound into a double chignon on the nape of her neck. She was wearing a rather shabby, but clean, navy-blue suit and white blouse, wool hat, and a flannel-lined raincoat. Her shoes were sturdy and rather the worse for wear . . . normal here. While I would not call her "pretty," she is attractive. Her eyebrows are dark and bushy, but her eyes, which are large and gray, are rather sad. She was a good conversationalist with whom I felt comfortable from the onset.

Our companion was a Catholic priest, Father Barney, who wore a black wool suit with a cleric's collar, topped by a gray wool overcoat. He said his name was Bernard Fogelman and he'd been born in Berlin and lived there until the age of twelve. His English mother, now deceased, had sent him to boarding school in England. He and Mrs. Kendall have been friends for years. She told me that Barney, as she calls him, speaks five languages fluently. He's about thirty-eight, I suppose, and has a mop of wavy blond hair and the most remarkable eyes. They're neither green nor blue, but a stunning combination like the sea at sunset, what an artist might call *shimmering teal.* He nodded occasionally during our conversation, but kept pretty quiet. Mrs. Kendall, on the other hand, was quite friendly and asked me questions about where I was from and why I'd come to London.

We traveled through sun-dappled hills in an area known as the Hampshire Borders until we reached Basingstoke. There, we left the main road and headed west into the New Forest where we happened upon a small group of wild ponies and Rutledge slowed the car so I could get a good look at them before we turned onto a muddy path of wagon ruts that had deep ditches on either side. About a half-mile in, the road opened and I could see a copse of greening beech trees ahead. Presently, we came to a farmhouse of sand-colored stone that was crowned by a scalloped thatched roof and surrounded by those magnificent trees. Four mullioned windows lined the front of the house, the sills of each hung with wooden boxes I assumed would soon be planted with spring flowers. It was the kind of place one sees pictured in travel magazines—stunningly beautiful, idyllic, and serene on this rare sunny day.

An attractive middle-aged woman of impeccable bearing was waiting for us just inside the front door. She held her hand out to me and, and when I took it, she told me she was Mrs. Cargill, the manager of the farm. As Father Barney came in she gave him a peck on the cheek. Then she and Sylvia hugged each other with genuine affection. She led us down a long hallway to the back of the house where Stoney was seated at a large table in the center of a spacious room flooded in sunlight. He greeted us in his usual affable manner and invited us to join him at the table. I was surprised when Mrs. Cargill took a chair, and more so when Rutledge removed his double-breasted jacket and donned an Argyle sweater that was hanging on the back of the chair he eventually sat in.

As soon as all of us were comfortable, Stoney turned directly to me and said, "Welcome to Beech Tree Farm, Miss Sands. You've probably introduced yourself to Mrs. Kendall and Father Barney as Evelyn Sanderson, but they know you're Eve Sands. And like me, they hope to be able to call you by your given name, Evelyn. Will that be all right?"

"Certainly," I said, smiling at everyone. "I'd prefer it."

"Good. We hope you'll come to love this farm, and what it represents, as much as we do. I don't want to alarm you, but there simply is no other way to explain why we've invited you here. After much thought and discussion, we want to ask if you'd consider joining us in what some would call a clandestine operation. We are a unit of C131—a civilian underground operation whose sole purpose is to undermine the enemy in every possible way while remaining totally outside the military and its objectives. We have thirty-two members, most of whom live and work in France."

My stomach turned over while a flush spread across my cheeks. Stoney remarked upon my reaction and hastened to tell me that our meeting was being held in the strictest confidence and that I was under no obligation should I have no interest in the work of the group.

At that point, Mrs. Cargill went to the sideboard and poured a cup of tea. As she handed it to me, she said, "We're sorry, my dear, that this is such a surprise. We did not intend to startle or frighten you. But Lord Beeton-Howard feels strongly that you'd make a good courier and we need good couriers badly. . . and the sooner, the better." She gave me a gentle pat on the shoulder before she went back to her chair.

I sipped the tea to give myself a moment to think and, as I did so, glanced over the rim of my cup at each of their faces. All eyes were on me, so I put the cup down, leaned into the table, and addressed Stoney. "I don't understand. What's this about?"

But it was Sylvia Kendall who answered. "Johann Claus," she said, in a flat tone as if I would know her meaning. "Lord Beeton-Howard has told us about your unusual abilities, Evelyn . . . your keen observation skills and your gift for details."

Father Barney, who was seated on my right, reached over and squeezed my hand. "We've been told by reliable sources at the war office that what you saw and heard on the *Althone* helped save the lives of thousands of British soldiers fighting in tank battalions in North Africa. That kind of valuable information is key to our survival in this war. Comprenez-vous, mademoiselle?"

I cocked my head at him and asked, "Porquoi voudriez-vous me voulez?"

Stoney chimed in, "Well, for one thing you have an excellent command of the French language, as you've just demonstrated. And with a few simple lessons and some practice, we feel confident that you could pass yourself off as French *in France*, where we need you."

"Oh, no! I couldn't possibly!" flew out of my mouth. "Why would you think I'd be foolish enough to go to a country swarming with Germans? What woman in her right mind would consider such a thing?"

Rutledge got my attention when he cleared his throat. "Before you decide about venturing that far, Evelyn" he said, "perhaps you'd consider spending time with us to learn more about our group and the work we do. I'm sure Barney can provide you with all the information you'd need to help you make your decision."

I was suddenly aware of Rutledge's erect bearing, his aristocratic speech—much like that of Lord Beeton-Howard. I'd assumed when I'd first met Rutledge that he was an East Ender, but I was obviously wrong. I suspected that Rutledge and Father Barney were neither chauffeur nor priest. This was confirmed when Rutledge turned to me and said, "The Red Cross uniform you used to wear, and your knowledge of that organization and how it operates, can give you entree into places not everyone can go."

I looked around the table again, taking a moment to study the people there. "Are any of you actually the person you told me you were? Or, are all of you someone else?"

Sylvia Kendall laughed. "Yes," she said, "some of us really *are* the people we said we were. I actually work as a transcriptionist for the Prime Minister. And I truly did grow up in a vicarage in Warwickshire. And Mrs. Cargill *is* the manager of Beech Tree Farm. But it would only be fair to tell you that, as a young woman, she was not only a nurse, but also an underground agent in Belgium during the last war. Oh, and Lord Beeton-Howard is who you think he is—Sixth Earl Croxdon. And yes, he owns factories in and out of London, and has an estate in Staffordshire. Father Barney, however, is not a priest, nor is he Catholic. He's a French historian and a professor of Greek and Latin. Oh, and a pugilist . . . the best boxer in his class."

Barney interrupted. "That was many years ago, Evelyn. I was just twelve when my parents sent me to Harrow the summer after the Austrian archduke was assassinated in Sarajevo. Stoney was our house captain and took me under his wing and taught me all things British. And he insisted I accompany him to Stoneham Feld for school holidays when it was too dangerous for me to go to Berlin. He also helped me get through Eton. And while I'm very fond of everyone around this table, I don't know what I would have done had it not been for my friend Stoney."

He made a little bow to Stoney before continuing, "Rutledge is William Rutledge here in England, but Artur, Count Zielinski, in Poland. He came here in the '20s to boarding school and finished law studies in Warsaw in 1935. Then he returned to England through an underground network like ours and went to work for Beeton Consolidated Industries. He's also a pilot, fluent in German, and reconnaissance is his specialty. Three years ago, his parents were forced out of their home in Gdansk and transported to a Nazi labor camp."

Mrs. Cargill touched me on the arm. "Since Rutledge came to school here, as did Barney, you'll be the only outsider, my dear," she said, "the only one of our group here who was not educated, to some extent, in England. We think of Father Barney, who is half German, as one of us because his mother was English and he's lived here most of his life. We need someone from the outside. Someone clever like you who'll see the things we don't, as they may appear normal to us." She smiled then and her green eyes twinkled with mischief. "Oh, we know you'll stick out like the proverbial sore thumb. You're so pretty with your dazzling white teeth and that gorgeous auburn hair. Are you sure you didn't pose for Titian in another life?" She paused to raise an eyebrow and others around the table laughed. "We think your looks will be an asset in this business. Nothing compared to your brains, of course. We know you've had a successful career on stage, Evelyn, and that will be an invaluable asset, too. You're used to being someone you're not—at least some of the time." She smiled at me and rose from her chair. "I must see about lunch."

Stoney stood up, nodded to Mrs. Cargill, and invited me to walk with him. I followed him down a hallway to the scullery where he took off his street shoes, put on a pair of hunting boots, and selected a Meerschaum pipe from a half dozen arranged on a stand on the zinc-topped counter. He handed me a pair of Wellies, which fit perfectly, and opened a door that led to a large terrace where the sun's bright rays made geometric patterns across the flagstone. Stoney stopped to light his pipe while I pulled on my boots, and as he began to draw on it, the air around us filled with a lovely smell that reminded me of dried peaches.

As we walked away from the house, he turned to me and said, "I've been meaning to ask you how you learned to speak French so well?"

"My mother taught me. She had a governess who grew up in Paris and came to North Carolina in the 1890s. She taught my mother French, Italian, piano, and voice."

"Well," Stoney mused, "you obviously take after your mother." He headed toward a stand of large trees and, after we'd gone a few yards, turned to give me a very serious look.

"When your president declared December 7, 1941 a date which will live in infamy, it was an understatement," he said. "Few people knew then, nor do they realize now, what's at stake for *all* of us, Evelyn, for we are on the eve of Armageddon. It isn't generally known, but all of Europe is to be destroyed and rebuilt as one huge German empire. That's Hitler's plan. Napoleon had nothing on this bastard. Alexander, either. And we British, and you Americans, are all that stand between this monster and his bloody grand design."

Stoney took another drag from his pipe, blew the smoke skyward, and continued. "Johann Claus and his contact, John Blackstoke, are in prison. And you were right. Claus is not his real name. It's Heinrich . . . Heinrich Arndt. He's the nephew of a Wehrmacht colonel. And the cigarette lighter Blackstoke left for him on the bar that night at the Rose and Crown contained a roll of microfilm with twenty four photocopies of diagrams outlining tank deployments in North Africa. Blackstoke is Gunther Holz, the son of

German immigrants, who moved to England after the last war. Four other men are members of their particular group and they've also been arrested. The tall man in the white suit is dead. Sylvia's sources have confirmed that he was Carlos Vasquez from Madrid. Two weeks ago, British agents killed him in a shoot-out in a village in the Pyrenees."

"Sylvia . . . Sylvia told you this about the man in the white suit?"

"Yes. Sylvia. Mrs. Kendall. While she's officially a transcriptionist, her job is much more involved than that. She's the prime minister's liaison with one of Great Britain's most important underground organizations, which I'm sworn never to divulge."

"Why haven't you told me this, Stoney?"

"Because I haven't felt the time was right. You've been busy with your new job at St Mary's and I thought it best to wait a little longer because there was so much more I felt you needed to know. There are rings of spies operating all over England, Evelyn, and it's not only the Germans. Unfortunately, many English are sympathetic to Hitler's cause. They think Germany was treated unfairly at the end of the last war . . . that inflation has ruined the German economy, and we British, and you Americans, are to blame. The Germans have always despised the French, and Hitler has cleverly stirred the flames of that simmering hatred to a boil.

"Week in and week out, the Nazis are transporting thousands of people, mainly Jews, out of Warsaw, Prague, Budapest, and other cities in Eastern Europe. Last winter, Barney and Rutledge made two trips into Poland and returned with hundreds of photographs showing people being loaded onto trains and taken away. From what we know now, they're being forced to work in the camps that produce weapons and equipment for the Nazi war machine. And just as hard as we're working to uncover these things, there are factions all over Europe, and in America, too, trying to cover them up . . . to bury the whole dreadful business.

"We've had an awful winter here in England, as you know, one of the coldest on record," he went on. "And it's been just as cold in France. But there's no heat in France. No coal, no food, no medicine. Everything in France is going to support the German military. Our sources tell us that this past winter more than twenty-five hundred planes were manufactured by French factory workers for the Luftwaffe. And anyone who resists is simply shot. There are no court systems in France now. Are you, by chance, familiar with the word *maquis*?"

I nodded. "A bit," I said. "Doesn't it mean brush or bush . . . something like that?"

"My understanding is that it originated on Corsica where inland areas are covered in thick scrubby underbrush. Anyway, a group of French men trying to escape labor conscription fled into the southern mountains where they set up camps from which they carry out clandestine operations against the Nazis. While they have no central organization, they've been highly effective. Over the last two years Barney has made numerous trips into France in order to establish connections for us. His contacts in Rouen say that thousands of men and women are living out in the bush all around the countryside fighting the Nazis every day. You'd be surprised what a large network they have, and the ingenious methods they've devised to thwart the Germans and destroy their equipment and weapons. One of their most successful ruses is an underground newspaper, *Defense de France*, which produces false identity cards, ration books, birth and death certificates, stamps and seals . . . any kind of document that might save a life.

"These are the courageous people the Beech Tree Group is trying to help, Evelyn. These maquis groups need food and medicines, and weapons and explosives . . . and simple things like jackets and boots and shoes, which are so very difficult to get these days in France. They're risking their lives every day. Not only for the sake of France, but for *all* of us."

As Stoney shared his concerns, I tried to imagine what it must be like to live out in the open, unprotected from the cold and rain, ill-clad and hungry, and vulnerable to an aggressive enemy with unlimited resources. This produced such raw, untouched feelings in me that I teared up. Stoney handed me his handkerchief and I stepped away. I felt an absolute fool standing there blowing, but couldn't help myself. When we'd walked out onto the terrace I'd been clearly frightened at the prospect of joining his group and determined not to. But over the last little while a veil had been lifted and a new world had been opened to me—a world about which I knew little beyond the fact that it was incredibly dangerous. I wasn't sure what to say, but I knew in my gut that I couldn't ignore what I'd heard.

I slipped Stoney's used handkerchief into my pocket to wash later and walked back to where he was waiting. "I'm not sure what I can do to help, Stoney," I said. "I know nothing about weapons or explosives."

"And you don't need to know much about those things, Evelyn. Our job is focused on getting resources to people and what we desperately need is an experienced actress. You're used to camouflage, to disguises, you've worn them for years. And you have the ability to slip into a role and become another person."

"But I can't do that at the drop of a hat. That takes time."

"There isn't much time, my dear," he replied. "But we here at Beech Tree Farm will do everything in our power to help you, to teach you, to prepare you. Your French is flawless, but it would never work among the French. It is too stilted, too studied. Parisians would be unlikely to betray you unless they were caught in a trap and had no alternative. But the Vichy would arrest you in a second, and they are only slightly less brutal than the Gestapo. We have colleagues in London who can pass for almost any kind of Frenchman, or Frenchwoman, from almost any walk of life. They will help you become more French than Coco Chanel! And Barney Fogelman will be chief among them. Instead of being in front of the footlights, you'll be working backstage. You're familiar with that aren't you?"

I nodded. "Yes, indeed. I've spent considerable time backstage. But I've never actually *worked* there."

"There's no need to worry about that because Barney will act as your stage manager. He'll be the director, too. I'll take the role of producer and provide funding for your missions. And you'll be doing what you do so well . . . acting. There's no pay, Evelyn, no monetary compensation, because all our resources go to help the Maquis. But the Beech Tree Group can offer you room and board, clothing, and all the supplies and equipment you'll need. Can you handle a gun?"

I tried to disguise the shock I felt and hurried to answer. "Yes, my father taught my sister and me to shoot. We shot quail, rabbits, that sort of thing, out at our farm. I never liked it, but I did it to please him. I had a pretty good eye, but it's been years."

"We'll talk more about that. While your work will not involve direct use of weapons, you may need a pistol at times for protection." He took one last pull on his pipe and tapped the bowl on the side of his hand to empty the ashes before taking my arm. "You're living in a boardinghouse in Piccadilly, aren't you?" I nodded, and asked how he knew. "Oh, we've had our eye on you for a while now. Would you mind moving?"

"I'm not sure," I answered, wondering what he had in mind.

"We have a cottage near Maida Vale. Mrs. Kendall moved there last week along with another colleague, Miss Jerusha Tuttle, whom I've hired as housekeeper and cook. It isn't very large, but I think it will be adequate for the three of you. You'll have a room of your own and share a bath with Sylvia. The nearest tube station is only two blocks away. We want you to continue working at your present job at St

Mary's. Please ring me at the factory at any time." He drew a business card from inside his jacket and handed it to me.

Charles Edmund Stoneham Beeton-Howard,
President
BEETON CONSOLIDATED INDUSTRIES
No. 65 Osterley Place
London, England
Tel: R – 1713

"And we'd like you to remain in an unofficial capacity with the Red Cross because, as Rutledge said, your uniform opens doors. I've already discussed this with Marjorie Reynolds."

We finished our walk back to the house in silence. Stoney stopped outside the back door. "Sylvia Kendall is a widow," he said. "She lost her husband, Robert, during the evacuation of Dunkirk. Rob was a platoon leader bringing a group of men from Armentières to the evacuation area on the beach. Three of his men fell behind. One of them sprained his ankle and two of his friends were helping him. Rob went back to find them. Some German soldiers came out of nowhere, trained guns on them, and began shouting that they were prisoners. Rob stepped toward them and they shot him in the chest. Two of those boys . . . they were only seventeen and eighteen . . . were taken by the Nazis, but one managed to get away and eventually made it to the beach. Otherwise, we would probably never have known what happened. Sylvia was pregnant at the time and lost the baby.

"Sylvia is twenty-five years old, the daughter of a vicar of some renown, the Right Reverend Dr. Richard Blessington. Several of his sermons have been published in highly respected magazines and journals. She has a cousin in Parliament, Harold Makepeace, who happens to be a solicitor on retainer with my firm. Sir Harold introduced Sylvia to the prime minister and she made such an impression on him that she was hired immediately at Whitehall. During their conversation, he muttered something in Latin, an offhand remark, and she responded—in Latin. Not many people would have had the expertise, or nerve, to do that. But Sylvia, regardless of her quiet unassuming nature, has plenty of *chutzpah* as the Jews say."

He was quiet for a moment, which added a bit of weight to his last remark. "Would you consider moving into the house with Sylvia tomorrow?" He did not wait for a reply. "I could have Rutledge call for you and your things at the boardinghouse late tomorrow afternoon so you wouldn't have to leave the hospital too early."

"I suppose I could, but how am I to explain this to Mrs. Sutcliffe at the boardinghouse? I wasn't supposed to move out until the end of the month. She'll want to know why I'm leaving."

"Don't concern yourself with that," he replied. "Marjorie Reynolds has another RC worker moving into your room at Mrs. Sutcliffe's day after tomorrow. Everything's been properly arranged."

"Goodness! Well, I suppose I could be ready by then," I answered.

"Splendid! Now, let's go see what Mrs. Cargill has laid on the board."

As Stoney reached for the doorknob, I touched the sleeve of his jacket. "Before we go in, may I ask you something?" With his hand still on the knob, he turned to look at me.

"What will happen to Johann Claus?"

"He, and his colleagues, went before a military tribunal two weeks ago. They'll be hanged next Wednesday at Scotland Yard."

"Hanged!" I cried. "Oh, Stoney! How awful! Just like that . . . they'll be hanged. But Claus is married and a father."

"Yes, he is. Most of those men are. But the punishment for treason in Great Britain—as it is in America—is hanging."

I took a step back, hoping to separate myself from the fact that I'd had a role in such a horrible situation. "I can't do this," I said, lifting my hands to expose my palms as I began to move away from Stoney, praying that he would change his mind about my joining his group.

Suddenly, he was at my side grabbing both my hands and pressing them inside his with such force I winced. "Suppose the situation had been reversed," he whispered, as his fingers tightened. "Suppose that day we had lunch at the Savoy Grille I'd told you that three thousand British soldiers had been massacred by the Germans because a woman who knew what was going to happen to them failed to act? Suppose those young men had died because that woman couldn't face the fact that the criminals who'd planned and organized the act of killing them would be hanged as traitors to their country?"

I jerked my hands away from his and covered my face with them. "I don't know," I hissed from behind my shield. "I don't know what to think."

Stoney moved closer, gently pulled my hands away, and looked down at me. "Let me ask you something, Evelyn. If you'd heard two *American* men talking in the storeroom on the *Althone* instead of Claus and the man in the white suit, would it have made any difference? If two Americans had been talking about blowing up British tank battalions in Africa, about killing thousands of soldiers, would *that* have kept you from telling someone about their plans?"

I jerked my hands from his, turned on my heel, and walked across the terrace in an effort to get away from the desperation I'd felt while trapped in the *Althone's* hold with Claus and the man in the white suit. Kicking at small stones, I tried to put a bit of distance between me and Stoney's nagging question and kept walking toward a copse of trees. As I struggled for an answer, I looked up into a mighty beech where dozens of strong limbs formed a canopy over my head. Along the ridges of the tree's delicate branches tiny green buds the size of squirrel's ears were beginning to unfurl. Spring was right around the corner and before long people would be going on picnics and boat rides and enjoying the outdoors.

The day before at St Mary's, Miriam and I had been overwhelmed by an unending stream of mutilated soldiers from the British 70th Division who'd been garrisoned throughout the winter in the Libyan deserts west of the port city of Tobruk. Despite the massive wounds and horrible burns they'd incurred during fierce fighting there, hundreds had survived the sea voyage home to England. One young man, with hair the color of pine straw and eyes as dark as huckleberries, had been at death's door when the orderlies laid him on the table in front of me. I'd removed a filthy bandage from his upper chest and stared at what looked like a pile of raw hamburger with edges oozing black where deadly gangrene had set in. I began cutting away his rotted flesh, but it had melted in my hands like jello, releasing an awful stench that made me gag. I'd not had much hope for him, but later that day Miriam had come to assure me he was on the mend.

I stood there beneath that beech tree thinking about that boy, and it hit me like a bolt out of the blue that he could easily have been one of thousands of British soldiers killed if I'd not told Stoney about Claus and the man in the white suit. That poor boy would not have been brought home to England. Nor would he have lived to see another spring.

I turned and walked back to where Stoney was waiting by the door. "No," I began. "It would not have made any difference if the two men I saw in the storeroom on the *Althone* had been American. We'd better go in now and tell your group I've decided to give this a try. But I've never done anything like this before, Stoney. You'll have to give me some time to prepare."

Relief flooded Stoney's face. "Absolutely nothing will happen until you're ready, Evelyn," he said. "We'll tell Barney not to plan any operation that involves your going into France with him until this summer."

* * *

A fine mist wrapped me like a cocoon as I trudged home the following afternoon to find Rutledge waiting with the Bentley. I'd left my packed suitcase and trunk in the hallway at Ma Denny's and was a bit embarrassed by the size and weight of the old trunk, but Rutledge had no problem hoisting it down the steps and into the back of the car.

He headed north to Hyde Park, and about twenty minutes later turned onto a cobblestone drive just off Hertford Street. A moment later, we came to a three-story house of tawny stone that had fancy lintels over the large doors and windows. All were filled with black-out curtains.

"That's Croxdon House," Rutledge said as we drove past. "Lord Beeton-Howard and Barney and I live there, along with Lord Beeton-Howard's man, Hatch . . . the majordomo, cook, house cleaner, and all 'round what-have-you. Hatch was m'lord's dogsbody during the last war and has been with him ever since."

We continued down the path and around a curve to a much smaller building located in what the English refer to as a mews, the alleyway between the two houses. Like the larger house, this house was made of beige stone, but had only two stories. And even though it hadn't any fancy hedges or lintels, it did possess a certain charm. Rutledge stopped just in front of the door and turned to me. "This is Corrie Cottage. It was named for the first couple who came to work here from Stoneham Feld when Croxdon House was built in the early 1800s. Miss Jerusha Tuttle will be keeping house and cooking for you and Mrs. Kendall. She was Lord

Beeton-Howard's nurse from the time he was born. They are completely devoted to each other."

The front door, located on the left end, opened and the fairy godmother from *Cinderella* stepped out, her cheeks glowing like pink satin beneath sparkling violet eyes. She pulled the heavy black shawl she was wearing closer around her plump shoulders before she took my hand and said, "I'm Jerusha Tuttle and never in all my born days did I ever think I'd be living with a celebrity! Lord Beeton-Howard has told me all about you, Miss Sands." Her little hands fluttered, and I smiled as an image of her changing his lordship's nappies while his little legs pumped and his naked bottom flashed filled my head. Embarrassed by this sudden intimacy, I quickly brushed it aside and followed her from the front hallway into a long rectangular room.

Like the house at Beech Tree Farm, this one was comfortably furnished. Two armchairs covered in faded chintz, and a humpback divan, were positioned to take advantage of the simple fireplace on the far wall. The wallpaper was a soft yellow, lavender, and green print that complemented the hooked rug in front of the hearth. Opposite was a curved archway that led to an intimate alcove containing a drop leaf table, six chairs, a server, and sideboard.

Out of the corner of my eye, I saw Rutledge come into the hallway and start upstairs with my trunk, so I assumed he knew which of the bedrooms would be mine. "Won't you have some tea?" Miss Tuttle asked, as she placed a tray with cups and a pot on the table in front of the sofa. "I've been saving this tea for a special occasion. You see, I've never really known an American before and this is a special day for me."

I couldn't help laughing. "I hope you won't be disappointed when you discover that I'm no different from anybody else," I said. "What might I do to help?"

"Not a thing, dearie. Just sit here by the fire and enjoy your tea. I know you've had a busy day at the hospital. I'll be back in a jiffy." She hurried from the room in her gray wool slippers with cuffs around the ankles, the kind my granddaddy had always worn. While I drank the lovely tea, I thought about the letter I'd be writing to my mother about Corrie Cottage and Jerusha Tuttle. A moment later, Rutledge bounded down the stairs. I got up and went into the hall to thank him and Miss Tuttle rushed in to tell him good-bye. As she closed the front door, she said, "Would you care to see your room now, Miss Sands?"

I followed her up the stairs to the landing, where she opened the door to a small but spotless bath. On the left a narrow hallway led to two bedrooms. "Mrs. Kendall moved in last week," she said, "and she took the bedroom at the end of the hall. She said she thought you would be more comfortable having the inside bedroom as it will be warmer and you're not used to our cold, English winters."

"How thoughtful," I remarked.

"She is thoughtful, Mrs. Kendall is. About the most thoughtful person I've ever known, especially for one so young. Now, come on inside and make yourself to home."

While the room was small, in one corner there was a fireplace that contained a grate filled with coal—an unbelievable luxury. Against the interior wall were twin beds covered in green chenille spreads. Opposite them under a large window, was a simple lady's desk and chair. On one end of it, framed by bronze bookends, was a collection of old books. Curiosity got the best of me and I crossed the room to find a volume of Shakespeare's sonnets, Jane Austen's *Sense and Sensibility*, Hardy's *The Return of the Native*, and a copy of *The Essays of Elia by Charles Lamb*.

Miss Tuttle stood quietly while I read the titles out loud. "His lordship brought those by this morning on his way to work," she said. "He wanted to be sure you had something nice to read after a long day at St Mary's." How kind, I thought, as she opened the doors of a double wardrobe to show me how she'd arranged my things.

"Mrs. Kendall will be along any minute," she said. "She's usually here about six. Would you like to take off your uniform and slip into something more comfortable while I put the final touches on dinner?" She walked over to one of the beds, turned back the spread, and fluffed the pillow. "We Londoners eat our evening meals earlier now. Because of the blackout, I suppose. Would dinner at six thirty suit?"

"Whenever you and Mrs. Kendall are ready, Miss Tuttle, just let me know. I'm not likely to miss a meal if I can help it. Thank you so much for preparing this lovely room for me and for your kind words of welcome. You've made me feel right at home."

At six thirty, I went down dressed in a Fair Isle sweater and wool slacks to find Sylvia Kendall in a dressing gown sitting on the striped sofa opposite a blazing fire. She looked a bit weary and mentioned that she'd had an especially busy day. I asked about the prime minister and she told me he was suffering with a dreadful cold, doctoring it with regular shots of brandy and Beechams Powders, and bustling about with a bee in his bonnet as usual.

Miss Tuttle came in carrying a small silver tray that held two glasses of sherry. Each of us took one and I settled into a chair near the fireplace. Neither of us spoke while we sipped our drink. Soon, Miss Tuttle was back to tell us that dinner was ready.

The dining table had been set with beautiful china and white damask napkins. After Sylvia and I seated ourselves, Miss Tuttle served plates of brown-crusted lamb chops and a casserole of leeks au gratin. "Lord Beeton-Howard wanted you to have something special on your first night together," she said. "I suggested lamb. I hope you like it, Miss Sands. You probably won't see another meal like this for quite a while."

"Oh, Miss Tuttle, this is glorious," I exclaimed. "Please convey my appreciation to Lord Beeton-Howard. I didn't think one could even get lamb chops here now."

Sylvia smiled. "Stoney Beeton-Howard can get anything he wants, can't he, Miss Jerusha? If he can't buy it, he can charm someone out of it. Isn't that right, Miss Jerusha?"

Jerusha Tuttle nodded. "Himself could charm me into anything his little heart desired when he was three years old . . . and he still can. He's the one brought me that Darjeeling tea, Miss Sands. I expect these lovely chops come from Beech Tree, or mayhap, Stoneham Feld. I know he's made trips to both places in the last few days."

As she started to the hallway, she turned back and said, "You lassies relish every bite. Tomorrow night we'll be back to fried eel and brussels sprouts. There's afters on the sideboard. Just leave everything as is when you've finished."

As soon as Miss Tuttle was out of the room, I turned to Sylvia. "What's *afters?*

"Sweets. Tonight it's biscuits and coffee, what you Americans call dessert."

I nodded. "Please help me remember to say biscuits, not cookies. Sorry to be so full of questions, but what's Stoneham Feld?"

"It's Lord Beeton-Howard's estate in Staffordshire. His mother, the Dowager Countess Millicent Altha Elizabeth Howard, lives there. And that's where the potteries are." Sylvia pointed the end of her fork at my plate. "You're eating from the famous Royal Beeton china. This particular pattern was made on the estate more than a hundred years ago."

"It's so lovely with those little violets around the rim. I feel honored that Miss Jerusha wanted to use it for our first dinner together."

Sylvia shook her head. "I think Lord Beeton-Howard made that decision. He's very concerned that he's uprooted you, so he's making an extra effort, I expect."

"Well, he need not. I think he's a very nice man regardless of his famous china from Stoneham Feld. Is that where his wife lives?"

"No. She's in an asylum in Cumbria."

96

"An asylum? Why is she in an asylum?"

"It's all very hush-hush, but the term that is politely used is *mentally unstable*. I'm sorry, Evelyn, but I don't know the circumstances. Since Miss Tuttle was living on the estate when Lady Lydia was taken away, I'm sure she knows all about it. But I've never felt I could ask. All I know is Lady Lydia suffered some sort of trauma several years ago and has been institutionalized ever since."

"What a tragedy. And Stoney's never mentioned it?"

"No, never. And those of us who are aware just avoid the issue. It's as if it never happened." Sylvia turned away and began cutting into a piece of lamb.

"What about Barney? Is he married?" I asked.

Sylvia paused to swallow. I thought she was about to say something, and when she didn't, curiosity got the best of me. "Does he have a girl friend? Is he involved in a relationship?"

"No," she replied, "there's no girl friend. Barney was married, but his wife was killed in a bus accident. One morning she went to visit her parents in Reading and never came home. Christina was a lovely girl and I've always thought when it happened that she was pregnant and on her way to tell her parents the good news. It was quite a blow for all of us. After the funeral, Barney left London and got a job working as a fisherman on the south coast. He took a little room-let in Falmouth and the only person who saw him during those years was Stoney."

Well, I thought, no wonder our priest is so quiet. I concentrated on my food and it wasn't but a moment before Sylvia changed the subject.

"How long did you live in New York, Evelyn?" she asked. "I understand you had quite a career on Broadway."

"I was there eleven years and loved every minute of it. But one day at rehearsal, I had a rude awakening when I realized that it wouldn't be long before I'd be replaced by someone younger."

Sylvia nodded. "And were you? Were you replaced by someone younger? Is that why you left New York?"

I wasn't ready to share the details of why I'd left New York, so I said, "No, that didn't happen. Last fall, a friend introduced me to a woman who'd been working for the Red Cross here in London. If you'd asked me five years ago if I would consider going to England to work for the Red Cross, I'd have laughed. Did you think, five years ago, that you'd be doing what you're doing now?"

Sylvia shook her head. "Even in my wildest dreams, I could never have imagined that I'd be working for the prime minister. Could anyone ever imagine such a thing?"

"You told me you grew up in a village where your father was the vicar. What about your mother? Did you have any brothers or sisters?"

"Actually, I grew up on a farm called Hullerbank Hill near the village of Delbridge. My mother died when I was five and I had no siblings . . . something I've often regretted. My father was a kind, gentle scholar of a man who taught me Latin and Greek and mathematics and all sorts of valuable lessons. But I was raised by our housekeeper and her husband, the farm manager. My father died in 1932 when I was fifteen and that's when I met Lord Beeton-Howard. He came to the funeral and told me how much he'd always admired my father. You see, they were stationed together in Cornwall in the last war."

"After the funeral, I came to London to live with my father's first cousin, whom I call 'Uncle Harold,' and his wife, 'Aunt Vera,' while I attended Queen Alexandra's Academy for Girls. After I finished there, they hired me to teach Latin. When the Nazis began overrunning Eastern Europe, I volunteered evenings at a settlement house to try to help the thousands of refugees coming here. In the spring of 1938, I was working with twin brothers from Vienna trying to help them get jobs. And one night, Rob Kendall showed up at the settlement house to interview people for jobs with the city.

Rob grew up in Delbridge, too, so we'd known each other all our lives. But he went off to school in Cirencester. And when he finished, he joined the faculty of a boys' school here in London. We left the settlement house together that night about ten o'clock and sat on a park bench talking for hours. He invited me out to dinner the next night. After that, we were never apart. We were married in June of 1939 and went, quite unexpectedly, to Vienna for our honeymoon."

"A trip to Vienna? How lovely. Why was it unexpected?"

"The Jewish twins we were trying to help at the settlement house, Ethan and Aaron Kohlberg, had family members still living in Vienna and they hoped we might be able to get them out. You see, the twins were able to buy their way out of Austria when that was still possible . . . back when Adolf Eichmann was head of Austrian Emigration. They paid an enormous sum and it left them destitute. But they hoped their brother and sister-in-law, and their father and two maiden aunts, could get out, too, and join them in London. When Barney heard about the family members still living in Vienna, he went to Stoney for help. Stoney suggested that he take Rob and me when he went to Vienna so we could help bring them out."

"Had you known Barney Fogelman long? When did the two of you meet?"

"Barney and my Uncle Harold had been friends for a number of years when I moved in with Harold and Vera. One afternoon we were all having tea at their house and Lord Beeton-Howard was with us. That's when we planned the trip. In Vienna, Barney passed himself off as a German businessman, which was not difficult as his command of the language is that of a native. And he's perfected the mannerisms of devotees of the Third Reich for that kind of work. Rob spoke fluent German, too, so it really wasn't all that hard."

"But even so, weren't you scared?"

"Yes. But I had Rob and Barney along to protect me and I thought that would be enough. I was so gullible, Evelyn. You'll remember that that was before Hitler invaded Poland, so England was not at war yet and travel visas were still available."

Sylvia raised her hand to try to stifle a yawn and her eyes glazed as she slumped against the back of her chair. "I'm sorry, Evelyn," she said. "I'm just so tired. What time is it?" She took a quick glance at her watch. "Oh, dear, it's after nine. We mustn't keep Miss Jerusha up any longer."

I picked up my empty plate with one hand and my silverware with the other, but Sylvia shook her head. "No," she whispered. "We must leave it for her. Otherwise she'll feel she's not doing her job . . . and her job is to look after the two of us."

"Where is she?" I asked. "Does she live at Croxdon House with Lord Beeton-Howard?"

"No," Sylvia replied, pushing her chair under the table. "Her rooms are downstairs next to the kitchen. I'm sure she's sitting patiently down there now waiting for us to finish."

As I followed Sylvia into the hallway, she turned to me and asked, "Aren't you off tomorrow?"

"Yes," I nodded. "I plan to be here all day writing overdue letters."

"Well, I have to work in the morning. But after I get home, we could have lunch together and I'll tell you about our mission to Vienna."

CHAPTER 10

The Judenplatz

Vienna, Austria • August 16, 1939

After Rob and I were married in June, I was terribly excited about going to Austria and wanted to go right away. But it was mid-August before we were able to arrange our schedules. Barney suggested that Rob and I carry only one suitcase between us, so I decided to take my old book satchel, too, because it had two big compartments where I could stash my underwear, stockings, toiletries, and a small purse. We crossed the Channel from Portsmouth on a Tuesday morning and arrived in Le Havre that afternoon where we caught a train that took us to Paris. The next day, we went on to Vienna.

At the Swiss border, we had to disembark so our visas and identity papers could be checked. This meant an hour layover, which we spent in a coffee shop near the station. While we were there, Barney went into the men's room and stayed for quite a while. When he finally came out, he was wearing a different suit and a fawn-colored Homburg I'd never seen. He'd colored his blond hair with some kind of dark tint, put on a pair of horn-rimmed glasses, and was holding a lit cigarette in a long black holder. I would not have known him had he not sat down with us. Even his voice sounded different.

He gave Rob and me a set of newly forged visas and identity papers and explained that from now on he was a German businessman from Cologne, who was showing a

British cousin and his wife around Vienna. His new name was Bernard Lutzman and our new names were Robert and Sybil Watts. The story line we developed involved Rob's make-believe mother, the sister of Barney's German mother, who had married an Englishman and moved with him to London after the Great War. After Barney collected our *real* British visas from the border patrol, he put them in an envelope, and mailed them to himself in care of a hotel in Zurich.

A little while later we boarded another train and went to the dining car for a wonderful lunch. I was concerned about the cost of all of this, especially after Barney told us that everything was a wedding gift from Lord Beeton-Howard.

When we arrived in Vienna, I felt as if I were on another planet. The train station in Vienna is very grand—floor-to-ceiling windows and marble floors with a big glittering dome rising in the center. The ceiling of that dome is about thirty feet high, and the whole area is defined by a dozen marble columns that form a circle beneath it. Hung in the spaces between those columns were larger-than-life posters of Adolf Hitler, Goebbels, Goering, and all the Nazi mucky-mucks. We got out of there as fast as we could and were herded into a narrow corridor where Nazi guards checked our papers and shouted at us to keep moving. I watched as they ordered the couple just ahead of us from the line and sent them into another room. When that happened, I took Rob's hand and held on to it until we were safely out the doors. I was shocked to see Vienna's lovely old buildings covered in blood-red banners emblazoned with spidery black swastikas and I shivered as we passed beneath them on our way up the street.

"Keep smiling," Barney whispered. "Remember we're on holiday. We're here to have a good time." He led Rob and me around the corner to our hotel and as soon as we'd washed up a bit, we went to view the splendors of St Stephen's Cathedral. We spent about an hour there going from room to room, marveling at all the gold leaf and red marble while nodding to each other and making small talk like the other tourists around us.

From there, we walked several blocks to the Kohlmarkt to satisfy one of Barney's passions—Viennese coffee and pastries. He introduced us to his favorite place, Demel's. We had to wait in line about twenty minutes, but were finally seated at a table on the back wall. As soon as the waiter brought our order, we fell on it as if we had not had a thing to eat all day. Demel's was crowded with happy, smiling customers all talking and laughing and enjoying themselves. But when a half dozen Nazis came through the front door, all those cheery faces vanished. Everyone seated at the tables around us jumped to their feet as the syncopated scrape of hundreds of chair legs drummed across the floor. They thrust their right arm forward at an angle and, in perfect unison, shouted Seig Heil! Barney was immediately on his feet with his right arm in the air while Rob and I remained seated. A moment later, the Nazis turned away and began chatting with the headwaiter and the customers began searching their pockets and handbags for papers. Then the Nazis circulated among the tables making sure everyone was properly credentialed.

As an officer started toward our table, Barney saluted. He pulled a business card from his jacket pocket, handed it to the officer, and in flowery German phrases told the man about his business in Cologne and explained why he was in Vienna. Then, as cool as a cucumber, he introduced Rob, who greeted the man in German. When he introduced me, the officer took my hand and kissed it. He asked to see our visas, but paid scant attention to them. Barney invited him to join us, stepping quickly into the aisle and snapping his fingers at a waiter. Moments later, we learned that the officer was a colonel who'd grown up in Berlin. This was the perfect situation for Barney who had spent the first twelve years of his life in that historic city and could talk about it with ease. Rob offered both of them cigarettes and joined in their conversation, making comments now and then. I just smiled and smiled. Then the colonel, whose name was Josef Greban, turned to me and said in perfect English, "And how do you like our fair city, Frau Watts?"

I mumbled something about Vienna's magnificent buildings while Colonel Greban downed the last of his coffee. He shook hands with Barney and Rob, kissed my hand, and bowed to us before he led his men out of the café. When the last soldier closed the door, I breathed a sigh of relief.

From Demel's, we went to an ancient Scottish church where we were met by a monk who invited us inside to view a gallery hung with rare medieval art. While Barney and the monk engaged in a whispered conversation in a corner, Rob and I strolled down the walls admiring the paintings. Just before we left, I saw Barney remove a small cloth bag from inside his jacket and give it to the monk.

That evening we had a late dinner. At eleven, Rob and I met Barney in the lobby of our hotel and the three of us walked several blocks toward the river to an old stone church built in honor of St. Ruprecht, the patron saint of Vienna's salt merchants. We were met in the entry by a monk in robe and cowl. He led us down three flights of damp gritty steps to a small room where he gave each of us a set of gray cotton coveralls that smelled of fish. I had to hang my handbag from my belt and stuff it, along with my skirt, inside the coveralls before I buttoned them up. Barney gave Rob and me black caps to wear. Everything must be covered, he reminded us as we pulled them on. Wearing these disguises was the first step in our plan to try to find the family of the Kohlberg twins.

The man in the cowl took us through another passageway that went under Marc-Aurel-Strasse. Then we went back up three flights of steps to Stern-Strasse—the entrance to the Jewish District—or *ghetto*. About twenty yards away from us, a group of Nazi soldiers was standing outside the main gate that led into the compound. A moment later, three of them jumped into the back of a truck and it rumbled through the gate. Our monk turned to whisper something to Barney and Rob. Then Rob pulled me close and told me that the soldiers in the truck were on their nightly round to flush-out and arrest hapless victims, whom they would beat out in the open on the streets of the Judenplatz as a kind of warning to the hundreds of people they'd imprisoned there. We continued down Stern-Strasse praying we wouldn't be seen as we hurried to hide behind a tall hedge that ran alongside it. Finally, we came to another entrance so obscured by overgrown vines and weeds that we would never have known it was there. From his robe, the monk drew out a large key, and with great patience, opened an old-fashioned wooden gate. While he and Barney had a brief exchange, Rob glanced at his watch and whispered, "midnight." Rob told me that the man in the robe and cowl had reminded Barney that he would be waiting for us at that same gate at exactly three o'clock. Barney nodded, and we set off down the gloomy streets. There was no moonlight, no streetlamps, and the air felt heavy and damp as if a storm were brewing.

Barney had cautioned Rob and me that we must be as quiet as mice and stay as close to the buildings as possible. I could hear the sound of a truck engine in the distance and the continuous squeal of its brakes set my teeth on edge. I just knew it would careen around the corner any second and we'd become the hapless victims.

Long minutes passed before we arrived at Building 46 where we crept inside a dark stairwell that smelled of blood and human waste. As I turned the corner onto the fourth floor landing, a cobweb reached out and grazed my cheek and I all but climbed the wall. Barney grabbed my hand and whispered a rather loud "Shush!" and the three of us froze, barely breathing for a moment, before we began tiptoeing down the hallway to apartment 4-D, the address we'd been given by the twins. "Calm down, sweetheart," Rob cautioned, "before I let them know we're here." The three of us had decided earlier that I would be the one to whisper outside the door, as a woman's voice might not be as threatening as a man's. I'd been told to identify myself as a friend of "Flying Squirrel," the nickname of the younger Kohlberg brother who had been a rock climber in his youth. Rob scratched on the doorframe off and on for about thirty seconds. Then I began calling "Flying Squirrel" in German just as he'd taught me to say it. The door opened a crack and a raspy voice said, "Who is it?" I repeated that I was a friend of Flying Squirrel and had an important message for him. The door opened a crack and a young man stuck his head out.

We explained who we were and why we'd come. After we were inside, the twins' younger brother, Flying Squirrel, whose real name was Hiram, introduced his father, Malachai, and two women who'd been sleeping on a pull-out sofa, Aunt Misha and Aunt Marta. Even in the gloom I could see that they were twins, also. We found ourselves in what had once been a roomy flat now crowded with cardboard boxes, wooden crates, trunks, and suitcases. Hiram's wife, Karin, appeared in her bathrobe just as he offered us a glass of water. "We have only water to offer you," he said. "I'm sorry. Please come into the kitchen where we can have a little light and sit down." He made his way through a maze of cartons in the semidarkness and we followed his shadowy form. Hiram lit two candle stubs in the brass menorah sitting in the middle of the kitchen table, and his aunts, father, and wife joined us there.

Barney began speaking to them in German, with his flawless Viennese accent, about the Kohlberg twins we'd met in London. At the mention of Ethan and Aaron's names, the aunts began to cry. Grandfather Kohlberg stood up, lifted his hands, palms up toward the ceiling, and began praying. I heard Hiram whispering to Karin, "They're alive! They're alive!" He turned back to Barney and said, "We've heard nothing from my brothers for almost a year. We had no idea where they were or even if they were still alive." He grabbed Barney's hand and shook it. "Thank you, thank you for bringing us this good news." Barney told him that Rob and I were the ones who deserved the credit, as we were the ones who worked at the settlement house where his brothers were now living. And when we'd heard they still had family living in Vienna, we'd begun working on plans to try to get them out. Rob translated all of this quietly to me.

Barney then turned to the grandfather, old Herr Kohlberg, and told him that we could provide new identity papers for all of them and that, over the next few weeks, they could be smuggled out of Vienna to Switzerland, and from there to England. But the old man just shook his head. "You're too late, my son," he said. "They have issued us tickets for an internment camp." He paused to look at a ticking clock on a nearby shelf. "We have to be outside with our suitcases ready to leave at seven." He pulled a brown piece of cardboard from a stack on the table that had the number 481 written on it. "That's me," he said, "number 481. That's all we are to them anyway, a number scratched on a piece of cardboard. We have a list of rules, all of which begin with *you shall not*, that we must follow if we are to stay out of prison."

Rob read it and continued to translate for me as the old man talked to Barney. "We're going to a place where we'll have a house with heat and lights. We've had neither here for over a year. They say they're going to save us, protect us from our enemies . . . the British, the Communists, the French. They're sending us to a place, they say, that is safe from the bombs of the Englanders. They've told us we'll have plenty to eat and warm beds to sleep in. At least we're not going to prison. They're coming here after we leave to pick up our household possessions to store them until we come back here to live . . . when the war is over."

Barney made no effort to hide his surprise. "Surely you don't believe this, Herr Kohlberg. Given all that has happened over the last couple of years, the fact that you've been living here with no heat, no electricity, rotting food, no medical care . . . surely you don't believe them. Have you forgotten

Kristallnacht? We're not at war and we Englanders are not your enemies."

Flying Squirrel broke in, "No, mein herr, you are not our enemies *yet*. But it is just a matter of time. Your government won't tolerate the expansion of the Third Reich much further."

Barney nodded. "War is inevitable and I expect all hell to break loose before Christmas."

Flying Squirrel agreed. "We think so, too, and we want to be as far away from here as possible when it happens." He pulled up his shirtsleeve, revealing a long scar on the outside of his lower arm. "I got that last year in a confrontation with a bunch of Nazi thugs who attacked our rabbi. They put me in jail for two months. Hundreds of people whose families have lived here for generations have been beaten and taken away . . . including our rabbi who had the courage to speak out publicly against them. They've burned down every synagogue in this city. Thousands are committing suicide every day. I know because I'm forced to help bury them. We have no choice but to do what the Nazis tell us. Austria is our home and we have no desire to go live in a foreign country. I'm sorry, but we do not want to be at the mercy of strangers."

I heard a whimpering sound from the other side of the wall. Karin, the wife, excused herself and left the table. A moment later, she returned with a little boy in her arms. "Our only child," she said as she sat down. He was about three, small for his age, with a face as thin and pale as a fingernail moon. His mother hugged him to her breast. "He's not been able to play outside for the past year. None of us is allowed on the streets. The parks and squares are verboten. We've not had any protein for months and we're not allowed to have meat now, at all. But when we move to the internment camp, we have been told that we will have meat at least twice a week . . . and eggs. And there is a school there for the children and a playground with swings and a carousel."

She rubbed her son's head and pulled him closer. "We have to get him out of here, don't you see? He's all we have. He's our only hope for the future." I turned away so she would not see the tears welling in my eyes.

"Come with us tonight," Barney said. "We'll take you down the river with us."—the first I had heard of a river trip—"All you need do is put on some warm clothing. We'll help you."

"No," Hiram said. "There are too many of us. If we are caught, all of you will be instantly charged with assisting Jews and that means death by firing squad. No, it's out of the question."

But Barney would not give up. "Is there *anything* we can do for you?" he asked.

Hiram nodded. "Yes. Tell my brothers that we will all be reunited when the war is over. We'll be living here again, where all of us grew up, when they come back home to Vienna."

The old man rose from his chair. "I have something I want you to take to them," he said. He went to the gas stove and inserted a knife into the edge of the metal panel on the back. It popped open on one end and he slid his hand inside and brought out a leather bag about the size of his fist. "We have kept this hidden here for several years," he said, "because we thought we might need it someday. They told us to pack up our valuables, our silver and jewelry, so they could store it for us. But we decided against that. Since we're coming back here, God willing, in a year or so, we thought we'd just leave it hidden in the stove. From what you say, Ethan and Aaron need resources in England."

The old man opened the bag and three broaches the size of hen's eggs spilled onto the table. Two were gold, very elaborate and set with diamonds, rubies, and emeralds. One was shaped like a bird; the other, a flower. The third broach was made of platinum, in the shape of a star with a large center diamond ringed by sapphires. "These," Herr Kohlberg said as he pointed to the two broaches made of gold, "came from a tiara that once belonged to the Grand Duchess Marguerite." He poured the rest of the jewelry out of the bag. There was a gold stickpin set with a single yellow diamond of at least two carats, a pair of linked bracelets made of platinum set with pearls and rubies, two collar pins made of white gold in the shape of leaves set with emeralds, and an exquisite platinum ring with three large diamonds. The dazzling assortment all but blinded me as I picked up each piece and examined it in the candlelight.

The old man sat back down and said, "My father was a jeweler. He and Mama brought my sisters, Misha and Marta, and me to Vienna from Munich in 1878. They set up a nice shop just around the corner from the Herrengasse where they made a good living. Please take these pieces to Aaron and Ethan. They will be safer with them." He picked up the platinum ring that held the three large diamonds. "Tell them they may sell this ring right away to help them get started in your country. It should bring enough to finance a new business and keep them and their families going until they can get on their feet. By then, maybe the war will be over and we'll all be together again. Tell them not to sell any of the other pieces because we will need them to start our new lives when we return here to our home." He scooped the jewelry back into his cupped hands and offered it to Barney. "Please take all of this with you, sir."

Barney looked at Rob and me and asked, "Are you willing to take it? You know it will be a great risk. What do you think we should do with it?"

"I could pin it inside my underwear," I blurted, surprised that I'd voiced such an absurd notion.

Aunt Misha got up suddenly and left the room. In a moment she returned with a brassiere that she threw on the table in front of me. "I think Sybil's idea is a good one," she said in flawless English. "We can secure the jewelry inside the two cups and make it smaller around so she can wear it. Get your sewing kit, Marta. Help me do this."

Misha told the men to leave the kitchen and asked me to take off my coveralls. My heart began to beat a little faster as I backed my way into a corner where there was no light and pulled off the heavy covering. Then I unbuttoned the blouse I was wearing, silently thanking God that it had a full ruffled bodice roomy enough to accommodate someone larger than I.

Marta waved me into the light of the candles and slipped a sewing tape around my back. "Thirty-four inches," she whispered to her sister. The brassiere measured forty inches. So they folded and sewed together two inches of fabric from under each arm. Then they folded a wide seam down the center between the two cups and sewed that up, being sure the cups were in the right position. They separated the jewelry and decided where the pieces would fit best and divided it accordingly. Misha wrapped a scrap of cotton wool around each piece of jewelry and then Marta sewed it into the lining of each cup. I took off my slip and they put the new brassiere on over the one I was wearing and secured the clasp in back.

It was heavy and uncomfortable, not to mention embarrassing. I'd never had much of a bust and I could not imagine how ridiculous I must look with one that stuck out like the prow of a ship. I put my blouse and suit jacket back on, and buttoned the coveralls over them. They were big and bulky, so I felt confident that no one would know the difference but me.

Parting with the Kohlbergs was very difficult. I was haunted by their desperate situation, but felt I must respect their decision. I knew that Barney, Rob, and I had done all that we could in the brief time we'd had. After a tearful farewell, we left as quietly as we'd come. Our monk was waiting behind a column at the Stern-Strasse gate, and the four of us hurried back to the church and went straight down a muddy corridor that smelled of rusting metal and salt. When we arrived at a stone landing just above the Danube

Canal, Barney pulled a small cloth bag about the size of a large fig from inside his coveralls and gave it to the monk. They hugged one another and the man hurried off.

A long narrow boat was moored at the dock. Barney pointed to it and said, "How about a ride, my dear?" He took my hand and helped me down into it, indicating that I should sit on the bench in the middle. I was surprised to see two monks in robes and cowls already seated on the bench behind me, oars in hand. Our suitcases had been secured with ropes along the inside hull. Barney and Rob hastened to the bench nearest the bow and each took an oar. We pushed off at exactly 3:15 a.m. No one said a word for the next two and a half hours. Barney and Rob rowed the entire time, keeping a steady rhythm with the two men behind me. I was amazed at how swiftly we went through the water, but it was obvious that the boat had been built for speed.

Just as a thin sliver of gray light began spreading over the horizon, we pulled in below the monastery at Melk. "Hurry!" Barney said as he helped me get my footing. "We don't want to be seen here." As we scrambled onto the dock, he waved to the monks who had brought us, and we fled up a set of stone steps. There was hot tea and toast with plum jam waiting in the stone-walled room I shared with Rob. We ate quickly, stripped off our smelly clothes, and stretched out on the two narrow cots in the room. Rob put the jewelry-laden brassiere under his pillow.

A few hours later, Barney knocked on our door. "Lunch will be served in thirty minutes," he called. "Come down when you're ready."

We slowly awoke to the smell of fresh bread baking. Light streamed into our room and I stretched for a couple of minutes, luxuriating in the quiet while I took in my surroundings. Then I got up to peek behind a curtain of dark heavy fabric hanging from a rod in one corner of the room. Behind it, I discovered a claw-foot tub, basin, and toilet. Nearby, a small shelf held bars of fine-milled soap and bottles of lotions. I ran several inches of water into the tub, washed my hair with the soap, and had a quick bath while Rob stood at the sink shaving. Then he had a bath. We found our clothes cleaned, pressed, and lying neatly on the beds. Even my underwear had been washed and was, miraculously, dry.

Lunch was served by two brothers in a walled garden. When we left, I saw Barney give one of them a small cloth bag. I learned later that the little bags he'd given the monks along the way contained a dozen diamonds, each about three quarters of a carat—large enough to be valuable, but small enough to pass undetected through the hands of money changers. The diamonds, supplied by Lord Beeton-Howard, helped finance a network of underground activities designed to thwart the Nazis. Rob told me later that the men who'd been dressed in robes and cowls were not monks at all and two of them were women.

Barney arranged for us to be taken by car from Melk Abbey to Innsbruck and had done this on purpose. "We must be seen in Innsbruck," he said. "You'll remember that I told Colonel Greban that we were going to Innsbruck. He will have his spies out to be sure we are doing what we said we would. I know you must be tired, I certainly am. So we'll visit only a couple of cathedrals and call it a day. We must be ready to leave at seven in the morning, so we need to get a good night's sleep. Perhaps we should order a bag lunch at our hotel for the train tomorrow. We'd be wise to lie low and stay out of sight before we cross the border again."

Early the next morning, Rob helped me put the jewelry-laden brassiere on over my regular bra. Then he and I met Barney for a hearty breakfast. Afterward, we ordered four ham sandwiches and three slices of crumb cake to take with us on the train. I asked the hotel staff to pack all of it in a brown paper sack. The trip through the Austrian countryside was uneventful, but when we reached the Swiss border, we were ordered off the train. Barney reminded us that he was still Herr Lutzman and that Rob and I were still the Watts.

We watched from our compartment window as soldiers in brown uniforms began with the passengers in the two third-class cars ahead of us just behind the engines. Two of the soldiers disappeared into the first car. A few minutes later, the passengers began to file out. Men passengers were ordered to one side of the station, and women and children to the other.

"Oh, hell," Barney said, standing up to get a better look. "They're doing searches." He turned to me. "Where's that sack of sandwiches?" I opened the clasp on my book satchel, drew it out, and handed it to him. "They're going to strip you, Sylvia. I just know it." His hands shook as he pulled the long black cigarette holder from his breast pocket and twisted off the mouthpiece to reveal a razor-sharp stiletto. I gasped as he thrust the tip toward me. "You've got to get Aunt Misha's brassiere off. We have to do something with that jewelry." He looked at Rob. "Get up, my boy, and help her," he ordered. "We haven't a moment to lose. Hurry! Hurry!" he kept saying while I fought to get the straps of my slip down over my shoulders. Rob, who'd had little experience with women's brassieres, fumbled with the clasp on the back for several seconds but finally pulled the heavy garment away and dropped it onto Barney's lap. Barney slid the stiletto into the clumps of cotton wool, slashing the threads that held the pieces of jewelry. "Get the sandwiches out of the sack, Rob," he said, "and unwrap them. Open them up."

Rob took the four ham sandwiches out of the paper sack and removed the wax paper from around each one. All were filled with several layers of thin sliced ham spread with thick stone-ground mustard. Rob carefully removed the top piece of bread from each to expose the contents and then laid each ham-filled piece on the seat across from Barney.

While I hurriedly redressed, Barney began separating the stacks of delicate pink ham with his fingertips. Then he slid the elegant broaches, the bracelets, the diamond-studded pin, inside the slices of ham, pushing the gleaming finery away from the edges of the bread and toward the center. "Close them with care," he said to Rob. "And be sure the wax paper fits snugly around each sandwich."

While I finished buttoning up my jacket, Rob rewrapped the sandwiches. Then Barney took the sandwiches, slid them into the paper sack, and put the three undisturbed slices of wrapped cake on top of them. He closed the end of the sack, creased it between his thumb and index finger, and handed it to me.

"If they ask you what it is, tell them," he said. "Offer them some. I cut the top sandwich diagonally on purpose. If someone wants it, unwrap the paper slowly and feel around to be sure you give them the side that isn't bumpy. Don't put those sandwiches back in your book bag, Sylvia. Keep that paper sack right out where they can see it." He held up the platinum and diamond ring. "Now, suck the mustard off this thing and put it on," he said. "It wouldn't stay inside the sandwich."

I put the ring in my mouth, winced at the sharp taste of the mustard, and tried to clean it as best I could with my tongue. It was too large, so I took off my wedding band, put the ring on, and slid the band back on to keep it in place.

Barney sighed. "Well done," he said, "and just in time, too. Here they come!"

After he'd screwed the stiletto back inside the cigarette holder, he dropped it into his breast pocket, grabbed Aunt Misha's bra and the scraps of cotton wool, and stuffed them down between the seat and the wall. Then he took my arm at the elbow, opened the door, and pushed me out into the corridor ahead of him and Rob. "I know it isn't in your nature to be nonchalant, my dear," he murmured. "But you must try." He leaned into me and the hair on the back of my neck stood up. "Look those Nazi boys right in the eye, Sylvia," he whispered. "Charm the socks off those damn bastards!"

I was shaking like a leaf as I followed the other women who'd alighted from our train car. Most were alone like me, but there was one young mother with two children. I heard her speaking to them in French, warning them to be still and quiet. I stared at the tops of my shoes while I stood in line and waited. A young officer, seated behind a desk, took my visa and asked me where I'd been and what I'd done there. His English was excellent. He asked if my husband were with me and wanted to know our destination. I knew he was a sergeant, but when I replied, I addressed him as major. He asked about the paper sack I was carrying and I told him it contained our lunch . . . ham sandwiches and slices of cake. I offered it to him, but he declined. "Just leave it here on my desk while Frau Michen completes your inspection. Go into the room behind me and she'll call you in a moment." He took my book bag and poured my underwear, toiletries, and hairbrush onto the desktop. Frau Michen barked an order and I jumped. She led me into a small room and told me to take off my skirt, blouse, jacket, and hat.

As soon as I had everything off, she began patting me with the palms of her large hands, going slowly over my torso, around my breasts, and down my hips. Then she thrust both hands into my hair, pulled the pins from it, and ran her fingers all the way through. "Get dressed," she said. "And wait on the bench until the sergeant calls you."

I dressed quickly, hurried out of the little room, jacket and hat in hand, and sat down on the bench beside the Frenchwoman and her children. Normally, I would have spoken to them, would have said bonjour, but neither of us spoke.

The sergeant got up from the desk, picked up my book bag, and brought it over to me. "You may go, fraulein. Your papers are in order. Have a pleasant trip."

I turned to leave and suddenly remembered the brown paper sack. I glanced over my shoulder to see it lying, wide open, on the desk. Nearby, cake crumbs were scattered across a piece of rumpled waxed paper. With my heart in my throat, I quickly made my way back across the room. I picked up the sack, closed it, and said "Danke," before hurrying out the door.

I slid the sack back inside my book satchel and there it stayed throughout our brief time in Switzerland, through an overnight in Paris, through the French countryside, and across the Channel to Southampton. Needless to say, those sandwiches were covered with smelly green mold by the time we got home. As soon as we arrived in London, we went straight to Lord Beeton-Howard's office and gave him the jewelry. Later, he had it professionally cleaned and stored in an underground vault at his bank.

That evening, we went to the Lighthouse Center where I gave the platinum three-diamond ring to the Kohlberg twins, related the wishes of their father regarding it, and explained that we'd given the rest of the jewelry to Lord Beeton-Howard for safekeeping.

We told the Kohlberg twins about our visit with their family members and made a point of saying that they were bearing up well. But we did not mention that they'd not had any electricity, heat, nor decent food for the past year. The most difficult part was trying to explain why they'd not accepted our offer to try to get them out of Austria.

CHAPTER 11

The Mouth of the Fish

Roscoff, France • June 10, 1942

Chateau du Pin was a glorious baronial splendor set deep in a wood off the coast of Brittany. It was home to a very intelligent woman, Lily Suchette, Comtesse de Valoire, and her ailing husband, Henri. While I never saw the interior of the chateau, I spent an afternoon hidden behind a mural in the fifteenth century chapel of that lovely estate. Nearby, beneath the chateau's massive kitchen, was a stone keep. There, a burlap bag containing dirty clothes, four fish, and an eel nestled beside a brace of plucked ducks. Inside the mouths of the four fish were twelve flawless diamonds—the contraband I was carrying into Occupied France.

While the chateau was not meant to be a stop on my first mission to France with Barney, it proved to be the most important destination of our journey. On the day we'd left London, Rutledge had driven Barney and me to Dartmouth where Stoney was waiting on his yacht, *Flying Griffin*. Because of the tremendous amount of equipment his factories produced for the British military, Stoney was one of a dozen Englishmen who had permission to travel in his car, or on his boat, without restriction. To that end, he'd turned his once-graceful yacht into a war machine. The hull, which was one-hundred-eighteen-feet long, had been refitted with sheets of steel and the entire body painted battleship gray. The lighted instruments in the wheelhouse were shielded by nonreflecting glass; all the ship's exterior lights were covered with canvas. *Flying Griffin* was equipped with depth finders, mine detectors, and one of those new heat-seeking devices that can detect objects in the water from up to a quarter of a mile away. Designed and produced in the machine shops of Stoney's factories, these modern devices allowed him to make regular runs across the Channel carrying stores of precious arms, equipment, and supplies for our Maquis contacts. In addition, Stoney had retained the services of an expert pilot, Philipe Pacon, who'd grown up in Caen and knew the Normandy coast and its dangerous shoals and channels like the back of his hand.

Thanks to Sylvia and the resources of the Quaker Lighthouse Center for Refugees, Barney and I were attired in French clothing like that worn by residents of the fishing communities nestled in the coves along the water. To help with his disguise, Barney had let his blond hair grow below his ears and dyed it brown. Over it he wore a blue knit cap like those worn by French fishermen. His pants, which had been made in France of a heavy cotton fabric called duck, were tucked into a pair of hip waders. He wore a blue plaid shirt and a navy cotton jacket. All contained French labels. For this mission, he'd adopted the name Stephan Montigu.

I broke down and cried when he told me I had to dye my hair. While the dye wasn't permanent and would fade after two or three washings with strong detergent, dying it broke my heart. Afterward, Sylvia cut two inches off to create a shoulder-length brown page boy and dyed my eyebrows brown to match. On the morning we left, she'd divided my hair into a dozen sections, rolled each into a circle, and pinned the circles all over my head. I wore a floppy brimmed hat, along with rough trousers, a man's shirt, a dark brown jacket and a pair of men's brogans that were a bit too large but not bad with extra socks. Sylvia and I had bound my breasts with a length of wide cotton bandage I'd brought from St Mary's, with hopes that I'd be able to pass as Maurice Doland, the fifteen-year-old boy my carte d'identité said I was. I had had a lot of fun in the lab at the hospital creating a dozen fake pustules for my face, which I applied very carefully to my chin and forehead using dabs of artist's cement.

The week before we left, Barney had told me that I was not to bathe, nor wash my hair, nor use any deodorant. I must run up and down the length of the path between Croxdon House and Corrie Cottage several times a day dressed in the pants and shirt I'd be wearing for this mission because I must smell like a working-class teenage boy. He reminded me that France was a Catholic country—something I must be aware of at all times. To that end, he gave me a simple strip of leather hung with a small wooden cross. The kind of thing a boy would wear, he'd said, as he showed me the brass chain and cross hung around his neck.

That same night, he'd surprised me when he asked me to come up with a plan for secreting diamonds into France. Stoney would have the diamonds ready, but the two of them had agreed that it would be best if I came up with an idea about where to hide them. I tossed and turned all night that night trying to come up with a plan. When I saw Barney a few days later, I told him that since I was supposed to be a fisherman, why not hide the stones inside some fish?

Barney had also insisted that I swim regularly in the large indoor pool at Croxdon House. We'll be traveling through some dangerous waters, he'd said, and I'd feel better knowing you can swim for at least a half a mile if you have to. (I spent so much time in the water, he took to calling me *Ducks*.) A set of slightly bucked teeth completed my disguise. Made of thin strips of wood, they fit closely over my upper teeth and were very uncomfortable. During the week before, I'd worn them as often as I could in order to practice eating and talking with them in my mouth. Barney had asked me if I'd like to come up with a password for this mission, and I told him that when I was young I'd fished the creek at Sand Hill for large-mouth bass. He found this funny, given the looks of my mouth filled with my very obvious new teeth, and laughed at me when I mentioned it. But in the end he agreed and *basse de bouche large* became the pass phrase of the day.

As Barney, Stoney, and I stood on deck that warm summer evening, Philipe moved *Flying Griffin* out of the harbor at Dartmouth and headed west. The fog lay over us, thick and gray, like wet meringue—the perfect cover for our crossing. About an hour out, Philipe cut the ship's engines and we began to drift slowly toward an outcropping of rocks just south of the Isles of Scilly. A thin beam of light flashed low within them and Barney answered sending a split-second beam from his torch. A moment later, the dark blue prow of a trawler came into sight. When it pulled up beside us, I saw the name *Yvette* painted on the bow. Barney lowered *Flying Griffin's* rope ladder, and two middle-aged fishermen came aboard and introduced themselves as Pierre and Leon. Pierre was carrying a brown burlap bag, which Barney told him to give to me. Leon was trailing a length of rope, and soon he and Barney had tied it off the stern of *Flying Griffin*. In order to make good time our boat would pull their trawler across the Channel.

As soon as we were under way, Stoney took me down below into the curtained galley. I sat down at a table to do my work within an arc of light coming from a lantern. He sat down on the bench opposite, holding a leather pouch in one hand and the bottom half of a round cookie tin in the other. Inside the tin were several needles, a small pair of scissors, strips of pink satin, and several spools of thread—green, light blue, pale pink, and a silvery gray.

"I have some jewelry," Stoney said, "that was left me by my grandmother. I'll never have any need for it, so I've decided to try to put it to good use. A friend of mine removed these particular stones from an old necklace. Beech Tree has never done this kind of thing before, Evelyn, but we think you have what it takes to get these stones to the people who need them." He tipped the bag and out poured a dozen diamonds. Large, round, and brilliant, they reflected light from the lantern in a dazzling array of vivid colors.

"Oh, Stoney," I began, "they're magnificent! But what if I get caught and the Nazis find them? You'll be out of a lot of money and I'll be in prison . . . if I'm not dead!" I put my forehead down on the table top and mumbled, "What will you tell my mother if I'm caught?"

Stoney reached over and put his palm gently against the side of my cheek. "You won't get caught, Evelyn," he whispered. "I know you're scared. Who wouldn't be? But you look French, you sound French, you are French. I'm sure Barney has thoroughly prepared you for your role as a young French fisher boy. When you came aboard tonight, I was simply amazed. I would never have recognized you!"

He reached down, opened the door to a small compartment beneath a bench, and brought out a bottle of brandy. "Let's drink to the success of our mission," he said as he filled two small glasses. While that amber liquid burned all the way down, landing with a searing thud in my gut, I soon felt relaxed enough to do my work.

I divided the diamonds into groups of three and, using a length of pink thread, sewed each bundle of stones into one of the four tiny circles I'd cut from the pink satin. Then I opened the burlap bag Pierre had brought on board and removed the dirty clothes, the long gray eel and the four fish. There were two scrawny blowfish, the kind no one wants to eat. The other two I could not identify, but their skin was mottled with gray splotches making them extremely ugly. One by one, I opened their mouths and stuck a tight little pink silk bundle into each, pushing it as far back into the gullet as I could. After changing the thread to silver gray, I sewed the mouths of the four fishes back together. Unless someone looked very, very closely my tiny stitches would not be seen. I put the smelly clothes back in the bottom of the bag, added the fish, and laid on top the long smoky eel—a delicacy loved by the French as well as the Germans. If I were caught with the bag, the best I could hope for was that they'd take my prized eel and leave me with the four trashy fish.

After I'd finished arranging the burlap bag, Stoney remarked on what a fine job I'd done and told me he had something important to discuss with me. "I have an old school chum," he began, "who once worked as an agent for British Intelligence. In 1917, he was captured by the Germans and spent seven months in a POW camp in France where he was tortured, starved, and deliberately exposed to virulent strains of tuberculosis and diphtheria. I expect that grueling experience influenced his decision to study medicine. I'm talking about Mortimer Platt-Simpson, Evelyn."

"My big boss . . . Dr. Platt-Simpson at St Mary's? He's your school chum?"

Stoney nodded as he rose from the bench and opened the door to a compartment above his head. He withdrew a white metal box and set it on the table in front of me. "I went to see Mort last week in his office at St Mary's where I told him, in the strictest confidence, about the Beech Tree Group and how we operate outside MI6, the SOE, and the military. I explained that I was having trouble getting medical supplies for our missions . . . especially morphine. I explained that we needed some basic medical supplies onboard *Flying Griffin* in case we're ever attacked. I asked him if St Mary's might be able to provide us with a small, but steady, supply of only the most necessary things. And he said that under the Emergency Powers Act, he and other hospital administrators, have a certain amount of discretion regarding situations like this. Then he suggested that I work with the Emergency Surgery Unit at St Mary's, as he felt strongly that I could take the head matron of that unit into my confidence. He praised Miriam Broadhurst as one of the most able people on his staff and made no bones about the fact that he trusted her completely. You work with her, Evelyn, so I want to know what you think."

"I agree with Dr. Platt-Simpson. Miriam would never divulge anything about the Beech Tree Group or our work. I would trust her with my life."

"Good! Good! That's all I needed to hear. Would you please check the contents of this box, Evelyn, and let me know if we need anything beyond what's here. Matron Broadhurst packed it, and when I picked it up at her office, she and I had a little talk. She thinks as much of you as you do of her. I hope you don't mind, but I asked Sylvia to run a check on her and your boss came out clean as a whistle. I've discussed this with the other members of our group and we feel confident that Matron Broadhurst is a keeper."

The box was neatly arranged and contained bottles of carbolic, packages of sulfonamide powder, hypodermics, morphine ampoules, rolls of gauze and adhesive, lancets, and all manner of small instruments. As I repacked it, Stoney made us a cup of tea and brought out a packet of Jerusha's ginger biscuits. The two of us sat and talked for about an hour in the quiet of that confined space with only the low hum of the Rolls Royce engines and the sounds of the sea around us.

"I know you must be worried," he said, taking my hand in his, "and a little frightened. The first mission is always the hardest, Evelyn. But you'll be fine because you and Barney are a good team. The two of you have enough brains and guts to take over the whole world!"

I laughed at that, but what came out was more a nervous giggle. When we'd come aboard *Flying Griffin* at Dartmouth, I was so nervous I feared I might throw up. But being in the galley with Stoney, and hearing his encouraging words, helped steady my nerves. And knowing Miriam was now a confidant of the Beech Tree Group had had a calming effect, too.

Stoney took the remaining biscuits up to Barney and the other men, and I went off to one of the staterooms where I dozed until Barney knocked on the door and told me we were close to our destination. I grabbed the smelly burlap bag and joined him and the others on deck just as we neared the Île de Batz, a small island off the coast of France where *Flying*

Griffin and *Yvette* would part. Just before I went down the rope ladder behind Barney, Pierre, and Leon, I waved good bye to Stoney. As soon as the four of us were safely aboard *Yvette*, I turned back to watch as *Flying Griffin* disappeared into the shadowy fog. Soon, *Yvette* was approaching the rocky beach at Roscoff.

Even though I had no way of knowing, I thought it was about five o'clock when a boat started slowly toward us. Pierre left the wheel and ran to where Barney and I were standing near the stern. "Boche!" he cried. "It's a German patrol boat! Stephan, get down!" Barney grabbed me by the shoulder. "You're going over the side with that bag," he blurted.

"No, I'm not!" I screamed as I tried to push him away. He snatched a length of rope from the deck and told me to hush as he began wrapping one end of it around the mouth of the bag. He tied it off, grabbed my shoulders, and jerked me around so that my back was to him. "Hold the bag against your chest," he whispered as he brought the rope over my shoulders, crisscrossing it like a bandolier over my wildly beating heart. I winced as he pulled it tight, knotting it at my waist. Even though the bag was secure and my arms and hands were free, I could not stop shaking. Barney clamped down on my shoulders and leaned close to me. "There's a dock off the starboard about twenty-five yards away," he said. Suddenly the beam of a searchlight from the German patrol boat began sweeping toward us and we ducked down and waited for it to pass. Barney squeezed my hand. "Go down the ladder on the stern, Evelyn, and swim as if your life depends on it. Because it does! Do *not* come into town. Get to the woods as fast as you can and stay there. I'll find you. Now go!"

The searchlight was coming toward us again, so I waited until it had passed before I began feeling for the handles at the top of the narrow wooden ladder attached to the stern. The last thing I saw before I slipped over the gunwale was Barney strolling up the deck of *Yvette* to join Pierre and

Leon. I dropped perhaps five or six feet from the bottom rung into the drink and began swimming. It wasn't but a moment before the beam of light began its trek toward me and I put my face in the water and went dead still, praying my dark clothes would not be seen. As soon as the light passed, I started swimming toward the boats moored at a dock. I chose the nearest one and slipped behind it to try to catch my breath. I knew the Germans had boarded *Yvette* because I could hear them yelling. I moved away from the side of the boat where I was hiding and swam under the planks of the dock, making my way toward the end of it. My boots touched bottom and I crouched and slithered like a snake all the way to the end. From there I saw the Schutzstaffel, with pistols drawn, take Barney, Pierre, and Leon into custody.

A wet gray dawn was easing itself over the rock-strewn shore as a crowd of townspeople began to gather. Most were quiet, wary of the black uniforms, but one old man kept repeating the name Leon until one of the SS came over and hit him in the head with the butt of his rifle. The poor man went down on his knees and a woman rushed forward to help him. The German raised his rifle and swept the crowd with the barrel. "Go home," he shouted, "and mind your own business before we arrest all of you! Schnell! Schnell!" The crowd scattered and the Germans forced Barney, Pierre, and Leon into the back of a truck and drove off.

For the next hour, I sat shivering in cold water. And while I dreaded the thought of what might be out there on dry land, I knew I could not stay under that dock. I had to move. Barney had cautioned me that if we became separated for any reason I was to stay away from towns and travel only in the woods. So, I slipped out from under the dock and crawled down inside a crevice between three large rocks where I waited until the fog lifted and the sun eased out. As soon as I was satisfied that there was no one around, I made a dash to the back side of a warehouse where I hid behind a pile of trash. Then I waited . . . and waited . . . and waited. Finally,

I stole along the outer wall of the warehouse to the loading area at the front. About twenty feet away was a dirt path lined on both sides by tall hedges. I ran up that path until the woods came into view. Moments later, I was scampering around like an animal beneath their cool dark cover.

I knew the ultimate destination of our mission was Taule, a town about eight kilometers south of Roscoff, so I picked my way through the tangled brush and kept heading south. I came to a stream where I paused to drink a couple of handfuls of briny water before I gave in to what seemed a frightening exhaustion. I sat down to rest with my back against a pine tree and after a minute or two, began to cry. I knew it was just a matter of time before the Nazis found me and hauled me off to jail. I'd be stripped naked and the diamonds would be found, and the best I could hope for was a firing squad. Suddenly an image of Barney and the other two men being shot by the Gestapo filled my head, and I buried my face in my hands and gave in to wrenching sobs. I must have worn myself out crying, because I lay down on the pine straw and went to sleep.

I dreamed that I was back in New York with my lover, Larry Christian, and we were in a fancy nightclub high above the city whirling 'round and 'round across a floor of clear glass. I was dressed in a wretched wedding gown, its lace tattered and torn, and wearing the pearl choker he'd given me for Christmas. On my left hand was the emerald and diamond engagement ring. While tears rolled down my face in great shiny blobs, Larry ignored me. His eyes were fixed on the horizon where menacing clouds kept piling up, one atop the other, as jagged streaks of lightning bolted across an ever-darkening sky.

When I awoke, I couldn't get that dream out of my mind. I thought about the thousands of dollars Larry had paid to have his wife, Giselle, released from the clutches of the Nazis after they'd stormed France. And I marveled at the irony of it all. She was safe and sound now with him in New York, while

I was stuck in France desperately trying to escape her former captors. Who could have imagined such a paradox?

A growling stomach reminded me of my desperate circumstances. I was famished, having had nothing to eat since Stoney and I'd enjoyed Jerusha's ginger cakes on the ship. I had the fish, but the thought of eating raw fish made me cringe. I was thirsty, too. And added to that was the burden of knowing I had to pee. I took a step away from the tree, unbuttoned my trousers, and squatted beside a bush. The rush of warm urine against my salt-laden skin set me on fire.

With a heavy heart, I buttoned up my damp clingy trousers and set out once more. The clothes I was wearing had rubbed me raw from shoulders to elbows to hips, and the bandage we'd used to bind my breasts had chaffed my nipples so badly that they were beginning to bleed. There were blisters on the tops of both my big toes, but I knew I had to keep walking.

A few minutes later I made my way to the edge of the woods where I peeked through leafy branches to see a field of freshly turned soil. On the opposite side a tractor was nearing the end of a row. I crept along, hidden by the brush, trying to match the pace of the tractor and keep my eyes on the man driving it. Then a farmhouse with a dirt road in front of it—a road that might take me to Taule—came into view. I straightened up, glanced quickly around, and ran.

The sound of a car engine startled me and I jumped. I started back toward the woods but was too late. The car, a huge black Renault, cut in front of me, plowing into a hedge as it went, to block my path. The back door opened and a tiny woman with silver hair stuck her head out. "Garçon! Garçon! Dis donc!" she hissed. "Basse de bouche large." She repeated these words a bit louder and I stood as if struck dumb, wondering how some little old lady in a twenty-year-old Renault would know. "Come," she said, "come with me before they find you. They are patrolling everywhere. You must come with me, child."

All the things Barney had warned me about flashed through my mind and I knew I was not supposed to speak to *anyone,* much less get into a car. But this was different. Why would this woman know the password if she wasn't a friend? She kept waving, beckoning to me. When I threw the burlap bag on the floor and climbed in beside her, she held out her hand. "I'm Lily Suchette and you must not tell me your name, my boy. It is better that I don't know." She tapped the driver on his shoulder and said, "Gerard, vite! Vite! You know they're coming. There isn't a moment to lose!"

As soon as I'd settled in beside her, she reached over and gave me a pat. "Do not worry, mademoiselle. We'll take good care of you. I have a place to hide you until this blows over."

I shook my head. "How do you know who I am?"

She smiled. "I don't know exactly who you are, but I do know what you and Pierre and Leon and your friend, Père Barney, were trying to do . . . bring resources for our network in Rennes, right?"

"Père Barney?" I asked.

"That's what we call your friend, your colleague. We have no idea of his real name, but since he appears often in the robes of a priest, we call him Father Barney."

This was news to me. I had no idea the French knew about Father Barney. I thought that getup was one he used only in England. But what surprised me most was how much this elegant woman knew about our mission. Barney had gone on and on about what I should do if I were arrested by the Milice or the Gestapo, about what to do if I became lost, about how to deal with the French people I might meet, and how necessary it was for me to remain silent in any situation. I'd probably said too much already, so I sat there mute as a statue holding on to the edge of my seat while Gerard sped down a bumpy tree-lined path.

Soon a large stone manor house came into view and I thought surely we'd stop there, but we careened around the circular drive in front of it and kept going until Gerard hit the brake and we came to a stop outside a chapel. Made of faded orange brick, it had a dark slate roof crowned by a magnificent gothic steeple. Gerard sucked long and hard on the cigarette hanging from his lips before he cut the engine. The countess opened her door and told me to take off my shoes. She then reminded Gerard to take his off, too, and to be sure to hide both pairs down inside the engine of the car. She turned to me. "No shoe prints must appear on the floor of the chapel but mine." I was surprised at how quickly she covered the distance between the car and the chapel entrance, pausing just outside the door where she deliberately walked through a puddle of mud.

Gerard took a moment to flip the butt of his cigarette into a rose bush. Then he took me by the arm and hurried me up the aisle of the chapel. "See that woodcut," he said, pointing to the breathtaking triptych of *The Last Supper* hanging on the wall above the altar. "That's where you're going." He put his index finger under the edge of the first panel on the left and pulled it away to reveal a rectangular opening about a yard square. Then he pushed aside the elegant linen cloth that covered the top of the altar table, braced himself against it, and laced his fingers together to give me a boost up. "Climb onto the end of the table first," he said, "and then put your foot in my hand." I did as I was told and he heaved me up into the narrow space. On the floor inside were a mattress, a blanket, and a mug of water. Gerard closed the panel plunging me into darkness.

After I heard him close the chapel door on his way out, I sank down onto the mattress, leaned against the wall, and dared to breathe. About five minutes passed before I heard the *chug, chug* of a truck, and le comtesse began saying her beads with great fervor. A moment later, the sound of heavy footsteps came closer and closer and I knew the Nazis had arrived. Le comtesse must have remained kneeling at the altar praying, because the soldiers did not speak for several minutes. When she stopped, one of them asked her if she had seen any strangers in the area, if her workers had seen anyone. She answered no to both questions and said to them, "Why would anyone come here? We have nothing of interest."

One of the soldiers laughed. "I think Hauptmann Osterlitz would find your response amusing, madame. He has sent us here to search the chateau." Le comtesse invited them to search anywhere they liked, but asked politely that they not disturb her sick husband who was in the end room on the second floor. "You must come with us," one of the men said, and I heard her reply, "As you wish." There were more footsteps and then I heard the door to the chapel close.

I let out a sigh of relief and took a sip of water from the mug. Because I had no idea where I was, or how I would find my way back to Roscoff, I stretched out on the mattress and tried to sort things out.

The sound of the truck engine scared me, and I sat up and listened as it pulled away. Gerard opened the triptych and light flooded my hiding space. "I'm sorry, mademoiselle, but you must stay here for a while . . . at least until dark." He set a metal bucket of water on the mattress and handed me a white canvas bag. "Please take off your wet clothes so the women can wash and dry them," he said. "Le comtesse says you must eat something as well. Now, if you'll be so kind as to remove the things from this bag and put your wet clothes . . . all of them . . . back inside it, I will take it to the chateau. Try to sleep now, as you won't be sleeping tonight." He handed me a single candle in a glass holder and a box of matches. "Go on and light it while I'm here. You need to be able see what's in the bag. But when you're finished eating, you must blow it out and rest."

I set the glass holder on the floor at the end of the mattress, lit the candle, and opened the bag. Inside were a cotton robe, a towel, and a small bar of soap. On the bottom I found a thermos, a sandwich wrapped in paper, and two apples. I stuck my head around the opening where Gerard was waiting and said, "Merci, monsieur, merci!"

"You must hurry and undress, mademoiselle, so I can close the triptych. We wouldn't want anyone to know you're here. And I have much to do before this day is over."

I did as I was told and stripped off my salt-laden wet jacket, trousers, and shirt. I felt ridiculous removing the fabric that had bound my breasts . . . and my underpants. But I did and knelt down naked behind the panel to hand the bag of clothes to Gerard. He gave me a *humpf* just before he closed the triptych and walked away. I waited until I heard the chapel door close before I dipped the cloth into the bucket of warm water, lathered the soap, and scrubbed the fake pimples off my face. What a luxury it was to finally remove the salty residue from my body. I tied the cotton robe around me, sat down on the mattress, and removed the paper from around the sandwich. It consisted of two slabs of fresh bread with a thick slice of blue-veined cheese in between and was delicious and the tart cider from the thermos was the perfect accompaniment. I decided to save the apples for later, which proved to be a wise decision.

The afternoon wore on. I lay on the mattress and thought about Barney and his companions and wondered where they were and what was happening to them. It was hard to imagine they'd been imprisoned, hard to accept the fact that they might die. How could I, lying there in the dark behind a magnificent work of art, help? What could I do? Do what Gerard told you, I thought. Get some sleep.

I heard the door of the chapel open and Gerard's growly cough before he opened the end of the triptych. He thrust the white canvas bag inside and told me to get dressed. "Leave that bag on the mattress," he said. "I'll get it later. And don't light the candle . . . it's too dangerous this time of night." I asked him what time it was and he told me it was just after midnight.

I found my clothes clean and dry, as were my shoes and socks, and hurriedly put them on. I pulled the black hat over my head and put the two apples into the pockets of my jacket.

"I'm ready," I whispered. Gerard helped me climb down onto the altar table and from there to the floor. With a flourish, he handed me the smelly burlap bag of fish, which he'd taken from me and hidden in the chateau's stone keep.

I followed him down the aisle of the chapel and out into the night. As we made our way along a stone wall, le comtesse stepped from behind a bush frightening me so badly that I almost cried out. She put a finger to her lips and shook her head as she pulled me to her side. "I know you've been warned that this mission is very dangerous," she said. "But there are things one can do to protect oneself. Use your senses, child, as you make your way through the forest. Stop and listen . . . and take time to smell things around you. Before you go, I want to tell you something that is paramount to your safety here in France. When I was a little girl, we played a game we called *night bird*. It's sort of like the old game of hide-and-seek that all children play. But the key to this game is the repetition of certain bird-like calls." She drew a quick breath, turned away from me, and whistled three light notes in succession that sounded as if they were *b*, *c*, and *e* above middle *c*.

From perhaps ten yards away someone whistled those same three notes. "That's Gerard," le comtesse said. "He's over by the well having a cigarette." I felt a fool, as I'd had no idea that Gerard was not still standing right beside me.

Le comtesse took my hand. "That trio of notes is similar to a particular call made by a woods thrush . . . one you're likely to hear when you're in the woods *if* you're listening. This is how the game works. The child who is 'it' tweets the three notes and moves into the woods to hide. The other children answer her and all parties continue tweeting the same notes, back and forth, until the searchers find the child who is 'it'." During the warm months of the year, my siblings and I played this game every night as did many other children in France. My parents played it and so did my grandparents."

"You try it," she said. I mimicked the sounds she'd made hitting the same notes as closely as I could. Gerard answered again.

"Always whistle as quietly as you can, cheri. The bushes will be listening."

I pursed my mouth into a thin line and executed the three notes again, but softer. Le comtesse nodded. "C'est si bon. Little birds must be quiet at night."

"You mentioned smell," I reminded her. "Is there a particular smell I should be wary of?"

"Ah, yes . . . I did. You see, our enemy has a certain smell. Their uniforms smell like flax—like ripe wheat. And the men themselves smell like the dairy. They have a sweet milky smell like a cow shed. In contrast, our comrades in the brush smell of sweat and tobacco . . . and garlic, of course. The Germans have more of a sour smell . . . like an over-ripe pudding."

I covered my mouth to stifle a giggle. I wasn't sure le comtesse meant to be funny, but I found her description amusing.

"You must go now," she said. "You have many miles ahead of you and I pray that God will guide you to safety."

"Merci beaucoup, madame. I'll never forget you, nor your great kindness to me." Suddenly Gerard was at my side urging me on, and before I could shake her hand, le comtesse had melted into the shadows.

Gerard and I went straight into the woods and tramped through them in a zigzag fashion, moving left to right, then right to left, for about an hour. When we came upon an abandoned barn, Gerard stopped and motioned for me to be still. A moment later, a man came from around the side of the building and Gerard walked toward him.

"Bonsoir, Cholet," Gerard whispered. "Here she is with the package. Someone must take her to the drop-off tomorrow morning at five. I must return to the chateau now and help le comtesse with her plan." He took my hand in his and said, "Give the bag of fish to Cholet, mademoiselle. He will see that it arrives safely at the correct destination. Bonne chance!" He turned and started back the way we'd come.

I was relieved when I handed the bag to Cholet and had no trouble following him through the woods because the scent of garlic permeated his clothes. As we walked along, I kept thinking about what Barney had told me about the resistance network in France. You'll probably never see one of these people, these *convoyeurs*, more than once, he'd said. They work alone and are not part of a cell, although they know how to reach the other cells in their particular area. They all use code names which change regularly. That way, if one of them is questioned by the Nazis, he can truthfully say that he doesn't know any others.

Cholet stopped in front of a massive tangle of brambles where he grabbed a handful of thick vines covered with bracken and pulled. As soon as I was through the opening, he turned and walked away. I found myself in a space that reminded me of the hollow in a bird's nest. On the ground two men and a woman sat on a bed of pine straw filling dynamite casings by the light of a paraffin lamp. They greeted me with *basse de bouch large*, bade me sit down, and offered me a bit of bread and cheese. I brought out the apples, and the woman picked up a knife and sliced them into several pieces.

"I am Simone," she said, leaning into the light of the lamp. She had beautiful almond-shaped eyes and luminous skin the color of cinnamon. Her mouth was small and dark, and when she talked, she nervously pursed her lips in an effort to hide her slightly bucked teeth. "We've heard that your friend Father Barney and his companions are at Gestapo headquarters in Roscoff."

I choked on a bit of apple as I sputtered, "Mon Dieu!"

The woman, who seemed unmoved by my response, went on. "We know they're still alive, because our contacts told us that they were questioned all afternoon by that bastard Osterlitz and his thugs. Late today, Osterlitz allowed the woman who feeds the captives to go into the cells and she saw all three of them. In a little while, the two of us will go to Roscoff where you'll board a boat and be taken to safety."

She paused to give me a stern look. "This is serious business, mam'selle," she said, opening another empty sleeve and quickly filling it with powder. "It's not that we don't appreciate what you're doing, but you and your partner have been separated . . . and that's very dangerous. You must always have someone nearby to cover for you, to help you evade the damn bastards who're out to get you. In this place they take many forms . . . as do we . . . we, who are called *la resistance* by you who are on the outside. We're all manner of resisters—communists, Gaullists, monarchists, republicans, socialists—and French Algerians like me. And our enemy is not only the Boche, but the Milice, the Feldgendarmes, and our various countrymen spying for the Germans. You got lucky when you were picked up by le comtesse." The woman paused and reached over to place two of her sooty fingertips atop my wrist. "Do not worry. I'll get you out of here. Now, eat your food and rest for a while before we begin our journey. You can lie here on the straw beside me."

Simone woke me from a hard sleep. "Time to go," she said, sliding a hatchet down inside her belt. She grabbed a long-barreled German Mauser from a stash of rifles behind her, pulled away the vines that covered the bramble opening, and led me, once again, into the night. It was a long, frightening walk, but Simone proved a clever passeur who was aware of every movement, of every sound, of every breeze rustling around us as we made our way through miles of tangled brush. A couple of hours passed before we came upon a well-worn path marked with tire tracks. "The Boche use this road often," Simon whispered to me. "Following it will make our journey easier, but we'll stay well off to the side hidden like a couple of cats keeping an eye on the mouse hole."

A few minutes before five, we arrived at the same warehouse that I'd run to when I'd climbed down inside the rocks on the beach the day before. Simone led me to the far side of the building and said, "You must wade into the water, mademoiselle, and go along until you see *Marseille*, a brown boat with a red stripe painted along her side. Go up the ladder on her stern and lift the hatch to the first compartment on the port side and get in. It's the one nearest the wheelhouse. Do not come out until you hear someone say 'basse de bouche large.' Comprenez-vous?"

"Oui! Oui!" I whispered, and grabbed her hand. "Merci, Simone."

She nodded. "Thank *you*, mademoiselle. Until we meet again." As soon as she'd slunk away, I waded into the water, found *Marseille*, and climbed her ladder.

It was at least an hour before I heard the sound of heavy footsteps crossing the deck. The engine came to life and soon we were underway. Then the lid was lifted from off the compartment and a man's voice said, "Basse de bouche large." Someone handed me a cup of hot water and a roll and I smiled my appreciation. We moved slowly into the wet gloom of a heavy fog and headed north. Late that afternoon we arrived at the Isles of Scilly and one of the men on the *Marseille* held the rope ladder while I climbed up the side of *Flying Griffin*. I gave Stoney and Philipe a big hug and got down on my knees and kissed the deck of the ship that took me home.

* * *

Four days later, Barney was brought to the Emergency Surgery Unit at St Mary's. He had a deep gash above his left eye, one on his lower lip, and numerous deep cuts and bruises all over his torso. His right wrist was swollen twice normal size, and the fingernail was missing from the index finger of his right hand. Dozens of dark sooty rings were embedded in the skin of his face and neck, evidence of the torture he'd suffered. It was nothing short of a miracle he was alive.

When Stoney brought Barney in that hot June day, Miriam and I left the patients we were tending and hurried to his side. I'd never seen Miriam cry, but she had tears in her eyes, as did I, while we helped Stoney get him onto a gurney. When he realized I was there, Barney took my hand, and through battered lips, whispered, "Basse de bouche large, Ducks. You saved the day . . . *again*. Last night, the train tracks in Rennes exploded and all those huge guns and tanks headed to North Africa were blown to bits along with three hundred German bastards."

I gave him a weak smile and squeezed his hand. "Hush now and let us take care of you."

Stoney stepped away from the table, and Miriam began removing the filthy bandage from around Barney's wrist. "Compound fracture," she said, "and gangrene has set in . . . as well as the end of his finger where the fingernail's missing. Better get Dr. Ansley. Lots of crushed bone in that wrist, I'm afraid."

While Miriam cut the foul-smelling pieces of clothing from Barney's body, I filled the hypodermic. When I turned back, she was removing the ragged remains of the blue plaid shirt from his shoulder. I stood as if hypnotized while she cut the cloth away, exposing an expanse of purple skin laid open to the bone. A jagged gash, perhaps eight inches long edged with clumps of dried blood, coursed its way toward Barney's heart.

It took Dr. Ansley four hours to set Barney's crushed wrist and repair and sew up the gash in his shoulder. Nothing could be done for the place where his fingernail had been pulled out except debride the gangrenous flesh and apply a new dressing and bandage. After Miriam and I tended the smaller gashes on Barney's chest and arms, and dressed the cigarette burns on his face and neck, I pushed his gurney into the recovery ward. When I walked back out, Stoney was waiting in the hallway.

He took me in his arms and gave me a long, tight hug. As I clung to him my feelings got the best of me and I began to sob. "Oh, Stoney," I said. "It isn't worth it! He could have been killed! They could have shot him! We can't do this anymore."

Stoney pressed his lips against my temple and whispered, "He'll be better tomorrow, Evelyn. You'll see. He's strong and he's a fighter and he'll be up and about before you can say 'Go to hell, Hitler!'" Then he cupped his palms around my shoulders, stepped back, and looked at me. "I'm sorry, my dear, but I must go. Will you please call me when he awakens? I'd like to come back later this afternoon if he's conscious. There's nothing more I can do, so I'll go along now and take care of a few things I've neglected over the last few days."

Two days later Barney got up, and with help, was able to make two rounds up and down the hallway. His appetite returned, and it wasn't long before he was flirting and joking with the nurses and sending the orderlies to hunt for special treats, chocolate bonbons and fruit jellies, which he shared with all of us. After dinner, Barney kept the other men in our ward in stitches, telling stories about the pranks he pulled while in boarding school, and the creative little lies he'd told to keep his classmates out of trouble. He was the most popular patient we'd ever had.

Our ward was never meant to be a regular hospital ward, because our patients—wounded soldiers and sailors who required immediate attention—never stayed in our recovery area more than three days. After that, if they were still alive, they were moved to regular wards on the second floor of the hospital. The time was fast approaching when Barney would have to be moved, and this presented a problem. He wasn't military and that meant he would have to go into a civilian ward. Stoney was concerned about this, worried that Barney might talk in his sleep as patients on morphine often do.

Stoney went to see his friend, Dr. Platt-Simpson, and asked that Barney be released into his care for the duration. Once Stoney described the kind of care Barney would get 'round the clock, Dr. Platt-Simpson agreed to release him.

That night, Sylvia moved her clothes and personal effects into my bedroom at Corrie Cottage. With its extra bed and oversized wardrobe, it was plenty large for the two of us. The next morning Barney was brought to the cottage by ambulance. Miriam rode in the back with him and helped the orderlies move him upstairs into Sylvia's room. Jerusha was beside herself at the thought of cooking and caring for Barney, as he was one of her favorite people.

On a Saturday evening two weeks later, Barney joined Sylvia, Stoney, Jerusha, Rutledge, Miriam, and me around the table in the alcove for a joyous celebration of his return. The Friday before, Stoney had received a call from the butler at his estate, letting him know that the dowager countess had suffered a fall. So Stoney had gone to Stoneham Feld the next day to visit his mother and meet with her doctors. He'd returned to London with a trunk full of loot, so the dinner Jerusha prepared that evening for Barney's homecoming was a rare feast of chicken fricassee, all manner of fresh vegetables, and a towering raspberry fool.

Barney had asked Stoney to bring all of us together because he wanted to tell us about the success of our mission and the unusual circumstances that led to his release. After dessert, I picked up a tray containing the sherry decanter and glasses and went into the lounge. The others followed me, pulling their chairs into a circle around our storyteller.

Stoney thanked Jerusha again for the fabulous meal she'd prepared and said, "I want to thank all of you, as well, for your part in this mission and for the excellent care you've given Barney." He paused for a moment to look directly at Miriam. "And I want you to know that even though Barney has suffered terribly in carrying out our objectives, it was a great success. Not only because the diamonds made their way into the right hands, but because a French lady with an engaging manner and quick mind, le Comtesse de Volaire, put her life in danger to help Barney, and our French colleagues, escape the clutches of the Gestapo. Barney wants to tell us what happened after he was arrested in Roscoff. And, I hope he'll tell us about the remarkable woman who saved his life and orchestrated his safe return to England."

Barney gave Stoney a nod and took a moment to acknowledge each of us before he spoke. "I've had the great pleasure of being in the company of Lily Suchette, le Comtesse de Valoire, on several occasions . . . and Evelyn knows her, also. You've probably never heard of her, but she and her husband, Henri, are descended from families who've grown the famous pink onions of France for centuries. Unfortunately, they aren't available here in England now because of the war. Le comtesse continues to grow many acres of onions on her estate, and her reputation as a farmer is known far and wide. You're probably wondering why I mentioned those onions. Well, after Leon and Pierre and I were arrested, we were taken to Gestapo headquarters in Roscoff. The front part of the building is an office where the world's most arrogant bastard, Waffen-SS Captain Freidrich Osterlitz, holds court. Behind his office there are four cells where prisoners are held. Down below is a large cellar where the Geheime Staatspolizei carry out their most delicate work . . . like that done to my right wrist and index finger.

"After we were arrested, we were questioned for hours. And for the next two days, were subjected to all kinds of persuasive methods. Most of this intense work was done at night so no one would hear our screams. Hah! Each morning, we were taken back upstairs, chained to walls in a cell, and given a filthy gruel of fish guts and a small piece of moldy bread. We languished through the hot afternoons trying to conserve our strength for the next round of persuasion. On the third afternoon, we heard someone come into Osterlitz's office and address him by his German rank, SS-Hauptmann Osterlitz . . . someone with a light step and a very pleasant feminine voice. It was le comtesse, and rumor has it she'd brought SS-Captain Osterlitz a basket of fresh pink onions from her fields and strawberries from her garden. My two companions and I were in the cell just behind Osterlitz's office, so we heard very clearly what was said. Osterlitz speaks French well and le comtesse's German is superb, so they chatted back and forth in both languages.

"Le comtesse told Osterlitz that the three men he was holding were innocent and she could prove it. She said that the Jews who'd escaped from Roscoff had been helped by three men who'd come that night from Saint-Brieuc . . . that they had been employed at an estate there called Les Essarts. The captain interrupted her to tell her that no one had been living at Les Essarts since the war began, that it had been boarded up when the family fled France. She told him she was aware of this, but the three men who'd helped the Jews escape from Roscoff had hidden in a cellar under the garage at Les Essarts for several months. She told Osterlitz that the men he had in custody—Leon, Pierre, and Stephan—worked for her, and they were working for her the night the Jews escaped. Osterlitz took his time, but after a moment he said, 'The three men we have in custody claim to be fishermen. Just what were they doing for you and why were they doing it when they should have been out fishing?'

"Le comtesse cleared her throat. 'They *are* fishermen, mein herr,' she said. 'And I have known them all their lives. Stephan Montigu is one of the most expert seiners in this area. The men in his family have been fishers in this region for centuries. During harvest season, he and Pierre and Leon work in my onion fields digging and packing onions for market. But last year, I hired them to help me run a different kind of enterprise. You see, I realized I could sell my onions, and all the other things we grow at Chateau du Pin, for a much better price than I can get in the city markets.'

"Osterlitz shifted in his chair, and I surmised that he'd moved a bit closer to le comtesse, because his voice sounded much softer. 'Are you telling me, Madame Suchette, that you've been selling goods on the black market?'

"The countess made no audible reply, so she must have nodded. The captain got up then and walked around a bit. 'This is most irregular,' he said. 'You of all people must know the seriousness of this offense. We have very strict laws governing food production and distribution in this country. Why would you do such a foolish thing?'

"'My husband is very ill,' the countess answered, 'and his medicines are very hard to come by. He suffers terrible pain without them and I could not bear to see him in such agony. The chemist who makes them for me has so much difficulty getting the necessary ingredients that I thought I might have something that could be traded for whatever he needed. I started hoarding certain foods from my farms and gathering other things like wine and cigarettes so I'd have more bargaining power. Stephan, Pierre, and Leon helped me clean out an old cottage where Henri's gamekeeper used to live. That's where I've been storing these goods. There are crates of salted oysters and fish, and jars of canned peaches and pears and cherries, and casks of wine . . . and bags of potatoes and onions. I've managed to store at least six dozen eggs there every week for the past three months.'

"A chair groaned in protest as Osterlitz sat down again. 'You realize, madame, that you will have to surrender all of these goods to the authorities, don't you?'

"'Oui,' the countess answered. 'I know this is the end of my little enterprise.'

"The captain went on. 'And you'll have to pay a fine as well. Not only for your involvement in this crime, but also for each of the three men involved.'

"'Ja, I understand. I know this is highly irregular. So, I brought along a little token of my appreciation to give to you with my most sincere apologies.' The room went quiet for a few moments and then we heard Osterlitz say, 'Monsieur Cartier . . . what a lovely box.'

"He must have opened it because the next thing we heard him say was, 'Ah, the red crowned parrot—one of the finest and most beautiful designs from his collection. Just look at the lovely way those rubies curve to define the head, and how realistic the bird's eye seems with that blue sapphire at its center and the diamond bezels forming the white ring around it.'

"Then the countess spoke again. 'My grandfather had it commissioned for my grandmother and she left it to me. I'm glad you like it and I hope your wife will, too.'

"We heard Osterlitz close the lid on the box. 'Why don't we consider your fines paid, madame? But we have a final bit of business that must be dealt with . . . the contents of the gamekeeper's cottage. In accordance with the laws, you know we must confiscate any items considered contraband.'

"There was no audible answer from Lily. A moment later, she said, 'I'll have my man Gerard drive you to the cottage. May I assume that you'll release the prisoners as soon as you collect the goods stored there?'

"Osterlitz hesitated. 'I have one more very important question of you, madam. I would be remiss if I allowed the prisoners to go free before you tell me the names of the three men who helped the Jews escape. Who were they?'

"'I had a very reliable source,' Lily said. 'But all I know is the last name . . . Leroux.' Osterlitz repeated the name Leroux twice as if he'd been surprised. Then he said, 'There's a nest of criminals named Leroux near Drain. I hope you're right, madame, for if you aren't . . .' His voice trailed off as Lily made her way to the door.

"We could hear Osterlitz's heavy steps as he followed her out. 'You may tell your man to come for the prisoners at five o'clock,' he said. 'We'll have a look at your store of goods so I can report that what you've told me is true.'

"At five fifteen, Osterlitz and Gerard came back to SS headquarters. Osterlitz ordered the guard to release us, and Pierre and I lifted Leon from the floor and dragged him out of the cell because the Nazis had shattered his right kneecap with a length of pipe. Gerard took him from us—just picked him up like a baby—and carried him out the door and down the steps to the car. Lily had told Osterlitz that the three of us would continue to work for her and live on her property, so Gerard had no choice but to take us directly back to the chateau. We stayed there only long enough for Lily to clean and bandage our wounds and feed us bowls of mutton stew and strawberries with cream. And while it was difficult for us to eat with our broken bleeding mouths, being in that kitchen and savoring that delicious food was pure heaven after our travail.

"Gerard brought clean clothes for all of us and, within an hour, Pierre and I were crouched down on the back floorboards of the Renault headed north. Because of his more serious injuries, Leon had to remain at the chateau. But Gerard told us that Lily had arranged for him to be cared for by a couple who had a farm near Rochefort. The farmers there were harboring a Jewish doctor who'd been forced by the Nazis to abandon his practice. He would tend to Leon.

"Gerard also told us how Lily managed to pull off the story she'd told Osterlitz and convince him that she was trading on the black market when she wasn't. The night before, as we were being nearly flayed to death by Osterlitz and his thugs, Lily had arranged for Gerard and two other men from the estate to collect all the produce, canned goods, and casks of wine they could find in the various households within her farm holdings. She told them they must divide up, as there was so little time, and visit every house on every farm—there were six—and remove any portable foods they found. They were to assure the farm workers that Lily would repay them for everything they'd had to give up. In the interim, Lily went to see the chemist she knew and bought from him twelve cartons of Gitanes to add to her cache, as cigarettes were a most valuable product for anyone dealing in black-market goods. The storeroom and larder at the chateau were emptied of all their canned goods. Dozens of bottles of priceless aged wine, hidden since the invasion, were unearthed and packed dusty and dirty into wooden crates. In the wee hours of the morning, all the loot that had been collected from all over the estate was loaded onto wagons and taken to the cottage in the woods where it was unloaded so when Osterlitz came the next afternoon, he'd find it there.

"After we'd finished our meal in the chateau's kitchen, Gerard brought out a package of cigarettes and we sat talking and smoking for a few minutes while Gerard caught us up on the activities of our Maquis colleagues in Roscoff. He thanked us for our contributions to their efforts over the last couple of months. Then we left the chateau, and he led Pierre and me to a mill on the river and helped us settle into a narrow wedge in the wall just to the right of the turning wheel. He gave me a bag filled with bread and cheese, and a bottle of water, and told me that someone would come along in a while whistling 'Lillie Marlene.' But I was not to move until I heard the password.

"It was a warm night and the air was as heavy as wet wool. Despite heavy thunder in the distance, both of us dozed for a while. We awoke to the sound of someone whistling. Then a voice said, 'Basse le bouche large,' and we crawled out of our hiding place. The whistler told us his name was Reynard, and he took us to a camp deep in the forest where three men and two women were cleaning a cache of pistols and rifles. One of the men said they'd received a package—a burlap bag with four fish—for which they were very grateful. He led Pierre and me through the woods to a farmhouse. There, a farmer and his two young sons helped us up into the back of a wagon and covered us with a load of pink onions. They pulled a canvas tarp over us and secured it with rope. Just as we were leaving, a heavy storm rolled in and we lay under those smelly onions and sweltered in their fumes all the way to Roscoff. But at least we were protected from the rain. Unfortunately, the farmer and his poor horses were not. Before dawn, we arrived at a dock, and Pierre and I crawled out and went our separate ways. He went immediately to a dory where two men he knew were waiting. I stood and looked around until a man in a trawler beckoned to me. He never said a word, but took me down into the hold and locked me inside a small compartment. And there I stayed until we reached the Isles of Scilly where Stoney and Philipe were waiting."

At that point, Barney raised his glass to Stoney. "To the Beech Tree Group!" he said. "Onward and upward!" There was not a dry eye among us as we raised our glasses. Even Rutledge was visibly overcome at that moment and had to look away to regain his stoic composure. Sylvia and Jerusha excused themselves and began clearing the dining table. Barney and Miriam said good night to each other in the hallway before he started up the stairs to his bedroom. Soon everyone but Stoney had drifted away.

When I gave him his hat, I asked if I might have a private word with him and he followed me across the hall to the front door. "Barney is already talking about going back," I began. "I fear he's determined to continue on this fool's errand. Oh, Stoney, can't you make him see how dangerous this work is? He was almost killed, for God's sake. Can't you talk to him?"

Stoney stood quietly running his fingertips along the brim of his hat. Finally, he said, "I don't think it would do any good, my dear. You see, Barney's parents were arrested in a roundup of prominent Jews in Berlin in 1938. Their home and businesses were confiscated and they were sent to prison where both of them were shot one morning during roll call. We don't know why. Barney's sister, Elise, and her husband, who live in Paris with their two young children were arrested a couple of weeks ago and sent, with hundreds of others, to the Vélodrome d'Hiver—an indoor bicycle arena. Many there died from lack of food and water . . . and from the heat. Sylvia told me yesterday that information about that particular situation is still coming in. Stoney shook his head. "I can't think of anything I could say to Barney. He's determined to help Elise and her family and others like them. I fear nothing short of his own death will stop him."

He put his hat on and leaned toward me. "Oh, Evelyn," he whispered, "how difficult all of this has been. I don't think I've ever felt more helpless, for there was nothing I could do. We'll talk about this later when Barney is better and we'll devise a plan for our next mission that's not as complicated as this last one." He surprised me when he kissed me on the forehead. "Good night, dearest Evelyn," he said before he walked out into the night.

CHAPTER 12

That Simpson Woman

Stoneham, Staffordshire • September 18, 1942

When Rutledge came for Jerusha, Sylvia, and me early one Saturday in September, I felt I was not sufficiently prepared for our much-anticipated visit to Stoneham Feld. In the days before, there'd been a lot of excitement at Corrie Cottage as the three of us bustled about deciding what clothes we might need, what gift we should take to Stoney's mother, the countess, and how to deal with the unpredictable weather in the midlands. Sylvia and I had carefully chosen our gowns for dinner that evening and an array of rather worn leisure togs for tennis and croquet, as she felt sure we'd engage in those activities while there. Stoney had asked me to bring something to ride in, so Sylvia helped me find an out-of-date, but beautifully made, pair of jodhpurs with matching jacket at the Quaker Lighthouse Center for Refugees. I had to dip into my savings and buy a pair of riding boots, as Sylvia's were way too small. Jerusha had wrapped a dozen packages of *city goods* (lisle stockings, perfumed soaps, Kirby Grips, toothpowder, etc.) for members of her family, many of whom still lived and worked on the estate. She'd hoarded her sugar ration, along with ours, for the past few weeks so she could make a small box of treacle candies for her grandnieces. I had one remaining pint of pear preserves from the Christmas box my mother had sent and I wrapped it in floral paper with Lady Millicent in mind, although I did not know if she liked preserves. Sylvia was taking her a box of nice dusting powder from Mark & Spencer.

On our journey, we passed through the city of Stafford, famous for its potteries, and continued north into the town of Stone. After meandering down a narrow country road for about three miles, we crossed a bridge over the River Trent, and entered the village of Stoneham. Rutledge slowed the car to a crawl as dozens of folks came out of pretty cottages and quaint shops all along our route. They called and waved to us and we waved in reply. I heard several people calling Jerusha's name, and she beamed with delight at seeing her old friends and relatives. We turned a corner and Jerusha, who was sitting beside Rutledge, pointed to the church on our left whose bell tower rose from the center of the roof.

"That's Stoneham Chapel, which was built by Lord Beeton Howard's great-great grandfather, who was an officer in His Majesty's Hussars what went to the Crimea. Dreadful that was. My parents were married in that chapel and all my siblings and I were christened there. M' lord's grandmother, Lady Flora, made the tapestry that hangs over the altar. It took her thirty years. Perhaps you'll attend services in the morning." She turned around to look at me.

"I hope so," I responded. "It's such a lovely chapel . . . all those huge stone blocks and magnificent windows."

Jerusha giggled. "It's a little thing in comparison to The Castle. That's what we ordinary folk here 'bouts call the manor house."

Presently we came to a cottage where the window boxes would have evoked envy in every gardener I'd ever known, including my own mother. Dianthus, bluebells, purple flox, and trailing arbutus burst from them in vibrant colors that brought life to the cool stone façade of the house. Rutledge pulled into the side yard and turned off the ignition just as a woman wearing a green plaid dress and pink apron emerged from the open door carrying a curly-haired baby on her hip. Behind her came four young girls, the oldest perhaps eight.

"Mercy, what a sight!" Jerusha exclaimed as she stepped from the car. "That's me sister, Faith," she announced. "The one I told you about what has all the grandbabies that is girls. That's them . . . all five of 'em. Their mam works as a parlor maid at The Castle, so my sister takes care of her bairns. You and Miss Sylvia come on over here so's they can see my friends."

Faith, who had Jerusha's twinkling eyes, came forward and bowed to each of us and invited us in for a cup of tea. But Jerusha told her that Sylvia and I couldn't stay, as we were expected at The Castle for lunch. The four little girls, who'd remained shyly off to one side, began jumping up and down singing "Auntie, Auntie" in unison.

"Ain't they something," she said, "chirping and bouncing about like a flock of magpies." It was obvious she was just as happy to see them as they were to see her. "Come here, you little biddies," she called, "and meet these ladies. This is Miss Evelyn and Miss Sylvia." She placed her hand gently on top of the head of the oldest girl and told us her name was Catherine of Aragon. Then she patted the heads of the remaining three telling us, in turn, they were Anne Boleyn, Jane Seymour, and Anne of Cleves, who's called Annie. She pointed to the cherub in Faith's arms. "The baby there is Katherine Parr, but we call her Katy. We think our little girls is as beautiful as Henry's queens."

Rutledge came from the rear of the car carrying Jerusha's old portmanteau and she called to the girls saying, "Now, let's go in the cottage so you can tell me all about the new lambs what come this spring." With her queens trailing regally behind, she started up the walk. Just before she crossed the threshold, she turned and said, "I'll see you ladies in the morning at services. Have a wonderful time tonight. I know you'll look ever so beautiful in your lovely gowns."

We'd been back in the car about three minutes when Rutledge turned onto a long drive lined on either side by stately evergreens. To the east, clouds were piled high like fluffy blobs of meringue above a lush green meadow where dozens of fat sheep grazed. Off to the right a line of ancient chestnut trees glowed in the afternoon sunlight, their deep burgundy leaves twirling in the breeze. A moment later, we topped a rise and I gasped as the manor house came into view. I'd expected it to be grand, but had not expected to see such a sprawling expanse of architecture. Medieval, Georgian, and Regency—all were represented in a graceful façade of ancient stone. Rutledge stopped the car before a set of massive doors that had brass knobs as large as dessert plates.

A moment later, those doors opened, and an elderly man came down the steps, followed by several women in black uniforms and crisp white caps and aprons. "Good morning, Mrs. Kendall," he said to Sylvia, with a slight nod of his head. Sylvia introduced me to Durham, the butler, and he, in turn, introduced each of the maids—Hettie, Fiona, and Gillie. After he'd handed them our suitcases, they hurried off. "Lord Beeton-Howard is conversing with the manager at the potteries," he informed us. "But he'll return soon. Now, if you'll kindly follow me."

We entered what Durham called the Great Hall, where enormous blocks of cream-colored stone rose more than twenty feet inside a room at least fifty feet square. Gleaming suits of polished armor stood in each of its four corners, and colorful displays of crested flags draped with silk halyards hung above the four doorways that led to various sections of the house. The floor was laid in black-and-white marble, and a pair of massive stone fireplaces sat on either end of it, their cavernous interiors stacked waist-high with oak logs.

When I stopped to stare, Sylvia came over to where I was standing to tell me that this stone keep had been the original house, and the area where we were had been the cow byre, the pig sty, the chicken box, and the stable. "During the winter months, they would have kept the sheep in here," she said. "Can you imagine the smell, the piles of manure, the vermin?"

There had been a second floor in those years, she went on, where the family lived. She pointed to a line of wooden stobs that rose at an incline up the right wall. "The stairs would have been there," she said. "And the cooking would have been done on the hearth of that fireplace beneath them. There's a date carved there if you care to see it."

I walked over to the fireplace and looked down to a slab of stone inscribed *Beeton House 1412*. Before Columbus discovered America, before Columbus was even born, Stoney's ancestors had built this keep, had made it their home, and had held on to it for five centuries.

Durham interrupted my thoughts, telling us that luncheon would be served on the terrace in half an hour. "If you'd care to follow me, I'm sure you'd like to freshen up."

From the back wall, he led us through a door that opened to a reception room decorated in the Regency splendor of George III. Life-sized portraits in elaborate gilded frames were much in evidence, including one of Stoney as a young boy. Other walls were filled with works by Gainsborough, Reynolds, Holbein. We followed Durham up a set of broad stairs to the landing, then down a walnut paneled hallway that seemed to go on for miles. Near the end, he opened a door and bowed to me. "Queen Anne's Room," he said, giving me a thin smile. He then continued down the hall to the next door, which he opened for Sylvia.

The room I entered was centered with a magnificent bed dressed in a gold satin coverlet. Gold and peach jacquard drapes hung on either side of a pair of tall windows that looked out on a stone terrace, toward the elegant gardens of an inner courtyard, and further to a sweep of pasture where a herd of red deer were resting. A fire burned brightly in the marble fireplace opposite the bed, and a stunning landscape by Turner graced the wall above it. To the left, a pedestal dressing table had been neatly arranged with my makeup cases, comb and brush, and bottle of perfume.

I found my clothes hung in a wall-sized wardrobe, my shoes and boots resting beneath them. Near the wardrobe was a green damask wing chair, and beside it a table that held a brass lamp and a crystal vase of silver bells, purple flox, and apricot chrysanthemums.

After running a brush through my hair, I put on fresh lipstick and hurried back down the stairs to find Stoney and Sylvia seated at a table on the terrace. When we'd finished our lunch and were savoring cups of *real* coffee, Stoney asked if the two of us might join him for a ride around the estate. Sylvia thanked him but declined. "I have to do some work this afternoon," she said. "I promised Sir Winston I'd call after he awakens from his nap and give him an analysis of some data we received last night. You go ahead. I'll see you for drinks before dinner, I promise."

Stoney and I went separate ways down the upstairs hall to change into our riding clothes. As soon as he saw me, he commented on my handsome boots and led me off the terrace to the stables where the cornerstone at the entry read 1640. A groom brought out a handsome black gelding, a restless beast that kept trying to dance his way to freedom.

"This is Satan," Stoney said, as he hoisted himself into the saddle. He took the reins, gave them a jerk, and Satan settled down. At that point, a second groom emerged from the stable leading a lovely bay filly. Stoney told me he'd bought her just the month before because he couldn't help himself. "It's her coat, you see," he said. "It's the same glorious color as your hair! I've named her Eve's Flame in your honor, and she'll be here waiting for you when you visit."

"Oh, Stoney, you're such a dear," I said, emphasizing the word *dear*. "She's gorgeous. But I haven't ridden in years. I hope I won't make too much of a fool of myself today. Please don't gallop off and leave me."

"I wouldn't leave you, Evelyn Sanderson, for all the tea in China! Now, come along and I'll show you some of my boyhood haunts."

The path from the stables led to a row of low, thatch-roofed buildings. All were open-sided and filled with men working at a particular job—the estate blacksmith, the wheelwright, the carpenter—and all were so busy that none saw us ride by. In the last section, a man and two teen-aged boys were loading wooden crates with apples. They tipped their hats and spoke to Stoney in a friendly voice, and he called each of them by name.

Just beyond the end of the building, Stoney took a path and we entered the cool cover of a forest of majestic beech, oak, and chestnut. "I want to show you something special," he said. "At least it's special to me. It was built by my great-grandfather, Lionel Beeton, for my great-grandmother, Cristobel. I think you'll like it." He urged Satan up a slope to the right.

Just ahead stood a three-story Palladian-style manse, the sort one might imagine when reading Jane Austen. Built of soft yellow stone, it had a columned porte cochere and two sets of crenellated chimneys on either end of a gray slate roof. Stoney guided Satan onto the gravel drive that led to the front door and I followed. After dismounting, he came over to help me down, and we went inside.

I was as charmed by the interior of the house as I'd been by the outside. Sunlight poured through tall windows making patterns across a large expanse of gleaming wood floors. While the drawing room and dining room on the front of the house were formal rooms that boasted Adam mantelpieces, the sitting room beside the large bedroom on the back was furnished simply with a comfortable sofa, chintz curtains, and overstuffed chairs. It reminded me of my mother's sitting room. I told Stoney this and he said he'd felt sure I'd be at home in Cristobel's Dower House.

"My motives for bringing you here are not entirely altruistic," he said. "I've a confession to make and I've been much too slow in making it because I've dreaded telling you."

I laughed when I saw the look on his face. You'd have thought he was a three-year-old who'd been caught with his hand in the cookie jar. "Telling me what?" I asked.

"Telling you that I knew who you were the moment you boarded the boat train in Southampton last December."

My mouth dropped. I was so flabbergasted by this revelation I couldn't speak.

Stoney looked down and nervously fingered a button on his jacket. "I've seen you on stage twice, Evelyn . . . once in the spring of 1937 and again in June of 1938. The names of those shows I've forgotten, but I've never forgotten *you*."

While I was intrigued, I was not upset. What really mattered to me was the last bit when he revealed how he felt. I suspected that if I'd given him any encouragement at all there in the Dower House, I'd have found myself in another relationship like the one I'd had with Larry Christian—one that would end with me getting the short end of the stick. When I'd left New York, I'd made a vow never to become involved with a married man again no matter how attractive I found him. And Stoney Beeton-Howard was a most attractive man. I tried to play it cool by shrugging my shoulders. "Why didn't you tell me that night?"

He shook his head. "I don't know. We were so late leaving Southampton and you were tired from your long trip, and I was a bit out of sorts over a letter I'd just received. The time wasn't right. I wanted to wait until the two of us were alone together, but that has never happened until now!"

I reached over and took his arm in mine. "Oh, Stoney. You're a quirky old bird, aren't you? There have been plenty of times when we've been alone together. We've had a dozen or so lunches and dinners alone when you might have summoned up the necessary courage to tell me. But I understand, I think, why you haven't until now. I think you wanted to wait until we were together in a special place like this where you felt at home and more comfortable."

"Perhaps you're right. I used to run away from my mother if she scolded me for some little infraction and seek solace here in the Dower House with my grandmother Flora, who lived here for twenty-two years after my grandfather died.

She was a sweet, affectionate woman and my brother and I adored her."

"Your brother . . . you have a brother?"

"I *had* a brother . . . James Revere. He was killed on the Somme in 1917. James was brought up to be the next earl, so he spent only four years away at boarding school. He had no need for university because his job in life was to provide employment to a large number of workers and to make the most productive and efficient use of thousands of acres of farmlands and woodlands. He was reared to support not only the estate, but the village and the church, and to represent this district in Parliament . . . and most importantly, to marry the right kind of woman and produce an heir. He did none of these things, God rest his soul. And neither have I."

I stood quietly for a moment trying to process another revelation from a man I *thought* I knew, and wondered why neither Jerusha nor Sylvia had ever mentioned James Revere.

Stoney cupped his palm under my elbow. "Shall we go? My mother adheres to a strict schedule and we must be in the library for drinks at seven thirty. I want you to have time to relax when we return and soak in a bath tub filled with all the hot water your heart desires."

* * *

As we rode home, I told Stoney how honored I'd felt at being invited to his estate and how impressed I'd been by all I'd seen. "The hearth slab in the Great Hall says 1412," I said. "Has your family actually been here since then?"

Stoney turned slightly in his saddle. "Yes," he said, "but three generations of Beetons lived on this land before that stone keep was built. My original ancestor was a Frenchman named Giles Bethune, who came here as a prisoner of war following the Battle of Poitiers, which was fought in 1356. Edward III, whom history called *The Black Prince*, took an army to France with the sole purpose of killing or capturing

French King John. And he did. John's surviving soldiers were brought back to England, and the Englishman who was given Giles as a spoil of war also received two hundred acres of land. He brought Giles to that parcel here in the Midlands and they began farming. The Englishman died several years later, and Giles, who was freed at his master's death, married the man's widow. They had a son whom they named Giles, which was later Anglicized. Over the years, Giles Bethune became James Beeton.

"James Beeton and his wife had a son they named Riviere . . . which eventually became Revere. It was Revere and his wife, Matilde, who built the stone keep in 1412. The Beetons lived here as farmers over the next three centuries, growing the same crops that we grow now—oats, wheat, rye, and barley. During those years, a wing was added to either side of the Great Hall. Not much changed until the 1720s when one of my ancestors piled up such massive gambling debts that he was forced to sell off large tracts of land. Things continued to get worse and around 1765 another of my ancestors, Charles Beeton, went to work for Josiah Wedgwood at his pottery works near Stoke-on-Trent. Charles learned all he could from old Josiah and, in 1774, he came back here and started his own business in a shed by the river. By 1800, he had more orders than he could produce because he'd made the very wise decision to manufacture goods for the growing middle class. Charles had a son, Edmund, for whom I'm named. He developed an abiding friendship with Lionel Rothschild and named his son—my great-grandfather—for him. And I, in turn, named my son for my great-grandfather. I suppose Jerusha has told you the tragic circumstances of my son, Lionel's, death."

I shook my head. "No, she's never mentioned it. But I know that your wife is . . ." I stopped there, not knowing exactly what to say.

"My wife, Lydia, is in an asylum for the insane in Cumbria. She's there as a result of what happened to our boy, who was our only boy and our only child. Lydia gave birth to two baby girls as well, but both died before they could walk. Lionel was ten when he died. He was a bit small for his age but a fine horseman, nevertheless. So, the fact that he died because of an accident with a horse is another example of how our lives are shaped by destiny.

"Lydia and our son, Lionel, went riding together one morning and Lionel complained that he'd not tightened the girth on his saddle sufficiently. His mother offered to correct it and got down off her horse just as Lionel dismounted. For some odd reason he went around behind his mount, and just as Lydia heaved on the girth, the horse kicked Lionel in the forehead knocking him unconscious. One of the farmhands happened to be working in a field just off the path where they'd stopped. He saw the whole thing and ran immediately to his mistress and offered to carry Lionel home. But Lydia put our boy across her saddle and started back home with him. The farmhand took Lionel's horse and rode as fast as he could to the pottery factory to tell me what had happened. I managed to get to the house just as Lydia arrived in the stable yard. When I took Lionel from her he was still breathing, but he died early the next morning. The front lobe of his skull was crushed, you see, and he'd suffered a massive concussion.

"When the time came to bury him, Lydia fought me and the servants tooth and nail. And even after we'd removed Lionel's body from atop his bed, she refused to leave his room. She lay on the bed for days in the exact spot where he'd lain. She wouldn't eat, she wouldn't let anyone bathe or dress her, she wouldn't speak . . . not even to me. I spent the next week conferring with all sorts of specialists and trying to get her to talk to me. It's been eight years since the accident and she hasn't uttered a word. She stayed in a hospital in London for two years. Finally, the doctors told me there was no chance she would ever recover. That's when we took her to a facility near Grasmere. She has a nice private room and excellent care 'round the clock. She eats very little. Fresh oranges were her favorite food and I've bought a cartload over the years and taken them to her over and over but she hasn't touched a single one. She's as thin as a pencil and her hair's gone gray."

"Does she know where she is?"

"The doctors say she hasn't any concept of where she is, nor any idea of what's going on in the world. I visit her every month and I might as well be a ghost because she has no idea I'm even in the room."

"Oh, Stoney, I'm so sorry. What an awful thing. Not only Lionel's death, but the loss of his mother, too."

"Yes, it's very difficult at times. Divorce is out of the question as it's against the law in England to divorce someone who's lost their mind. But let's not talk about that anymore. It's enough that you know about Lionel and Lydia. Please don't feel sorry for me, Evelyn. I've accepted the fact that nothing can be done and I must go on with my life."

We rode quietly on, each of us harboring our own thoughts. I found it difficult to imagine being in Stoney's situation and wondered what my life would be like if I were married to someone who'd lost his mind, if I'd lost my only child in such horrible circumstances, if I'd had to shoulder the incredible responsibility Stoney had for the lives of others. It was more than I could comprehend.

As we pressed homeward, we passed hedgerows dark with blackberries where little yellow butterflies flitted in and out among the dusty leaves, their tiny wings aquiver as they searched for latent blooms. We wound our way through a chestnut grove alive with chattering squirrels and the raucous cries of rooks as they warned others of our presence in their territory. From the crown of a hill, we started down into a valley of endless fruit trees—peaches, apricots, apples—where land girls were hard at work gathering the abundant harvest. Like the other workers we'd encountered at Stoneham Feld, they smiled and waved to us as we rode by.

* * *

I'd brought the burgundy chiffon gown I'd bought in New York to Stoneham Feld on purpose. It was at least ten years old now, well-worn and a bit dated, but still in good condition. I knew Sylvia would be quietly dressed, as usual, in something unassuming, and I didn't want to appear flashy when I met the countess and her friends. I knew she was in her seventies and not well, so I'd chosen the burgundy gown and a pair of garnet earrings, thinking their understated style would please her. I could not have been more wrong.

On our way downstairs for drinks in the library, Sylvia told me about the other guests. "I know all of them," she said, "because of my father. The Marchioness of Claremont, Lady Jane Howard, has been here for a week. She and the countess are first cousins and visit each other often. Because she's the daughter of a duke, she's addressed as 'Your Grace.' Next in line on the social ladder is Bishop Francis Sheffield. He's a bit stuffy as one would expect of a man of his station in the church hierarchy. Low man on the totem pole is the Right Reverend Dr. Bevan Wilson Whitfield, the Vicar of Stone. Rutledge will be joining us, too."

We entered the dark gleaming recesses of the library and found the marchioness and two churchmen standing together near the fireplace. Sylvia introduced me to Lady Jane Howard and as I sank into a curtsey, she took my hand and said, "Hello, my dear. I've been ever so keen on meeting you. You're even lovelier in person than your pictures."

Lady Jane had a rosy round face and sparkling blue eyes and a crown of gingery hair dressed with pearl barrettes and blue satin bows. I was completely at ease with her from the start. Bishop Sheffield was an entirely different matter. He looked down his long nose at me with obvious curiosity and a hint of disdain. I smiled sweetly in return and moved toward the little gray-haired man with the warm smile, Dr. Whitfield, who kissed my hand and told me what an honor it was to meet me.

Fiona appeared with a tray of drinks, and I was surprised and delighted when the marchioness chose a gin fizz. I selected the same and so did Sylvia. The men took glasses of amber liquid which I assumed was whiskey. We stood in a circle and engaged in the kind of meaningless conversation one always has in such circumstances. Both clergymen asked Sylvia about the prime minister, and Lady Jane asked after his wife, whom she called "dear Clemmie."

Rutledge came in looking ever so handsome, his black hair smooth with pomade, his tuxedo resting perfectly on his slender frame. Lady Jane took a step toward him and said, "Good evening, Count Zielinski. It's so nice to see you again." Rutledge bowed and kissed her hand and moved on to shake hands with the churchmen. Fiona appeared instantly, bearing a silver tray with a lone glass of scotch for our Polish count.

A moment later, Durham entered the room, went directly to the marchioness, and said, "Pardon me, Your Grace, but Her Ladyship has asked that as soon as it pleases, would you be so kind as to lead her guests into the small dining room. She and my lord will be down shortly." About five minutes later Lady Jane smiled at me and said, "Shall we go in?"

The small dining room was quite large and in its center was a beautiful Georgian table set with an exquisite pattern of Beeton-Howard china, immense silver candelabra, and footed crystal bowls of fresh flowers. On the long wall opposite the windows, a heavily carved sideboard held dozens of commemorative silver pieces bearing the Croxdon crest. Behind it, covering the entire wall from walnut wainscoting to crown molding, was a finely executed pastoral scene of rolling pastures, woodlands, and a herd of red deer—the view from my bedroom window. Sylvia sidled up to me and whispered the name *Cristobel* as she pointed to the signature in the lower right corner. Lady Jane suggested we seat ourselves, and soon two elderly footmen dressed in livery began pouring wine into one of four elegant glasses at each of our place settings.

I heard a *thump, thump* and looked toward the doorway where a woman dressed in a silver moiré gown was slowly making her way toward us with the help of a cane. She was tall, square-shouldered, and handsome. Her hair, marcelled in a style that had been popular in the twenties, was arranged with elaborate diamond clips. Around her neck was a stunning choker of diamonds, amethyst, and pearls. Ignoring her other guests, she came directly to me. I rose quickly from my seat and, with much trepidation, sank into a deep curtsey.

"So this is the famous Eve Sands," she said, her voice as bland as oatmeal. "I've heard so much about you from my son and I must admit that you certainly live up to what he's told me. Welcome to Stoneham Feld. I trust you found your accommodations adequate?"

Stoney, standing behind his mother, made a motion indicating I should stand. As I rose, I said, "More than adequate, m'am. They're lovely." I dared look back at her and discovered the coldest eyes I'd ever seen. Pale gray, ringed with lavender, they bore into mine revealing her true nature—suspicious, cautious, wary of strangers. Her Ladyship turned away from me and addressed her other guests. "Shall we dine?" she asked, dismissing me in a thrice.

Lady Jane sat in the seat of honor on Lady Millicent's left; the bishop sat on her right. I sat between him and the vicar. Stoney sat on the far end down the table from his mother, and Sylvia and Rutledge were seated across from the churchmen and me. Conversation centered on the village, the farms, and news of members of the community. The vicar brought everyone up to date on the latest engagements and christenings. The bishop went on to say that a new airfield was being built just north of Stoke-on-Trent. Stoney commented on the growing relationship of FDR and Churchill, and Sylvia informed us that General Montgomery was making significant advances against the Germans in North Africa.

I nodded, smiled, or laughed as necessary, and concentrated on the delicious foods we were served. By the time dessert arrived, I was miserable and hardly touched the luscious almond pudding with apricot brandy sauce.

Lady Millicent picked at her food and ate little. Stoney had told me earlier that she was not well, but I hadn't realized how serious her condition was until I saw the cane. When the footmen brought trays of fruit and cheese, she looked at me and said, "I understand you're a nurse, Miss Sands, at St Mary's. Did Edmund tell you that he was born there?"

It took me a moment to realize she was talking about Stoney. "No, m'am. He didn't," I answered, giving Stoney a quizzical look.

Lady Millicent went on. "Well, he arrived a bit earlier than expected. I had been at Croxdon House for the season and was preparing that very morning to return to Stoneham Feld to await his birth, which was a month away." She gave Stoney an adoring look. "He was the prettiest baby, and the sweetest child, I ever had. And, unlike my two daughters and his older brother, he lived. I recall St Mary's being a busy bustling place, and I understand from my friends in the city that it's busier than ever these days. I'm sure all the hospitals in London are treating the horribly wounded young men being brought home from the battlefields of North Africa. Tell me, Miss Sands, isn't it difficult to deal with those poor hideous victims each day? Surely you weren't brought up to do such things. Does your mother know what you're doing?"

I lifted my chin. "My mother's quite supportive, actually. It was her idea that I go to school to become a nurse in the first place. All I wanted to do when I was young was sing and dance onstage. But my mother insisted that I had to train myself for a real job before I tried to break into the entertainment business."

"But weren't you in the entertainment business for quite a few years? I was given to understand that you'd had a successful career on Broadway. Why did you leave New York to come here?"

"My father died unexpectedly," I said, all but stepping on her question. "His death was so sudden that I felt I needed a change."

"So you left your forward-thinking mother, and your family and friends, to come here to help us fight the Germans?"

I nodded.

"And you've never married?" she asked, letting the word *married* hang like a noose above the table.

For some reason, I cut my eyes at Stoney. Then I looked quickly back at the countess. "No, m'am, I haven't."

Her Ladyship turned to the man on her right. "I don't understand young people today, Bishop. Do you?" She looked around the table as she folded her napkin and placed it beside her plate. "Shall we go through, ladies, and leave the gentlemen to their business?"

Stoney rose, embarrassment plain on his face, and made his way to the head of the table where he helped his mother out of her chair. Our hostess braced herself on the edge of it with one hand and grabbed her cane with the other, trying hard to disguise the obvious pain she felt as she struggled to stand. She took Stoney's arm and said, "Perhaps, Miss Sands, you'll favor us with one of your show tunes after the gentlemen join us."

* * *

As far as I was concerned, Sunday and the trip back to London could not come soon enough. I'd never felt such a fish-out-of-water as I had in the presence of the countess and Bishop Sheffield. When we women joined the men in the drawing room the conversation continued much as it had at dinner, sprinkled with little stories about past lives when people knew their place and kept to it. Stoney intervened occasionally, remarking that conditions for the British working class had improved greatly, and that he felt the situation would bolster the economy when the war was over.

Lady Jane smiled and nodded at everything Stoney said. She was sweet and kind, and so incredibly different from the countess, that I marveled they had the same blood in their veins. She went out of her way to make me feel welcomed, asking me all about my family and digging for details about my job at St Mary's.

While it was larger, the west drawing room reminded me of our living room at home. The walls were a soft celadon green decorated with elaborate Wedgwood plasters featuring flowers, fruits, and vines. A magnificent Bösendorfer grand sat in the far corner beneath a wall of mullioned windows. Sylvia had told me earlier that the piano had not been played since Stoney's grandmother Flora died, and that he'd had it tuned just days before because he hoped I'd sing.

As we sat together on sofas near the fireplace, Fiona served cordials from a tray. The countess occupied what I assumed was a centuries-old chair upholstered in plum-colored damask with elaborately carved wooden arms. From this seat, she commanded the room, and everything and everyone in it. Every few minutes, Stoney asked his mother if she needed anything, if she were comfortable, if he could get anything for her.

After a while she told him, yes, she would appreciate it very much if I would entertain the guests with a couple of songs. She looked over at her cousin who jumped up and hurried off toward the piano. "Come along, darling Evelyn," Jane called to me as she sat down on the bench and began executing a series of running chords. "What shall it be?"

Hoping that the others would be familiar with them, I chose a couple of Mr. Porter's more well-known compositions. Lady Jane provided a skilled accompaniment for "What Is This Thing Called Love?" and "In the Still of the Night." The countess requested an aria and I worked hard, but managed to pull off a decent rendition of "O Mio Babbino Caro," something I hadn't sung in years. When Vicar Whitfield asked for "The White Cliffs of Dover," I smiled and said I'd be happy to do it, but only if everyone sang along with me. They did, and this joining of voices moved the proceedings to another dimension. Soon the bishop came forward to sing "Jerusalem" and I happily sat down.

At precisely ten thirty, the countess heaved herself out of her chair and nodded to each of us. Stoney handed her the cane and escorted her out of the room. The vicar and the bishop followed, and I walked out with Lady Jane thanking her again for her hospitality and fine musicianship.

I felt a great sense of relief when I closed the door to my room and began to undress. Soon, the old burgundy gown I'd worn with such unrealistic expectations was hanging in the wardrobe with my fancy evening shoes beneath. I put on a robe and sat down at the dressing table to take off my makeup.

There was a soft knock on the door. Thinking it must be Sylvia, I hurried to open it. But it was Stoney, and as soon as I saw the look on his face I knew why.

"I'm so sorry," he said, "so very sorry if my mother seemed rude. She's not well and her condition is taking a much greater toll these days. May I come in for a moment?"

He sat down in the green chair by the fireplace and spread his hands atop his trousers by way of explanation. "My mother has changed so much, Evelyn. She wasn't always this way. When she was young, she could be a lot of fun. She was a fine horsewoman, very daring . . . with expert hands. And she was a gracious hostess with many friends and admirers. But my brother's death, and my father's, coming so close together took a great toll. Then, her only grandchild was killed. And Lydia's situation has only exacerbated her fragile emotional state. As you saw tonight, everyone in this house puts her well-being and comfort above all else . . . as do I."

"I know this must be difficult for you, my dear, because, truth be told, you're young enough to be her granddaughter.

And you're so in touch with what's happening in the world right now and my mother isn't. She is definitely of another era . . . an era of high-top shoes, daring hats at Ascot, and riding in an open carriage through Hyde Park on Coronation Day. My mother was presented to Queen Victoria in 1892, the absolute height of the British Empire. She can't seem to comprehend what's happened to her world, and she's furious that four of her footmen deserted her and went to war. And she still hasn't accepted the fact that we have several young girls living here *on their own*, caring for livestock, and harvesting crops. She refers to them as 'street girls,' if you get my drift."

Since I'd never known anyone quite like Millicent Beeton-Howard, I wasn't sure how to respond to these personal revelations. I rose from the dressing table bench and knelt down in front of Stoney. "You mustn't take on the burden of your mother's behavior. It won't do any good. We human beings carry around a lot of baggage . . . the things we *think* we know, the people we *think* we are, the insecurities that plague us throughout our lives, the problems we have with other people . . . even the people we love. You can't take on another burden, Stoney. You're already carrying more than your share. And you need *never* apologize to me."

I went back to sit on the bench. "I don't think I could ever be a member of the British aristocracy," I said. "I come from such humble roots compared to yours. My folks were farmers and merchants and horse traders."

Stoney stood up and gave me a smile. "Well, that's one thing we have in common, my dear. I come from the same. Aristocracy is just a bunch of ballyhoo. It's just trappings and masquerading around in costume trying to be somebody you're not. We all started the same way, jockeying for a position as close as possible to the rich, the powerful. And while we were at it, we lived in a pig sty and grubbed in the muck like everyone else!"

He walked back across the room to the door. "I hope you rest well," he said as he opened it. "By the way, we'll be leaving tomorrow right after services are over. I have a meeting at three with several men from the War Ministry to talk about a new technology called RADAR. It's a sort of tracking device, a system for detecting enemy planes. I'm converting a section of the London factory to the production of parts for these systems. I'm sorry we can't stay longer as there were other things I wanted to show you. Perhaps next time."

As he turned to go, he said, "Regardless of what you might think, you were splendid tonight, Evelyn. Please forgive my mother. She just isn't herself."

* * *

I had breakfast on Sunday morning from a tray in my room, followed by another leisurely bath, and met Sylvia in the hallway at quarter of ten. Rutledge took us to the village chapel, and when we entered the sanctuary, we found it already full and hurried up the aisle. The organist struck a chord and began a Bach prelude, and the congregation rose as Stoney came down the aisle with the countess on one arm and the marchioness on the other.

As I sat most comfortably on an embroidered cushion in that lovely centuries-old chapel where Stoney had married Lydia, I felt a great sadness for all the losses he'd suffered and the fact that he'd had to face the ultimate parting with so many loved ones in that beautiful space . . . his only son, his baby daughters, his father, his brother, his beloved grandparents. My heart went out to him—and to everyone else around the world— who were sitting in a place of worship that Sunday morning praying for loved ones, many of whom would never set foot in a church again.

When we returned to the manor house, we found Durham directing two teenage boys who were hauling crates from the house onto the drive. Rutledge came to where Sylvia and I were waiting at the back of the car to be sure the boys placed a roomy metal box in the center floor of the trunk. "That's filled with fish caught this morning," he said. "It's been packed in ice, along with ten pounds of butter. We'll collect Jerusha in the village on the way home."

Just as Rutledge closed the trunk, Durham came and whispered to me, "The countess is in the west drawing room, Miss Sands. She'd like a word with you before you leave."

I hurried off and made my way through the maze of corridors to the drawing room, where I found Lady Millicent seated on the fancy plum chair she'd sat in the night before.

"Won't you come sit for a moment, Miss Sands," she said, indicating that I should take the chair opposite her. As soon as I sat down, she started talking, her words piling one upon the next in the same impatient cadence my father had used with my mother when he was displeased. "I know you must think our country customs strange," the countess began, "and so different from the hustle-bustle life you Americans lead. But, you see, we English are old-fashioned and in our society, a young unmarried woman would never have considered accepting an invitation to visit someone in their home without a chaperone. And she would never have been so bold as to sing a song such as those you sang last night to *any* man."

My mouth opened slowly and I tried to think of something to say while the countess ignored me and went on. "My son, Edmund, has enormous responsibilities and a reputation to uphold. And while my daughter-in-law, the Countess Croxdon, is temporarily incapacitated, she will recover one day. You must have many admirers, Miss Sands, but Edmund cannot be one of them."

I heard a soft click as the door to the hallway opened. "Ah, Durham," the countess said. "Miss Sands was just leaving. Please show her out."

I stood up, but remained rooted to the spot in front of my chair. I've asked myself a dozen times why I didn't respond to her accusation, why I didn't tell her that I had no interest in Stoney, nor any man. I suppose it was the conversation Stoney and I had had in my room the night before. Perhaps it was the sympathy I'd felt for him. A hot flush settled on my cheeks as I reluctantly started across the room. But the countess was not finished.

She tapped her cane on the side of her chair to be sure she had my attention. "You Americans obviously think you have the answers to all the world's problems . . . including ours," she said, her voice dripping venom. "Women like you, and that ridiculous Nancy Astor, assume the cream of British society is yours for the bidding. Well, I'll not see my son's life ruined by some flashy bit like that Simpson woman."

CHAPTER 13

Apple Farmers

Cobourg, France • October 11, 1942

On October first, the Beech Tree Group gathered at the farm in Hampshire to plan the strategy for our next mission to France. While there, Sylvia provided us with detailed information about Allied and enemy troop movements in North Africa. The target now was a place called El Alamein—a desert outpost no one had ever heard of—to which the Luftwaffe was flying a supply of equipment, weapons, and troops from its air base in Caen. If we could help slow the flow of resources from Caen, the Allies could take the area around El Alamein and push the Germans east. So Caen Air Base became the target for the next Beech Tree operation.

Barney told us, that because he and I would be operating in the apple-growing regions of Normandy, the password for this mission would be *bonne hotture*—the name of a well-known russet-colored apple grown there. He did an excellent job of preparing me for this mission by drumming into my head ordinary idioms and phrases used by French country folk, teaching me to sup my soup like a French farmer, showing me how to stoop and shuffle like an old lady, and how to appear modest and humble (What a feat!) in my role as the wife of a simple apple grower. Our adopted names were Antoine and Hortense Laurent and, according to our carte d'identitiés, we were born and still lived in the town of Montivilliers several miles inland from the sea.

Sylvia supplied us with disguises, bringing a store of French-labeled clothing from the Quaker Lighthouse Center for Refugees. When we set out, Barney was dressed in wide-legged blue trousers, a heavy black jacket over a rough homespun shirt, and a pair of *sabots*—the wooden clogs worn by French farmers. He'd combed ashes and baking soda into his hair and moustache, which he'd grown just for this mission. It aged him considerably.

Sylvia suggested that I dress in something that would disguise my youthful stature, so I wore a long slip, camisole, heavy cotton blouse, and a bulky black skirt—all made in France. To this, I added the brogans and socks I'd used on our fish mission back in June. The biggest challenge, as usual, was my hair. Sylvia helped me rub handfuls of ash and baking soda into it until it was fully coated, and afterward I put it in a bun and pulled a black knit cap over it. Then I brushed ash and soda into my eyebrows. Both Barney and I wore metal-rimmed glasses, their lenses so scratched we could hardly see through them. Eyeglasses were all but impossible to get in France and people had to wear their lenses much longer than usual making magnifying glasses worth their weight in gold.

Just before we left Corrie Cottage, Barney gave me a sheepish grin and I gasped when I saw that he'd darkened his teeth to a muddy beige and colored an upper middle one completely black. Raising an eyebrow, he said, "I'm not the only one who must shed the impertinence of personal vanity for the sake of this mission." Into my palm he laid a rather disgusting set of false teeth. Made of some kind of rubber, they lay crooked against one another, were grayish in color, and appeared very realistic. It took a few minutes for me to work them on over my own teeth, but the effect was good as they made me look older and rather unhealthy. Barney cautioned me to keep them in at all times. "Every molar in that set has a one-and-a-half carat diamond hidden in the bottom of it," he said.

"Oh, no," I groaned. "Do I have to?"

"I'm afraid you do, old thing. You see, the Nazis are much more likely to examine *my* mouth than yours. I'm praying they won't find you worth the time or effort, and you must do your best to make them think you're slow-witted."

"That will be the easiest part," I laughed. "I wish that was all I had to do."

Barney handed me a bundle of five thousand worn franc notes (about two hundred-fifty dollars American). "You'll need to hide these in one of your shoes," he said. "That money is real and we'd rather they find *it* than the diamonds hidden in your gorgeous new teeth! And if they do, just blubber about your old aunt's dying and leaving the money to you. Remember, Evelyn, the two of us are uneducated, hardworking farmers, and we've always been poor! I know it will be a stretch, but you've been acting for years."

"Yes, I have," I agreed. "But my life has *never* depended on it!" I hoisted a prop, a barrel-shaped canvas apple bag, to my shoulder and said, "Lead on, Macduff!"

In the weeks before our departure date, Sylvia had been in constant touch with the meteorologists at the War Ministry to be sure that, when we embarked, we'd have the perfect conditions to conceal our Channel crossing aboard *Flying Griffin*. Channel weather can be lovely and clear right into mid-October, so we had to wait almost a week before we could start. Sylvia told us that a front would be moving in around October 9, bringing heavy fog that would saturate the area for several days—an ideal situation. So Stoney readied his yacht and we all waited for Mother Nature to cooperate.

When we finally got under way, our progress was slow due to all that pea soup, but it gave us the cover we needed. About three miles out of Le Havre, Stoney told Philipe to cut the engines and drop anchor because he'd spotted the fishing trawler that was waiting for us. I had a hard time getting down the rope ladder in my bulky skirt, but when I reached the last rung, I was lifted off by a small, but strong, Frenchman who helped me climb over the gunwale onto the deck of the trawler. An hour later we put in at heavily fortressed Le Havre, and we fisher people left the trawler and presented our papers to the Nazi guards waiting on the dock. Then Barney and I helped the other folk off-load their catch into the back of a waiting truck. I sat in the front of the cab between Barney and the driver, who took us along muddy back roads through farmland and forests all the way to Honfleur. There, we crossed the Seine and headed south. We stopped in a little village of perhaps a half dozen houses where we were given a bowl of the best potato soup I'd ever eaten (slowly and painfully due to my cumbersome false teeth!) and a cup of delicious fresh cider. After we'd finished eating, the man from the truck shook Barney's hand and drove away.

Another man appeared leading a horse hitched to a low-sided rickety cart—what the English call a "bone shaker"—packed with wooden crates of apples. Barney gave the man some money and helped me climb up onto the cart's bench before taking the reins. He gave the horse a gentle tap and we headed away from the village. Our destination was a little town called Dives, which was about twenty kilometers west of Caen. The trip was slow due to the heavy load of apples, the day gray and cool, and the road rough. For a couple of hours we followed a route up through the hills and down through the valleys of that beautiful farmland until we came to a crossing that led north to Cabourg. Just beyond this intersection, Barney pulled off the road and urged the horse across a pasture and into the stand of woods on the far side. Once there, we climbed down and had a drink of water from the bucket roped inside the back corner of the cart. When we finished, Barney took the bucket to the horse and held it so the animal could drink.

We were moving about, stretching our weary legs, when a young woman dressed in men's clothing stepped out of the brush, rifle in hand. "Bonjour, monsieur," she said to Barney, who called her by her code name, Michelle. As she nodded to me, three men came from behind her, and Barney turned and whispered, "Take out your false teeth, Hortense. Hurry!"

The top set came out easily, but I struggled with the bottom. I finally handed both parts to the woman. She quickly wrenched diamonds from two of the eight molar cavities and swallowed them. Then she pulled out the other six diamonds and handed two stones to each of the three men who also swallowed them. Without a word, she gave the empty false teeth back to me and, in the wink of an eye, she and the men were gone. I could hear them making their way deeper into the brush as I worked my jaw forcing the teeth back in place. God, how they hurt! Barney and I got into the cart, crossed the pasture to the road, and headed back the way we'd come.

Just beyond the turn to Cabourg, a truck suddenly roared into sight. Dark green and obviously Wehrmacht issue, it headed straight toward us. Barney jerked the reins and pulled to the side of the road as the truck ground to a stop.

The driver jumped out of the cab and approached us. "Aus! Aus!" he yelled as Barney turned to me and whispered, "Remember, Hortense, you're a dim-witted fool. Go slowly and keep your mouth shut!" He helped me down as the SS driver demanded our papers.

I kept my eyes on the ground while Barney handed him our cards. I heard the truck door open and close, and soon another pair of black boots was standing in the mud across from me. I looked up as the driver turned to the man beside him and said, "All seems to be in order, Lieutenant. Their papers say they are farmers from Montivilliers."

The lieutenant snatched our papers from the driver. "What are the two of you doing here?" he yelled. "Where are you going?" Barney took off his cap, hung his head, and told the lieutenant that we were on our way to Cabourg with our apples.

The lieutenant stepped to within inches of Barney and said, "You're moving in the wrong direction, idiot! Cabourg is that way!" He pointed north.

Barney nodded. "Yes, mein herr," he said. "I know. But you see my wife needed to relieve herself, so I was going back toward those woods so that she could have some privacy."

The lieutenant raised his riding crop and slapped it against the side of the cart, frightening the horse. When Barney turned to grab the reins, he was knocked to his knees. "Check his jacket pockets," the lieutenant told the driver, "and her pockets, too. Take off your shoes," he demanded while the driver rifled our clothing. Barney slipped out of his clogs with no problem, but it took me a few minutes to unlace the brogans. The driver had no trouble taking them apart and soon found the hidden franc notes. He handed them to the lieutenant, who looked at me and said, "What do you think you're doing with all this money? You know it's against the law for you to have such a large amount in your possession."

I started to tremble and quickly summoned up the saddest possible scenario I could imagine—the death of my mother. When I began crying, emitting a string of wrenching sobs, the lieutenant began flicking the end of the riding crop against his trousers. He stomped away, and from a distance of perhaps five yards yelled, "What the hell is wrong with you, stupid woman?"

Barney got to his feet and told the lieutenant that I'd recently lost my aunt and that it was she who'd left me the money. Then my French husband grabbed me by the arm and, with a burst of profanity, told me what a stupid cow I was. As the lieutenant walked back toward us, his mouth curved into a smile. "Oh, what fun Hauptmann Osterlitz will have with you!" he sneered.

We were forced into the back of the truck, manacled to a bar, and taken to SS headquarters in Cabourg. On the way, Barney reminded me of who Captain Osterlitz was and the manner in which le comtesse had duped him during our fish mission. But when we arrived at SS headquarters in Cabourg, Osterlitz wasn't there. He was out chasing other *terrorists*.

Our cart and horse were confiscated, along with the load of apples, and Barney and I were questioned by Schutzstaffel for several hours. Nazi officials in Montivilliers confirmed that a couple named Laurent had an apple farm there and that Hortense Laurent's aunt, Brigette Doual, had died two months before and left her niece, Hortense, five thousand francs. It was close to midnight before they let us go. They kept the money, of course.

Barney and I crept through the back streets and meandering alleys of Cabourg, making our way east toward the woods. I was miserably tired and hungry but Barney refused to stop, so we tramped on through the brush until my toes were crowned with oozing blisters. Just before dawn, we reached the outskirts of Merville, a small town whose residents worked in the Nazi factories building war materials for the air base at Caen. "We have friends here," Barney said, "and we'll be able to rest and find food."

We entered the town the same way we'd left the last one, through the deserted alleys. Barney soon stopped at a small cottage and knocked twice, then twice again, on its wooden door. A voice came from within and Barney opened the door. I followed him into a dark dusty room where a man was sitting at a metal table carefully pressing a rubber stamp onto the blank lines of what I assumed were fake identity cards.

"Ah, monsieur," he said to Barney. "Welcome! It's nice to see you again."

Barney introduced me as Hortense, and the man, whose name was never mentioned, offered us an apple and a cup of water for breakfast. In between bites of his apple, Barney told the man what had happened to us. The man shook his head, obviously surprised to hear that the Gestapo had let us go. "There are rumors around town that Osterlitz is searching for two British agents," he said. "You must have fooled his lieutenant and gotten away with it simply because Osterlitz was not there."

"It was Hortense," Barney said. "If only you could have seen her moaning and groaning trying to convince them of her innocence. She got down on her knees in front of the lieutenant and begged him to let her keep her money. He screamed and yelled and called her a *filthy stinking whore* and laid his riding whip across her back. Then the most marvelous thing happened . . . she started drooling." Barney turned to me, eyes shining with admiration. "I don't know how you managed that, Hortense. All that drooling down your chin and sweater. It was disgusting—and wonderful! Apparently that did it because the lieutenant yelled, 'Aus! Get them out of here!' He lashed about with his riding crop while he told us to stay in Montivilliers where we belonged or next time he'd set the dogs on us. When he said that, Hortense hung her head and made these awful sounds from deep in her throat. That drove the Nazi bastard mad and he grabbed her by the scruff and shoved her out the door. What a wonderful performance!" He grinned as he looked back at me. "You're all I dreamed you would be, Hortense," he beamed. "Brilliant, just brilliant!"

The man shrugged his shoulders. "As soon as that stupid lieutenant tells Osterlitz what happened, they will come for you. They're a ruthless pack of wolves who take delight in creating interesting methods of torture for their prey, so I suggest you rest for a while because you're sure to have a perilous journey ahead. You are welcome to bathe, if you wish, at the kitchen sink. But first, I want to show you a way out of here just in case Osterlitz orders a search. Come with me."

He opened a door at the back, led us down a set of steps, and pointed to a ramshackle enclosure several yards away. "There," he said, "that's the well. If the Boche come, you must get to that well as fast as you can. Grab the rope at the top of the bucket and lower yourselves down. There's an opening about two and half feet wide on the far side of the well's wall that's an escape hatch." He looked at me and frowned. "I'm afraid your skirts will weigh you down, mademoiselle. But this is the only way out. Drop down into the water and keep your head below the surface while you use your hands to feel around the wall for that opening. Then swim up into it. You won't be able to see, but the well is small enough that you can find your way through. I've done it many times. When you surface, you'll be inside a tunnel that's forty-three meters long. I know because I dug it myself. And I've been down into the well and swum up into that tunnel several times. When you get to the end of the tunnel, it opens on a ledge above the river. Follow the path to your left that goes into the woods. Do you understand?" he asked, looking directly at me.

"Oui, monsieur, I understand. But dropping down into a well sounds risky. Isn't there another way to get to the woods?"

"No, mademoiselle, there is not. You see the Boche have guards posted at regular intervals along the paths that lead from this part of town into the woods. You and Father Barney will just have to take your chances in the well." He turned and started back to the house. "I must go now to try to find help."

Once we were back in the house, the man put on a faded blue jacket and worn cap. "You will have to stay in the cellar," he said, handing me another cup of water. We went across the room to a corner that served as the man's kitchen. A greasy woodstove stood on one wall. On the opposite was an old-fashioned sink mounted in the center of a plank counter. A length of flowered fabric hung in front of it like a skirt. The man pulled it aside to reveal a small trap door in the floor. "There," he said. "Go down these steps to the cellar and stay there until I return."

Barney and I lay on a bed of pine straw in that tiny cellar through a miserable afternoon of oppressive heat, carefully sipping from the cup of water when we could bear our thirst no longer. The man finally returned about dusk and opened the trapdoor to tell us that he hadn't been able to get any help. "But I have some sheep's broth and a small loaf of bread," he said, "and you are welcome to join me for dinner and rest here for the night."

After Barney and I finished our meal, we thanked the man, and went back down the makeshift ladder to the cellar. I removed my boots, and all the clothes I dared, and took out the false teeth. Wearing nothing but my slip and underpants, I lay down on the pine straw once more. Barney took off his boots and stripped down to his trousers and T-shirt. The sound of thunder in the distance lifted my spirits, and I told Barney that it had always rained in the evenings during the summer when I was growing up in Baker. "Yes, he said, "what a relief a bit of rain would be, Ducks, especially in this midget's Hell hole." Soon both of us drifted off to sleep.

Sometime during the early morning hours, I awoke with an urgency to pee. There was no chamber pot, no bucket in that little cellar, nothing I could use. So I went up the ladder, tiptoed past monsieur snoring on his cot, and crept out the back door. The feel of wet grass on my blistered feet was so soothing that I paused for a moment to gaze longingly at the stars and think about my mother. Since there was no outhouse, I squatted there in the yard. I'd been warned not to wipe myself with grass or leaves, so I gathered up the lace-trimmed tail of my slip and used it to dry between my legs.

As I stood up, an arch of light flashed overhead. From a distance, I heard a man's voice shouting in German. Another man answered in a high-pitched, thin voice that sounded like that of the lieutenant who'd arrested Barney and me outside Cabourg. I ran quickly into the house and shook monsieur. Then I hurried to the trapdoor, where I found Barney coming up the ladder. He was fully dressed and handed me my boots and clothing. "The well," he said. "Run to the well. I'm right behind you."

I slipped the blouse over my head, pulled on the skirt, and tied it at the waist while monsieur crept to the front door and opened it a crack. He looked at me and whispered, "Osterlitz" before sprinting to the back door. I grabbed my boots and followed. When we reached the well, Barney jumped in front of me. "Let me go first," he said. "I'll wait for you down under in case you need help getting into the hole." He grabbed the knot above the bucket and monsieur hauled back on the long rope and lowered him into the drink while I put on my boots. A moment later, I clasped the knot and went as far down as the surface. I took a deep breath, forced myself under, and thrust my hands out in front of me to try to find the opening. I could feel my skirt rising around me, billowing like a parachute, and in an instant it had wrapped itself around my head, covering my face like a shroud. I kicked back from the stone wall and began clawing frantically at the fabric. Barney snatched me by the arm and hauled me up, up, up into the hole. As we surfaced, I gasped for air and his hand closed over my mouth like a vise. "Hush!" he whispered. "They'll hear you."

An hour passed before we decided it was safe enough to crawl out of monsieur's tunnel. When we finally reached the opening at the ledge, my feet were so sore I could hardly move. Barney put his arm around my waist and held on to me as we made our way along the narrow path that led to the woods. We'd not been walking more than a few minutes when I told Barney I'd heard something. He paused to listen, but whatever I thought I'd heard was no longer there. "I'm sure the Nazis are combing these woods like an army of ants," he whispered. "We'd better not take any chances."

A few yards from us stood a large low-lying shrub and we quickly covered the distance between it and us. "Wrap yourself around the root as tightly as possible, Hortense," Barney said, "and I'll wrap myself around you. Our clothes are dark so maybe they won't see us."

I scuttled down into a bed of moldy twigs, dead leaves, and bird droppings, and wrapped myself so tightly around the roots of the plant that the tops of my knees were all but touching the end of my nose. Barney followed, covering me like a heavy cloak, and as we lay there in the dirt wound as tight as a bobbin, I prayed I wouldn't sneeze. A few minutes later, I smelled cigarette smoke and heard footsteps coming down the path. My heart drummed in my ears as two sets of shiny black boots went by, their owners conversing quietly with one another. Barney told me later that one had told the other that Osterlitz had offered a reward for the capture of the British agents and he intended to get it.

When we finally dragged ourselves out from beneath the bush I was so stiff I could hardly move. Barney tried to sooth me saying we would soon find help, but we had to keep moving. My feet were in such bad shape that I begged him to wait a moment while I took my boots off. The blood from the blisters on my toes and heels had dried, and my socks were stuck to them, so I couldn't take them off. I could think of nothing but to wrap something around them to try to cushion the pain. So, I took off my slip and Barney ripped it into two pieces so I could swaddle my feet. He picked up my boots and I held on to him as we started out once more.

Somewhere in the distance an owl hooted. I surprised myself by tweeting the three notes le comtesse had taught me, and Barney all but knocked me down. "What in the hell are you doing?" he hissed. "Somebody might hear you."

Somebody did. When they answered with the same three notes, Barney jumped. "It's a code," I said. "When I was with Lily Suchette, she told me what to do if I heard that whistle in the woods. I have to answer back now to find out where our contact is." I turned away from him and whistled again. A moment later, someone answered. Barney pointed to a grove of large trees and said, "Over there."

There was a sound like wind rustling through dry leaves, and from a distance of about twenty feet, the woman Barney had called Michelle dropped down from the branches of an oak. "Bon jour, mes amis," she said. "Fancy meeting you here. I thought you went to Montivilliers."

"We had to make a little detour," Barney said.

"And lucky for you mademoiselle knows the song of the night bird, huh?"

"Oui," Barney nodded. "Very lucky indeed." He turned to me and said, "Oh, Hortense, darling, forgive me. But your little tweets scared the crap out of me!"

Michelle took us to a bramble camp where she fed us stale bread, cold sausages, and crude red wine. After the three of us had had a nap, she led us deep into the forest once more and we crawled behind her through the tall grasses beneath an archway of old grape vines that led to a farm. The owner was very kind and brought us bunches of grapes, apples, and a jar of water. Then we were hidden behind a waist-high stack of burlap bags against the back side of his truck's cab. Once we'd settled in, the farmer and his son loaded the truck bed with crates of apples and covered it with a tarp for the three-hour trip to Le Havre. There, the fruit was unloaded and put on a cargo ship destined for Bremen.

Barney and I remained in our hiding place behind the bags while the work was done, and when the crew had finished unloading all the apples, we settled back against the wall of the cab and tried to relax. But the stifling heat and constant buzz from clouds of flies kept us awake through a long, scary afternoon. Dozens of German soldiers were stationed on the docks, and they kept walking up and down beside the truck, badgering each other and making jokes. What if they decided to crawl into the back of the truck? What if they removed the stack of burlap bags that shielded us from sight? All I could think about was the SS lieutenant and the sting of his riding crop.

Late that night, two men climbed up into the truck bed and whispered, "Bonne hotture." We were taken aboard their boat and given bread and cheese before they put us in a storeroom behind a bulkhead. The trip across the Channel was quiet and slow due to a heavy fog, and Barney and I slept like babies. The next morning we rendezvoused with *Flying*

Griffin off Pointe de Barfleur, and Stoney and Philipe took us home.

* * *

Kommandant Walthur Bauer
14 October, 1942
SS HQ 26 rue Saint Marthe
Caen, France

Herr Kommandant: My office is aware that British agents posing as apple farmers are transporting contraband to the terrorist element operating in and around Caen Air Base. Rest assured I will apprehend these anarchists.

Heil Hitler!
Friedrich Osterlitz, Hauptmann
SS HQ Cabourg, France

CHAPTER 14

In the Shadows

London, England • January 2, 1943

Dearest Mama,

Happy New Year! Thank you for the nice long letter about your Christmas holidays and for news about Claire and Charles and Maddie and Fletcher and all the family. I love the beautiful hat and scarf you knitted for me, the wonderful Blue Gardenia dusting powder (dusting powder doesn't exist in England any more) and the gorgeous lace slip. Everyone at Corrie Cottage was so happy when I opened the box of oranges, sweet potatoes, and bags of shelled pecans (manna from Heaven!). Thank you, too, for the added bonus of three more composition notebooks, which are very scarce here. You'll be pleased to know that so far I've filled seven.

You and Maddie deserve standing ovations and bouquets of roses for hosting six airmen on Christmas Day. I know the time and energy it must have taken to prepare and serve that meal, to decorate the house, and put up a tree. And to have a nice gift wrapped for each of them under it. Oh, Mama, what I would have given to have been there with you.

My Christmas was very busy. My boss, Miriam, and I worked on Christmas Eve as well as Christmas Day so the

nurses in our unit with families could have that time off.
Like all hospitals in London, St Mary's has been overrun
with wounded men being transported home by ship and
plane from the major battle areas—which I'll not mention
due to censorship. But I know you're aware of where the
heavy fighting has been in Europe since the end of October.
Thank God it is finally coming to an end and our foe has
retreated east.

Members of the St Mary's Women's Auxiliary spent
several days decorating the hospital's wards with greenery
and putting Christmas cards in all the windows. On
Christmas morning, Miriam and I were on duty at seven,
so we enjoyed watching our patients awake to find their
stockings filled with packages of razor blades, socks,
handkerchiefs, toothbrushes, small candies, and delicious
apples. My friend, Stoney Beeton-Howard, had crates of
various apples shipped to St Mary's from his estate. He has
asked me to call him "Stoney" as his friends do, so I'll refer
to him as Stoney in my letters from now on.

Miriam and I had to work through the following
Wednesday, but on Thursday morning, New Year's Eve,
we took the train from Paddington to Stoke-on-Trent.
Rutledge and Sylvia met us there with Stoney's car and
took us for a late lunch at a delightful pub right above
the river. Sylvia encouraged me to try the quintessential
English dish, jugged hare, and I did. It was served in a
crockery bowl with lots of rich gravy and was delicious!
The reason it's so tasty, she said, is because they marinate
the meat in red wine for twenty-four hours before putting it
in the oven.

When we left the pub, a heavy snow was falling and
the trip to Stoneham Feld was a journey through another
world—the meadows white and glistening and all the fur

trees looking as if they'd been sprinkled with fairy dust.
Oh, how the sight of that delighted us! We were so happy
to be out of London with its soot-blackened buildings and
piles of gray rubble.

That night, Stoney hosted a dinner party that included
our friend Barney, and Sylvia's Aunt Vera and Uncle
Harold who'd come from London, and two couples who
live not far from the estate. We ate from beautiful bone
china produced a century ago in Stoney's factory—a
cream-colored background with the Beeton crest in the
center and a garland of greenery and red berries 'round the
edge.

Our dinner was a feast fit for the gods—followed by
real coffee and an ancient bottle of French brandy. Stoney
had hired a trio of musicians, so after dinner (when we
could hardly move!), we gathered in the Long Gallery for
dancing. The trio was really good and I sang with them—
several jazz tunes and a couple of compositions that were a
bit more formal. Everyone begged for "A Nightingale Sang
in Berkley Square," so I did that, too.

At midnight, we toasted in 1943. Then we sang "Auld
Lang Syne" followed by "God Save the King" and "Rule
Britannia"—which are always sung in England on New
Year's Eve. The trio went right into "I'll Be Seeing You"
as the finale, which brought all of us to tears. Stoney
startled everyone by clapping his hands rather loudly and
announcing, "Have I got a surprise for you! Look out the
windows!" We looked out to see two stable boys leading a
pair of magnificent Morgans pulling a large red sleigh. The
horses were decked out in red blankets, silver trappings,
and garlands of greenery. Soon we were "dashing through
the snow" in a Winter Wonderland—and singing that
delightful song at the top of our lungs.

We didn't return to the manor until five in the morning, and when we arrived, Stoney invited us back into the dining room for hot chocolate and an elaborate breakfast buffet. Afterward, we dragged ourselves up to bed and slept for six hours. We gathered again at one o'clock the following afternoon for our last meal together—sandwiches and pickles, etc. And Rutledge took Miriam and me back to the train station to catch the three o'clock to London.

Mama, how I wish you could've been with us at Stoneham Feld to ring in the New Year. One day I hope I'll be able to introduce you to Miriam and Sylvia, and Rutledge and Barney—and especially Stoney, one of the most remarkable people I've ever known. He has vowed to do all the good he can for as long as he can, and you can bet he makes an effort to live up to that promise every day.

Miriam and I had lunch at Harrods last week where we talked about what we wanted to do when this dreadful war is over. We've decided we'll both move to a city where we'll try to get jobs in the same hospital—Atlanta, Richmond, or maybe Washington, DC. It's hard to imagine what things will be like then, but both of us are sure we want to be nearer our loved ones. Just think of the millions and millions of people in every corner of this poor benighted sphere who are hoping (and praying) for the same thing right this minute!

I must close, take a bath, and get ready for bed. I'll be out of here tomorrow morning by six thirty as usual, and not back until seven thirty. But Saint Jerusha will have dinner ready then, and Sylvia and I will visit and chat about our day—and solve all the problems of the world before we lie down to sleep and wake up tomorrow to start all over again.

I do hope you're sleeping well and getting enough rest. And that all your Christmas activities did not take too great a toll. Please give my love to Aunt Hepsi and Uncle Robert and to Maddie and Fletcher. I'll write to Claire later this week.

Longing for the day when I can see your beautiful face and sending you hugs, hugs, hugs.

Your loving daughter,
E

I carefully folded the ink-lined sheets of onionskin paper and sealed them in an airmail envelope ready to drop off on my way to work the next morning. In the bathroom I turned the tap above the tub, and while it filled to the regulation five inches, undressed and pinned up my hair.

As I lay in that little pool of water, I thought about all the things I *hadn't* told my mother in the letter. I didn't tell her that Stoney was married—just as I'd never mentioned that fact about my former lover in New York, Larry Christian. I didn't tell my mother how many times I'd danced with Stoney on New Year's Eve, nor the hundreds of times I'd danced with him over the twenty four months we'd known each other. Nor did I tell her how he'd taken me to Claridge's for dinner the week before and given me a very special gift—a beaded silk evening bag that had belonged to his grandmother, Flora.

I'd been careful not to tell my mother how Stoney and I had cuddled as close as two peas in a pod on the front bench of the big red sleigh, or the way he'd taken me into his arms and kissed me when I'd gone with him to take the horses and sleigh back to the stable.

The thought of that kiss and the way it happened had ignited a flame in my core that raced to the top of my head and all the way down to the ends of my fingers and toes. Stoney had driven the sleigh up to the front door so that our friends could alight there and go inside to get warm. He suggested that I go with him to return the sleigh to the stables. As we'd trudged our way through the snow from the stables back to the house, Stoney led me away from the light streaming from the windows and into the shadows beneath them. He'd held tightly to my hand, his movements so abrupt and demanding that I'd felt as if I were being led by a stranger, for I'd never known Stoney to be so insistent. He kept repeating my name, *Evelyn, Evelyn* as he pushed me up against the wall, pressed himself into me, and covered my mouth with eager lips. That's when a fire like Vesuvius erupted, and I surprised myself by returning his kisses with equal passion. It had finally happened and, truth be told, I'd relished every sensation.

That kiss, there in the shadows, gave me the courage to tell Stoney how relieved I'd been that his mother, the countess, was visiting her cousin, Lady Jane, for New Year's. He laughed and pulled me closer and said, "Oh, darling Evelyn. I cannot imagine you being intimidated by anyone . . . including my mother. Besides, she doesn't mean you any harm." But Stoney had no idea what Millicent had said to me when she'd dressed me down in front of Durham.

Her words: My son is a *married* man, a *married* man, a *married* man kept ringing in my head like a gong and I knew I'd never forget the way she'd compared me to *some flighty bit like that Simpson woman.*

Edward VIII's ultimate affair had been the scandal of the century—the man who would be king ruined because he wouldn't give up the woman he loved, Wallis Simpson. Well, I was not going to be *some flighty bit like that Simpson woman.* My dream of a life with my former lover, Larry Christian, had gone slowly down the drain in a swirl of yellowing tulle and faded orange blossoms. And in the end, I was the one who'd been left with a hurt that cut so deep that I promised myself it would never happen again.

I left the bath and hurried back to my room where I reread the Christmas card I'd received from Larry two weeks before. I tore a sheet from a new composition notebook and sat down on the side of the bed. It was high time I brought that relationship to an end, and I wasted no time telling Larry, in a single paragraph, that it was over. I felt a great sense of relief as I slid the note inside an envelope and gave the seal a quick lick.

As I crawled into bed, I realized I'd never told Stoney anything about Larry beyond his name and the fact that our relationship had lasted for eight years. Stoney deserved more than that. He and I were meeting for lunch the next day—my last day off before I returned to work at St Mary's. As I snuggled down beneath the covers, I thought about all the things I wanted to tell Stoney about the night I'd arrived in New York: the sodden air that saturated my clothes as I'd stepped down from the train, the dollar-a-mile taxi ride from Grand Central Station to Carnegie Hall, the warm smile on Freddie Trask's face as she'd welcomed me into the tiny apartment that would be my new home.

CHAPTER 15

Just Another Hoofer

New York, New York • June 7, 1929

At eighteen, I was too old to cry myself to sleep, but that's what I did when I got to New York. Every night I lay on a daybed in a studio apartment on the ninth floor of Carnegie Hall and cried myself to sleep. I tossed and turned, fuming about the light that poured in from a hotel across the street. Horns blaring below on Seventh Avenue drove me crazy. But it really wasn't the light or the noise so much. I was just plain homesick. For years I'd dreamed of living in one of the world's most glamorous cities. I'd left Baker with two suitcases and a trunk—and grandiose ideas about taking New York by storm. I'd spent hours practicing dance steps and songs, preparing for all the auditions I knew I'd have. My mother had bought me a lovely dress as a going-away gift, a snug-fitting sheath the color of champagne that stopped at my knees. I'd convinced her I needed it for all the parties I'd attend. I was devastated when I realized how silly my dress looked among the latest Fifth Avenue styles that featured plunging necklines, fitted waists, and long flowing skirts. The age of the flapper was over in New York, but how was I to know?

While that apartment was the smallest I'd ever seen, I had the great fortune of living there with an amazing woman, Winifred Trask. I found she'd aged little since I'd seen her six years before at my cousin Emily's wedding. A short brunette with a straight nose and welcoming smile, she was waiting for me when I emerged from a taxi at midnight in front of Carnegie Hall. A tall Negro man, whom she introduced as the building's maintenance supervisor, Sam Perkins, was with her. She told me that her friends called her Freddie and asked me to call her that, too. Then she took my big suitcase from me while Sam hoisted my trunk onto his shoulder, and we made our way to the service elevator and up to her apartment on the ninth floor.

After Sam wished us a good night, I walked up the hall to what was the most compact living room imaginable, a space not nearly as big as the foyer at home. Fortunately, the ceiling was high, about sixteen feet. On one wall there was a daybed. A three-legged table that held a radio sat beside a wing chair under a set of double windows that filled the front end of the room. "This is the kitchen," Freddie said, pointing to the area opposite the living room. Beneath a dropped ceiling stood a tiny sink, a two-burner stove, and a small icebox. The whole area was about the size of the playhouse my sister Claire and I had had in the backyard in Baker. A black wrought iron table, with a surface hardly bigger than a cake plate, separated the kitchen from the living room. Two ice-cream parlor chairs were tucked beneath it.

Freddie motioned toward the hall where we'd come in and said, "The bathroom and closet are there. I know you must be tired after that long trip. Please make yourself at home. I've put sheets on the daybed so it's ready when you are. I'm going on up now. We can talk in the morning over coffee. I hope you sleep well and please call me if you need anything." She took off her coat, hung it in the hallway closet, and went into the bathroom for a few minutes. Then she started up the narrow set of steps that led to a loft over the kitchen that was her bedroom.

Freddie Trask proved to be one of the nicest women I'd ever known, and one of the kindest and most helpful. She gave me a shelf in the tiny bathroom and half of the closet in the hall, and she got up each morning and made a pot of coffee and toasted bagels for us. She did her best to make me feel at home. As secretary to a successful booking agent named Al Meyer, she had access to valuable information about theatre auditions and helped me get my first job dancing in a review called *Happy Hearts* that was staged down in the village. In September, Freddie arranged another audition for me, this time for a big Broadway production called *Wake Up and Dream*. I was only one of a horde of dancers, but it was a job and I needed the money.

Freddie was the one who introduced me to Laurence Christian, one of the show's producers. Larry, as everyone called him, invited Freddie and me to dinner one night in October to celebrate my first job on Broadway. We met him at a swanky place he'd suggested on Eighty-Second near Central Park. Over dessert, he asked me what my whole name was.

"Anna Evelyn Sanderson," I replied.

"No, that won't do," he said, frowning. "I think you should consider using a stage name. Evelyn Sanderson sounds a bit stodgy, don't you think?"

Freddie jumped right in and suggested that I use Eve instead of Evelyn. "Eve is so evocative," she said, "so forbidden."

Then Larry said, "What about Sands as a last name?"

Freddie said, "Hmmm . . . Sands . . . sounds like a shimmering desert, like swaying palm trees. I like it."

Larry piped up again. "Eve Sands?" he asked. "Eve Sands," his voice questioning as his eyes scanned the crowded restaurant for a moment. Then he looked back at me. "Well, what do *you* say, pretty girl? Can you live with another name now that you're a star?"

I raised my glass and said, "Eve Sands it is!" And the three of us toasted my new name.

Larry told us over a dessert that he would be sitting right up front behind the orchestra on opening night, and invited us to a party he was hosting afterward at his apartment, which was just a block north of the restaurant.

Later, when Freddie and I were preparing for bed, she told me that Larry was married and that his wife had been living for a number of years in her family's villa in France. "He's quite the man about town, invited to all the right parties given by all the right people. He had an affair with a well-known showgirl that went on for four or five years."

Larry Christian was a handsome, fascinating man, no doubt about it. Well over six feet tall, he had gray-green eyes and a thick mop of golden hair that was just beginning to gray. But he was older even than Freddie, and I couldn't imagine him as anything but a father figure.

October 29, 1929 became known later as "Black Tuesday," but Freddie and I knew nothing about the stock market crash until the following day when I turned on the radio before dinner and we heard about businessmen jumping from office windows killing themselves.

Like everyone else, we knew that the entertainment world would suffer badly if the market did not recover. So we were encouraged when *Wake Up and Dream* opened on December 30 as planned with me in the chorus. It got rave reviews and became the hit of the season. Cole Porter wrote most of its songs and his famous composition "What Is This Thing Called Love?" remains a particular favorite. I met Mr. Porter at a party at Larry's penthouse on opening night. *Wake Up and Dream* ran for 136 shows and closed on April 26, 1930.

That's when I found myself without a job and no prospects whatsoever. Freddie and her boss, Al, were worried about their business, as the lights on dozens of theatre marquees remained dark throughout the spring and summer of 1930. I made the rounds of local businesses, but they weren't hiring. Mama had written to tell me that things were very bad at Daddy's bank, but still okay at his mill. Daddy was working late almost every night now and having to fire many of his employees. She continued to send me a check each month, but her thirty dollars covered only the rent I owed Freddie.

One morning as I was heading out the lobby to job hunt again, I saw Sam Perkins coming from his office. I mentioned that I was desperate for a job, and he told me that he had one but I was certainly not qualified. I pressed him and found out that he needed a man to scrub the floors in the lobbies outside the building's three theatres during the hours of 1:00 and 4:00 a.m. It paid six dollars and fifty cents a week.

I've never worked harder than I did at that job. Learning new dance routines, practicing them nonstop during rehearsals, and performing every night is very demanding. But scrubbing floors with a heavy, water-filled mop, back and forth for hours, is murder. Freddie was upset with me and told me that she was going to call my mother if I didn't stop mopping floors. I knew things were not good at home and begged her not to say anything until I could find another job. So, she put her thinking cap on and came up with an idea.

One night in early June, we were sitting in the living room when she said, "Hoofers are a dime a dozen, Evelyn. You've got to face the fact that you're just not the hoofer type. You're graceful and willowy. Your hair is so gorgeous and you have a certain saunter when you walk. I think you should try modeling."

I looked at her as if she had lost her mind. "But I'm a dancer! I want to dance and sing. I've got a good voice and I can tap off a routine with the best of them."

"Do you know how many dancers come through my office every month? Hundreds! And all of them want to do the very same thing you want to do. But most of them don't have that special quality you have, Evelyn. It's called class!"

Freddie got up and went to the bookshelf behind the wing chair. She pulled out a copy of *Harper's Bazaar* and handed it to me. On the cover was a handsome young woman in an exquisite gown. "You could do that," she said. "You've got the perfect figure and face for that kind of work. And your hair would look divine in an elegant chignon like hers."

I stared at the cover trying hard to imagine myself posing before a camera. It was so foreign to me, so scary. "I don't know if I could. But I do know I've got to get some sleep now so I can get up at one o'clock and practice my dance routine with that smelly old mop."

The next evening, Freddie came home with a brown envelope full of pictures of models wearing all kinds of clothing, selling all kinds of products—hand cream, perfume, lipstick, gloves, soap. I was busy making an omelet. "How much money do you have?" she asked.

"About thirty dollars," I answered.

"Well, I want you to take ten dollars of it and have some photos made. I have a friend who says he'll take fifty shots of you for ten dollars. We'll pick out a dozen or so, have him make some copies, and you can take them around to the modeling agencies in town."

I turned to her, exasperation plain on my face. "You win!" I said, scooping up the omelet. "Now, let's eat."

Freddie had a friend named Margo Rennick who was an award-winning costume designer who'd worked for some of the biggest names in the business. The two of us went to see her the following afternoon. As soon as Freddie introduced me, Margo took my chin in her hands and turned my head left to right. "Good bones," she said, "and wonderful coloring. You have great skin and I love the color of your hair and eyes." I felt like a horse in a stockyard, but stood still while she walked all the way around me giving me the once-over. Then she invited us to have some tea. Margo and Freddie continued to talk about my assets, and how I might make the most of them, while they drank tea. I listened.

Margo had gone down to the warehouse earlier and gotten a couple dozen costumes and hung them over the furniture around the room—period gowns, cocktail dresses, suits and hats, ski togs, lingerie. I stripped down to my underwear and began trying everything on. I was surprised to find that most of the pieces fit remarkably well. Freddie and Margo decided which were the most becoming and the most suitable for photos.

Freddie called her photographer friend and made an appointment for the following Saturday. Then she called Sam and told him to hire someone else to mop floors. When she hung up, I began to protest, reminding her of how much I needed that job, but she told me to hush. "You've got to get some rest, Evelyn. You've got circles under your eyes. You're not going to go hungry anytime soon and I'm not going to kick you out. At least not until you've got a job."

The photos turned out much better than I dreamed possible. But I didn't get a job modeling. At least not then. In late June, I learned that Melissa Welch, who lived down the hall from us and ran the perfume counter at Altman's, was leaving her job because she was pregnant. As soon as she told me, I selected three photos from my stash and headed to the personnel office in the basement of that huge department store. Then I received a call telling me I got the job.

Freddie came by at lunch the next day to check on me. She tried out all the testers and bought some Chanel body powder. Larry Christian came a couple of days later and bought three bottles of an expensive brand that he said he needed as favors for his dinner parties. "You should come from behind that counter, sweetheart," he said, "and let everybody see you. You could sell a lot more perfume out here in the aisle." I took his advice and was amazed at the results. The amount of perfume I sold to women didn't change much, but sales to men more than doubled.

Larry came in almost every week and bought a couple of bottles each time. One day, he brought along the store's manager, Mr. Klein, and introduced him to me. In his hand, Mr. Klein held the three photos I'd taken for the job interview. He told me that I had the kind of wholesome, all-American look he wanted for a project and asked if I would be willing to pose with a bottle of perfume for the store's holiday ad which would appear in the November issue of several fashion magazines. It added an excellent item to my portfolio, and the check I earned went into an account which became a deposit on an apartment where I could live alone.

I was amazed at the number of people who recognized me in the perfume ad when it appeared in *Collier's, Woman's Home Companion, Vogue,* and *Harper's Bazaar.* The graphic designer dressed me in a green chiffon outfit with a short skirt that made me look like a leprechaun. The hairdresser put my hair up, tied it with several ribbons, and curled it around the back of my neck a la Little Bo Peep. I had to stand, stoop, and kneel for hours with a huge bottle of perfume called "Eternity" at my feet.

In August, Larry invited Freddie and me for a long weekend at his house at Mill Neck on Oyster Bay. Both of us took Friday off and went by train up Long Island to Centerville, where we were met by his chauffeur. There were about a dozen of us at the house party and we were a congenial lot. At dinner that night, I sat beside a Broadway director, Howard Lindsay, who told me that casting would begin soon for a new show called *Gay Divorce.* Cole Porter would compose the songs and Fred Astaire would play the lead. I could feel my toes tingling. Be still, my heart!

After dinner, Larry went over to the baby grand near the fireplace and started playing popular tunes like "I Found A Million Dollar Baby" and "Blue Skies." Freddie sat down beside him on the piano bench and was soon singing along. "Come on over, Eve," he called.

I excused myself from the group on the sofa and went to stand beside the piano. Larry played "By the Light of the Silvery Moon" and Freddie and I had a lot of fun with it. Then he said, "Let's let Eve sing this one." He broke into the catchy, syncopated rhythm of "What Is This Thing Called Love?" and I fell right in on cue. I was transported back to *Wake Up and Dream* with no problem at all, and really belted out the chorus. Howard Lindsay never took his eyes off me.

When I finished, he came over and said, "Auditions for *Gay Divorce* open September fifteenth. Please come."

* * *

This time I was not *just another hoofer*. I got to sing. *Gay Divorce* began with a two-week pre-Broadway run in Boston in November; then we moved to the Shubert Theatre in New Haven. We finally opened at the Ethel Barrymore Theatre November 29, 1932. Fascinating Mr. Porter wrote the songs and topped the charts again with another huge hit called "Night and Day." A florist's box of a dozen yellow roses arrived every Wednesday evening through the show's long run. There was never a card, but I knew who'd sent them.

Larry hosted an opening night gala for the production's sponsors and members of the cast at his penthouse and Freddie went with me. There was a huge crush of people, lots of imported champagne that had been smuggled in from Canada, and well-wishers galore. I bought a gown of burgundy crepe de chine and a pair of stunning earrings set with garnets just for the occasion, which was one of the most glorious nights of my life.

Freddie pooped out about 2:00 a.m., but I stayed. Just before light broke over the East River, Larry offered me a ride home. "Fantastic," he said as we settled into the backseat, "you were just fantastic, Eve. And you look like the star that you are in that gorgeous new frock. I could not be more proud if . . . if you were . . ." There was a sudden jolt as the car pulled away from the curb and I fell against Larry's chest. He put his arm around me, drew me to him, and kissed me rather passionately for a long time.

It was only a matter of moments before we reached Carnegie Hall. I thanked Larry in a small voice that sounded completely unlike mine and sprinted out of the car. I could feel a warm flush spreading across my face—and up my thighs. I tried to sleep, but I was too excited. I spent a restless couple of hours while "What Is This Thing Called Love?" went 'round and 'round in my head, and my mother's sweet face loomed like a ghostly shadow above the bed.

I didn't hear from Larry for a few days, but he called the next week to tell me that he'd heard about a nice apartment that had come available. "It's a second floor walk-up," he said, "in an old brownstone. The rent is eighty dollars a month and that includes heat and water." He offered to pick me up the next afternoon to go see it. I could not have been more pleased when we pulled up to the curb and I got a good look at the house and neighborhood. The apartment had a furnished living room with two French doors on one side that opened onto a balcony with a black iron railing. On the front end of the room was a fully equipped kitchen. Between the living area and the kitchen sat an oval dining table and four chairs. The bedroom, with its tiled bathroom and walk-in closet, was on the opposite end. I lit the oven, flushed the toilet, ran water in the bathtub, and turned on the radiators to make sure everything worked while Larry laughed.

"Let's go put down a deposit before someone else grabs it," he suggested as he locked the door on our way out.

He sent his car to Freddie's apartment on Monday afternoon and his chauffeur helped me move all my stuff to the brownstone. I was surprised to find a gorgeous bouquet of yellow roses on the coffee table. Tucked among the leaves was an envelope with a card that said, *Leaving for France Tuesday; be back end of Feb. STOP. Missing you already. Love, Larry.*

I'd not been home to Baker in two and a half years and promised Mama I'd come home for Christmas. There had been many changes during that time. My brother-in-law, Charles, had lost his job in September and left for Chicago to try to find work. Claire had gotten a job teaching in Raleigh and was living in a boardinghouse there. She had left four-year-old Wally, and toddler Cliff, whom I'd never seen, with Mama. I felt I had to go help Mama and give her support through a busy holiday, especially now that she had two little grandsons to look after. But I was in a quandary about how to deal with it now that I had a steady job. On top of everything else, I'd gotten a letter from Mama the week before telling me how Daddy was down with a fever brought on by a case of severe diverticulitis.

I went to Howard Lindsay's assistant and told him that my father was very sick and I needed to go home. He was sympathetic and told me to get one of the girls on the call list to fill in for me. "People are desperate for jobs," he said, "so you won't have a problem finding a stand-in. I'd ask Janet Barstow if I were you. And tell her to get down here ASAP to learn the routines. She's a quick study and she'll do a good job. Since there's no performance on Christmas Eve, or Christmas Day, you won't lose as much pay as you might have otherwise. You've got one week, Miss Sands . . . that's the rule. Even if your dad dies, you have to be back here ready for an eight o'clock curtain on January first."

I found Daddy much improved when he met me at the station on Christmas Eve morning. Gosh, was I happy to be back in Baker! Mama was waiting on the front porch to welcome me with Claire's two boys in tow, and right behind her was her new helper, Maddie Gaston. They fed me a lovely lunch and sent me upstairs for a nap so that I would be fit as a fiddle for the "Welcome Home, Evelyn" party they'd planned. That night, I gave Mama a magazine that had the perfume ad in it, which she proudly passed around for all our party guests to see. Afterward, I showed everyone the playbill for *Gay Divorce* where my new name appeared. I went on and on about Freddie, Larry, and my new apartment. I desperately wanted my parents to know that I was settled, and at age twenty-one, finally capable of making a living.

When it came time for me to leave, Mama gave me a big hug. She promised to come spend time with me in my new apartment and see the show. But that never happened.

* * *

January 1933 was one of the coldest, most miserable winter months on record. Two shows had to be cancelled due to heavy snow and sleet the first week of the month, and two more were cancelled the third week. I saw Freddie only twice and remained holed up in my new apartment until six o'clock every evening when I had to get to the theatre. Although most of the performances were sold out, many people who had tickets could not get into the city, so the audiences were smaller than usual.

February was just the opposite. We had a string of lovely, spring-like days that spoiled us for the rest of winter. I met Freddie several times in the park where we shared a picnic lunch. We went on a shopping jaunt down in the Village and spent a long weekend seeing the sights in Philadelphia. And, off and on, we talked about Larry. I had told Freddie that I was afraid I was falling in love with him and didn't know what to do. Freddie was convinced that Larry would never leave his wife, Giselle, who had been born in France to an American mother. Her father, a German Jew named Jacob Rathmann, was a well-known French businessman who'd made a killing in champagne and table wines. Following the Prussian War, his family had immigrated to France and Giselle had inherited a fortune from Jacob's parents before she even met Larry. "He will never leave her," Freddie said, "because Giselle controls the purse strings. Larry makes money on his own investments, but not the kind of money that would support his current lifestyle. Things would be very different for him if Giselle were not in the picture."

"Why doesn't she come to America?" I asked.

"She doesn't like it here," Freddie replied. "She grew up in France and went to school there. That's home. Giselle and Larry spent the first thirteen years of their married life here in New York. She sent their son to boarding school at Phillips Exeter. Then she sent him to a school in London when she went home to France." I was surprised to hear this. Larry had never mentioned having a son. "Yes," Freddie continued, "they have a son named Monte who lives somewhere in England. He's just about your age."

That stunned me. I had no idea that Larry had a child *my* age. "How did they meet?" I asked.

"Larry grew up in Buffalo where his father was the head of the utilities commission there. During college, he and three of his classmates went on a tour of Europe. One night they were in a club in Paris where they met a group of girls who were students at the Sorbonne . . . Giselle was one of them. She and Larry hit it off and he decided to stay in Paris to be with her. He got a job working as a gofer at the American Embassy and rented a garret where he and Giselle spent weekends together. Larry went to her father and asked permission to marry her, but he got thrown out on his rear. So, he and Giselle eloped to America. Since both of them were twenty-one, the captain of the ship married them. Monte was born six months later."

* * *

When he returned from his trip to France on March 3, Larry called from his apartment above Central Park and invited me to dinner the next night. "We'll celebrate FDR's inauguration," he said. "I brought back some wonderful champagne I want to share it with you."

I hesitated. I was so upset about what Freddie had told me about Larry, Giselle, and their son, *who was my age*, that I'd decided not to see him again. I hemmed and hawed, trying to think of an excuse. Finally, I told him I had to take something off the stove and I would call him back. I did not have a performance the next night and Larry knew it, so I couldn't use that as an excuse. Just buck up, I said to myself. Just tell him you can't see him anymore. Tell him you've got a boyfriend. Tell him you're going out with the girls. Tell him you've got to wash your hair.

In the end, I told him none of these things. His chauffeur picked me up and deposited me at the door of his building about the same time Eleanor and Franklin were receiving guests at their pre-inaugural gala.

I was a bit standoffish when I arrived at his apartment, still upset about what Freddie had told me. But I didn't stay that way long. Larry was his charming self, asking me about the people I'd seen and the latest gossip. He prepared a tray of Stilton on rye and smoked oysters, and a couple of tasty, but strong, highballs made from his stash of bootleg whiskey. We continued drinking and talking as we made our way through his savory beef medallions, which were accompanied by a robust burgundy from the stock in his wine cellar.

I ended up on the sofa with Larry, and my skirt and blouse on the floor. Too much bourbon, too much burgundy, too much champagne. I pushed Larry off of me and went to the bathroom to wash my face.

When I returned to find him relaxing in front of the fire wearing nothing but a bathrobe, I knew I should leave. He walked over to me and cupped his hands around my shoulders. "You're a big girl, Eve, and you've known all along that I'm crazy about you. I want you very much and I thought you wanted me, too."

I pulled away from him and plopped down on the sofa. "Yes, I know I'm a big girl. But all of this is new to me. And you're married."

He raised one eyebrow and gave me a curious look. "That's never been a problem before," he said, his voice as smooth as silk. "I didn't think it would be a problem for you."

I got up and went into the kitchen to get a drink of water. Larry followed me and sat down at the table. I drank the water slowly, taking a moment to gather my thoughts. "When I was in high school," I said, "my nickname was String Bean. I was this gawky kid with long arms and skinny legs and bushy red hair. I had freckles all over my nose and a gap between my two front teeth. I was fairly popular with girls, but the boys stayed away in droves. I was so tall, you see. Five nine by the time I was thirteen. The only thing I had going was the fact that I could sing and dance . . . and that kept the boys away, too. I never dated much, just a few times during my last year of school. I guess what I'm trying to tell you, Larry, is I don't have much experience with this kind of thing. I'm nuts about you and you know it. But you're old enough to be my father. How would I ever explain that to my mother?"

Larry took a long draw from his cigarette, crossed his arms over his middle, and stared at me for several minutes. Finally, he spoke. "Are you telling me you're a virgin?"

"Yes, Larry. That's exactly what I'm telling you."

He stood up. "Get your coat. You're going home."

We rode all the way to my apartment without speaking. He got out and opened my door and walked me up the steps. "This isn't going to work," he said. "I'm sorry, but I had no idea. You're so lovely, Eve, so put together. And you seem so mature. I thought . . . well, I thought the wrong thing, didn't I?" With that, he turned and walked back to his car.

When I arrived at the theatre Wednesday evening, I found a florist's box sitting on my dressing table. Inside were a dozen yellow roses and a note. *Darling*, it read, *I'm such a fool! I spent the last two months in France totally miserable, thinking of nothing but you, and realize now just how much I love you. Trust me . . . we'll find a way. Please, please join me for dinner tonight with friends at Julian's. Freddie is coming. I'll have the car waiting for you behind the theatre at eleven. From the idiot who worships the ground you walk on.*

After the show that night, I went to dinner with Larry and Freddie and another couple who described themselves as just good friends. Laura Mennick and Bill Framson worked together in a well-known publishing house, she as a secretary and he as an editor. As soon as everyone had finished their appetizer, Freddie excused herself to go powder her nose and suggested that I go with her. As soon as we were alone, she asked me why I'd come. "I thought you said you weren't going to see Larry anymore. What happened?"

I told her about the yellow roses and the note.

"Don't be a fool, Evelyn," she sniffed. "He'll never divorce Giselle."

"He said we'll work it out," I protested. "He told me he loves me!"

"Oh, I have no doubt that he loves you," she replied. "But that doesn't mean he'll give up the things he's accustomed to . . . not even for you. You're a grown woman and I'm not going to tell you what you already know. Just try to be sensible, kid. Do you have a diaphragm?"

"Wh—what?" I stammered. "A diaphragm? I've never even seen one!"

"Well, you'd better get one," Freddie hissed. "And it had better be sooner, not later. I'll call Dr. Lashley's office tomorrow morning and make an appointment for you to be fitted right away. Now, swear to me that you'll not go to bed with Larry until you not only have a diaphragm, but know how to use it. Swear!"

I did what she wanted and picked up my new diaphragm three days later. By the end of the week, I was no longer a virgin.

Mama called the following week to tell me that some men from the Banking Commission in Raleigh had come to Baker the day before and closed the bank. They had sent Daddy and the staff home, without telling any of them why they were closing the bank or when they might be allowed to return. Mama said that Daddy had spent the entire day drinking in his study and, just before dinner, had gotten in his car and left. She had no idea where he'd gone. I tried to reassure her, but didn't know what to say. Poor Mama. She had no one to talk to but Claire and me. I hated telling her that I needed to leave for the theatre but had no choice. I promised to call her the next day and prayed that Daddy would be back home by then. I went off to work and forgot about the Bank of Baker. In a few days I'd slipped back into my regular routine and completely forgot to call Mama.

After *Gay Divorce* had had a successful run in New York, the producers took it to London the summer of 1933. Larry suggested I take a little time off before I auditioned for a new show. In August, he sent his sloop, *Adventurer,* and her crew south. Then he and I drove out to his place on Oyster Bay for a week. Freddie, Laura, and Bill joined us for the weekend. We had a nice dinner party on Friday night that included a number of Larry's business associates and their wives. Larry and I went back to the city on Sunday afternoon and left early Monday morning by train for Miami. *Adventurer* was waiting for us when we arrived at the dock in Fort Lauderdale on Thursday morning. We spent the next two weeks sailing through the Keys and the Bahamas.

As soon as we got back to New York, I called Mama. She told me that the mill had been closed and Daddy had been gone for two weeks. I asked if she wanted me to come home. But she said absolutely not, that I was to stay in New York, continue with my work and my life. She kept telling me not to worry, that everything would be all right. After I hung up, I sat down and wrote a check for a hundred dollars and sent it to her.

Then I called Freddie and told her everything. I knew she would call my Aunt Bethany and Uncle Bryson and tell them that Daddy had left. They needed to know that my folks were in trouble, and since they lived in Raleigh they were close enough to go check on my mother.

In the course of our conversation, Freddie told me that auditions for a new show called *Anything Goes* would begin the following week and that Ethel Merman had been cast as the lead, Reno Sweeney. I got a wonderful part as one of Reno's four angels, which meant I got to sing as well as dance. Miss Merman, or *The Great Ethel* as the producers called her, gave me valuable tips on how to exaggerate facial expressions, things to do with my eyes, my hands, my mouth to get a point across to the audience. She thought Larry Christian was the bee's knees and invited us to all her parties in the Waldorf Towers where she kept a penthouse apartment. That's where I met Ernest Hemingway and Scott Fitzgerald, the Whitneys, the Goulds, Walter Winchell, and John D. Rockefeller III. Cole and Linda Porter were regulars at Ethel's. Prohibition had ended the winter before, and high above the city gallons of champagne flowed from silver fountains while endless bread lines wound through the streets below.

Anything Goes was one of the longest running shows in the history of Broadway with a record number of 420 performances. In spite of hard times, it was a huge success and took all the top awards including *The Fresh Face Award*, which I won that year. When it finally closed, Miss Merman asked me if I would like to work with her again. She had been approached by the producers of a new show and hoped I would join the cast. I was elated, and told her I would sign up as soon as auditions began. But she told me there was no need for me to audition as she had already given me her personal recommendation.

Red, Hot and Blue was the hit of the new season and I got my first speaking role. Only eight lines, but they were a start. We made our usual trial runs in Boston and New Haven before opening in New York on October 29, 1936. When I arrived at the theatre on Wednesday nights, a bouquet of beautiful yellow roses was always waiting for me. And there were parties galore until we closed on April 10, 1937.

Larry took the opportunity of my being without work to plan a trip for us. I sublet my apartment for the months of July and August, and we took the train to Montreal, then out west through the Canadian Rockies. Larry had an old friend from college who lived in Vancouver, BC and we spent two weeks with him and his wife in their palatial home above the city. They seemed completely at ease with the fact that Larry and I were not married, and gave us adjoining bedrooms separated by a bath. I learned later that they had known Giselle since the early days when both couples lived in the same apartment building on Seventy-Fourth Street. It was obvious that I was not the first girl Larry had brought there. He was his usual fun-loving, gallant self and we had a wonderful time. But there was something about it that made me feel cheap. One night, I told Larry how I felt. He shook his head and said, "Don't worry, darling. It won't always be this way." Then he took me in his arms and started singing "You'd Be So Easy to Love," my favorite tune from *Anything Goes*. I swallowed my feelings and helped him finish the song while we waltzed into bed.

I had a letter waiting from Mama when I got back to New York, telling me that both the bank and the mill had been closed permanently and that Daddy was very ill—which I took to mean he was drinking more than usual. Mama had sold some of her jewelry to keep the wolf from the door, and was teaching piano and voice lessons three afternoons a week to try to pay the bills. She went on to say that Daddy had begun staying out all night with his friends and came home only to take a bath and change clothes. I could sense the desperation in her words and I wasted no time getting packed for a trip home. I left two days later.

I saw my father only once while I was in Baker. He staggered up the steps one morning sporting a black eye and reeking of alcohol. Dressed in a suit streaked with stains, I would not have known him had he not been wearing the shirt I'd sent him for his birthday the year before. I opened the door startling him so badly that he grabbed the newel post to keep from falling. As soon as he realized who I was, he stumbled back down the steps and fled across the lawn to the street. I left Baker the next day and never saw my father alive again.

Just before Christmas, I met Sophie Tucker at a dinner given by Douglas Fairbanks, Jr. (whom Larry called Doug) when the two of us were seated beside each other across from Gertrude Lawrence and Danny Kaye. Mr. Kaye went on and on about what a great job I'd done in *Anything Goes* and *Red, Hot and Blue*. He invited me to sing with him after dinner and I learned that he was just as much fun in private as he was onstage. Mr. Kaye and Miss Tucker were excited about a new show that was being cast and, as of yet, had no name. Eventually it became *Leave It to Me*. I found a box of yellow roses waiting on my dressing table on opening night, November 8, 1938. Mr. Kaye and Miss Tucker played the leads. I managed to land my biggest role ever, which included singing back up for Mary Martin in her tour de force, "My Heart Belongs to Daddy." Fake snow fell around us as we danced and sang our way across the wintry stage, she in a silver fox jacket that barely covered her fanny, and the rest of us in tight-fitting Tyrol-inspired jackets, very short skirts, and sassy red boots. To celebrate, Larry gave me a fox stole for Valentine's.

* * *

On July 4, Larry hosted an Independence Day celebration aboard *Adventurer*. He'd been tied up at work most of the week and we'd not seen each other for several days. So I bought a new outfit—navy-blue tap shorts, a sleeveless white middy embroidered with red stars, and white wedges that tied around my ankles—rather daring, but very patriotic. I also bought a new nightgown in pale yellow chiffon, which I packed along with my makeup, in a straw bag Larry had bought for me in Nassau. I tied a little skirt on over my new shorts and took the train out to Centerville Station where I was met by Larry's chauffeur. When I got to the dock, I was surprised to see so many people on the boat. Larry never invited more than a handful of friends when he went cruising, but there were at least two dozen people milling about on deck.

I went straight down the steps to the salon where I knew I'd find him. He was back in a corner with Freddie and Howard Lindsay and a handsome dark-haired young man. I walked over and gave Larry a peck on the cheek. He laughed and said, "Why here's Little Miss Sunshine now. Eve, allow me to introduce my son." He turned to the young man beside him and said, "This is Monte. He's taking a break right now from law school at Eton. Monte, this is Eve Sands."

I looked into the eyes of Larry's son and saw absolutely no resemblance to his father. His hair was as black and shiny as coal, his skin as golden as honey, and his eyes were a subtle but penetrating shade of gray. Monte flashed his perfect white teeth, took my hand, and kissed it. "Enchanted!" he said. "Welcome aboard, Miss Sands. My father has told me so much about you. I can't wait to see you perform Wednesday night."

I tried to regain my composure and heard myself saying, "It will be my pleasure. Please come back to my dressing room afterward for a nightcap."

Monte smiled again. "I wouldn't miss it for the world. Would you care for a drink, Miss Sands?" Taking me by the arm, he led me through the crowd toward the bar where he removed two flutes of champagne from a tray. We went back up on deck to a small area off the galley that contained a banquette. "Let's sit here away from the crowd," he suggested, "and get to know one another. Have you lived in New York long, Miss Sands . . . it is Miss, isn't it?"

I nodded as I took a sip of champagne. "I've been here almost ten years. I lived with your dad's friend, Freddie Trask, for a while, but now I have my own place."

Monte looked at me with interest. "Oh, good," he said. "And where is it?"

I told him about my walk-up apartment in an old house on Sixty-Fourth. He laughed. "My dad's brownstone . . . the one with the black iron railing overlooking the street and the big oaks out back? Is that where you live?"

I felt as if the breath had been knocked out of me, as if I had been punched in the stomach. I'm sure my face went white because I could feel my hands getting cold.

"Are you okay, Miss Sands? You don't look so good. Here," he said, taking the flute from my hand. "Let me get you a glass of water." He jumped up and hurried off toward the door to the galley.

I wasted no time going the other way, up a narrow flight of stairs to the sundeck, and straight out the gangway. I called a cab from the corner bait shop, hid in the back of the store until it came, and fled to the privacy of what I had thought, until now, was *my* apartment.

The phone started ringing a couple of hours later, but I ignored it. About midnight, I heard Larry calling my name outside the door, heard his key in the lock, but I'd bolted it from the inside so it wouldn't open. I sat on the camelback sofa, *his* camelback sofa, and fumed, and cussed, and cried until I wore myself out. At some point I must have fallen asleep, because I found myself stretched out on the sofa at dawn, still wearing my wrinkled nautical finery. I put on a pot of coffee, stripped off my clothes, and washed my face. Then I sat at the table in my robe drinking coffee, thinking, thinking, thinking through most of the afternoon. I'd never felt such a sense of betrayal and was at a loss about how to deal with it. I knew I'd have to find another apartment and dreaded moving. Finally, I called Freddie and asked her to meet me for lunch the next day. She wanted to know if I had heard from Larry, but I told her I would talk to her about it at lunch.

The phone rang throughout the afternoon and eventually I took it off the hook. I toasted a bagel for dinner, soaked in the tub for an hour, and went to bed before eight. I lay there for hours, thinking about all the wonderful times Larry and I had had in *his* apartment, how we had gotten to really know each other within *his* four walls and on *his* bed. Larry had always met me with his car after the show on Saturday nights when I felt as if I'd been beaten from doing both a matinee and an evening performance the same day. As soon as we got home to the apartment, he always brought me a brandy, took off my shoes and massaged my feet to help me relax enough to go to sleep.

We always spent Sunday afternoons in bed. Larry was a wonderful lover—sensitive, attentive, and very affectionate. About five o'clock, I'd drag myself out of bed and get into the tub for a good soak. Larry would put on his robe and sit on the toilet lid and read the funnies to me—*the Katzenjammer Kids, Bringing Up Father,* and *Li'l Abner*—and we'd laugh and laugh. Larry always closed with Eleanor Roosevelt's column, *My Day.* I went to the theatre at six and left there about eleven. Larry and his car were always waiting for me at the stage door.

Now, all of that was over. I'd been living a fantasy for more than eight years, had loved and trusted a man who'd betrayed me, who'd used me, who'd taken my love for granted. That was what I told Freddie the next day when we met for lunch. But she bought none of it.

"You're a grown woman, Evelyn," she said, "and you can't say I didn't warn you. I told you he'd had a long affair with a dancer. Her name is Janet Barstow. And she lived in his brownstone apartment for five years, the same one you live in."

I frowned, trying to place that name. Janet Barstow. "That name rings a bell," I said. "How do I know Janet Barstow?"

Freddie gave me a little smirk. "She's the one who stepped in for you in *Gay Divorce* when you went home to Baker for Christmas back in '32. Remember?"

"Oh, God. Of course. She's a tall brunette, right?"

Freddie nodded, took a bite of her sandwich and said, "Before that, it was a dancer named Louise Lambeth. And before that it was a secretary named Peggy Delong. Larry had numerous affairs before Giselle ever went home to France . . . and she's had her share, too."

I pushed my fruit salad away. "Well, it's over as far as I'm concerned. I never want to see him again."

"Oh, but you will," Freddie assured me. "You'll see him because you love him and because he keeps promising that the two of you will be together. Right?"

I nodded. "Yes, he tells me that all the time."

Freddie ate the last bite of her sandwich, and using her napkin, dabbed at the corners of her mouth. "Wise up, kid. It ain't gonna happen."

I sat there, my thoughts swirling in a sea of doubt, trying to take it all in. "What am I going to do about the apartment? My lease isn't up until the end of December," I fumed.

"Just stay there, Evelyn," Freddie said, her voice as smooth as butter. "Don't waste good money moving out just because you're disappointed in Larry. There's really no reason why you should give up that nice place just because of what *he's* done."

The phone rang, off and on, every afternoon for the next two weeks, but I never picked it up. I avoided the places Larry and I had frequented and worked like a dog to stay on top of my role in *Leave it to* Me. I found a new apartment, a walk-up in the Seventies and made a deposit so that I could move into it on December 30. I called Mama and told her I was coming home for Christmas. I knew she was terribly worried about Daddy, about the financial situation she found herself in, about the larger issues that were looming over us all. Claire and Charles had moved to California a couple of weeks before so that Charles could take a supervisor's job in a factory, and Claire had found a teaching job, so they were doing well. But Mama had had a hard time accepting the fact that Claire and her grandsons were now twenty-five hundred miles away.

On top of that, the papers that fall were filled with disturbing news from Europe. Despite the restrictions the Treaty of Versailles had placed on Germany, Adolf Hitler had amassed an army of several million and was wasting no time building his new empire, the Third Reich. He stormed Czechoslovakia and began preparing for an offensive that would bring all the German countries taken by the Allies in 1918 back into his realm. Many Americans felt that this fight was between Germany, France, and England and none of our business. And since it was happening so far away, it was easy to ignore most of the time. But I was terribly frightened that September when I saw newsreels showing Hitler's army marching into Poland.

In October, I landed a role in a new show, *Very Warm for May*, which opened at the Alvin in November. I found a box of yellow roses waiting on my dressing table on opening night. As Lila Lee, the director of a dance troupe, I had a funny scene with the star, Eve Arden, in which we ended up in a crazy, laugh-a-minute argument while we tapped circles around each other. The audiences loved it, but the show was a flop and closed the week before Christmas.

On Monday, December 18, I went to Grand Central to pick up a ticket for my trip home to Baker. I'd be leaving the following Thursday and returning on December 28 so I'd have time to pack before I moved. After I left the station, I had dinner in a little Italian place and caught a cab for home.

When I got to the brownstone about eight, I took off my shoes and settled down on the sofa with the paper. I thought I heard something scratching and paused in my reading for a moment to listen. I heard it again. It was right outside my door. Then I heard a little whine like a puppy makes. I opened the door to find a cocker spaniel lying on the floor and Larry holding its leash. "Please don't close the door, Eve," he pleaded. "Please, please just hear me out. I'm here to tell you how sorry I am. I knew you wouldn't open the door if you knew it was me, so I borrowed Jasper from your neighbor. Can I please come in for just a moment?"

Larry took Jasper to the kitchen and tied his leash to one of the cabinet pulls. He removed his overcoat and threw it over a chair. I sat quietly, wondering how I was going to deal with another of his shenanigans. Lord, but he looked good!

Larry sat down beside me on the sofa and asked if he could take my hand. I let him, but remained as still as stone and dared not look him in the eye.

"Eve Sands," he began, "I love you and I'm miserable without you. I want us to be together."

I pulled my hand from his and gave him a sideways glance. "You've said that before, Larry. Many times. Why should I believe you now?"

"I've been meeting with my attorney and he says Giselle's leaving me and going home to France almost seven years ago is definitely in my favor. He says that it's a strong indication of abandonment, the kind of evidence I need for a divorce settlement. I want us to be married, Eve. I cannot tell you how much I want to be with you . . . forever." He put his hand in his trouser pocket, pulled out a blue leather box, and opened it. Inside was a magnificent ring, an oval-cut emerald of at least two carats, surrounded by diamonds. Larry removed it from the box and slipped it on my finger. "Will you please marry me?"

I called Mama the next morning to tell her I wouldn't be coming home for Christmas after all, that I had to work for someone who was ill. I knew that broke her heart, but I couldn't help myself. I wasn't ready to tell her about Larry or the ring. All of that had to wait. That very afternoon, Larry and I took a train to Miami and spent the holidays in the lap of luxury at the Riviera Hotel. I lost the deposit I'd made on my new apartment, but I got my man.

* * *

Larry and I rang in 1940 in the club car of the Silver Star, Ltd. on our way back to New York. The night after we returned we had dinner with Freddie. She told us that one of the girls singing backup for Ethel Merman in *DuBarry Was a Lady* was dropping out. So I went down to the Alvin the next day to see Miss Merman and got the part.

In spite of the worst blizzards in ten years, of miserable weather day after day, *DuBarry* was a success, and the next three months were some of the happiest of my life. Larry and I took to spending some of my days off in his penthouse, where we curled up before a fire and talked about the kind of place we wanted to share after we married. Neither of us wanted to stay in our current residences; mine was too small and his was too large. Plus, he had a friend who was ready to buy his as soon as Larry was ready to sell. I wanted to live in one of the apartment houses that overlooked the East River, so Larry contacted a friend who was a realtor and we began looking. We haunted the antique shops searching for old European pieces and oriental rugs because I wanted to get away from the Deco look that had been so popular. We spent hours gazing at china and linens, at silver serving pieces, and kitchen appliances.

Blissfully immersed in our own little world that spring, Larry and I were oblivious to the chaos erupting in Northern Europe when, in April, Hitler crushed Norway and Denmark. A few weeks later, his seemingly unstoppable forces invaded Luxembourg, The Netherlands, and Belgium.

Larry's birthday was May 30. To celebrate, we headed to The Paramount to see Vivien Leigh's new movie, "Waterloo Bridge." Just after we'd settled into our seats, a newsreel appeared on screen showing masses of troops being evacuated from a beach at a place called Dunkirk. "Oh, no," Larry whispered. "The British are pulling out of France!" He rose from his seat and turned to put a trembling hand on my shoulder. "I have to find a Western Union office," he said. "Wait here, Evelyn. I'll be back in a little while. I'm sorry, but I need to send a cable." He didn't say to whom, but I knew.

On June 14, Freddie and Larry and I were having dinner at my apartment when the music on the radio stopped suddenly and the announcer informed us that Edward R. Murrow had just sent a wire saying the German army was marching down the Champs-Élysées. Larry jumped up from the table, told us he'd call as soon as he could, and ran out the door.

Freddie and I left our dinners unfinished. We continued to sit at the table, but neither of us spoke for several minutes. Then Freddie pulled a cigarette from her case, lit it, and said, "Well, I guess that's that. I just hope Giselle and Mrs. Rathmann got out in time."

"What do you mean? Do you think they've left France?"

Freddie took a long draw. "I certainly hope so," she said. "Giselle is half Jewish, and in the eyes of the Nazis that's enough to cause serious problems."

But I was confused. "Why wouldn't she have told Larry if she were leaving?"

Freddie shrugged her shoulders. "She would have if she could have. Larry told me last week that he'd not heard from her for a couple of weeks. He's been very worried because Giselle's mother is ill."

I got up from the table and scraped our leftovers into the garbage. "Where do you think he went just now . . . to his apartment?"

"I've no idea," Freddie answered, "but he's going to try to send a telegram, I expect."

I didn't see Larry again for four days. When he finally showed up, he looked as if he had not slept the entire time he'd been away. He told me that he'd taken the train to Washington to see an old college friend, Ronald Hughes, who was a big shot in the State Department. But Ronald had not been much help. He'd told Larry that the US Embassy in Paris had been closed and there were no lines of communication open in France for any organization except the Third Reich. The phones, telegraph offices, and post offices had all been closed.

There was no fancy party on July fourth that year. I spent the day washing throw rugs at the Suds-O-Rama. That evening, Freddie and I met at the Rainbow Room where we watched the fireworks over the river from our table by the window. Larry was holed up at his office through the night making calls to Europe, trying desperately to find a connection to anyone who might know the whereabouts of Giselle and her mother. Freddie reported to me over dinner the details of his latest trip to Washington. Larry had gone back to see his friend Ronald again, and told him of his plans to go to France at the end of June. But Ronald told Larry that he would not be able to get any closer to France than Switzerland. "The Germans have the borders to France securely closed," he'd said. "We are in constant communication with the Swiss and it would be useless for you to try something like that. You'd end up in a Gestapo prison. My advice to you is to stay put and let us keep working on it. These things take time, my friend. Now, go back home and try to keep your mind on your work. And rest assured I'll call you as soon as we learn anything."

All of us were miserable, and I couldn't keep dragging around the burden of knowing what Larry was going through without it affecting my work. I let him call the shots about when we would see each other. I instigated nothing and stayed away as much as I could without hurting his feelings. *DuBarry* was demanding, with rehearsals a couple of times a week, and parties at Miss Merman's almost every weekend. The Germans had begun bombing London on September 7, killing five hundred civilians in one night, and their Blitzkrieg continued night and day throughout the fall.

I had to work on Thanksgiving Day and when I arrived at the theatre, there was a note from Larry asking me to meet him that evening for dinner at the Plaza. He and Freddie were waiting for me in the lobby, and I knew the moment I saw their faces that something was up. Larry hugged me, and the three of us went into the dining room to be seated. As soon as a waiter appeared, I ordered a cup of coffee. Then Larry ordered the special for us—turkey and all the trimmings with pumpkin pie. Freddie and I exchanged glances and waited. Finally, he spoke.

"I had a call from my friend Ronald Hughes last night. Giselle and her mother are in Sierra Leone. He doesn't know why they're there, but their names showed up on the manifest of a freighter when they disembarked three days ago. Ronald's trying to find out more. I offered him money but he said it won't do any good. He said it may be months before we hear anything else. We just have to sit tight and wait." Larry balled his fist and slammed it on the table. "Goddammit! What in hell has this world come to? I can't find my wife, for Christ's sake!" His head slumped to his chest as he heaved a sob.

I got up to put my arm around his shoulder and leaned down to kiss him on the cheek. But he ignored me, stubbing his cigarette out with a vengeance before he jumped up and hurried off to the men's room. Neither Freddie nor I spoke while he was gone. When he returned he apologized. He had washed his face and his eyes were clear, but I knew he would not sleep that night. The waiter brought our dinners, and what little we ate, we ate in silence.

We dropped Freddie off, but neither of us spoke as we rode on to my apartment. Larry unlocked the door, and as soon as we stepped inside he began removing his clothes. He dropped his overcoat on the sofa in the living room, his jacket, trousers, and shirt in the hall on the way to the bedroom. He stopped at the bathroom and was soon sprawled across the bed in his boxers.

"Come over here, gorgeous," he said. I took off my dress and slip and started to unhook my stockings. "No, leave those on. You look so sexy in a garter belt."

I melted into his arms and he began to kiss my neck and shoulders. After a few minutes, it was obvious that it wasn't going to work. Larry sat up and put his head in his hands. "Dammit," he said softly. "Now this of all things. This has never, ever happened before. Never!" He got up, walked down the hallway as he collected his clothes, and started dressing.

I got up, too, and put on a robe. I removed the emerald ring, offered it to him, and said, "You don't need the added burden of worrying about me. Please take this, Larry."

"No!" He shook his head. "I love you, Eve Sands, and that ring is the symbol of our bond. I want you to keep it and wear it. And remember that one of these days, there will be a plain gold band beside it. Just bear with me a little longer. I promise you this nightmare will be over, and you and I will be together." He grabbed me suddenly and held me tight against him. "Oh, I do love you so," he whispered. Then he put on his coat and hurried down the stairs.

* * *

DuBarry closed in mid-December and I made plans to go home to Baker. But I came down with a horrible cold, sore throat, and fever a couple of days before Christmas Eve. I called Mama to tell her I was too sick to come home, and in the course of our conversation, she told me that Daddy had been arrested for drunk driving again and had spent the weekend in jail. Uncle Robert posted bail on Monday morning and brought him home, where he'd stayed for two days. But the night before I'd called, he'd told Mama that he had no intention of spending Christmas with her and left in his car that morning carrying an old suitcase and his attaché, which she assumed was full of liquor. She had no idea where he was. I offered to come home, but she told me there was nothing I could do. "You must take good care of *you*, dearest," she said in a trembling voice. "Don't worry about me. Your Aunt Bethany and Uncle Bryson are coming Christmas Day and Maddie will help me get everything ready for them. We'll all miss you, darling, but you mustn't worry. I'll be fine." After we hung up, I went back to bed and cried myself to sleep.

Freddie arrived about eleven on Christmas morning and let herself in with her key. She'd brought a quart jar of chicken soup, a congealed salad, and a loaf of fresh bread. While she heated the soup, I got up and washed my face and brushed my hair. When I walked into the kitchen, she said, "Oh, lord, you look awful. I'll bet you haven't eaten anything for days."

My throat hurt so badly that I didn't feel like talking so I shook my head. Freddie pointed a long-handled spoon at the table and told me to sit down. She handed me a beautifully wrapped package, which I tore into. Inside was a gorgeous tweed scarf in muted shades of green, brown, and rust.

"Thank you," I muttered. "I'm sorry I haven't been able to get out to get yours."

"Never mind," she said. "All I want is for you to get well. This is from Larry." She put another box on the table. Made of robin's egg-blue leather and topped with a silver bow, I knew it was from Tiffany's.

"I'll open it later," I said. "And I'll call and tell you what it is."

"I know what it is," Freddie laughed. "But I hope you'll call me anyway. Now, eat your soup and salad." She set a bowl of hot soup and a saucer of salad in front of me. I was surprised at how quickly I consumed all of it.

By Friday, I was feeling much better and agreed to have dinner on New Year's Eve with Larry and Freddie, Laura Mennick and Bill Framson. The final days of 1940 had been difficult for all of us and I was anxious for the New Year to begin, hoping things would be better. I wore Larry's favorite gown, an emerald-green taffeta, along with the stunning pearl and diamond choker from Tiffany's he'd given me for Christmas. We met the others at his favorite restaurant above Central Park. It was a bitter night with a light sleet falling, and I'd worn nothing over my gown but the fox stole.

We ordered soup to begin and I wolfed mine down in an effort to get warm. Suddenly I began to cough and could not stop. I could feel myself getting hotter and hotter and knew my face was flushed. Finally, I excused myself, grabbed my stole and evening bag, and went to the ladies' room. Freddie followed.

"I have to go home," I sputtered between coughs. "Please get me a cab and don't tell Larry till I'm gone. I don't want to spoil everyone's evening." I took the long way out, skirting my way around the back side of the banquettes so no one would see me. I had another coughing spell in the elevator and was relieved when I finally slid into the back of the cab. Barely fifteen minutes passed before I was in my flannel nightgown snuggled down in bed.

I awoke about four thirty in a pool of sweat. I dragged myself out of the bed and held onto the furniture as I made my way to the bathroom. As I slowly lowered myself onto the toilet, my head began to swim and I clung to the edge of the sink in an effort to steady myself. When I finished, I found I hadn't the strength to get up, so I sat there in a stupor trying to decide what to do. I knew I had a high fever and was much sicker than I'd been the week before. And I knew I needed help. I staggered back to my room and called Freddie. She arrived less than ten minutes later and brought the cabdriver in with her. Freddie rolled me up in the wool blanket from the bed, and the driver picked me up and took me down the stairs. I was admitted to Columbia Hospital just before six o'clock on New Year's Day, 1941. I remember nothing of the trip to the hospital, nor being admitted. I slept for the next three days and awoke to the disinfectant smell I knew so well. The sound of sleet tapping the windows startled me and I turned toward them. On the sill was a bouquet of yellow roses.

When the doctor came in, he checked my vitals, spat orders at his nurse, and patted my foot. "You've got a pretty severe case of ulcerated throat, Miss Sands," he said. "But it's better now. Your fever is down and your hemoglobin is up, but you're not out of the woods yet. You must rest, rest, rest. I've got you on a regimen of sulfur, but what you need most is quiet. I'm no specialist, but this kind of severe infection of the throat seems to plague people in your profession. I expect a lot of this is due to stress. And while it's none of my business, Miss Sands, may I just say you need a change."

I stayed in the hospital almost two weeks. When Freddie came to take me home on a Friday afternoon, she gave me the emerald ring, which she had taken off my finger and put on hers when I was admitted to the hospital. She told me that Larry had left on Thursday morning for another trip to see his friend Ronald Hughes in Washington. I'd seen Larry only twice while in the hospital, but a fresh bouquet of yellow roses arrived every few days. Over dinner I told Freddie all I wanted was to get well and go back to work. The doctor had laid down the law regarding both. I was not to appear onstage before March 15. And I was not to rehearse until February 15. He'd warned me that if I did not heed his advice, I might end up incapacitated for the rest of the year. I went home to my apartment with a list of strict orders buzzing in my head.

Mama called the first week in February to tell me that Daddy had disappeared for several days and was found passed out in the warehouse behind Sanderson & Son Mill with an empty liquor bottle in one hand and a revolver in the other. Uncle Bryson had come from Raleigh, and he and Uncle Robert had taken Daddy to the state hospital to dry out. The doctors suggested that Daddy needed long-term rehabilitation and admitted him to the psychiatric ward that afternoon.

"I never dreamed I would have a relative in the state hospital," Mama lamented, "much less my own husband. Life is full of surprises, isn't it? And some of them are downright cruel." I assured her that I was feeling much better, was eating as I should, and following doctor's orders regarding rest, rest, rest. But I felt terribly guilty that I couldn't go home and help her when she needed me so much.

Larry came to the apartment on Valentine's and brought steaks and champagne. We had a delightful time dancing to Fred Waring on the radio, sipping Manhattans, and savoring a delicious dinner. About ten we settled on the sofa in the living room with coffee. Larry lit a cigarette and strolled over to the French doors that led to the balcony. I looked beyond him to the heavy snow falling in the glare of the streetlamp on the corner.

"I've had some news about Giselle and her mother," he said, walking back toward me. "They're in Venezuela. They've evidently been there for a while, but no one here knew. My friend Ronald Hughes called after lunch today and he's arranged passage for them on a freighter to Miami, which won't happen for about three weeks. I'm going to meet them there sometime next month. My mother-in-law is very ill." He stubbed his cigarette into an ashtray on the coffee table. "Oh, God . . . why?" he asked, "why does everything have to be so goddam complicated?"

I didn't know how to answer him or what to say beyond I'm sorry. I'm sorry your mother-in-law is ill. I'm sorry your wife and she have had this horrible ordeal. These were the words that went through my head. All I said aloud was, "Is there anything I can do to help?"

Larry shook his head. "No, this is something I have to do alone. I'm sorry, Eve. So sorry all of this has happened . . . and right when you were sick and needed me." I put my fingertip over the emerald ring and began to pull it off. "No," he said. "No, don't do that. I want you to look at that ring every day that I'm gone and remember how much I love you. I have to do this. I haven't any choice. Giselle is the mother of my child. I have always cared deeply for my mother-in-law and she's going to need serious medical help when she gets to Miami. She may have to be hospitalized. Sometimes people coming here from South America are quarantined. I haven't any idea what kind of money Giselle might have with her, or if she has any at all. I sent Ronald Hughes a check this afternoon to pay for their passage on the freighter coming from Caracas. I don't know what to expect, but given what has happened, I don't see how it can possibly be good. Now, I've got to go home and try to get some sleep. And you, my darling, must stay here and take good care of yourself. I want you to be completely well when I get back." He put on his overcoat, gloves, and hat, and kissed me on the forehead. "I'm not coming back here again before I leave. It's just too hard."

I walked him to the door where we stood holding each other for a long, long time. I think both of us knew in those few moments that the life we'd known over the last few years was at an end. I tried to push that reality aside, tried to hold on to my fleeting dream of happy days together in a vine-covered cottage. Larry whispered, "I will always love you." Then he slipped out of my arms and slowly made his way down the stairs. I waited at the door, thinking surely he would turn around. But he did not look back.

* * *

On the day Larry left for Miami, I went down to Freddie's office to find out what was happening in the world. I'd been away from work so long, was so out of touch that I knew nothing beyond what I'd read in the papers. *Panama Hattie* was getting wonderful reviews and a packed house every night. Freddie's boss, Al Meyer, told me he thought it would be the longest running show of the decade. Miss Merman was in the lead role and Mr. Porter had written all the songs, so it was easy to see how he might be right. Al surprised me when he said, "They have an opening coming up. Did you know? One of the girls is leaving and going to Hollywood to make a movie . . . Betty Grable, I think that's her name. Anyway, one of the producers told me they need somebody to take her place. You want me to call and see if they've filled it yet?"

I signed the contract the next morning and started rehearsing the songs and dance routines for *Hattie*, but went slowly, especially on the dancing. My first performance was scheduled for two weeks later, March 28. That night, a box of yellow roses was waiting on my dressing table when I arrived. All went well, but I was so exhausted afterward that I slept until two the next day. It took a couple of weeks for me to get back into the routine. I was careful not to overextend myself and turned down several parties as the weather got warmer that spring.

Larry called on April 5 and asked me to meet him at Freddie's apartment for lunch. He was going to pick up some Chinese food on the way. I dressed with extra care in new beige slacks and a pink sweater that brought out the burgundy tones in my hair. Larry was already there when I arrived. He'd lost weight and his suit hung on him in folds. The dark smudges under his eyes stood out like spent coals in his tired face. But he picked me up and twirled me 'round and 'round Freddie's little kitchen while I shivered with delight.

"You're a sight for sore eyes, girl!" he said as he put me down. "Prettier than ever!"

I clung to him and whispered, "Oh Larry, I thought I'd never see you again."

He led me to the little round table and opened the cardboard boxes that held egg foo yung and chicken chow mein. "Sit down, fair maiden, and let me wait on you." He found two coffee cups on the shelf above the stove and filled them with the hot tea he'd brought. "Now, tell me all about this new show you're in."

Between bites, I told him about the set—which was supposed to be a beach in Panama; and the costumes—which were supposed to be grass skirts; and all the silly songs I had to sing. He laughed and laughed, and I sensed that this was the first time in a month that he had been able to relax and enjoy himself. I was happy to see him, to be with him again, but I had this gnawing in the pit of my stomach. I ate very little and waited for him to lower the boom.

Later, I closed the empty boxes and threw them away, rinsed out the coffee cups, and went to sit on the daybed. Larry came and sat beside me. "Where are they?" I asked.

He took a cigarette from the box on the coffee table and lit it. "They're at my apartment. My mother-in-law is nothing but skin and bones. I'm afraid she's dying. You can't imagine how both of them look . . . like wizened old women who've never seen the light of day. Giselle has this haunted look about her . . . like a frightened child. God, it's been awful!"

"Tell me what happened," I said.

Larry took a long draw from his cigarette. "Evidently, the Nazis came out of nowhere. They just showed up one morning at the vineyards and rounded up all the workers at gun point and locked them, along with Giselle and her mother, inside a storage barn. They kept them there with no food or water for two days. Then they forced all the workers into trucks and took them away. A German colonel told Giselle that because she was a Jew, she had to pay the equivalent of twenty-five thousand American dollars for an exit visa for herself and her mother. They were taken to a ship moored in the harbor at Marseille and were told it was going to Lisbon. But the ship didn't go to Lisbon. It went to Sierra Leone. And, weeks later, they were put on a ship to Venezuela. That's why it took so long for Ronald Hughes to find them."

He took the last draw from his cigarette. "Darling, I hate to tell you this," he said as he pounded the end of the cigarette butt, over and over, into the bottom of an ashtray. "My attorney told me that as long as Giselle is in New York, you and I cannot be seen in public together. If Giselle got wind of our relationship, she could take everything in the divorce settlement. She doesn't even know that I've been working on one. So you and I can't meet for dinner in a restaurant and we can't be seen in the same room together at a party. What a hell of a mess this is!" Suddenly, he grabbed me around the waist and pulled me onto his lap. "But we can meet right here. Why don't we meet here for lunch exactly one week from today, okay?"

I nodded. But a week later I called his office to say I couldn't make it. Miss Merman was hosting a luncheon for Frank Sinatra and wanted me to be there. I was glad to have an excuse not to go to Freddie's apartment for a lunchtime tryst. I'd been the other woman for years. Suddenly I realized that I was not only *the other woman*, but the other woman in exile. I could no longer be seen in public with the man I'd loved for almost a decade. I was relegated to the back burner to sit and simmer until summoned.

The summer months passed slowly as I tried to adjust to life without Larry. It was miserably hot in July and August, so Freddie and I went to the shore as often as possible. I took two days off and we celebrated my thirtieth birthday in a little bungalow at Jones Beach. Audiences for *Hattie* thinned out as the dog days lay upon us like a fog. I saw Larry very little, only a couple of times at Freddie's when she'd told him I would be there. This was always difficult for both of us, and I came away from our rendezvous with a terrible headache each time. I couldn't stop thinking about what I was going to do when I finally got up the nerve to walk away from Larry and call it quits.

One day at the theatre something happened that got me thinking. When the director replaced one of the other dancers—a woman *my* age—with an eighteen-year-old, a light went off in my head and I stood there like a dolt trying to grasp the fact that I was no longer an ingénue. My Fresh Face Award had been gathering dust on a shelf in the closet for the past eight years! It was in that telling moment that I started thinking about how much longer I might get work onstage. That question led to others like: What can you do otherwise, Eve Sands? Who's gonna hire a has-been like you? Those were sobering thoughts, and while I hadn't time to dwell on them, they were always lurking in the back of my mind . . . just like Larry.

One gorgeous day in October, Freddie called and asked me to meet her at the Russian Tea Room for lunch. When I arrived, I found her with a dark-haired woman I'd never met named Betty Stevens. Betty was dressed in a Red Cross uniform similar to my mother's. Freddie mentioned that Betty had been in working London for a year and I asked her to tell us more.

"Well," she began, " I started out working in hospitals tending to the social and personal needs of the wounded soldiers . . . writing letters for them, playing cards, reading books aloud, or articles from magazines, that kind of thing. The last two months I was there I drove a van filled with hot coffee and doughnuts for soldiers leaving for the battlefront. I've only come home because my mother is very ill with cancer. She won't last much longer, God help her. I hope I'll be able to go back when . . ." Betty's voice trailed off and the three of us ordered lunch.

Freddie asked me if I'd heard from my mother. How was my father doing? Had I heard from Claire? I answered, talking about the farm and how busy things were at Sand Hill with the cotton coming off and the tobacco being sold. I told Betty about growing up in Baker and how I'd come to New York in 1929 to take Broadway by storm.

She smiled and said, "Well, you certainly managed to do that. People in London know all about you, Eve Sands. Everyone has seen you in the movie newsreels."

This came as a big surprise to me. "I had no idea," I said. "I had no idea there was anything about Broadway on the news in London."

"Yes, yes," she said. "You know the Brits live for our American shows and especially our movies. They just love them."

I nodded, my mouth full of ham. "You mean to say they're still showing movies in London in the midst of all that bombing?"

"Sure," Betty said. "I went to see *Gone With the Wind* just before I left. People go into the cinema houses and stay there all night while the Jerries do their dirty work. You can't imagine what London looks like these days . . . the destruction is just beyond belief. I'll be so glad when the US Congress gets off its duff and does the right thing and the US comes onboard."

Freddie frowned. "You really think that's going to happen?" she asked.

"Yes," Betty said. "It's just a matter of time. Do you have any idea of how many Americans are flying for the RAF right now?" Freddie and I shook our heads.

"Thousands," Betty answered. "And so are the Danes, the Norwegians, the Poles, the Australians, the French, and the Belgians. That's one reason the Red Cross in London is so important. We try to keep up morale for an international brigade of fighters. By the way, we're desperate for people who speak French if you know someone who might be interested."

"I speak French fairly well," I blurted, being careful not to look at Freddie. "Where does one apply for Red Cross work?"

"There's an office on Fifty-Fifth," Betty said. "You can pick up an application there, and once you complete it, they'll send it on to world headquarters in Zurich. It's pretty simple."

Freddie's fingers closed tightly around my wrist. "Don't you dare think about such a thing! You couldn't possibly leave your job and go to London. You couldn't, Evelyn."

But I could and I did. As soon as Betty left the Tea Room, I said good-bye to Freddie, gave her a quick hug, and headed to the Red Cross office. The woman behind the counter told me I needed to write a letter of intent to the director and mail it as soon as possible. "A well-known personality like you, Miss Sands," she said, "is usually accepted based on the information you include in your letter." Then she gave me an application and asked that I complete it and return it to her within the next two weeks. After I left the Red Cross office, I walked down the street to a travel agency and booked passage to England on the SS *Stockholm* which was scheduled to leave New York the Saturday after Thanksgiving.

On Thanksgiving Eve, I called my mother to tell her what I'd done. She cried, something she rarely did. And so did I.

But I felt so strongly that I'd done the right thing that I stuck to my guns and told her I'd write her from the ship. About an hour later I had a call from a woman at the Red Cross office who told me that a cabin had come available on the HMS *Althone,* a British transport ship sailing that evening. She said that other RC recruits would be aboard the *Althone,* so I decided to take advantage of that opportunity so I could meet some of my new colleagues as soon as possible. I spent the afternoon packing and worrying about what to do about Larry. Should I call him? Should I leave a note for him with Freddie? By the time my cab arrived at five, I'd run out of time and simply walked away.

CHAPTER 16

Sleet Storm

London, England • February 25, 1943

Whoever said "April is the cruelest month" got it wrong. Nothing in all my years in New York could compare to the cruelty of February in London. On Thursday evening, February 25, the Beech Tree Group gathered at Corrie Cottage for dinner. Jerusha had prepared a hearty soup of potatoes, cabbage, and spam balls—little nuggets about the size of large marbles that she'd first rolled and fried, then added to the soup broth along with the leftover grease. Alongside, we had the usual gummy brown bread, spread with tasteless margarine. All of us showered Jerusha with compliments, for she had done the best she could with what she had.

After dinner, Stoney, Barney, Rutledge, Sylvia, and I retired to the lounge to enjoy the fire and a tot of brandy. Sylvia began the conversation by telling us that the Germans had officially put into action *Service du Travail Obligatoire* throughout France to tap labor resources for their war plants, and were mercilessly recruiting Frenchmen by blowing up the caves and underground bunkers where they and their families had been hiding. "The Nazis are on a rampage," she said, "killing thousands of people, including women and children, in their quest for manpower. The small groups of independent fighters like those we've been helping are organizing themselves into an army. They're working with the Allies and the Free French, and are desperate for assistance from underground groups like Beech Tree."

Stoney, who'd been sitting quietly listening to Sylvia, jumped to his feet and went to stand in the center of the room. "This is a crucial situation, my friends," he began, a hint of exasperation in his voice, "as the fortune tellers at the War Ministry say *this* is the year the Allies will advance into the interior of Europe to turn the tide of the war! I feel we simply must do more to aid our colleagues in France. So far, the diamonds have been a safe form of exchange and they're easy to transport, don't you think?"

He looked over at Barney who replied, "Yes, but I think we've run the gamut on the false-teeth disguises. Perhaps Evelyn has some ideas."

That caught me off guard. I'd always depended on "Director Barney" for such things. I frowned and said, "I'll give it some thought over the next couple of days. Maybe I could wear my Red Cross uniform and hide the stones somewhere in my medical bag."

Barney shook his head. "Not a good idea, Duckie. The Nazis will tear your bag to shreds even if you *are* wearing your uniform. The Red Cross doesn't count for much in France these days. Besides, I think it's time for you to conduct a mission on your own."

"On my own?" I gulped. "You won't be going with me?"

Barney shook his head and said he had to be about twenty miles south of Paris in April. "That's when we're taking in a big load of ammunition and explosives to a network of free fighters near Melun. But I could meet you in Paris, Evelyn, as soon as that job's finished. Perhaps Marcel Guillion could help us. He works as a waiter in the dining room at the Hotel Albert. It's a favorite of the Germans, so we'll get a good dinner. Stoney can take you across the Channel on *Flying Griffin*, and I'll arrange for you to be picked up on the beach and taken to Caen. From there you can catch the train to Paris. Sylvia will keep us apprised of the weather conditions so you'll have good cover going in and I'll meet you at Hotel Albert the evening you arrive."

He paused for a moment and I could see the wheels turning as he continued to think his way through the plan. "Don't worry about your papers. I'll take care of them and coordinate our schedules. Maybe you and Sylvia can visit the Quaker Lighthouse Center to find a disguise that will conceal the diamonds. Stoney has several stones of exceptional quality for this particular mission."

Barney leaned back in his chair signaling the end of his part of the conversation and Stoney looked around at each of us. "Are we all agreed?" he asked. I watched as everyone nodded, and reluctantly accepted the fact that I would be going to Paris alone. Stoney got up and thanked us for a productive meeting before he, Barney, and Rutledge started toward the hall. Sylvia and I joined them while they put on their coats, hats, and gloves for the short walk to Croxdon House. When Rutledge opened the door to a frigid wind, Sylvia said, "Better get your woolies and wellies lined up. The weather wizards say we're in for it tomorrow." Rutledge groaned as he stepped out into the bitter cold.

I was so terrified at the thought of going alone to France that I could not sleep that night. I lay in the dark for hours while images of Barney, Leon, and Pierre, and the chapel at Chateau du Pin danced in my head. I trembled remembering the mission we'd undertaken to Cabourg in October and the fear that had consumed me while we were questioned by the SS lieutenant, the cruel names he'd called me, the maniacal look on his face when he'd lashed at me with his riding crop. I knew I'd never forget the miserable hours we'd spent in monsieur's steamy little cellar, the horrors of lying for hours in the tomb-like tunnel off the well, and the frightening moments Barney and I had spent wrapped together around the roots of that bush. What could I possibly do in France *alone?*

Those worries flew out of my head the next morning when I arrived at St Mary's where 216 horribly wounded men had been brought by ambulance to Emergency Surgery. I'd never seen such awful burns as those poor boys had. Burns are the most difficult wounds, the most demanding, and harder to heal than wounds caused by bullets or shrapnel. Burn wounds require more than disinfecting, stitching, and bandaging. They have to be bathed and have their dressings changed hour after hour for days on end. Injections of morphine help, but deep-tissue burns radiate an excruciating misery that even morphine cannot touch.

That morning, Miriam and I were not able to keep up with the unending number of burn cases and had to ask Dr. Platt-Simpson to pull nurses from other areas to help. By lunchtime, when we finally saw a light at the end of our tunnel, we fled to Miriam's office for a cup of weak tea and a biscuit. Afterward, I went down the hall to the WC where I found this posted on the notice board:

Due to worsening weather conditions, hourly staff whose shifts end this afternoon are asked to leave no later than three. Any staff member who is able to stay the night will be paid an extra shilling per hour. Doctors and nurses are urged to remain overnight due to possible weather-related accidents. Camp beds are available in the hallway outside the morgue.

From the WC, I went straight to the morgue where I picked up two folded camp beds. On my way back to Emergency Surgery, I made a little detour down to the ambulance entrance and walked out the double doors onto the loading dock. The wind had picked up considerably since that morning and a sleet-filled fog covered everything—a sure sign of what was to come.

I took the camp beds back to Miriam's office and stood them against the wall before joining her for rounds in the ward. The afternoon wore on, and every now and then an orderly would come by and give us an update on the weather. By three o'clock a sheet of ice a quarter-inch thick covered the ground and sleet was predicted to continue into the night.

Our relief staff did not arrive that evening until after nine, two hours late. At that point Miriam and I dragged ourselves to her office where she closed the door to give us a few minutes of privacy. While she opened a can of baked beans and set it to warm on a one-burner hot plate, I got out the tea and spooned some into the crockery pot we kept handy.

"It looks like I'll be going back to France again." I said. "Beech Tree met last night to plan another mission for April. This time, I'll be going alone. Stoney and Philipe will take me across the channel to a beach where I'll be picked up. Then I'll take the train from Caen to Gare du Nord in Paris."

Miriam kept her eyes on her hands as she spooned beans into two mugs. "Alone?" she asked, turning around to hand one to me. "Why would you go alone?"

"Barney's leaving a few days ahead of me this time and I'm supposed to meet him at this hotel. Oh, Miriam, I hate the idea of getting on a train in France. You know every car will be crowded with Nazi soldiers."

"Yes, but they'll be completely mesmerized by a pretty woman like you. Just go into actress mode, honey. You'll do fine. Now, eat up."

"I'm sure I'll be shaking like a leaf the whole time. Sylvia is going to look for an old French-made suit for me, and a hat, and all the things I'll need. Maybe it won't be so bad."

I gulped the last of my beans, licked the spoon, and dropped it down in the mug. "I won't be gone but a couple of days, so maybe we can arrange the April calendar so I won't have to miss work. I wouldn't mind missing work tomorrow, though. My feet are killing me! I'm not looking forward to sleeping on a smelly old camp bed, but it will be nice to give my dogs a rest."

"Things could be a lot worse, honey. We could be out in that ward covered in burns like those poor suffering boys. Burns are the worst, Evelyn. And I've had to deal with some so bad they made me throw up. I'll never forget one little girl who had third-degree burns over seventy percent of her body. We found her the day after the Germans began bombing

London. Elgin and I went down to the docks that morning where thousands of people had been killed and bodies were everywhere. You couldn't walk for the bodies. Little children were hiding under bombed out automobiles and crawling around in ditches and huddled under steps crying for their mamas. There were so many of them," she paused, "and so few of us."

"That's when you lost Elgin, isn't it? The day after the Germans came? Oh, Miriam, how I wish I could have known Elgin."

"I wish you could have, too. You would have liked each other. Everybody loved Elgin. He was kind and good and his patients adored him because he took the time to talk with them, to get to know them. And he was fun!"

Miriam downed the last of her tea and went over to the sink to rinse her mug while she kept talking with her back to me. "It was a beautiful September day . . . and Elgin and I had been looking forward to some time together for weeks. You see it was his birthday and I wanted it to be special . . . you know, memorable. I had no idea when we started out just how memorable it would be."

CHAPTER 17

The Good Morrow

London, England • September 7, 1940

On Saturday morning, September 7, 1940, Elgin and I awoke to find bits of bright sunlight along the outer edges of the black-out curtains at our bedroom windows. What a glorious sight that was! He and I always tried to arrange our schedules at St Mary's so we could spend at least two Saturdays a month together. But that didn't happen often, which made that particular Saturday, with its bright sun and blue sky, more precious. After a quick breakfast, we skirted around piles of sandbags as we meandered through the cozy little shops in our neighborhood. Then we went our separate ways because I had a special mission I needed to conduct alone. When I arrived at Burnheim's Jewelers, I saw a package wrapped in yellow paper, tied with a white bow, sitting on the counter. I somehow knew it contained the sterling silver cuff links I'd purchased and had engraved with Elgin's initials for his birthday. I put the pretty box in my purse as I went out the door. Elgin was waiting for me and we continued browsing the shops off the Strand.

Eventually, we made our way to a teahouse where we had a late lunch. When we'd finished dessert, I brought out the yellow box and wished Elgin a happy birthday. I could tell he was pleased with the cuff links. After he removed the old ones he'd been wearing, he gave them to me to put in my purse. Then he put the new silver pair in and shot his cuffs so I could admire them. "What an elegant gift," he exclaimed.

"You are the light of my life, darling Miriam." As he pulled a wrapped package from inside his jacket, he said, "My mother taught me that I should always give someone else a gift on *my* birthday, so this is for you." Inside the elegant paper was *The Collected Poems of John Donne*. I was not familiar with the works of Mr. Donne, but I knew he was my husband's favorite. Elgin reached across the table, squeezed my hand and said, "No poem could ever capture my feelings for you better than 'The Good Morrow,' which is the first poem in this collection. Perhaps I'll read it to you, dearest, this very afternoon."

From the teahouse, we strolled up to the Temple gateway and down past Temple Church, a lovely area filled with stately Georgian mansions. Workmen were high on ladders taking down the awnings above their big front windows—a sign that summer was at an end. I'd never before been in this part of the city, which Elgin had once described as the most spiritual place in London. It was not long before I realized what he meant. I soon felt as if I had escaped to another world. The hustle bustle of Piccadilly and Trafalgar, and the noisy crowds along the Strand, had disappeared. All I heard was the soft patter of shoe leather along the pavement, the chirping birds as they flitted from tree to tree, the high-pitched laughter of children as they chased balls across the lawn.

Elgin and I walked through the Temple grounds to the site of the magnificent Round Church. I gazed up at the towering stained-glass windows, the balustrades, and stooped to read the date inscribed on the cornerstone: 1185. Elgin said, "You know this church is very famous. It was built during the reign of Henry II and completed not long after the murder of Thomas Becket. Just think what this place was like before Henry got a foothold and a crown, and laid all this brick and mortar that, through the centuries, became the city of London. Just imagine what it must have been like when the Roman legions first arrived here."

I closed my eyes and tried to picture the Temple grounds as they must have been two thousand years before. In my mind, I saw fields of tall swaying grasses, and clumps of bluebells growing where Elgin and I now stood. Surely, there had been woodlands in the distance where deer and boar raised their young. I went back to a time when the Roman legions, led by Emperor Claudius, had made their way across this very ground in 44 AD. I could almost smell the heather as their long legs brushed against it, could almost see the sun glinting off their shields as they trudged across a rich virgin plain to a ford on the Thames known as "Lyn-din." Elgin had once shown me a coin that had been a gift from his grandfather. A profile of Emperor Claudius and the inscription, *De Britt*, were engraved on the heavy gold piece, which had been minted in Rome about the time Saint Paul set out on his missionary journey. London was an old, old city, with a venerable history, and I felt honored to be standing in what must have been the heart of it.

We left the Temple grounds and started toward the Victoria Embankment. As we rambled along the wide stone pavement, Elgin pointed out two barges, a merchant ship, and a sloop in full sail going down the river. "Queen Victoria and her ladies once strolled here," he said as he paused to look at his watch. "It's four o'clock, darling. Do you still want to go to the cinema tonight after dinner?"

"Yes. I almost forgot about that. We'd better catch a bus and head home." No sooner had I gotten these words out of my mouth than Moaning Minnie began to wail, her plaintive warning filling the heavy air. I frowned and shrugged my shoulders. "Probably another false alarm."

Elgin turned toward me and put a finger to his lips. "Listen," he whispered. From a distance came a droning, a low reverberating noise like the hum of a thousand swarming hornets. Elgin scanned the sky, looking first to his left, then to his right, seeking the source of that sound. "Look!" he shouted. "Look there!" I turned around to see dozens of fighter planes coming straight at us. Behind them, their fuselages gleaming in the sunlight, was a squadron of bombers. I felt the ground shake beneath my feet as they passed overhead. Like birds of prey, they circled upriver and banked in formation to begin their descent. "Stukas!" Elgin shouted, grabbing my hand. "Run, Miriam! Run for the Temple Underground!" Suddenly we found ourselves carried along like flotsam on a stream as hundreds of people joined our desperate flight.

While scores of Dorniers and their escorts blocked the sun, flocks of songbirds rose out of the tops of trees and swept north. Pages from newspapers catapulted over the lawn as readers abandoned them and ran for safety. Mothers jerked sleeping babies from peaceful naps and sprinted away as if shot from cannon. Picnickers foresook their comfortable blankets, their baskets, their unfinished meals, and rose to run. Businessmen in suits picked up children who were obviously not theirs and lunged toward the gaping maw of the Temple Underground.

As we neared the entrance, people began to push and shove, and suddenly Elgin and I were separated. I started down the steps, but found myself pinned against the wall. A man behind me put his hand around my waist, picked me up, and took me down to where Elgin was waiting at the bottom. A horn began to blare and we jumped away from the tracks as a train roared in. Crowds of passengers poured from its doors forcing us further back. No one got on the train, but it started up again and moved out of the station as quickly as it had come.

Elgin found a piece of stray newspaper, put it down on the floor beside a concrete pillar, and bade me sit. I was wearing the lace-trimmed suit I'd been married in two years before and didn't want to get it dirty, but I was so exhausted from running, and from fright, that I gave in. We sat down together and leaned against the pillar, watching as droves of people continued to stream into the station from the streets above. No one had a blanket, of course, nor any food or water. They were as unprepared as we were. But once they found a spot and claimed it, they quieted down. The woman next to me sobbed quietly into a handkerchief. Then she began to pray. Dozens of people were on their knees, heads bowed, lips moving in prayer, begging God to save them. I thought about my mother and Aunt Delma and what they would hear on the radio the next morning while they were getting ready for church.

About eight thirty, the lights went out, plunging us into complete darkness. People began to complain of the cold, whispering to one another what they'd give for a blanket. A steady staccato of artillery fire came from the big guns mounted on rooftops around us. Their sound heartened us while the constant *thud*, *thud*, *thud* of German bombs brought tears to our eyes. Soon the shrill of sirens added to this din. Elgin squeezed my hand. "Hear that?" he said. "Ambulances. As soon as the All Clear sounds, we'll go see what we can do to help."

About midnight, Elgin stood up and told me that he was going topside to see what was happening. "Not without me, you're not," I answered. I could feel the muscles in my calves burning as I struggled to stand up. Hours on a cold concrete floor had taken a toll and my back felt as if I'd been chopping cotton. We carefully made our way through the crowd and started up the stairs. As soon as we cleared the covered entry, we turned east toward the docks, and I gasped at the sight of the inferno blazing in the distance. Monstrous flames, layered in brilliant hues—purple, red, blue—filled the horizon. Gigantic balls of fire rose and fell like shooting stars over the rooftops of factories, warehouses, and tenements. Artillery fire from hundreds of fighter planes, ours and theirs, danced like lightning across the smoke-filled sky. A barrage of explosions *boom*, *boom*, *boomed* and funnels of fire began rising in dozens of places beyond the Southwark Bridge.

"Gas lines," Elgin commented. "Only broken gas lines could cause explosions like that. Oh God . . . those poor people. Not only the Luftwaffe, but those gas lines running under their houses. Come on, darling, we'd better go back down. I wish I had my medical bag! Why didn't I bring it? There's nothing we can do until they sound the All Clear. But as soon as they do, we'll head down there to see if we can help."

The All Clear finally sounded the next morning at 9:48. People gathered their belongings, but no one pushed or shoved to get up the stairs as they had going down them the day before. We all dreaded what we might find. Once Elgin and I were topside, we made for the east end. We were stopped by Civil Defence workers several times along the way, but were allowed to pass when we presented our credentials from St Mary's. By the time we reached Tower Green, a cloud of dark smoke lay over everything. I quickly covered my mouth and nose with a handkerchief to keep the deadly fumes at bay. Thick, greasy blobs of ash fell like wet snow, matting our hair and drenching our clothes. Pile after pile of smoldering rubble stretched ahead of us as far as we could see. High voltage wires hung like jungle vines, their frayed ends throwing deadly sparks above the jagged pavement. The steady scrape of shovels and the *ping, ping* of pickaxes as diggers hit their marks were the only sounds we heard.

Not a single building along the way had escaped damage. Broken beds, chairs, and legless tables lay haphazardly atop yards and yards of shattered glass. Feathers from pillows floated down from open spaces that had once been upstairs windows. Crooked door frames stood free of the walls that had once adjoined them. Baby dolls and toy trains lay smashed amid pots and pans, photograph albums, broken china, dead pets. Elgin and I carefully picked our way toward what we thought was a sign for a bus stop. A few yards beyond it lay the scattered remains of a city bus—strips of twisted metal, lacerated tires, horsehair stuffing, women's purses, a string bag filled with turnips and potatoes. From the denuded branches of nearby trees hung the shredded remnants of human torsos, fragments of bone, blood-drenched strips of skin, and torn clothing. I saw a strand of pearls draped over the top of a boxwood as neatly as if someone had laid it there.

It was in this Hellish landscape that we finally encountered people not in uniform. Their hair, clothing, and faces were coated with a film of heavy gray dust that made them look as if they were living dead. Unsteady on their feet, they swayed as if drugged and wandered aimlessly back and forth crying for loved ones . . . *Mum, Dah-Dah, Granny . . . where are you?*

Nearby a dozen Civil Defence workers were bent over piles of rubble. I heard a voice come to me as if from a dream, a strange, indistinct mutter that sounded like *help, help*. One of the firemen knelt down and addressed a pile of broken concrete slabs. "We're coming, dearie," he said. "Hold on. We'll have you out in a jiffy."

In the next block, several wardens were clustered near a fence that was still standing, even though the front wall of the house behind it was missing. Elgin asked the men if there was anything we could do to help. "No help for it, sir," a warden answered. "She's dead, and so is that poor little baby." He pointed to the remains of what had obviously been a dining room. We looked up to see a hole in the broken ceiling where a woman's body dangled, her skirt blown to shreds, a baby's bloody head caught between her legs. The dining table, set for dinner, was undisturbed.

I did not want to leave that woman and baby, but I knew Elgin and I had to get to the hospital. Elgin asked a fireman if any buses or trains were running. "No," he answered. "There's nowhere for them to run. All the streets in this area is impassable. All the electric lines is down and no one is allowed to drive a private vehicle anywhere 'cause of all the broken gas lines. Them Nazi bastards really did a number on us last night. West Ham took the worst of it from what I hear. The Beckton Glassworks is still burning, and the Surrey Docks and the West India Docks is all but gone. A gent come by this morning and told us that ten thousand tons of tobacco, sugar, wool, and rubber just went up in smoke."

Elgin and I began walking again, hoping to find our way through the hideous remains of a night in Hell. The smell of gas assaulted us as we turned the corner and headed up glass-strewn pavement toward a stretch of jagged, smoldering ruins. Soon, we were overcome by the sweet, cloying scent of burning flesh. Charred, blood-streaked bodies were flung up and down the broken sidewalk in front of a section of badly damaged row houses. Two dead dogs, their fur singed almost completely off, lay sprawled across a set of steps. The spade finials on the black iron fence beside us had melted into shapeless blobs that resembled chunks of coal. I reached out to touch one, but pulled away as I stumbled over the remains of what appeared to be a human leg. I had seen blood before—lots of it every day at the hospital—and horrible burns and dead babies. But I'd never seen anything like this. What we'd dreaded for months had finally come to pass, but with a fury that was almost beyond human comprehension. How does one describe the destruction caused by 330 *tons* of bombs dropped during a single night? Little did we know then that this horror would continue, unabated, for the next fifty-seven nights.

Through the smoky haze, Elgin and I saw the outline of an ambulance and made our way toward it. There was a house still burning nearby and Elgin went straight to the front door and called out for anyone who might still be inside. Not far away, I saw one of our colleagues, Dr. Markham, kneeling on the ground beside a man who was bleeding profusely from his shoulder. Markham yelled, "Morphine! Where's the morphine?" As he tried to quiet the poor thrashing man, I stooped down, opened his bag and found a hypodermic and a vial of morphine. I quickly prepared it for him. "Thank God," he said. "You're an angel of mercy, Broadhurst." He thrust the needle into the man's thigh.

Elgin came down the steps of the house with a little girl in his arms. She was completely nude and had severe burns all over her buttocks, legs, and feet. Her eyes were closed, but

I found a faint pulse. Elgin took off his jacket, wrapped her inside it, and laid her on a blanket beside the injured man. I prepared another hypodermic and Dr. Markham gave her a shot. An orderly came from the other side of the burning house and helped Elgin and Dr. Markham put the man and little girl into the back of the ambulance. A moment later, another ambulance from St Mary's pulled up behind it. The driver jumped out and yelled to Dr. Markham that he had three passengers who were critically injured and he needed to go. He looked over at me and said, "Come on, Matron Broadhurst. You can ride up front with me."

I knew the driver, Mr. Kitteridge, had seen him many times at St Mary's, and wasted no time getting in with him. I watched as Dr. Markham got into the cab of the ambulance in front of us. Then Elgin climbed in beside him. I could hear the sound of glass crunching beneath our tires as we moved ever so slowly for about a mile, easing our way through mountainous piles of rubble and clouds of dark smoke. We came to a clearing, but Civil Defence workers would not let us pass. "Gas lines broken up ahead," one said, waving his torches to the right to send us in that direction. We continued to follow the ambulance containing Elgin and Dr. Markham around a corner and found ourselves stuck behind an Army truck.

All I remember from that moment was what I saw when the ambulance in front of us exploded. The roof buckled first. Then the whole thing flew apart and my husband was thrown out the front window. Several seconds passed before I was able to move. For some reason, I couldn't get my door open. So I rolled down the window and climbed out. I found Elgin lying near some trees. He had been thrown on top of a sign . . . some painted boards . . . I don't know what it was. And he had this piece of metal through his neck. Not completely through, but almost. I remember that it was silver . . . probably aluminum. I think it must have been a length of frame from around the windshield. Elgin was still alive when I sat down beside him and took him in my arms. His eyes were open and I'm sure he knew who I was. I kept talking to him, telling him how much I loved him, and how he was going to be all right. But I knew he wasn't. That jagged strip of aluminum had gone right through his carotid artery and blood was gushing like a fountain. I knew it was hopeless and just sat there holding him, crying "Elgin, Elgin . . . don't leave me, Elgin."

My husband was not the only one who died that day. Dr. Markham was also thrown by the blast and suffered a broken neck. The driver of their ambulance died from third-degree burns to his head and chest. Three soldiers in the back of the Army truck were also killed.

I sat on the ground with Elgin's head in my lap for an hour or more. Mr. Kitteridge offered to cover Elgin, but I told him I wanted to look at my husband's face as long as I could. About two o'clock, another ambulance arrived and I got up and helped the few who'd survived the blast get aboard. Soon after, an Army truck arrived. Two soldiers had been sent to collect the victims. The three of us wrapped the bodies in blankets and put them in the back of the truck. The soldiers helped me climb in and I stayed with Elgin all the way to St Mary's.

Elgin's body was taken to the morgue where his clothes were removed and I was allowed to wash his body. After the attendants put him in a canvas bag, Dr. Platt-Simpson came in to offer me his condolences. He gave me an envelope that contained a wide gold wedding band, a black leather wallet, and a pair of silver cuff links that were testimony to the happiest years of my life.

CHAPTER 18

French Clutch

Paris, France • April 23, 1943

I saw her before she saw me. And in that split second, I managed to slip in front of a tall heavyset gentleman and melt into the crowd. Hundreds of us had poured from the train and were moving like batter through a funnel toward the south exit of Gare du Nord. A wary school of fish, we careened quietly to the left, then to the right to avoid the Feldgendarmerie stationed at intervals along dun-colored walls. Only an occasional soft murmur could be heard drifting on the stale, smoky air of that narrow passage. More obvious were a dozen Nazi officers laughing and joking as they loped, like healthy gray wolves, just ahead . . . *Eh, Gerhardt? Hah! Hah! Jawohl, Mein Kompanietruppführer!* Be calm, Evelyn, I kept saying to myself. Keep your head down and be calm. When I dared look up, I saw a sign for the women's restroom and a shudder of relief passed over me. I ducked in, made for the first available stall, and quickly slid the lock. I laid my suitcase across the open toilet seat, sat down on top of it, and pulled my feet back on either side praying she couldn't see me.

It wasn't long before I heard the ringing *tap, tap, tap* of her steel-toed boots striking the marble floor and cocked my head to listen. She began walking up and down the room, and through a crack in the door I caught a glimpse when she paused to look around. She was not nearly as tall as I, but had broad shoulders and wide hips, and was at least twenty pounds heavier. Dressed in a dark gray suit, she wore a snap-brim fedora pulled down over her short blonde hair. She kept opening and closing her large hands, which were knotted with bulging knuckles like those of a fighter. Over her right shoulder was a black leather bag, and I shivered to think what she might have hidden there—a Luger, a length of piano wire, a hypodermic filled with strychnine.

Women began emerging from stalls nearby and several started toward the sinks to wash their hands. But they changed their minds the moment they saw her and made for the exit instead. There, they were met by dozens of other women who were flooding the restroom, making it more difficult for me to see her. I slid off the suitcase, leaned forward to press my forehead against the little crack at the side of the door, and squinted. I looked left and right, but she was nowhere in sight. The ringing blare of a whistle sounded in the corridor. Then a voice called "Halt!" From the other side of the room came the unmistakable *tap, tap, tap* as she hurried out to investigate.

Only a few minutes had passed since I'd entered the stall, but I felt I'd been there for hours. I longed to stay behind that little door to try to regain my composure, but I knew I couldn't. I allowed myself the luxury of one small sigh before I turned around and opened the suitcase. It contained a French-made nightgown and underpants, toiletries, two sanitary pads, and a brown snakeskin clutch that had been purchased years before at a well-known Paris department store. On one end of the suitcase, I'd stowed a paper bag that held a thermos of water and the two bread-and-jam sandwiches that Jerusha had kindly made for me. On the other end, I'd rolled up a worn tapestry bag, the kind Frenchwomen take to market.

I removed the beige knit hat I'd worn, turned it inside out to reveal the black material inside, and pulled it down on my head like a cloche. I unbuttoned the beige gabardine jacket I was wearing, took it off, and slipped out of the matching skirt. I turned both inside out and put them back on. Now

I was clad in a suit of olive-green and black check. I said a silent prayer thanking God for Jerusha's fine sewing skills. She'd taken apart two old suits and made them into these shabby, reversible garments, because new clothes catch the eye in war-ravaged Europe. Both pieces had inconspicuous, but legible, French labels. As a final touch for my masquerade, I added a pair of horn-rimmed glasses. The contents of the beige leather purse I'd carried on the train fit neatly into the snakeskin clutch. They included a tube of lipstick from a shop near the Louvre, a receipt for the repair of a necklace from a jeweler in Caen, a set of keys to my apartment there, and several worn Franc notes all punched with telltale holes like those made by tellers in branch offices of the French National Bank.

I took out my *new* carte d'identité, and went over the information written there one more time. I was now Helene Collette Dumont, a recently widowed teacher who'd come to Paris to visit her aunt. Helene Dumont had taught at a girls' school in Caen for the past ten years, and I had a school identification card among my recently acquired possessions to prove it. The photos on both of my identity cards looked remarkably like me, but I was not the person in those pictures. I'd memorized the names of my now-deceased parents and grandparents from Caen and knew exactly where they'd been born. My mother, Mignon Collette, had been a housewife. My father, Jacques, had worked in an auto factory. My husband, Gaston, had died the year before fighting with the Free French in Algiers. I had a small photo of him in my wallet, too. Folded behind it was a letter from my aunt, Celeste Noet Dumont, who supposedly lived in a flat on rue Abbeville near the basilica of Saint Vincent de Paul in the heart of Paris. A highly effective member of our underground network, she'd written a brief note begging me to come visit her during my spring holiday from school and mailed it to me at my fake address in Caen where it had been picked up by another operative and forwarded to Barney.

Over the past few weeks, Barney and I had deliberately handled my carte d'identité and my school identification card numerous times to be sure both were sufficiently creased and worn. He, Stoney, and Jerusha had been calling me Helene for more than a month to help me get used to my *new* name. Other members of our underground network in France had supplied me with several small, but important, items I would need to try to pass myself off as a Parisian. While I felt I was sufficiently prepared for this mission, I was terribly uneasy about being alone.

I unrolled the French market bag and filled it with the items from my suitcase. The underpants I was wearing were now stained with blood, so I removed them. Then I put on a fresh sanitary napkin and clean underwear. While I'd been busy changing myself into someone else, the restroom had emptied. All was quiet. Too quiet to make a move. So I waited. It was just a matter of moments before I heard another train chug into the station. The Germans were nothing if not punctual, and they had turned an unreliable French railway system into a finely tuned machine that moved their army and its deadly weapons at record speed. In a short time, the restroom filled again.

After removing the waxed paper from around a sandwich, I opened the thermos and tried to savor a bit of food while I concentrated on the information Barney had drummed into my brain. I reviewed the map he'd had me memorize showing me where to go after I left Gare du Nord—a map that didn't exist anymore except in my head. As the moments ticked by, I heard several women as they emerged from stalls and finally felt safe enough to venture out.

But before I did, I stood up, closed my eyes, and imagined myself standing in the wings beside the dark blue curtains backstage at the Winter Garden Theatre. This is just another play, Evelyn, I said to myself. It's just another show. You're a schoolteacher from Caen. So act like one. Gripping my suitcase in one hand, and holding the snakeskin clutch confidently under my arm, I walked from the wings down stage to the exit doors and turned left, as I'd been instructed, onto Place Napoléon.

It was late in the day and hundreds of Parisians crowded the sidewalks on their way home from work. I knew I had to walk four long blocks up Place Napoléon, then cross rue Saint-Denis, and walk two more blocks to the Hotel Albert. That's where I'd meet Barney. I slowed my step a bit and moved to the center of the sidewalk, hoping to be less conspicuous. I wanted to look behind me to see if she was there, but dared not. Soon, the eight o'clock curfew would be in effect, and I longed for the safety of the hotel's dining room and Barney's friendly face. It was there that I'd finally be able to rid myself of the precious contraband I was carrying.

Our mission had been delayed two days while I waited for my period to start. This was done on purpose because it meant I could carry five two-carat diamonds sewn into a tampon. The five flawless stones had been removed from a century-old Beeton tiara and were priceless. They would be sold on the black market to provide resources to hundreds of resistance fighters who would support British and American forces in *Operation Anvil*, the Allied invasion planned for early summer on the coast of Spain.

Stoney and Philipe had been waiting on *Flying Griffin* the night before when I arrived at a well-hidden makeshift dock near Dover. Only the three of us, and a ship's hand, were aboard as we made our way through a gloomy wet darkness across the Channel, riding a blustery sea that flooded the bow the entire trip. By the time we reached our destination, I was shaky, hungry, and a bit the worse for wear. I went down the side on a rope ladder and was handed into a small boat by a man dressed entirely in black. Another man in black took my suitcase. As soon as I sat down in the dory, they lowered the oars and made for shore. Fortunately, we were shrouded in a heavy mist that shielded us from German searchlights on the ridge above.

As soon as the hull of the boat began to scrape along the bottom, one of the men shipped his oar. He leaned toward me and whispered that I should stand up. After I did, he lifted me and my suitcase out of the boat and carried me in his arms through the surf to the beach. A moment later, a horse and wagon emerged from the mouth of a cave tucked beneath the rim of a sandbank. As the dory began to move away, the horse and wagon came closer. On its seat was a man dressed in dark clothing. He pulled on the reins and stopped the wagon. Then he hurried to the back of it and reached down to help me in. Barney had told me that I would be met on the beach by a man called Balzac, and that his wife was known as Madame Bovary. I was a bit surprised when Balzac told me to lie down, but did as he asked. He helped me wrap myself in a blanket for which I was very thankful, as the wind was bitterly cold there on the beach. Afterwards, he covered me and my suitcase with hay for the trip to his farm, located about three miles north of Caen. Once we arrived, Madame Bovary showed me into a small room that contained a single bed where I slept for the next three hours. She woke me at noon and gave me a bowl of thick mutton broth and a chunk of tasteless gray bread. Then Balzac took me in his wagon to the station in Caen where I caught the four o'clock to Paris.

Because I had a third-class ticket, I sat in a crowded corner amid dozens of women on their way to work in the German war factories. I nodded to a few and made small talk as necessary. Then I leaned back against the seat, closed my eyes, and let my mind return to all the things Barney had done to prepare me for this, my first mission alone. He'd told me what to do if I got lost, what to say, and to whom. He'd taught me how to tap out Morse code and how to use the tiny flashlight in my purse to signal SOS . . . dot, dot, dot . . . dash, dash, dash . . . dot, dot, dot. He'd drawn a map showing safe houses and insisted I memorize the routes to their locations.

One afternoon, several weeks before I was scheduled to depart, I was busy doing bed rounds at the hospital when Miriam called me into her office. I was surprised to see Barney sitting on the side of her desk. He offered me an orange biscuit from a tin he'd brought and bade me sit down for a moment. Miriam had prepared a pot of tea, and the three of us enjoyed a few moments together relishing our hot drink, the sweet biscuits, and bit of stimulating conversation. Barney gave us a brief, but heartening, update on the progress Allied forces were making in North Africa as they pushed the Germans and Italians toward Tunis. Because he'd interrupted our work, he didn't tarry. When he got up to leave, he asked me to walk with him out into the hall. Once there, he handed me a box of Chinese black tea with instructions to drink a strong cup of it three times a day. I was not to brush my teeth.

"Why does it always have to be my *teeth*?" I fussed.

"When you go to Paris," he said, "you must look Parisian. No one there would ever mistake your dazzling white teeth for anything but those of an American. And that won't do."

So, I drank the black tea until it left a gray stain on my teeth. Just before I left, I dyed my hair and eyebrows dark brown *again* to help me fit in. I'd dreaded the thought of dying my hair, but Barney had insisted, telling me my auburn color would draw too much attention, especially in Paris. But nothing about these preparations was harder for me than drinking that black tea and ignoring my toothbrush.

Barney had also taught me to eat in the Parisian manner, holding my fork in the left hand and my knife in the right throughout a meal. And even though I rarely smoked, he'd reminded me that I must not smoke at all, as women in Paris were forbidden by the Germans to smoke in public. I'd learned that cream must be poured into cups of tea only after the tea had been poured, the opposite way it was done in England. During the last few weeks, Barney and I had conversed only in French and I'd struggled to master the nuance of *street* French, learning from him dozens of expressions I'd never heard before.

A few days before I was scheduled to leave, Barney gave me a narrow gold wedding band engraved with the initials *HCD*, a small gold cross on a chain that I was to wear around my neck at all times, and a simple rosary strung with tiny black beads. When we parted, he kissed me on the cheek and said, "Remember, Helene, it is not our job to fight the Germans. It is our job to provide the resources for those who do. I'll see you at eight o'clock Thursday evening in the dining room at the Hotel Albert." He'd left London a week ahead of me, hitching a ride on an RAF Lysander that would drop him into a horse pasture just south of the gates to Versailles.

After Barney and I had had our dinner in the hotel dining room, I was to go to the lavatory, remove the diamond-laden tampon, and wrap it in the linen napkin I'd used. I was to return to our table and leave the dirty napkin beside my plate. Marcel Guillion, Barney's contact at the hotel, would collect it when he cleared the table. Now, all I had to do was get to that hotel.

As I continued up Place Napoléon, shadows lengthened and darkness began to fall. The crowd was thinning and soon, I feared, there would be no one on the street but me. I passed several market shops displaying boldly written signs in their windows that read *Nur für Deutsche,* shops where only Germans were allowed to purchase goods. The poor French *untermenchen* who served them barely survived on what little rotting fruits and vegetables and bits of meat remained after the conquerors had done their morning shopping.

Off to my left I heard a child crying, and the soothing reassurance of his mother's soft voice. A moment later, a man who was walking on my right began to cough. I glanced toward him, and as he placed his finger tip lightly on my wrist, he whispered, "En guard!" That's when I heard *tap, tap, tap* on the pavement behind us. I gave the man a quick nod and fled into the nearest open doorway—a butcher's shop. Behind the counter a woman in a blood-smeared apron was putting pigs' hearts into a large metal pan. I walked along the display case feigning interest in her small store of goods while I kept my eyes on the front door. When I reached the rear of the shop, I dropped the snakeskin clutch into the market bag, tiptoed down the hallway to the back door, and fled into an alley.

Then I ran. I ran and ran until I thought my lungs would explode. Finally, I reached the corner where it opened onto another street and I fell back against the wall and burst into tears. "Oh, God," I blubbered, covering my mouth with my hands. I stood there sucking air, wishing I were at Corrie Cottage sitting before the fire with Sylvia. I spent another minute or two grappling with the fact that I had no idea where I was. Then, from out of nowhere, I heard Barney's voice saying, *Steady on, old girl. You've got a job to do.* I wiped my nose on the back of my hand, straightened my rumpled suit, and reminded myself that over the next few days the lives of thousands might depend on whether I completed my mission . . . or not. Barney's map floated through my mind and I just knew I had to be near rue Saint-Denis. I started walking up the street, praying with every step, and was filled with gratitude when that wide boulevard opened up before me. I crossed against the traffic and quickly headed south.

The sound of gears grinding startled me. I turned my head ever so slightly and was dismayed to see dozens of trucks coming my way. Every few yards they slowed, and German soldiers jumped out, rifles at the ready. It was the witching hour, eight o'clock. I made an about-face and walked as quickly as I dared in the opposite direction. Several anxious minutes passed before I came to another street. I slipped around the corner and found myself in a cobblestoned passageway enclosed on both sides by a high stone wall. Overhead, leafy chestnut boughs meshed like an arbor, shielding everything in gloom.

From a distance, I heard the unmistakable tap of steel on pavement. I bent over, slipped off my shoes, and dropped them in the market bag. Then I scrambled around in the bottom of the bag until I found Barney's tiny flashlight. Flashlights, regardless of size, were strictly verboten in France, and if the Germans had discovered mine they'd have arrested me immediately. But I was much too frightened to think about that. I bent down and hobbled forward in my stocking feet, keeping my left hand flat against the stone wall for balance while I clutched the flashlight in my right. The tapping noise sounded again, closer this time, and I glanced over my shoulder to see a shadowy figure moving from one chestnut tree to another, coming closer with every step.

I rose to full height and my trembling fingers reached a surface that felt smooth and dry. My heart all but jumped out of my throat when I discovered that it was the top bar of a metal gate. Through it, I could see the outline of a large building. Although its windows were shuttered, there were figures moving back and forth behind them, their shadows playing against the soft light from within. Behind me, a twig snapped. I raised the flashlight toward those windows, but my right hand was shaking so badly, I couldn't press the button to flash the beam.

I laid my wrist atop the bar, gritted my teeth, and hit the button . . . dot, dot, dot . . . dash, dash, dash . . . dot, dot, dot. Above me, a shutter swung open and I screamed, "Ici! Ici!" That's when a searing jolt, like the blast of a furnace, struck my side. I tried desperately to hold onto the gate, but my legs gave way and I went down.

CHAPTER 19

The Sisters of Saint Lorraine

Paris, France • April 26, 1943

I awoke to find my face and hands bathed in sweat. My feet were blocks of ice, and try as I might, I could not stop my teeth chattering. I clawed at the heavy covering over me and tried to sit up, but a sharp pain in my left side kept me down. So I lay still with my eyes shut, dreading what I might find when I opened them: dank prison walls studded with leg irons, gray uniformed guards, straw-covered floors laced with urine, feces, and blood.

Breathe, just breathe, I kept repeating to myself. You know you're alive even if you don't know where you are. With the tips of my fingers I reached up and gently touched the area above my right cheek. Not only my eyes, but the top of my head was covered in strips of coarse fabric. A strong earthy smell, like pine straw, convinced me that I was lying on the floor of a prison.

A voice came to me . . . a woman's voice. Someone was talking in quiet tones asking questions. A moment later, I heard a swooshing sound like stiff fabric makes when it rustles, and as that sound came closer, it was accompanied by the scent of garlic.

"Anon, mademoiselle," a woman whispered, putting her mouth close to my ear as she placed her warm palm over my cold hand. "We were so afraid we might lose you, but it seems you've passed the point of danger. I'm so pleased to find you awake."

I opened my mouth to say merci, but couldn't speak. The woman lifted my head and held it while she fed me a few drops of water from a spoon.

"Don't try to talk," she said. "Just rest. I'm Sister Marie Louise and you are safe now in the Convent of the Sisters of Saint Lorraine. We are a small group of eighteen who operate a hospital on the third floor of our building. Over the years, we've had many patients come to us through a misfortune similar to yours. You mustn't worry, child, as it will only delay your healing. You're in a little room we dug out from under our chicken coop. You've been here for two days and your fever's finally broken, so we hope you'll be able to eat something now. But before you do, I want to change your dressings. I'm going to remove the bandages from your head. Just relax now and let me do the work."

Sister Marie Louise's hands were sure as she held my head and carefully unwound strips of bandage. I blinked several times before my eyes adjusted to a narrow space where the flickering glare from a trio of candles threw long shadows on dirt-packed walls. The face before me was round, had a turned-up nose, sparkling dark eyes beneath black brows, and a welcoming smile. As Sister Marie Louise lowered my head back onto the pillow, she said, "Your wound is healing nicely. I'm so sorry we had to shave off so much of your hair, but the gash was long and deep. Evidently, when you fell, you hit the left side of your head on the edge of the pavement. I'm afraid you'll have a scar there, as it took twenty-three stitches to close it."

"Merci," I whispered. "Thank you for all you've done. I don't know how you found me or why you brought me here. But I expect it was very dangerous for you."

Sister Marie Louise nodded. "Yes, but we've had a lot of practice and yours isn't the worst case we've ever had. I'm going to raise your shift now and remove the dressing over your wound."

While she snipped at a bandage on my left side, I tried to recall what had happened to me, but all I could remember was being chased by someone into a grove of trees. "I was being . . . being chased by someone," I stammered.

Sister Marie Louise's fingers felt cool against my hot skin as she lifted the smelly pus-filled bandage from my side. "Much better," she said as she began bathing the area with a solution that smelled of carbolic. "Only ten stitches here because the bullet went into your back side and exited out the front just below your rib cage. It lodged in an old sycamore tree near the wall. One of the sisters pried it out with the point of a knife and filled the hole with a mixture of sawdust and resin. One would never know that old tree had suffered such indignation. We wouldn't want the Boche to have any evidence of what happened, would we?"

"I don't know what happened, Sister. I was clinging to the top of a gate. Did you see me there? Is that where you found me?"

"No, child. When we found you, you were lying under the stone bench beneath the sycamore tree. You must have crawled under the gate and dragged yourself under that old bench. Don't worry about that. Just rest and get well."

I felt a tingling sensation as she sprinkled sulfa powder over my wound. "Lie still now," she urged, "while I put on a fresh dressing. Sister Marie Francine will come in as soon as I'm finished and bring some broth. By the way, we removed the sanitary pad you were wearing and put a fresh one on you. But your period seems to be over now."

My lips formed a silent O as I tried to think about how to respond. I wasn't sure that it was safe to tell Sister Marie Louise about the diamond-filled tampon. But I knew I had to do something, because it was probably reeking with rot by now.

Sister Marie Louise picked up the kidney-shaped pan she'd filled with my dirty dressings and the scissors she'd used to change them. "You look so worried, my child. Is there anything I can do for you?"

I asked if she had a pair of forceps handy and told her why I needed them. An hour later, the filthy tampon had been discarded and the diamonds safely hidden in the base of a brass candlestick that sat on the altar in the convent's chapel on the second floor.

As soon as Sister Marie Louise left me, another woman came into the little cave-like room. She was dressed in the same black habit and wore the same black-and-white wimple, but she was quite different from the first sister and much younger.

"I'm Sister Marie Francine," she said, giving me a sweet smile. Her skin was as pale as clotted cream, and the pink in her cheeks so iridescent they were barely there. A fringe of gold lashes set off her eyes, which were a soft watery blue like the sky on a hot August day. After setting a basin on the bedside table, she removed my shift and proceeded to bathe my face, arms, chest, my legs and feet with warm soapy water. Then she dried me with a soft towel and helped me ease into a clean gown. She sat down on the edge of the narrow bed, massaged my feet for several minutes, and dressed them in warm wool socks. "Don't try to sit up just yet," she said. "I'll raise your head and spoon the broth into your mouth. Go easy now and take your time."

I finished the entire cup of broth and felt much better thanks to the gentle ministrations of Sister Marie Francine. The last thing I remember from that day was Sister Marie Louise standing over me with a hypodermic in her hand. Soon, I'd drifted back to sleep.

The following day was much the same. As soon as I awakened, Sister Marie Francine washed my face and fed me broth. Then Sister Marie Louise appeared and removed my dressings, bathed and tended my wounds and redressed them. I asked where I was and how I'd come to be there. After Sister Marie Louise had explained all of it to me again, we talked briefly in quiet tones about the Boche, the local Gestapo, the underground network in the city, and the

Maquis. Then she told me how the Sisters of Saint Lorraine had organized themselves and their hospital and convent to combat the German war machine, and the Paris Police who worked so closely with them. She also told me how she'd learned about the legendary Father Barney and how he was called the Pied Piper because of his many followers.

She knew that Barney had contacts in many places in France and that he'd adopted various disguises to conceal his identity. She told me that the Gestapo and the dreaded Paris SS had been on a rampage during the past few months searching for him, and for the Englishwoman who was his accomplice. The police had been to the convent several times searching for an Englishwoman whom they believed lived in Paris, but who had not reported to the authorities as all foreign nationals were required to do. She also knew that Barney and this woman had posed as apple farmers in a village in Normandy the previous October, because she'd seen notices posted about the exploits of these two "criminals." Fortunately, the posters had not contained photos of the suspects.

"This is a good example of just how stupid the Germans really are," she said. "How could anyone ever believe that *you* were the wife of a farmer?" She pulled my carte d'identité from her pocket and showed it to me. "Helene Collette Dumont is a very pretty name, isn't it? Did you make it up? Or was it Father Barney's idea? Fortunately, we were able to retrieve the market bag you were carrying when you were shot."

I was so surprised by this I was speechless. She, and the other sisters who'd helped her, had known exactly who I was when they secreted me into the convent and hid me beneath their chicken coop. "Why?" I muttered. "Why did you help me? Why would you put yourselves in such danger?"

Marie Louise slid my identity card back into her skirt pocket. "There is not a sister here, not a single novitiate," she said, "who has not suffered in one way or another at the hands of the Boche. Some of us have seen our brothers killed, some our fathers. Our family members, our siblings, have been arrested and tortured. They've closed our businesses, our schools, taken over our homes, and confiscated our crops, our animals, our autos. Whatever they want, they take. Our young men have been forced into labor camps where they've been turned into skeletons. Our precious daughters, our future brides of the church, are now prostitutes, vessels of pleasure for animals lying in wait for any woman who is forced by desperate circumstances to search for food, while they gorge themselves on foie gras and champagne!

"The Boche come here often. They look under our narrow beds and in our empty cupboards and behind our ancient tapestries. They take what little food and medicines they find, and leave us with nothing. I suppose you know that France is forced to pay the German Army four-hundred million francs *a day* for their upkeep here on *our* soil! Our Reverend Mother, Marie Lorraine, gives their food collectors six dozen eggs every Monday . . . because she has to! She is a very savvy woman who speaks fluent German and she knows how to make the most of the fact that she had German ancestors from Alsace. What the Boche don't know is that her ancestors were Russian Jews who escaped the pogroms and fled to Metz in the 1850s, where they made a new life for themselves. And in the process of changing their identities, they converted to the *true* church."

Marie Louise let out a long sigh. "That's enough for today," she said, eyes flashing. "Now you know that we who live in this place are doing everything we can to oppose the Third Reich and the devil on its throne. One day this war will be over and all of them will burn in Hell for the reign of terror they've wrought on the sacred soil of France!"

As she pulled the blanket up around my shoulders, she said, "We're going to move you up to our hospital ward tonight. We have a flyer, a British pilot, hidden beneath the floorboards under the chapel altar. He has a broken hip and his right thigh is riddled with festering shrapnel. We must move him down here and put you elsewhere." My heart skipped a beat and I'm sure she saw concern on my face, because she took my hand and said, "Don't worry, Helene. We'll take good care of you." Then she gave me another shot and I slept through the afternoon.

That evening Marie Francine fed me broth and a crust of bread. As soon as I'd eaten, Marie Louise appeared and brought with her two men dressed in laborer's clothing. Both were short and stocky, at least sixty, and all business. They lifted me onto a canvas stretcher and hoisted me through an opening in the wall. The smell of fresh-baked bread wafted over me and I raised my head to look at my surroundings and realized I was being carried through a high-ceilinged kitchen. A group of young women dressed in the simple garb of novitiates stood at a stone sink scrubbing pots and pans. As the men who were carrying me turned to go around them, I craned my neck to see Marie Louise bend down and slide the door of a cupboard closed. Located on the lower right side of an immense hutch of numerous shelves of crockery, it was the opening I'd been passed through. Marie Louise began stacking plates and bowls back in front of the panel she'd just closed, and I marveled at the clever ruse the nuns had devised to conceal the underground room where I'd been kept.

The day before, Marie Francine had told me that the convent hospital comprised the entire third floor. When I entered it that evening, shutters were closed over the windows and the only light came from a few carefully placed candles. Several nuns were on duty, moving between the rows of beds, checking their patients. Two of them came forward and helped the two men move me from the stretcher to a bed. While one covered me with a blanket, Marie Francine bent over me and whispered, "I'm sorry, mademoiselle. We must cover your face again. We would not want anyone to see you, would we?"

As she reached for the gauze bandages, I raised my head for a quick glance around the room. It was about forty feet long by twenty feet wide and filled with two long rows of narrow white metal beds similar to those at St Mary's. The opposite side of the room had a row of tall windows aligned above the beds and was separated from my row by several fabric screens.

"That's the men's ward over there behind those screens," Marie Francine said. "Currently, we have thirty-two patients. The surgery is just beyond the wall at the back and there is a recovery area beside it where we have two additional beds." She began wrapping the length of gauze around my head, taking it over my ears and across my forehead. She paused for a moment before covering my eyes. "Is there something else you wish to see?"

"No, thank you. Maybe you can show me more of your hospital later. You see, I'm a nurse."

Her hands were still for a moment. "A nurse?" she whispered.

"Yes. I'm Assistant Matron in the emergency surgery unit of a large hospital in London."

At that moment, Marie Louise came down the aisle accompanied by a petite woman robed entirely in white. "How does it feel to be in a real bed?" she asked. She did not wait for my reply, but stepped aside so the woman in white could come closer. "This is our Reverend Mother," she explained, "Marie Lorraine."

I looked up, saw a pair of intelligent coffee-colored eyes set in a thin face etched with fine wrinkles, and managed a faint "bonsoir." The Reverend Mother took my hand. "Save your breath, my child," she counseled. "Conserve your energy for the days ahead. I'll be praying for you. Now I must go see about the British pilot and make sure he's comfortably situated beneath the chicken coop." She gave my hand a squeeze before she walked away.

Marie Francine ran the end of the roll of gauze over my eyes and secured it on the back of my head. I barely felt the needle as she administered the morphine, but was fully aware of the gentle sureness of her hands as she tucked the blanket close around me.

* * *

A *ding-ding-ding*—an annoying sound that would not stop—awakened me. I put my hands over my ears, but the *dinging* continued. A growl like that of a small dog rose in my throat and I squeezed my eyelids as tightly as I could against the disturbance. The bell stopped ringing as suddenly as it had begun, and I opened my eyes to bright sunlight and the sound of someone coming from the hallway.

The footsteps continued quickly down the center aisle of the ward and stopped at my bed. Marie Louise touched me on the shoulder and whispered, "Wake up, Helene." She turned to Marie Francine who was standing beside her. "Bring me the most disgusting chamber pot you can find," she said. "Get one that has vomit in it. And get the refuse bucket from the surgery."

She leaned over me and the scent of garlic filled the air. "It's the Boche," she whispered, " Lieutenant Colonel Osterlitz and his band of thugs. We're going to move you into the men's section. I have a space open for a bed there and an admittance form filled with false information. I want you to lie very, very still while I desecrate your nice clean bandages with blood. I'm going to give you a shot because I'll tell him that this patient is in a coma and I want you to appear as if you are. And then I'm going to pray to the Holy Mother and all the Saints above that he'll leave you alone." She turned from me and said, "Hurry up, Sister, with that bucket of blood."

The blood felt cool as it dripped through the gauze down onto the skin on the left side of my face. I felt several drops as they ran across my forehead just before I heard Marie Louise unlock the brake on the end of the bed. The wheels screamed in rusty protest as she and Marie Francine pushed it across the aisle and through an opening between two fabric screens. "Put that filthy chamber pot right under her," she said. "And bring me two blankets. Even if you have to take one from another patient, she has to have two more on top of her so her breasts won't show. Hurry, child, hurry. They're coming up the stairs!"

From the hallway came a loud voice, a grating voice, a commanding voice. Just as heavy footsteps started toward me, I felt the needle prick the skin of my upper arm. Quick light footsteps followed the heavy ones and a female voice said, "Guten morgen, Obersturmführer Osterlitz. To what do we owe this unexpected visit?" I could hear the Reverend Mother as she spoke in fluent German and what she'd said struck fear in my heart. Osterlitz. Surely it was not the same man, the Waffen-SS leader in Roscoff? The man whom Lily Suchette had outsmarted to save the lives of Barney, Pierre and Leon . . . the same man who'd come looking for Barney and me while we were hiding in monsieur's cellar in Merville.

The *clomp, clomp* of his heavy boots came closer and closer as my eyelids became heavier and heavier. Then I heard the Reverend Mother's clear voice again. "Surely you don't think we're giving aid to an Englishwoman here, Obersturmführer Osterlitz. This hospital exists to serve the good people of France, our good French Catholics. We would never give aid to a heretic Englander!"

"Shut up!" he shouted and his voice thundered through the room. "You think you're in charge of this miserable rat hole, but you're not! I am!" I tried to stay awake, tried to listen as he continued to berate her, but I gave up after I heard him say, "You'd do well to come to your senses, old woman, and realize that Paris is *my* city. And you, and your whores of the church, are nothing but filth in *my* gutters!"

* * *

Marie Francine awakened me at nine the next morning, told me it was Sunday, and handed me a cup of warm broth. With her help, I was able to sit up. "As soon as you finish your broth," she said, "we're going for a little walk. Not far because you must be careful and not overexert yourself." She pulled soft felt slippers over my feet and tied a worn flannel robe around me. We walked, arm in arm, very slowly up and down the length of the hospital ward twice. When a sharp pain stabbed just below the bullet wound, I jerked, and Marie Francine said, "That's enough for today."

She led me back to my bed and handed me a cup. I downed the water that had the slight taint of metal and knew she'd added a tablespoon of spirits of ammonia to help me relax. "No morphine today," she said, pulling a blanket up to my shoulders. "We must wean you off it. Before you go to sleep, I need to tell you that Reverend Mother has gotten a message to the BBC . . . *the school teacher is busy preparing her lessons* . . . I know your friends here in Paris, and in London, will be relieved when they hear it."

Before she could turn away, I grabbed Marie Francine's hand and kissed it. "For the Reverend Mother," I whispered, "and for all of you who are taking such good care of me." Moments later, I felt the warmth of the sun's rays spreading over my tired body, bringing with it a calmness that washed over me like a mother's love. And somewhere deep inside I knew that in that place of God, of care and healing, I could not have been in better hands.

I slept for several hours before Marie Francine woke me at two. She helped me sit up so I could eat a small bowl of broth with bits of potatoes and onions harvested from the convent's garden—the first solid food I'd had since I arrived—and held on to me while I squatted over a chamber pot. Afterward, she supported me as we walked up and down the length of the ward twice, which caused beads of sweat to break across my brow.

That's when she told me that while I'd been sleeping Osterlitz and his companion, a blonde woman wearing a gray suit and snap-brim fedora, had come again during the night and searched the convent, ransacking all the cupboards in the surgery and recovery area, as well as the cells of every nun. The next morning the Reverend Mother had asked Marie Francine to bring me to the kitchen at 8:45.

It was a beehive of activity when we went down. At the large wooden table, two of the youngest novitiates were wrapping freshly boiled eggs in a towel to take out to the Nazi guards who were going off duty at nine—something they did every morning in an effort to keep the two young men distracted while the sisters moved their secret charges to different hiding places.

Marie Louise bade me sit down at the table where a bowl of hot porridge—an unbelievable luxury—was steaming. "Eat! Eat, mademoiselle! This will be your only meal today." She pressed a crust of hard brown bread into my hand and set a saucer of hot water nearby in which to dip it. The porridge was tasteless and the bread so tough I could hardly get it down, but get it down I did. I finished just before the Reverend Mother appeared bearing a lighted lantern. She came straight to the table, sat down across from me, and in her comforting voice said, "We've prepared everything for you, child, for your stay in le cache—our safest hideaway. I regret that it is rough and barely habitable. But it will have to do until you're strong enough to get around on your own. Open the drawer, Sister."

As Marie Francine stepped away from the table, she made a slight bow to the Reverend Mother. She walked across the room, dropped to her knees, and pulled the handle on a large drawer at the bottom of a built-in cupboard. The Reverend Mother rose from the table and we followed her to where Marie Francine was waiting. I heard a clicking sound, metal against metal, and watched as she lifted the drawer from the rollers on which it had rested and set it aside on the stone floor. She turned back to the opening, and a moment later, drew out on the same set of rollers a wooden box large enough to accommodate a person six feet tall.

Marie Francine surprised me by removing her wimple and exposing her shaved head. She took the lighted lantern from Reverend Mother, sat down in the box, and gathered her skirts around her. She lay back, and while she pushed with her palms against the walls of the cupboard that were on either side, she and the box disappeared from view.

A moment later, the empty box rolled back into the kitchen and Reverend Mother held out her hand to me. I took it, stepped into the box, and slowly lowered myself onto the bottom. The thought of being confined in la cache filled me with dread, and several moments passed before I was able to make myself lie down and push off as Marie Francine had. I ended up inside a small space where the flame from the lantern threw shafts of light onto four dark walls. Just beyond the foot of the box, I could see the lower rungs of a crude ladder and followed the light up the wall with my eyes to find Marie Francine's sweet face peering down at me. "Slowly," she said from the opening above. "Come up the ladder slowly." And slowly I went because my left side felt as if the tines of a pitch fork had been buried in it.

After I'd finally reached the top rung, Marie Francine took both my hands and held on to me while I stepped off the ladder. My nose twitched at the odor of dead mouse. So, this smelly little hole will be my secret sanctuary, I thought, peering into a space no larger than a closet. The interior was about eight feet long, less than four feet wide, and the entire wall on my right consisted of curved brass pipes—the backs of the pipes of the chapel's organ. The wall opposite was made of rough boards that went straight up to a ceiling perhaps twelve feet high. The end wall, just under the eaves, was tall and narrow, and contained two small windows. A crude low-lying bed frame was attached to the wall opposite the pipes. It held a mattress and pillow, neatly arranged with fresh sheets, and two woolen blankets. In the far corner was a small upholstered chair and chamber pot. A tin pitcher and cup sat on a small shelf nearby.

Marie Francine got down on her knees and grabbed the sides of the ladder. She pulled it up through the opening and stood it against the wall. Then she closed the door and turned the hasps on the two locks that secured it. "The man who built this was a very fine carpenter," she said. "Even if someone were to discover the secret drawer in the kitchen cupboard downstairs, and the box hidden inside it, they would not know la cache is up here because they wouldn't be able to see it. The entire wall on the opposite side appears as if it were one unbroken structure. When I leave, you must draw up the ladder like I just did, slide the bolts on the locks, and be very quiet. You must not move around much. But do try to sit in the little chair several times a day. During the daytime, there's enough light coming from those two high windows for you to read, and as soon as you're well enough I'll bring you some books." She turned to go, but stopped to hand me a couple of brown eggs she'd drawn from her pocket. "Hard boiled," she said, "for later when you get hungry. There's water in the pitcher on the wall shelf."

She slid each of the locks, opened the wooden panel that served as the door, and carefully slid the ladder down to the floor of the opening beneath her. Just before she left, she said, "Don't forget to pull up the ladder and slide the locks, cheri. I'll come back at three in the morning to check on you. I'll knock twice, then twice again—four short knocks. It's the knock we use here at the convent . . . a knock for each sign of the cross. Say your prayers and rest, mam'selle. May God be with you." Then she disappeared down the ladder into the dark hole below. I heard the rollers hum as she pushed herself back through the opening that went into the kitchen. It took all the strength I had, and then some, to hoist the ladder back up. I broke into a sweat and had to sit on the bed for a moment to catch my breath. Several moments passed before I'd recovered enough to get up and lock myself in.

That was surely the longest day—and night—of my life. I lay on the bed for hours, until I could stand it no longer. Then I got up and sat in the little chair. Thunderstorms began in the night and continued off and on all morning, lashing rain against the two windows, producing an all-consuming gloominess that dragged me down. I had no idea of the time and longed for the pretty French-made watch I'd worn on the train. Where was it? I wondered. What had they done with it? Where were my clothes?

As storms raged outside, I wrestled with a storm in my head. I tried to remember what had happened to me. I knew I'd been on a train and had gotten off at Gare du Nord. I remembered seeing a woman in a gray suit on the baggage platform. I kept trying to figure out why she was following me. What had given me away? And how could I have even been so naive as to think I could complete this mission alone? But, according to Marie Louise, I had. She'd assured me that the diamonds were moving from one pair of hands to another securing equipment, supplies, and weapons to fight the Nazis.

That day passed so slowly I thought I'd lose my mind. There was nothing to see, no one to talk to, nothing to keep me occupied. I was fidgety and restless as my mind raced from one thing to another, a side-effect of the morphine. Waves washed over me . . . waves of loss, waves of hurt, waves of fear. The present, the past, the future danced like wraiths in my head.

Late in the day the rain stopped and sounds came from the kitchen below. I could hear the sisters talking, could hear the occasional scrape of metal, could smell the smoke from the fire. How I missed the hearth at Corrie Cottage and Jerusha's sweet face, and Sylvia's latest story from "The Hole." If only I could see Miriam in her crisp uniform going about her business at St Mary's. I was surprised to find that I missed Stoney's reassuring presence most of all.

While mice skittered in the wall beside me, I dozed for several hours. Marie Francine knocked four times and I slid the bolts on the door and lowered the ladder. She climbed only half way up and handed me two books: Victor Hugo's *Les Misérables* and *The Hunchback of Notre Dame*. "For tomorrow," she said, "when you have light. Marie Louise wants you to come down now if you feel well enough. She wants me to take you for a walk while the Nazi guards are asleep."

Once we were in the kitchen, Marie Francine handed me a cup of warm broth and a crust of bread that I devoured in two bites. She put her arm around my waist and together we walked up and down the hallway three times. This became our nightly routine, and eventually I was able to walk unassisted for fifteen minutes. Afterward, we often sat for an hour or so in the kitchen while she told me about her busy day nursing in the hospital, about how the British pilot was progressing, how he was up and walking. And I told her about Michelle, the woman who'd swallowed the diamonds, and Lily Suchette, and how she'd saved not only my life, but the lives of Barney, Leon, and Pierre. About five o'clock a thin sliver of light began creeping over the windowsill bringing our conversations to an end. I reluctantly lay down inside the long drawer and pushed myself back into the dark hole where the crude ladder stood waiting.

As the days passed, I found myself adapting more and more to a routine. In the mornings when the sunlight was best, I read. I knew when it was noon not only because I was famished, but because I could hear lots of activity from the kitchen below. I ate my boiled egg and drank a cup of water at almost the same time every day. Afterward, I took a nap.

When I awoke, I tried desperately to find something to occupy my mind. I practiced Morse code by tapping my fingers on the wall beside the bed. Then I played every recital piece

I'd ever learned on the piano in the same fashion. In my head I sang every line of every song from every show I'd been in and recreated all the dance routines that accompanied them. And I wrote dozens and dozens of imaginary letters—to my mother, my sister Claire, to Miriam, Sylvia and Jerusha, and to my old friend in New York, Winifred Trask.

Several days passed without a visit from Osterlitz. But one afternoon when I was sitting in the little chair reading about Jean Valjean, I heard a commotion and realized that someone was in the chapel. I recognized his booming voice immediately, and heard Marie Louise's contained words as she carefully answered his questions. A few moments later, his heavy tread pounded the floor above me and particles of debris began drifting down from the ceiling. I sat as still as a statue, the book open in my hands, while he paced up and down the hospital ward. Finally, he stomped away, but it was a while before I resumed my reading.

When I looked up again from my book, a thin ray of sunlight had stretched itself across the floor at my feet. I followed it with my eyes along the boards to a crack in the wall just beneath one of the windows. I was elated to discover that I could lift the little chair without help, and I set it down beneath that little crack. Then I climbed up on it, pressed my forehead against the rough planks, and looked out toward the garden. What a wondrous site . . . my first glimpse of the outside world in weeks. But my wonder changed to fear when I discovered Osterlitz standing just inside the gate arrayed in all his Germanic glory—spotless black SS uniform gleaming with whorls of shiny gold braid, silver lightning bolts on his collar flashing in the sun, and the menacing *totenkopf*, the hollow-eyed Death's Head insignia, glaring from his cap. I was surprised to see what a large man he was—at least six three—and sporting a substantial paunch, testimony to the good food he was enjoying at the expense of the French. I watched as he turned toward the convent, raised his right arm, and began punching the air in obvious defiance. He seemed the epitome of the Aryan superman and it was in that telling moment I realized, in a most fundamental way, what I was up against.

At three o'clock the following morning, Marie Francine appeared and we went down to the kitchen together where I drank a cup of broth and ate a bowl of cold gruel. From her pocket, she brought out an envelope of heavy cream-colored vellum and I knew right away what it was.

My dearest, dearest girl: How I miss your beautiful face, your lovely smile, your warm laughter. I'm utterly devastated by your situation, and feel totally useless. But B assures me that his contacts there say you're making progress and healing well. I'm holding you close and praying for you every moment. My precious darling—how I miss you. S

As I folded the note and put it in my pocket, I was suddenly overcome with a deep sadness and, without warning, my nose began to run while my eyes filled with tears, and I dissolved into a sodden mess. Marie Francine put her arm around my shoulder and followed me up the ladder to la cache where she sat down on the bunk beside me and fingered her beads over and over praying aloud for my recovery.

Three mornings later, I found Reverend Mother waiting for me at the kitchen table. "I want to have a word with you in private," she said, motioning to Marie Francine who slipped out of the room. I sat down, and as I bit into a slice of brown bread smeared with chicken grease, she lowered her voice. "We have another pilot who is dangerously ill and we need you in our hospital, mademoiselle. Not only do we need your skills and experience, but this will be a good way for you to build up strength while you're recovering."

I put the last bite of bread in my mouth and began to chew, hoping to give myself some time to think. I was not sure that I was strong enough to work. But before I could respond, Marie Francine came in again bringing a habit, a wimple, and a pair of old shoes. The Reverend Mother rose from her chair and took the items from her. "Three months ago," she said, "we lost Sister Marie Annette, lost her to pneumonia. This was her habit. She was about your size, not quite as tall. And she was considerably older, so we'll have to see to that. I have her papers and a few of her personal possessions. She was Annette Gervais and she came to us from Lyon." She put the clothing and shoes on the table and sat down beside me.

From under her habit, she brought out a pair of old-fashioned, wire-rimmed glasses and a tiny gray blob that looked like bookmaker's glue. I took it from her and asked, "What's this?"

She surprised me when she began to giggle. "It's a wart," she said, trying to contain herself. "Look closely, child. It even has a little gray hair in it. It's for your chin, to make you look older and less attractive. Marie Francine made it for you."

She touched her fingertips to the back of my hand and I looked into her kind eyes. "I'm very sorry, but we'll have to cut your hair. That gorgeous spun copper cannot be longer than two inches to accommodate our headdress. And we'll have to do something about your auburn eyebrows, as well." She set a small rectangular box on the table. Faded and worn at the edges, I could see that it had once been red. Inside was a strip of light brown mascara and a little black brush. How could such a thing exist in a convent?

Reverend Mother rose from the table. "One last thing before we say good night." She opened her right hand and in her palm was a thin gold band. She took my left hand in hers and gently pushed the ring over the knuckle of my left ring finger. "You must wear this ring at all times, Sister Marie Annette, for you now are a Bride of Christ."

I backed away and pulled the ring from my finger. "No, I'm not," I said, handing it back to her. "And I can't be even for you, Reverend Mother. You've been so kind to me. You, and the sisters, have saved my life. But I'm not worthy of the mantle of a nun."

Reverend Mother bade me sit down again and lowered herself onto the bench. "You told Sister Marie Francine that you were a nurse. Is that not so?"

"I *am* a nurse," I replied, nervously picking at a fingernail. "But I wasn't always. And the life I led before I came to London two years ago . . . well, it wasn't the kind of life a woman leads before she's accepted into an order of nuns. It would be a sacrilege for me to put on the habit of Sister Marie Annette and pretend to be the pious woman she was."

Reverend Mother turned to me and her dark eyes met mine. "How do you know she was pious? What do you know of Sister Marie Annette?"

"Nothing beyond the fact that she was good and pure and wholesome. She must have been, or she wouldn't have been allowed to join your order."

"On that score, my child, you're wrong. Annette Gervais was thirty-six when she came here and begged us to take her in. She worked as a charwoman scrubbing floors and doing laundry for six years before she asked if she might study to take her vows. Before that, she'd earned her living on the streets of Lyon to provide for her two children. Each had a different father and Annette had no idea who they were. Is that the kind of life *you* led in America?"

I was puzzled by Annette's story and not sure how to answer. But I was so uncomfortable at the thought of pretending to be a Bride of Christ that I felt I had to say something. "No," I said in a small voice. "I was raised in a close-knit family by loving parents who gave me a good education. When I was young, I dreamed of going to New York to sing and dance onstage. And after I finished nursing school, I did that. And I fell in love . . . very deeply in love with a married man. And I knew he was married when I started going out with him."

"So, you are a sinner," Reverend Mother said, "like the rest of us."

"Well, I didn't start out that way. You see I was very young, only eighteen, when I went to New York. I was different from the woman I am now."

Reverend Mother reached out to squeeze my hand. "Why don't you let us be the judge of the woman you are now?"

CHAPTER 20

The Ace

Paris, France • June 12, 1943

When I first saw her lying on a hospital bed, Ireni Igorsky was burning with fever and racked by delirium. Her white blonde hair, matted with gummy oil, lay close against her head like a cap. A patch of dark bruises dotted the right side of her face, a deep cut split her chin, and bloody lacerations carved a hatch work down the right side of her neck.

I hurried down the aisle between the hospital beds to the surgery where the Reverend Mother and Marie Louise were covering the operating table with clean sheets. Beside it the small workstation held towels, sutures, bandages of all types and sizes, various beakers, and rubber tubes. On the counter behind the worktable a sterilizer bubbled, purifying instruments while it filled the room with steam. Above all, in beautifully carved wood, was la Vierge Marie.

Marie Francine and Marie Louise wheeled our pilot in and I helped them lift her onto the table. As the Reverend Mother and Marie Louise removed the cotton blanket from around her, I drew a sharp breath and restrained myself from commenting about her injuries. How she had survived was beyond me. Her right thigh, swollen twice normal size, was loosely wrapped in layers of blood-soaked bandages. Her right shoulder was braced in a sling of makeshift splints that was held in place by strips of filthy cambric. I picked up a pair of scissors and began snipping at the bandages around her thigh while Marie Louise cut fabric from her shoulder. When our patient began moaning, Reverend Mother looked up and indicated we should keep going. "We have only two vials of morphine," she whispered. "I wanted to wait until the last possible minute to give her an injection because she'll need it more when we finish than she does now."

After I'd removed the last layer of bandage, I stepped away from the table. Never before had I seen human flesh so butchered. Shrapnel had torn completely through the muscles of Ireni's thigh, leaving long red gashes oozing with pockets of white pus. Around her kneecap was a pattern of radiating bluish streaks—the first sign of gangrene. As I began to probe the gashes, Ireni cried out and Marie Louise administered the morphine. I asked for a magnet but was told there was none. Reverend Mother called Marie Francine from the hospital ward and sent her out to find one. "Magnets are verboten in France," she said, "as you probably know. The Germans would never allow us to have anything as valuable as a magnet. So, we don't have one. But I think I know someone who does." She closed her eyes and her lips moved for a moment and I knew she was praying that the magnet could be found.

Ten minutes later, Marie Francine returned, removed a small magnet from inside her tunic, and handed it to me. Grasping it with a pair of small tongs, I dipped it into the boiling water of the sterilizer. Then I began passing it back and forth just above Ireni's thigh.

Tiny shards of dark metal surfaced along the pus-filled gashes, popping out like black ants on snow. Using a pair of tweezers, the Reverend Mother began removing them. While we worked on her thigh, Marie Louise washed Ireni's head with a solution of warm water and carbolic. When Reverend Mother was satisfied that all the shards of metal were gone, she cleaned Ireni's thigh, sprinkled it with sulfonamide powder, and I helped put on a new dressing.

Later, as we sat drinking mutton broth at the table in the kitchen, I commented to Reverend Mother that I thought our Russian pilot had a good chance of recovering. She shook her head. "Not unless a miracle occurs," she said in a matter-of-fact tone as if reading a bus schedule. "Our medicines are gone. Osterlitz took all we had the last time he was here searching for you. I had two vials of morphine and a packet of sulfonamide powder in the inside pocket of my habit which we used on the pilot today. Our last gallon jar of carbolic is reduced to an inch and our supply of ammonia is less than that. I've exhausted all my usual contacts. There's no one to help us. Osterlitz has screwed a lid down over this city and nothing comes in or goes out that he doesn't know about. And anyone caught smuggling drugs, or any item that is verboten, is subject to a firing squad. I don't know when I've been more discouraged. I've prayed night and day that God would help me find a way to save those poor souls in our hospital, especially that young Russian. Just think what she's been through, what she must have suffered to get here. But God has brought her to us and we must help her."

"Perhaps God does have a way," I said. "Perhaps He has given *me* a way to help. Where is the Hotel Albert? Is it nearby? Do you know of it?"

She told me it was two blocks south just beyond rue St. Denis. Her boney fingers encircled my wrist. "You cannot go anywhere, Annette," she whispered. "The guards will arrest you the moment you walk out the door."

I told her I had a contact at the Hotel Albert, a man named Marcel Guillion, whom I would visit that very night. "Please tell me how to get there," I begged.

Reverend Mother rose from the kitchen table and I followed her to the tall windows along the east wall. "There," she said, pointing toward the cemetery. "There, on the far side of the cemetery fence is a path that leads past those apple trees. You take that path through the orchard until it opens onto an alley. Walk up the alley as far as the stone building, La Cremerie. The back entrance to Hotel Albert is directly across from it. Knock softly twice, then twice again, just as we do here in the convent. Someone will answer that knock, I assure you."

She turned and started back toward the table. "This is madness!" she said, her voice laced with a shrillness that surprised me. "I can't have it on my conscience!" She looked at me with pleading eyes. "Please, my child, don't do this. You've escaped the jaws of death and now you want to tempt fate again?"

I shook my head. "I have to. Don't you see? I *have* escaped the jaws of death and I must help others do the same. You helped me . . . and I must help them."

She sat down at the table, cradled her head in her hands, and whispered, "God forgive me." I stood beside the table waiting for what seemed a long time. Finally, she looked up at me, eyes flashing, and said, "Speak to no one! There are German spies all over this city dressed as Frenchwomen, who speak French like they were born here. They pass themselves off as prostitutes and hotel maids and they're out and about in the night. They disguise themselves and they're clever . . . you know? Yes, I'm sure *you* do know."

Often at night Reverend Mother would go outside to talk with the four Nazi guards and take them something to eat or drink. They seemed to respect her and obviously appreciated that she spoke fluent German. That particular night, she held back four cups of broth from the usual amount allotted for our supper. At midnight, she and I flavored that broth with a touch of the last of our precious store of spirits of ammonia. Then she and pretty Marie Francine poured it into four mugs and took it out to those men. An hour later, all of them were nestled against the stone balustrades at the front and back doors sound asleep.

It was a clear night and I had no trouble finding my way through the orchard. I encountered no one, thank God, as I hurried down the alleyway to the back entrance of the Hotel Albert. I knocked twice, then twice more. A heavyset man with a beard opened the door and said, "What is it, Sister?"

"Monsieur Guillion?" I asked. He nodded and invited me into the safety of the kitchen. I told him my name was Helene and explained why I was wearing the habit of a nun. "And what a pretty nun you are, mademoiselle," he said, his eyes twinkling. "Barney sent word just last week telling me that you had completed the mission and had been rescued by the sisters. Why would you expose yourself by coming here to the hotel?"

I told Marcel about the Russian pilot, that she'd been shot down by the Germans and brought to Paris by the Maquis de Melun.

Marcel nodded. "The network says she's known as the white rose of Stalingrad," he whispered.

"White rose?" I asked. "I don't understand. What are you talking about?"

"Your pilot," he said. "She's from Stalingrad and she's famous . . . an ace."

I paused, taking a moment to try to figure out just what that meant. "All I know is this young woman, this pilot, is in a lot of trouble. And if we don't find some morphine and sulfonamide powder, she'll surely die."

Marcel nodded and said he might be able to get some of both, but it would take time. He walked me to the door and asked me to come back the next night.

So I went back through the alley and down the orchard path empty-handed to find the Reverend Mother waiting for me at the wrought iron gate. We walked past the sleeping guards and did not speak until we reached the safety of the kitchen. There, I told her I felt sure Marcel would try to help us. She fell to her knees on that old scarred floor and began saying her beads, and I went down beside her saying mine.

The following night when Marcel answered the door he was holding a burlap bag in his hand. He told me that it contained twenty-four glass vials of precious morphine, each wrapped separately in cotton wool, and two dozen envelopes of sulfonamide powder. He was sorry he'd not been able to get any ammonia. He asked that I take off my habit as quickly as I could, and after I had, he tied the bag around my waist with a piece of rope. He turned to a barrel of potatoes sitting on the floor behind him and added two dozen to the bag before he cinched it up. "The Germans have everything," he said as he pulled the rope tightly around my waist and tied it in a knot. "And they are so careless about their stores of food." Then he helped me get back into my habit and knelt to straighten the hem of my skirts so the bag wouldn't be seen when I walked. He took my hand and kissed it before I stepped out the door and ran to the shadowy path that led to the orchard.

Thanks to those medicines, Ireni improved. Marie Francine soon had her walking slowly up and down the ward with the help of a padded crutch. Her complexion brightened, her blonde hair shone, her appetite returned, and she began to talk. I asked how she'd come to be so far away from home, how she'd gotten so far west, how she'd been wounded. She gave me a blank stare and said in fluent French, "I don't remember. There was this young girl . . . I can't recall her name . . . but her father is Henri. I remember that I was flying above a forest and Katya and Lily were in the plane with me. We'd just completed a mission . . . a bombing mission over Saarbrücken in Western Germany. Every week, the Germans fly planes filled with food, equipment, and supplies into Saarbrücken where it's off-loaded onto railroad cars and sent across the border to their army bases in France. We'd just demolished those rail lines and were headed home when a couple of Messerschmitts came out of nowhere and started firing at us. Then, one day I woke up, and an angel of mercy was dressing the wounds in my thigh. That angel was you, Marie Annette. I remember *that* very well. But it's very frustrating not knowing what happened to me before."

Another week went by and Ireni continued to improve. Each morning after her wounds were cleaned and her dressings changed, she and Reverend Mother talked. They conversed in German, most of their conversation about conditions in Russia and the joyous news of the collapse of Hitler's eastern front. One morning, the Reverend Mother found Marie Francine and me in the kitchen and told us to come up to the hospital. "She's getting her memory back," she said. "Our pilot is beginning to talk about what happened, how she was shot down, how she was rescued. You'd better come. She's ready to tell us about it."

CHAPTER 21

Hog Trough

Catelle, France • June 23, 1943

That morning, Valeria Porovna and I were flying our two Yak-6Ms as a team. Katya Maisky and Lily Shulik were seated behind me in the positions of navigator and gunner. I was swooping around trying to draw a Stuka away from Valeria's plane so she could zero in on our target, the railroad below. Right after she'd made the hit, we flew off in opposite directions to get away. But two Messerschmitts came at us and started firing and everything happened so fast I lost sight of Valeria. I dove and veered west to try to escape, employing my usual trick by taking the plane down a thousand feet to try to hide. Suddenly, a forest rose up like a wall right in front of me. I spotted a break in the trees that I thought might be a road, so I threw the stick forward. I kept diving toward it until a mass of green branches came rushing up at me. I stood on the rudders, hauling back on the stick with all the strength I had, trying to hold steady as we zigzagged toward what I hoped was a strip of dirt. But I lost control of the stick—it jumped right out of my hand—and the right wing dug into the ground, spinning the plane around and throwing it against a tree. That's when I must have blacked out.

When I came to, I could hear the Messerschmitts overhead searching for us. My seat belt had disappeared into the wall of the fuselage, so I had to use my knife to cut myself free. That took a long time, and in the process, I discovered

I'd been hit in my right thigh. I had a hard time doing it, but after several tries, I was able to hoist myself up out of my seat. I called and called for Katya and Lily and tried to turn around to look at them, but my shoulder wouldn't turn. My thigh was a bloody mess, but my left leg and left arm seemed to be okay. I thought I'd never get the hatch over the cockpit open because I had to keep moving it back and forth, over and over, until it finally gave. Then I dragged myself up on the side of the rim and slid very slowly down onto a narrow span of canvas, the only thing that remained of the wings. From there, I eased my body down to the ground and slithered along on my left side like a snake.

I'd stuffed my pockets with chocolate bars and a small thermos of tea, and I had my knife and pistol. I used the knife to cut a strip of canvas from the plane that I wrapped around my thigh to try to stop the bleeding. Then I cut another piece I thought I'd use for cover because I was shaking with cold. I knew I had to get away from the plane and try to find somewhere to hide, but my thigh was throbbing so badly I could hardly move. Finally, I dragged myself under a bush and pulled the piece of canvas over me. I must have passed out again because I don't remember much after that.

Something moving through the brush woke me. At first, I thought it was a bird. But when I opened my eyes, I saw a young boy who appeared to be about ten years old. He told me his name was Jacques and that he lived on a farm nearby. I pushed the canvas cover off and when he saw my bloody leg he cried, "Mon Dieu!" and ran away.

About an hour later, he returned with another boy taller than he. The older boy was dressed in rough blue work pants and a homespun shirt and had a brown beret pulled down over his ears. When he knelt beside me and asked how I was feeling, I knew immediately that he was not Jacque's big brother, but his sister. She introduced herself as Suzette Charbone and told me the Germans were going house-to-house in Catelle, the village near their farm, and they would surely find me if I remained where I was. She sent Jacques to find two downed tree limbs. Then she took my knife and went back to the plane and cut three long strips of canvas from the struts.

After the two of them made a travois from the canvas and tree limbs, they dragged me onto a wide piece in the center and strapped me to it. I must have passed out again, because all I remember is the smell of clean bed linens when I awoke sometime that afternoon. Suzette told me she'd removed the bloody canvas from around my thigh, cleaned my wounds, and put on a fresh bandage. While she spooned goat curds through my broken lips, she said that she and Jacques had set my shoulder with splints. I slept off and on the rest of the day.

That evening, she stewed a chicken and boiled some eggs and fed me again. She said I needed a doctor and she was sending Jacques to get one as soon as he returned from Catelle, where he'd gone to try to learn what the Germans knew about the plane crash. Just before she blew out the candle on the bedside table, she held a mug of brandy to my lips. "You must drink all of this," she said, "for strength."

She awakened me at dawn the next morning and gave me a cup of warm water. After I'd drunk it, she helped me sit up and put a heavy shawl around my shoulders. "Jacques has returned, mademoiselle, and we must move you. The Gestapo is searching all the farms, so you must hide. We have only one place to put you and it is not pleasant. But we must do what we must if we are to live."

Jacques put his arm around my waist and Suzette lifted me under my left arm. They dragged me along from the bedroom through the kitchen and out the back door. It was a bit of a chore getting there, but we finally arrived at a hog pen beside their barn. Suzette opened the gate, pulled a handful of garbage from inside her pocket, and threw it to the far side of the pen. Four sows and their numerous progeny, a dozen or more shoats and piglets, squealed as they raced toward it. Jacques let go of me and knelt down at the end of a large feeding trough. He pulled the end plank straight up and completely out of the grooves that held it in place, exposing an opening that was perhaps two feet across and a foot deep. "You must hide in there," Suzette said, pointing to the hole. She snatched a feed sack from a nearby wheelbarrow, laid it in the filth beneath the edge of the opening, and she and Jacques helped me lower myself onto it. Then they grabbed the sides of the sack, lifting my head and shoulders first, and slid me into the opening. By using my left arm and left hip, I was able to wiggle further and further down inside it. The stench of hog feces and urine was so overwhelming I feared I'd throw up, but all I did was shake. Just as I drew my feet in, Suzette said, "Here they come!" and the plank on the end of the trough came down like the blade of a guillotine.

A *thump, thump* sounded above me and a disgusting odor made me gag as Suzette filled the trough with watery garbage. The hogs were snorting and snuffling and gobbling all around me, so I didn't hear the car when it arrived. But I could hear the sounds of men's voices when they began yelling at Suzette and Jacques. One man gave an order to search the house and barn. Another man, who sounded a bit younger, replied, "Jawohl, Mein Stabsfeldwebel!" I never heard the gate to the hog pen open, so I assumed that Suzette and Jacques were still standing in the muck near the trough and the Stabsfeldwebel remained outside the pen.

The soldiers returned to report they'd found nothing. This must have made Herr Stabsfeldwebel furious because he exploded with abuse. This was followed by a sound like that made when metal crashes into metal, and I assumed he'd picked up a shovel or a hoe and thrown it at the wheelbarrow. Then he started yelling again. He threatened Suzette and Jacques, telling them he would burn down their house and barn if they didn't tell him where the Russian pilot was. I could hear Suzette pleading with him, telling him they knew nothing, only what they'd heard in the village—a plane had gone down.

"Please, Herr Stabsfeldwebel," I heard her pleading, "we are simple ignorant farmers. We don't know anything about planes or the people who fly them."

Herr Stabsfeldwebel asked where their parents were and Jacques replied that they were dead. When Herr Stabsfeldwebel accused him of lying, Jacques began to cry and the master sergeant began cursing again. Mud-sucking footsteps came toward me and I heard the sound of a pistol shot, the squeal of the pig, and a *thunk* reverberated beside my head.

"Pick it up, you idiot," Herr Stabsfeldwebel shouted.

"Stay calm," Suzette whispered as she bent down beside the trough to retrieve the body of the dead pig. I heard the screech of the hinges when she opened the gate and another when the car's trunk was opened and shut. Moments later, the sound of the car's engine faded.

Suzette heated two buckets of water on the stove in the kitchen and poured them into a tin tub in the backyard. She undressed me, and she and Jacques held on to me while I stood in the tub and she scrubbed the shit off me using handfuls of sand, all the while apologizing because she had no soap. They covered me with an old robe and took me back to bed. Even though my thigh was throbbing and I was in a great deal of pain, I slept. Several hours later, Suzette woke me to introduce me to her father, Henri, and to another man standing nearby, Gaston.

"They are taking you away from Catelle, mademoiselle," she said as she removed the only blanket from the bed and wrapped it around me. Henri held an open bottle to my lips and whatever it was I swallowed had a bitter taste. He picked me up in his arms and went out the back door. Behind the barn, another man waited in a truck powered by a gasogene engine. Gaston opened the door for Henri, who somehow managed to slide in with me in his arms. We started down a path that took us into the woods and not long after that I went to sleep. I have no memory of them bringing me here to the convent.

* * *

One day my favorite patient surprised me by asking why I was hiding in a convent trying to pass myself off as a nun. When I told her I'd grown up on a farm near Lyon, she just laughed. "You're a fine actress, mademoiselle. But your demeanor and lovely hands give you away. You're not a woman who has toiled in the fields or scrubbed clothes on a washboard. Believe me when I tell you I'm intimately acquainted with women who've lived that life. There's nothing bourgeoise about you either. You may be a French aristocrat, a grand lady perhaps, fallen on hard times. You're not a nun."

I smiled as I nodded to her. "You're a clever girl, Captain Igorsky," I said, "and very observant. But I'm no hero like you and I haven't survived a plane crash. How frightening that must have been. I can't imagine having the skills, or the nerve, to fly a plane . . . especially a fighter. Where did you learn to fly?"

Ireni cocked her head to one side. "I learned at an Osoaviakhim—what you might call a camp—a place where young people in Russia compete in various sports, learn to climb a rock face, how to handle a pistol and rifle . . . and for some, master the skill of flying gliders and planes. Growing up, all I dreamed about was flying airplanes."

CHAPTER 22

Forget You're a Woman

Stalingrad, Russia • September 12, 1942

When I was little, my father worked in a chemical plant on the Volga River where he was the factory's carpenter. His name was Andrei Igorsky and he was born on a farm outside Moscow in 1899. He met my mother, Fanya, in 1919 when she was working in a glass factory there and they married later that year. In 1924, Comrade Stalin was named Leader of the Party and put into place the first of his Five-Year Plans, one that called for rapid industrialization and the establishment of economic collectives. My parents moved to Stalingrad so my father could work in a plant collective while my mother stayed home to look after us. I had a brother two years older, Volodya; and another, Anton, who was three years younger. I was seven when our little sister, Natalia, was born.

We lived on the outskirts of the city in a simple structure with a living area downstairs that included a kitchen with an indoor pump. There were two small sleeping rooms upstairs. On the back side of the kitchen was a stone-walled wine keep. Prior to the Revolution, our house had been part of an estate owned by a wealthy aristocratic family. The year I turned four, my father made a bargain with the head of a dairy collective and brought home a cow. He traded some of his beautiful carvings of the patron saints for a half dozen chickens. Then he spent hours converting the wine keep into a barn with a stall for the cow and, down one wall, nesting cubbies for the chickens. During the long winters, the stove in our kitchen kept it just above freezing.

Beneath the kitchen my father had a workshop where he did his carving and made furniture. It was just a small cellar with walls of clay that had been punctured with dozens of "weep holes" to let in air. My father spent long hours there in the evenings, working by lantern light, turning salvage lumber into simple tables and benches for our house. He'd built a rather ingenious little entry into the wall of the hallway on the first floor that led down into his secret place. It looked just like one of a half dozen crude panels he'd installed there, but if you pushed the top right corner with your fingertip, it would open. When this panel was closed, we were not to bother him . . . but if it was open, we could go down for a visit, which I did often.

At the age of seven, I was awarded a scholarship to one of the most prestigious academies in Stalingrad. When I climbed aboard the tram each morning, I felt very grown up crossing the city alone, and very fortunate to have been selected for this honor. I loved my classes, especially mathematics and languages. I excelled in French and German, probably because my maternal grandmother, who was from Brandenburg, had taught me both from the time I could talk. I made top marks in all my subjects. It would have been a disgrace for my family if I had not.

When I turned fourteen, I begged my parents to let me join the Osoaviakhim—an outdoor school where one could learn to fly. For free. I had several friends, girls and boys, who were studying to become pilots and longed to join them. On Saturday mornings, they went out to an old airfield that had been built during the last war and learned to fly gliders. That was all the rage then with young people. My parents were horrified at the idea and forbade me to even visit the airfield. But I sneaked out there often and some of my friends took me up with them. Oh, how I loved that feeling of complete freedom that came with soaring high above the earth! The thrill of looking down on treetops and watching the birds that came to fly alongside us spoiled me for ordinary things like riding in automobiles. Nothing in my life has ever compared to seeing farmers below stop working in their fields to wave to us as we floated silently overhead. I got into trouble at school for daydreaming about performing aerial stunts in a flying circus. I wanted to wear a suit and goggles like the pilots wore. I wanted to get into a real airplane, grab the stick, and do crazy-eights until I was giddy. Most girls my age dreamed of being another Pavlova, but I dreamed of being another Raskova, the founder of the Soviet Women's Air Force.

After my brother, Volodya, finished school, he was taken into the plant where our father worked and apprenticed to a master mechanic. The following year, our father was killed in a horrible accident. He and two other men were leaning against an outside wall when it collapsed on top of them. We never got to see our father again because they brought him home in a wooden box that had been nailed shut. After his burial, the Party gave my mother five hundred kopeks and told her to report to the factory the following week. She was assigned a job in the packing shed.

The year I turned sixteen I completed my schooling at the academy and began taking flying lessons at the airfield. The club had only three machines on which to learn, all old salvaged biplanes. There were two Anatra Ds, their fuselages covered in thin plywood; and one Lebed-VII, which had been manufactured in Russia, but fashioned on the British Sopwith model. The latter was my favorite because it was easy to handle and had such a sensitive rudder that I could maneuver it through the tightest spots. At first, I lied to my mother about where I was going when I went to the airfield, but after a few months my conscience began to work on me and I finally told her. One Sunday in late spring, she brought Natalia and my brothers out to the airfield to watch me, but she refused to go up. In June of 1941, I finished at the top of my class. A man from the newspaper came to interview me and take my picture.

That summer the Germans bombed the Baltic states—Latvia, Lithuania, Estonia—to rubble. They stormed into a large area of Soviet-held territory in Poland, where they brutalized thousands of Jews, dragging them from their hiding places, shooting them execution-style, and burying them en masse. They took hundreds of thousands of civilian prisoners, and those who were unfit to work in their labor camps were locked behind walls and starved to death. As soon as he learned about this, Volodya joined the local home guard and kept us informed with news from the front that came in every night on the wireless. Our army had massed to meet the German assault, but we were out-numbered twenty to one. Only one Russian soldier in two had a rifle. The first day of the assault, the Luftwaffe destroyed 1,800 of our planes; over the next three days, they destroyed 2,000 more.

In July, the Luftwaffe began bombing Ukraine because they needed that region's vast stores of grain to feed their army and air force. Winter was coming and they had no time to lose. In September, they took Kiev and began a drive toward Moscow. But our fiercest ally, Old Man Winter, dealt them a crushing blow. By mid-October, the nighttime temperatures were well below zero and the Germans' tanks wouldn't start. Their plane engines wouldn't turn over unless heated. Even when they ran, their pilots couldn't navigate through the sleet-filled clouds that covered the ground. The Nazi army was suffering frostbite, gangrene, insomnia. Their supplies and equipment sat in crates on the docks because they couldn't transport them in the heavy snows. The Germans managed to get within eight miles of Moscow and there they stayed for months, hunkered down against a frozen adversary they couldn't shoot, bomb, or imprison.

The following spring, the ground thawed and everything started again. The Luftwaffe renewed its bombing of Moscow flying as many as 3,000 sorties a day. Our air force was hard-pressed to keep up. We had lost so many planes, so many pilots. Boys and girls as young as sixteen were recruited into our military and Volodya went into the regular army. In an effort to slow the oncoming German tide, women were digging trenches and building barricades around all our cities.

By this time, more than a quarter of our vast country had fallen into German hands. Our major industrial and agricultural areas in the western provinces, our vast grain fields in Ukraine, our coal mines, and oil fields, were lost. It was then that Comrade Stalin ordered that millions of Russian women be taken east by train to build new farms, factories, airfields, and war plants. Once they arrived on the other side of the Urals, these tough and courageous women built crude sheds under which they slept each night on the ground. They lived off small rations of pickled cabbage soup and hard black bread. Wearing their babushkas, long aprons, and boots they cleared the rock-strewn, frozen ground with pickaxes and shovels. They planted hundreds of thousands of acres in wheat, potatoes, turnips, onions, and cabbage. They pulled the plows themselves, as there were no dray animals left to do it. Then they built the vast walls for the new war plants. Inside, they laid plank floors, where they slept for months while the snow mounded each night atop their blankets. After several months, they'd completed hundreds of these simple, massive structures. Then Comrade Stalin sent in the Army engineers, with their diagrams and layouts, to design the work areas where the same women who'd cleared the fields and planted the crops would now produce the guns, ammunition, uniforms, planes, tanks, and all manner of desperately needed war materials by working twenty-four hours a day, seven days a week. In the first six months of production, they doubled the output of any pre-war year. After they'd built the hangars and laid the runways for the new airfields, they erected the barracks, built and installed thousands of bunks inside them, welcomed the male recruits who'd been brought in for training, and *manned* the kitchens 'round the clock. These millions of Russian women, whom the Germans called "swamp trash," turned the tide of the war and forced Hitler to focus his attention and resources on a target with more potential for success: North Africa. But more than a third of the troops in his Wehrmacht and Luftwaffe—a million and a half men and their vast store of armaments and planes—remained in Russia.

I was feeding the chickens when bombs began screaming down with the fury of the anti-Christ. We knew the Germans would do everything in their power to destroy Stalingrad and blast us straight to Hell. This was the mission of the Nazis . . . destroy, destroy, kill, and destroy. There was no letup as the bombing went on, day and night, for weeks. The plant where Volodya had worked was an early target and many of our friends and neighbors died there.

Late on a cool evening in September, my mother and I were sitting across from one another at our kitchen table. Anton and Natalia were seated at either end of it on three-legged stools our father had made. We were eating our only hot meal of the day—boiled cabbage and potatoes, with slices of fresh black bread. From a distance, we could hear the constant *boom-boom-boom* of the large guns and knew they were coming closer. Anton slipped out the back door and went to the neighbors, where he learned that hundreds of thousands of German troops were marching toward us behind a phalanx of panzers.

I jumped up from the table and began putting all the food I could find into a bag while Mamochka got out her largest cook pots and filled them with water from the pump. She told Anton to get our father's pistol, and all of his clothes, from upstairs. Then she went to the larder and brought back a gallon jug of milk that, just an hour before, she'd brought from the barn. She blew out the lone candle on the table and put it, along with the box of matches, in her apron pocket and whispered, "Take the food to the cellar, Ireni. And get all the blankets you can find and the bear rug that belonged to your grandfather . . . and that old throw he made out of wolves' pelts. Gather our clothes, our boots and shoes, and tie them up in the sheet on my bed and bring it down. Get the soap and towels and all the bedclothes. Leave nothing, Ireni!"

She sent Anton and Natalia to the barn to check the hens' cubbies one more time, and to stuff all the straw stored there into feed bags, tie them, and bring them to the door of the cellar.

As soon as we finished our chores, Mamochka lit the candle from her pocket, and we followed her down to our hiding place. After we carefully placed our possessions on the floor, I spread the bear rug near the stairs where the air was warmer. We huddled in the center of it and pulled the heavy bags of straw over us. It wasn't long before we could hear tanks and artillery transports rumbling through our neighborhood. Planes were zooming back and forth overhead, their deadly bombs screaming down around us. Natalia began to cry, but there was no comfort for her. There was nothing any of us could do but hold her and whisper in her little ear that everything would be all right come morning . . . or some other lie. We shuddered with every *ack-ack-ack* from our anti-aircraft guns and huddled deeper into the bear rug, praying we would not be hit. Just before dawn, the guns stopped and my mother stole up the stairs. She returned with a bucket of milk, the last our cow would ever give.

That morning, soldiers broke down the front door and entered our house. They were not German. No, they were our own. We could hear them laughing as they discovered the chickens and cow in the barn. God help them, they were just as hungry as we. But it was still a bitter pill to swallow. Evidently, they found a pot, because we could smell the sweet scent of hot tea. We heard the unearthly screams of our beautiful cow as they dragged her from the barn and hacked her to pieces in the backyard. The leader of the group ordered his men to build a fire, so the stools and tables my father had made became a roaring blaze over which they roasted their prized chunks of beef. Dark, greasy smoke began drifting into the cellar and with it came the irresistible scent of meat. Our mother had told us we could not eat anything that night from our precious store of food. But a couple of hours later she relented, giving each of us a small ration of milk and a chunk of stale bread. I nibbled on it as long as I could while the soldiers stomped all over our house searching for anything of value. About an hour later, we heard the front door slam, and assumed they'd gone.

There was nothing we could do now but wait. We lay down again on the bear rug and Mamochka told us stories about what life was like when she was growing up. Later, as she sang the old lullabies she'd sung to us when we were babies, we fell asleep.

Heavy footsteps sounded on the hidden stairs and Mamochka and I bolted awake. The door to the cellar opened and a uniformed soldier appeared. Volodya! He was alive! My mother cried with delight as he jumped down off the last stair and we rushed to embrace him. He was covered with mud, but seemed to be fine otherwise. He pulled a chocolate bar from his pocket and broke it into several pieces for us. What a treat that was! Then he urged us to come upstairs with him, for he had much to tell us. "Our army is moving west," he said to our mother, "to try to keep the Germans from crossing the river." He put his arm around her and led her up the stairs to the kitchen.

"Thank dear St. Jonah," she cried. "Now we can bring our clothes and bedding back up here and get out of that nasty dark hole."

But Volodya told her that was impossible. "You cannot stay here because this area will be overrun with scavengers and they'll do anything, Mamochka, because they have nothing to lose. You must go somewhere else. I've brought a horse and wagon to move your things." Mamochka began to protest, but Volodya told her he had a plan. "I am going to help you pack your things," he told us, "and take you south to one of the caves above the river. That area will be safe while we engage the Germans north of the city." Then he asked our mother if she still had the wolf pelts that Grandfather always threw over us when we rode in his sleigh. She nodded. "Go and get them," he told her. "Bring everything from the cellar out to the wagon."

He turned to me. "I have a suitcase in the wagon for you, Ireni. Go out and get it and fill it with your warm clothes. Pack your nightgown, toothbrush, a towel and a bar of soap . . . if you can find one. Put in your books about flying, too.

"Why?" I asked. "Why do I need those books?"

He put his index finger to his lips. "I'll tell you later," he whispered. "Just do it."

Our mother brought out the old throw made of stitched wolf pelts, the bear rug, and her cook pots. Volodya threw the suitcase I'd packed on top of the piles of goods in the back of the wagon and swung Natalia up onto the seat. He took hold of the horse's harness and began walking, and we fell in beside him making our way through the wasteland that had once been our neighborhood.

All around us were bombed-out houses, some with only one wall standing. Shards of glass lay in the streets, along with jagged planks, kitchen sinks, mattresses and bedsprings, pillows spewing feathers and legless tables. Beneath these ruins were many bodies . . . the old, the young, babies with their heads blown off. Dogs and cats and even birds lay like stuffed toys tossed aside by careless children. Natalia began screaming and Mamochka took her on her lap and pressed my little sister's wet face into her ample breasts.

We soon left familiar terrain and turned south onto what had been the beautiful tree-lined Commissar Boulevard. Now the trees stood broken, their tops blown out, their graceful limbs flung helter-skelter along the bomb-pocked pavement. Until then, we'd seen no other living people. But now they came from behind the piles of rubble that had once been their homes and began walking with us. Volodya said nothing, but kept his free hand firmly on his rifle. It wasn't long before a company of German prisoners, perhaps two hundred, shuffled toward us, many with bloodied bandages wrapped around their heads. As they passed, several of the Russian guards who accompanied them gave Volodya a curt nod.

About three o'clock that afternoon, we made a sharp turn and went up a dirt path to an escarpment above the river. When the wagon could go no further, Volodya unharnessed the horse and took her down to the river to drink while we unloaded the wagon. The cave he'd chosen for us had a large opening down the face of the escarpment and another above it at ground level that was smaller. Inside, wooden crates were stacked near the back wall and there were charred remains from a fire. Volodya told us that, during the Revolution, these caves had been used by deserters in both the Red and White Armies. He pulled one of the wooden crates into the center of the space, lit the lantern, and sat it on top. "Just like home," he exclaimed. "You'll be fine here, at least until we push the Germans back into Germany before Christmas."

I could tell by the look on our mother's face that she didn't believe him, but she didn't argue. Then Volodya told Mamochka he had something important to share with us. So she sat down on one of the wooden boxes and Natalia crawled into her lap. "Come over here, Ireni," he said to me. "I have something to show you." He took an envelope from his jacket pocket. "This is for you. I hope you won't be angry with me." He lifted the lantern so I could see the envelope and told me to open it. Inside I found a letter written in a flowery hand.

Dear Miss Igorsky,

Your brother has kindly written to me of your expertise with gliders and airplanes. I am currently recruiting young women who understand the rudiments of flight and navigation for three special regiments in the Soviet Women's Air Force. If you are willing, we would welcome you to our program. You will find enclosed a rail pass that will allow you to board a train at the station nearest you, and travel to Engels Air Base free of charge. Thank you for your consideration of this request. Regardless of your decision, I congratulate you on your accomplishments and send warmest regards to you, your brother, and all your family.

Most sincerely,
Marina Raskova,
Commander
Soviet Women's Air Force

I could not take my eyes from the paper—especially the signature—Marina Raskova, the famous flyer who, in 1938, had made the longest nonstop flight ever made anywhere in the world by a woman. Colonel Marina Raskova, my heroine, had written a letter to *me*. She wanted *me*.

Natalia brought me back to the moment. "What's wrong, sister? You look as if you're going to cry."

I told her I thought I might. Then I handed the letter to Mamochka. As soon as she read it she said, "You cannot do this, Ireni. You're too young. Don't even think about it." She handed the letter to Volodya, "Burn it," she told him. But I grabbed the letter from his hands and stuffed it into my coat pocket.

"I'm eighteen, Mamochka," I said, "and I'm going!"

Volodya found the suitcase I'd packed at the back of the cave. He knelt down in front of our mother and said, "All of this is for the *best*, Mamochka. Ireni is the *best*. And Mother Russia needs the *best*."

I tapped him on the shoulder. "How am I going to do this? I'm filthy. I smell. I can't go anywhere like this."

He stood up and put his arm around me. "You can wash in the train station before you leave. You have soap and a towel, remember? I'll take you there now." Then he hugged Mamochka, Anton, and Natalia good-bye. "You're the man of the family now," he said to Anton before leading me out of the cave. I could hear our mother crying, could feel her eyes on me. But I did not look back.

Volodya took me to the only train station still operating in Stalingrad where I stood at a sink in the women's room and bathed with cold water and gritty soap. I put on a clean dress and a sweater, and sat down with him for a cup of tea and a roll. He was reluctant to leave me there alone, but I knew he needed to join his battalion that night and urged him to go. We gave each other a long hug and he left. Another hour passed before I boarded a train where I sat with two other young women who were also going to Engels Air Base. When we reached the station in Saratov, we stepped down from the train car to find a sergeant waiting. He began calling out names, including mine, and I joined a dozen other girls. He helped us into the back of a truck that had benches along the sides and room to put our suitcases on the floor. Not much was said, as all of us were tired. I leaned the back of my head against the canvas covering behind me and dozed off and on for the next hour.

Just before midnight, we arrived at a large compound. Armed guards stood at-the-ready on both sides of the road as we made our way through a metal gate. Moments later, the truck made a sharp turn and came to a stop. One of the men jumped from the cab, released the chain that opened the tailgate, and shouted, "All out!" He offered each of us a hand as we climbed down. "This is where you'll sleep," he said, pointing to a squat stone building behind us. A young woman dressed in mechanic's coveralls opened the door and motioned for us to come in. As we crossed the threshold, she pointed to dozens of bunks around the room and told us to take one. I walked across the rough-cut boards laid in what my father would have called a *slipshod* fashion, and made my way to the far side of the room. The naked gaslight above the bunk I chose illuminated a greasy frame of wooden planks that held a straw mattress, a lumpy pillow, and quilted coverlet. I looked at the open rafters above, and the rough poles that rose about fifteen feet to support them, and knew that it would be very cold in our quarters come winter.

Once all the girls were inside, the woman closed the door. "Welcome, comrades," she said, "I am Lieutenant Belik and I intend to mold you into the best fighting unit at Engels Air Base. As you may know, Engels was built in 1930, and over the last decade its flight school has become one of the finest in the world. I welcome you here and urge you to make the most of this opportunity! This," she said with a sweep of her arm, "is your new home. As you can see, it was once a barn for one of Comrade Stalin's collectives . . . a dairy farm. Each of you is assigned a bunk and the small chest to the right of it. You will find a bucket at the foot of your bunk. Please use it at night. There are toilets in the classroom building, the dining hall, and the recreation room. Pitchers of fresh water will be available here every morning for bathing, brushing your teeth, drinking, and general use. On your bunk, you'll find a feather-filled pillow and coverlet, a bar of soap, a tin cup, and two towels. After you use your towels, please hang them on the post of your bunk to dry. You are responsible for keeping your towels and personal effects clean. The straw in your mattress will be changed at the end of each month and you will be issued another bar of soap then, too.

"Before you go to bed tonight, please select two sets of long underwear and two pairs of woolen socks from the boxes marked USA near the door. You are to sleep in one set of the underwear and in one pair of the socks. I suggest you wear wool slacks and a sweater over the remaining set each day, along with the second pair of wool socks. I trust all of you brought heavy shoes. Since it is October, it will soon be very cold here with deep snows coming before the month is out. If you did not bring at least two pairs of warm trousers and several pairs of heavy socks, please let me know as we have a supply of Lend-Lease clothing from America. In the morning after breakfast, I'll take you on a tour of the base and to the classroom where you'll begin your instruction. Lunch will be served at 1200 hours in the dining hall, and afterwards, you'll meet our commander, Colonel Marina Raskova."

Soft murmurings rose among the group at the mention of our heroine's name. Lieutenant Belik paused for a moment and her lips spread slowly into a smile. "Tomorrow afternoon, you'll be issued a pistol and a rifle. Supper will be served in the dining hall at 1800 hours. You are allowed to play games or listen to records in the adjoining recreation area until 2000 hours. Or you may return here to do your homework. Lights out at 2100 hours."

At that point, she turned to the table behind her and removed cloths from atop trays of sausage-stuffed rolls and slices of poppy-seed bread. She pointed to the battered samovar sitting on one end of the table. "Please bring your tin cups and help yourselves to hot tea. Normally, you'd be awakened at 0500 hours tomorrow, but because of your late arrival, we'll wait until 0600. But day after tomorrow, you'll be awakened at 0500 to spend an hour marching, drilling, and exercising before breakfast. As soon as you've had your tea, I suggest you change into your long underwear and warm socks. I'll wake you at six in the morning."

No one spoke for a moment. Then there was a rush to the table as we scrambled for rolls and bread. All of it was stale and dry, but it filled us up and quieted our aching stomachs. The tea was not hot. It had been sitting too long. But it was strong and sweet and no one cared. We giggled as we changed into our scratchy new underwear and heavy gray socks. Not a crumb remained on the trays, not a drop of tea was left in the samovar when I put the light out above my bed.

* * *

A strong north wind buffeted us the next morning as we walked from the barn to a nearby field where a company of uniformed women was marching in formation, new rifles on their shoulders. Lieutenant Belik stopped, raised her hand to salute members of the flag guard, and turned to us. "This is where you'll be tomorrow morning at this time, comrades. One must be a well-trained, fully prepared soldier before one can be a flyer."

Hundreds of women and men were already crowded into the dining hall when we arrived, most dressed in uniforms or mechanics' coveralls. Lieutenant Belik pointed to two empty tables at the back of the spacious room and told us to gather there as soon as we'd picked up our trays. Dozens of other new recruits, dressed as we were in civilian clothing, were lined up along a wall. From an open window near the back of the room, each of us was given a small metal tray that held a bowl of steaming barley gruel, a cup of hot tea, and a thick slice of black bread spread with pickled onion and cucumber. After I'd finished eating this warm, nourishing food, I began talking with a couple of my classmates about where they'd grown up. Both had attended an Osoaviakhim, and it was obvious that they were just as eager as I to get back into a plane.

A few minutes later, Lieutenant Belik rose from the table and we followed her out into the cold. Armed soldiers stood at attention all along our path, their faces grim with the serious duty they'd been given. Every few yards, we saw mounted anti-aircraft guns with stacks of ammunition piled on each side as high as our heads. As we walked toward a cluster of hangars, Lieutenant Belik told us that over the last year, three regiments of four hundred women flyers had been trained at Engels and were now in the skies every day, and that our unit would be part of the third group of four hundred women who would be trained there. "As I mentioned earlier," she said, "you will be joined in the classroom this morning by a dozen comrades. There will be a total of forty young women in your company."

Ahead of us, spaced closely together along the tarmac, were five large hangars bustling with activity. Women and men dressed in pilots' uniforms were conferring with other workers dressed in mechanics' coveralls. Some were servicing the planes—checking the struts, filling the gas tanks, sliding the bombs into racks beneath fuselages. Lieutenant Belik motioned us to one side. "There will be a sortie this morning," she said, "over the Volga at an old chemical factory. The Germans have amassed large stockpiles of ammunition there and we intend to destroy it. Now, let's walk over and take a look at the planes you'll eventually be flying."

We walked beyond the hangars to a field where hundreds of planes were covered in a sea of netting that had been pierced here and there with long branches cut from trees—a kind of camouflage to keep German pilots from spotting them from the air. Lieutenant Belik put her hand on the strut of a small biplane covered with green and gray camouflage-painted canvas. "This is the PE-2. It is a new plane and you may not have seen one, but it will be a major fighter for us from now on. The innovation that sets it apart is the fixed machine guns front and rear." She paused to point out the mounted guns. "This plane is highly maneuverable, but it often takes two pulling on the stick to get it airborne. Hope you have good strong arms."

Lieutenant Belik stated again that a total of twelve hundred young women had been trained and engaged in combat during the past year. She did not say how many had died. "All of you," she continued, "will be trained for three positions: mechanic, navigator, and pilot. Then Colonel Raskova will decide who serves in what position. One is no more important than the other, as all of these jobs are required for a successful operation. Following graduation, you will be assigned to one of three regiments: the day bombers, the night bombers, or the fighters. Now, come along. It is time for your first class."

Most of the desks in the back of the classroom where Lieutenant Belik left us were already taken by the recruits who'd arrived ahead of us the day before. So my bunkmates and I sat down at the desks in front. I glanced over at a window nearby where a layer of ice as thick as my finger was banked on the sill. An officer wearing the insignia of a major walked briskly into the room and everyone rose to her feet.

"Please be seated," he said, throwing a folder down on the desk in front of him. "I am Major Koloski and I don't mind telling you that I do not approve of young women on this base except in the capacity of cooking or cleaning. I do not think women have what it takes to become airplane mechanics or navigators, and certainly not pilots. However, I've been assigned this job by the commandant and it is my duty to prepare you regardless of what I think."

As soon as he finished taking roll, Major Koloski went to a cupboard and took out a stack of large photographs. "Now," he said, "we'll see just how prepared you are for this kind of work. If you know the names of the planes in each of these photographs, please raise your hand." The first picture was of the German Dornier 24 and all of us raised our hands. All of us knew the Junker Ju 88 as well. Fewer hands went up for the Heinkel 111 and the Messerschmitt 109. Only two of us knew the Focke-Wulf 190, a fighter, and the Focke-Wulf 57, a bomber. No one knew the last two in the group: the Gotha and the Albatros trainer. I'd never seen pictures of either.

"Not too bad," Major Koloski commented as he put the stack of photos back into the cupboard. "But you must be able to recognize every single plane the Germans fly." He began walking up and down the rows of desks, handing out thick stacks of cards. On each was a photo of a German plane. There were no less than four different photos of each design, taken from various angles—front and rear—as well

as from both sides. The back side of each card was filled
with information about that particular plane: the length of
the fuselage, the width of the wing span, the horsepower,
the type of guns and ammunition it carried, the number of
crew. There were a total of 138 different cards in the stack
he handed me.

"When you come to class tomorrow," Major Koloski
continued, "I want you to be thoroughly familiar with the
planes on these cards. I expect you to know the difference
between a bomber and a fighter, between a trainer and a mail
plane, between a hospital plane and a spy plane. For those of
you who actually finish your training, and eventually engage
in combat, this kind of basic knowledge could mean the
difference between life and death. Now, put your photo cards
away and turn your attention to the front of the room."

Major Koloski walked to the wall behind him and pulled
down three large maps: one of Russia, one of Europe, and
one of the entire world. "Where is the fighting going on now?
Where are battles raging, comrades?"

I raised my hand and repeated what Volodya had told me
in the train station, "Guadalcanal."

Major Kiloski gave me a brisk nod. "Very good, Comrade
Igorsky."

This kind of questioning went on for the next two hours
as the major discussed the extent of the vast, worldwide effort
being made to stop Hitler, and the expanding importance
of the role Russia was playing. Major Koloski reminded us
that more than three million of our countrymen had been
taken prisoner by the Germans during the last year, and that
while much of our homeland lay in ruins, the Americans
had brought us hope with their program called Lend-Lease.
He asked us if we knew that the underwear and warm wool
socks we'd been given the night before had been sent from
America. "Did you notice," he continued, "all the green
trucks lined up behind the hangars on your tour of the base
this morning . . . Fords, Dodges, and Chevrolets? All were

shipped here from America. More than a million American soldiers, sailors, and airmen are stationed in England now. Can you imagine all those men and their equipment crowding that tiny island? A little smirk played on his lips, but it was not unkind. "Did you know that President Roosevelt has given fifty battleships to the British Navy? Do you know what all of this means to us here in Russia?" He paused to let us consider this question before he answered it. "It means that we are not alone in this war. It means that we now have two strong allies helping us push Hitler back to Germany. Mother Russia will prevail!"

Major Kolonski was suddenly quiet. "Ah," he sighed as he pulled the strings and returned the maps to their rolled positions. "We will not have another session like this," he said, his voice barely a whisper. "From now on, our map studies will focus on topographical drawings and aerial photographs. I expect you to become an expert at reading them. As a flier, your life will depend on it. After nine weeks, our map studies will come to an end. The nine weeks following, we will turn our attention to navigation. When you complete your classroom instruction and begin your flight training, you will assemble each morning after breakfast with the pilots and navigators in the map room to discuss the day's strategy related to which company will fly where . . . and why. But I'm getting ahead of myself here. It's time for you to join Lieutenant Belik for lunch. Don't forget your homework, comrades! One must know one's enemy. Class dismissed!"

* * *

Being in the dining hall again warmed us up a bit and we removed our heavy coats before we sat down to a meal of potato and onion soup, accompanied by thick slices of black bread and strong sweet tea. Lieutenant Belik led us back to the classroom building and down the hall to the map room where we sat down behind long tables arranged on each side of the room. The walls around us were covered with maps, large and small, some in color, but most in black and white. I could not take my eyes off the map of Stalingrad that hung near my table. I could see the street where our house had been, picturing my mother at the table in the kitchen kneading a loaf of bread dough and I wondered what she, Anton, and Natalia had eaten for lunch that day in the cave.

The sound of footsteps from the hall got my attention. I turned toward the doorway and my heart leapt as Colonel Raskova walked through it. Everyone in the room was on her feet cheering as the colonel stepped behind the lectern at the front of the room. After a few seconds, she began to murmur her appreciation. Then she signaled for us to quiet down and asked us to please be seated. Reluctantly, we obeyed.

Colonel Raskova removed her cap to reveal a fringe of dark curls over a broad forehead. She had a pert nose and rosy cheeks and the most beautiful dark blue eyes I'd ever seen—deep and clear like water in a lake. Her shoulders were broad, her hips trim, her uniform immaculate. Pinned to the left breast pocket of her tunic was a red-ribbon with gold star indicating her membership in Russia's most elite group—the Order of the Hero of the Soviet.

"Welcome, comrades," she began. "What a nice-looking group of young women you are. So healthy, so energetic! I appreciate so much the fact that you have left your homes and families to become a part of our home and family here at Engels Air Force Base. And I appreciate your courage and resolve as you face our enemies. I hope you have come with your feet firmly planted, as your time here will not be easy. This is no place for the faint-hearted, no place for those who desire recognition, no place for anyone who is not ready to work very hard from early in the morning until late at night . . . and sometimes through the night. I'm sure there will be times in the days ahead when you'll wonder why you came here. There will be days when you'll be hungry, days when you'll be so tired your eyes will not stay open, days when your fingers will freeze around the stick while you're trying to start your plane's engine. Because our enemies are the most well-trained, well-equipped men on earth, they are a formidable foe. You will have to learn to fight like a man, to go after them like a man, to kill like a man. Femininity is worthless here. Forget you're a woman. Forget about your hair, your skin, your nails, and concentrate on your job. Furthermore, you must face the fact that you may be killed, that you may be burned beyond recognition, that you may be blinded, that you may lose an arm or a leg and spend the rest of your life an invalid. If you cannot accept this possibility, then you must leave this place today. Do not fool yourselves into thinking that you will somehow avoid such dangers. If the Germans decide to bomb the base this afternoon, all of us could die. This will be your fate every single day as long as you are here."

Colonel Raskova was quiet for a moment. She lowered her head and when she looked up again there were tears in her eyes. "Our sisters and brothers are dying by the tens of thousands in Leningrad, in Minsk, in Kharkov. Millions of our comrades are prisoners of the Germans. But Hitler will not defeat us. With your help, Mother Russia will triumph." She smiled then and told us that we should get back to work. "Good luck, comrades!" she called as she left the room.

* * *

We went back down the hall for our last class of the day. Our instructor was Lieutenant Colonel Anastasia Nevelsky, a tall woman with thin brown hair and small green eyes. I knew immediately that she was serious about her work and was intent on teaching us as much as possible about the weapons we'd be using. On each of our desks was an open wooden box that contained a 9mm Makarov pistol. It was a handsome gun with a polished blue finish, fixed short barrel, and large trigger guard. I knew that Volodya carried this same Army-issue weapon in his hip holster. Lieutenant Colonel Nevelsky instructed us to remove the pistol from the box and let it lie in our hand. She talked about the weight of the gun, the length of the barrel, the magazine, and the trigger. She showed us how to open and close the magazine and, for once, I was thankful for my big strong hands. Several of the girls near me struggled with the slide return, which was stiff and hard to open.

Over the next thirty minutes, my hands became so swollen and sore that I could hardly move my fingers. I heard someone crying and turned to look at the girl next to me who sat with her reddened hands in her lap and her pistol back in the box on her desk. Lieutenant Colonel Nevelsky saw her, too, but said nothing. She told us to take a ten-minute break. We went out into the hall where we stood and talked quietly among ourselves until she called us back in. Along one wall was an open rack filled with semiautomatic rifles. The lieutenant colonel selected one for each of us and showed us how to position it correctly against our right shoulder. Under the barrel, there was a fitting for a bayonet and a ten-round detachable magazine. We were told to return to the hallway, guns on our shoulders, and march up and down single-file.

It seemed that an hour passed before Lieutenant Colonel Nevelsky called us back into the classroom. As we filed in, she showed us how to stack our rifles in the rack. "Tomorrow we will take our rifles apart and put them back together. When you have mastered assembly, I will teach you how to clean your rifles, and also your pistols. Soon you'll be experts in the use of both of these weapons, and you'll be expected to wear your pistol in its holster at all times. Tonight, I want you to become so well acquainted with your gun that when we meet tomorrow, you'll be able to assemble it and disassemble it with your eyes closed. Good luck, comrades! Class dismissed."

* * *

Autumn passed quickly as our days were filled with marching and drilling, classroom instruction in map reading and navigation, cleaning and practicing with our pistols and rifles, studying the planes of our enemy, and the techniques used by them in battle, and homework, homework, homework! There was no variation to the routine except when flight crews returned to base victorious. Then we were allowed to go out to the field to cheer them as they executed victory rolls above the tarmac before they landed. This happened about twice a week. There was some kind of soup and black bread every day for lunch as well as dinner. Occasionally, we were given a tin of fruit or chocolate bars from the crates marked USA.

In mid-November, heavy snows began to fall, covering everything in a deep blanket of white. The highest daytime temperatures hovered just above freezing. Somehow, hundreds of planes got off the frozen ground almost every day throughout the winter, the exception being two days when a heavy blizzard struck and planes and crews were grounded. Every plane, every pilot, gunner, and navigator who soared into the skies above the field carried our hopes for the future. Many did not return.

Soon I'd know what it felt like to have enemy planes coming at me armed to the teeth and determined to blow me out of the skies. I could navigate and I could read a map with the best of them. The rudder, the throttle, the oil pressure and temperature gauges—all of those were easy. But could I actually fire the heavy guns from the pilot bay with enough skill, and enough courage, to kill my enemy? This was the question that haunted my dreams as I lay in my bunk those cold winter nights imagining my fingers opening and closing around the trigger while the whistle of the slipstream hissed at me like a monster in the dark.

CHAPTER 23

Lizzie

Paris, France • July 8, 1943

Once the heat of a Parisian summer was upon us, we sisters spent hours sponging off our patients in an effort to keep them cool. Twice a week, we filled an oval-shaped tin tub in the privacy of the surgery and bathed those who were well enough to be lowered into the small amount of water we could spare. One afternoon, Marie Francine and I were giving Ireni a leisurely bath when I looked up to see Reverend Mother coming up the aisle of the hospital with Marcel Guillion. I quickly dried my hands, handed the towel to Ireni, and walked out into the hospital to meet them.

"Welcome, monsieur," I said. "To what do we owe this pleasure?"

"The pleasure is mine, I assure you, mademoiselle," Marcel said, smiling at me. "I have some good news and some bad news. I'll start with the good news. Father Barney is in France."

"That is *good* news. Is he at the Hotel Albert?"

"No. Today he is with the Maquis de Orsay. Now for the bad news. Osterlitz is at the hotel and he's unleashed a pack of devils with orders to take the city apart to find the Russian pilot. She shot down two Messerschmitt 109s in a dogfight over the border with Germany, killing eight of their airmen. In retaliation, Osterlitz selected eight Frenchmen he'd imprisoned at Drancy and had them beaten to pulp. Then he cut off their genitals, stuffed them into their mouths, and hung them by their ankles, alive, from the top of the wall on rue St Germaine."

He paused while Reverend Mother crossed herself before he continued. "Last night, I was working in the hotel dining room and overheard Osterlitz tell his lieutenant to begin searching tonight in the outer limits of St Denis. Tomorrow night, they'll be moving into the heart of the city. And they will spare no one," he glanced at Reverend Mother, "and that includes *you*, in their attempt to find the Russian."

"Osterlitz also mentioned *the British spy*," he said, looking at me. "He's convinced that you're still hiding in the city and has put a price of one million francs on your head, dead or alive. So, you see why it is critical that we get you out of here as soon as possible. Barney has arranged for a plane and you must go tonight because there's a full moon."

I stood there stunned. One million francs, I thought. How could I be worth one million francs? From the corner of my eye I saw Reverend Mother staring at me, so I turned back to Marcel. "What does the moon have to do with this?"

"The plane's a Westland Lysander, what the British call a *Lizzie*. For an operation like this, the pilot must fly in without instruments, so moonlight is critical. Please let me handle the details, mademoiselle. That's my job. You must be waiting at the end of the orchard path at eleven. My brother Rene will be there with his truck."

Marcel addressed Reverend Mother. "Do you have trousers, Mother, that will fit her? She cannot do this in a habit. She must have a jacket and sturdy shoes, as well."

I began to back away. "No," I mumbled. "I'm not ready. I have a patient and I need to stay here with her until she's well enough to travel."

Marcel leaned close to me and whispered, "The white rose of Stalingrad?"

I nodded. "I cannot leave her."

Marcel looked over his shoulder to where Ireni was sitting on a chair just inside the door of the surgery. "She's going, too," he said. "Both of you are going with Rene. Two men will be waiting tonight beneath the kitchen windows for the Russian pilot and they'll take her through the orchard to the truck."

"But she can't," I began. "She isn't well enough to walk that far."

"We assume you have material here to fashion some kind of sling by which she can be lowered down the outside wall. And I'm sure you have a blanket to wrap her in. She won't have to walk. The men will carry her and put her inside a hidden compartment in the back of the truck. After Rene drops you off at the agreed landing site for the Lizzie, he'll take your pilot to a safe house near Limoges where she'll rest for a couple of weeks. Later, friends in our network will transport her to a village near Toulouse, and from there across the Pyrenees into Spain. Your friend, Monsieur Beeton-Howard, has arranged overland passage for her from Barcelona to Moscow. It will be a long journey, but she will get the best of care." I glanced over at Ireni and knew she'd understood every word.

"What about the guards?" I asked. "I'm not sure I'll be able to get by them."

Marcel reached into his jacket pocket and brought out a small bottle of clear liquid. "Spirits of ammonia," he said. "I was afraid I wouldn't be able to find any, but an old friend came through at the last minute." He took my hand and said, "Do not worry, mon ami. All will be well. Rene will be waiting for you tonight at eleven o'clock on the far end of the orchard. Bonne chance!"

That evening at dinner, Ireni and I were given large servings of food while the others did without. It made both of us uncomfortable, but Reverend Mother would not have it otherwise. She and Marie Louise brought out from their myriad hiding places two pairs of men's trousers, jackets, precious boots, warm socks, and caps. While they packed all the food they could spare into two burlap bags and filled two canteens with water, Ireni and I dressed in the warm clothing. Ireni was so thin that all of it hung on her like rags on a scarecrow. I had to roll up the legs on the trousers I was given and secure them around my waist with a belt. Marie Louise had given me a knit cap—gray-and-black stripe—that I slipped over what little hair I still had and pulled down on my forehead to the tops of my eyebrows. Unlike the clothing, the boots we were given actually fit and I suspected that they'd belonged to two of the sisters.

At ten o'clock, Reverend Mother went out to give the guards a boiled egg and a cup of water that contained ammonia. When she came back in, she went to the big hutch in the kitchen and opened a drawer that had a false bottom. After closing it, she handed me a pair of goggles. "From the RAF pilot," she said. "You'll need them for the plane."

I shook my head. "No, he'll need them when he leaves."

"He's dead. The Maquis de Melun were able to get him as far as the harbor at Marseille, but the trawler where they'd hidden him was blown up by the Germans the night after he was taken aboard. Everyone on it was killed. He didn't take these goggles when he left because he said he wouldn't need them anymore and someone else might. Try them on, Annette, and make sure the strap is secure."

At ten minutes before eleven, I helped Ireni get into a sling we'd made from two bed sheets. On either side of it were long strips of fabric that would serve as ropes to lower her down the outside wall. Just before eleven, she hugged the sisters good-bye and thanked them again for all they'd done for her. Then it was my turn. Through tears I kept telling them that I'd come back to see them once the war was over. And they kept nodding and saying *oui, oui, Annette.*

Reverend Mother opened a window, poked her head out, and announced, "They're here." I hurried over to help Marie Francine lift Ireni up to the sill. She sat there looking down for a moment before she turned back to say she was ready. We wrapped the lengths of fabric that trailed from the sling around our hands and let them out slowly, watching as she went down. As soon as they'd removed her from the sling, one of the waiting men wrapped a blanket around her, picked her up, and walked quickly away. I grabbed the bags of food and canteens and hurried to the back door.

The two Nazi guards were snoring like pigs as I crept down the stone steps and raced toward the orchard. I caught up with Ireni just as the men were lowering her into the secret compartment beneath the truck bed. As I stuffed a bag of food and a canteen in beside her, I kissed her forehead and whispered, "I'll never forget you, Captain Igorsky." She squeezed my hand and said, "Dos vidaniya, Marie Annette." The men laid planks over the wooden box, secured them with lengths of wire, and stacked crates of fresh cabbages and potatoes on top and all around its sides. Then they disappeared into the trees.

As I climbed into the cab, Rene laid his heavy foot on the accelerator and we sped away. Neither of us spoke as the truck careened through numerous back alleys that led out of the city. For the next two hours, we wended our way down country roads. Just outside Orsay, Rene turned onto a stretch of muddy ruts that led to a farm. He drove behind a barn, cut the engine, and reached under the seat. "Come with me," he said as he drew out a pistol and crammed it inside his waistband.

We crossed the farmyard and, as we entered a wooded area, several women and men emerged from behind trees carrying wooden truncheons that smelled of petrol. For the next few minutes I followed along as they walked single-file beneath the overhanging branches of a hedge that eventually opened onto a long grassy field. I heard a droning sound and looked up thinking I'd see lights from a plane. But there were none. Rene touched the end of his cigarette to the crude torch he was holding and it burst into flame. As the sound of the plane grew louder, the others began lighting theirs.

Rene put his arm around me and drew me close. "Put on the goggles," he said. "And get ready to run. The plane will not stop. But it will touch ground long enough for you to get in. There will be a ladder extending from the rear cockpit—just behind the wing—and you must grab hold of it."

As soon as I secured the goggles over the black-and-gray cap, Rene took my hand and we sprinted to the far end of the field. I watched as the plane banked into a turn and heard the engine slow to a growl. Then it roared back to life and the torchbearers hurried into position along the outer edges of the long open space.

As the plane started its descent, Rene pushed me out into the middle. "Run," he yelled as the dark hulk raced toward me. It *whooshed* by with the force of a hurricane, pelting me with clods of muddy grass and sucking the breath right out of me. I began running, but stumbled in a rut, and Rene jerked me up like a rag doll. "The ladder!" he screamed. "Grab the ladder!"

A sliver of metal glinted in the moonlight and I lunged toward it, scraping the skin off the ends of my fingers as I scrambled to get a hold. My shoulders were all but torn from their sockets when someone hoisted me up into the cockpit.

"Hello, Ducks!" Barney screamed as the plane soared into the sky.

CHAPTER 24

Reasons to Smile

London, England • January 1, 1944

Happy New Year, Mama!

*Welcome 1944—thank goodness you've finally
arrived! Isn't it encouraging, Mama, when you think about
how far we've come over the last year? Many are saying
the end of the war is just around the corner and perhaps
next year this time, I'll be with you in Baker.*

*Your beautiful Christmas gifts lifted my spirits.
I love the vest you knitted for me and the birdcage
earbobs . . . don't know when I've seen anything so clever
as all those little pearls tumbling around inside those
dangling gold cages. And thanks so much for the books—
can't wait to get into A Tree Grows in Brooklyn.*

*You won't believe it, but oranges appeared in the food
markets here the week before Christmas. Then bananas
arrived. Both from South America. They were rationed,
of course, but sheer heaven to have just a few. We haven't
seen any coconuts yet, but I made ambrosia anyway with
canned cherries and pineapple chunks instead. It was
divine and, in between bites, we smiled and smiled.*

*We had a wonderful Christmas, Mama, but quite
different from the past couple of years. For once, Miriam
and I were not on duty at St Mary's on Christmas Eve or*

Christmas Day, because our staff insisted that we have those days off. As soon as we knew we'd be free, I told Stoney, and he and Jerusha started planning a Christmas Eve party and Christmas Day dinner at Croxdon House—Lord Beeton-Howard's three-story Regency-style manse built by Stoney's great-grandfather, the third Earl, and his wife, Cristobel. I've been there a couple of times for dinner, but I don't think I've ever written to you about it. All of the floors and mantels on the first floor are Italian marble and the walls are filled with works by Italian masters. On the back is a spacious conservatory furnished with chintz sofas and chairs, lots of white wicker, and all sorts of exotic plants. It's Stoney's favorite place and he spends most of his time there when he's home.

On Christmas Eve morning, Rutledge brought in a nine-foot fir tree and set it up in Stoney's library. Over the next couple of hours Miriam and I decorated it with hundreds of glass ornaments and dozens of old fashioned clip-on candles. Then we went into the dining room and strung garlands of juniper along both mantels and above the windows. Miriam has a real knack for flower arranging and she created beautiful arrangements of holly and ivy for the table. Sylvia's Uncle Harold and Aunt Vera joined the six of us for dinner that evening and what a wonder it was. All manner of dainty sandwiches and little pastry tarts and rolls stuffed with rare roast beef (the food Brits say they've missed most during the war) and cold pheasant and ham and lovely desserts—cakes, custards, and Plum Pudding.

Afterward, we gathered in the library beside a concert grand that had belonged to Stoney's great-grandmother, Cristobel. Barney surprised us when he sat down and played several Fats Waller compositions and two very jazzy *numbers he told us he'd seen Josephine Baker dance to in Paris. Then Sylvia's Aunt Vera played "Moonlight Sonata" and "Clair de Lune." Stoney asked me to sing and Barney accompanied me on "O, Danny Boy." It was so sad I thought I'd die before we finished. We lifted the mood after that with "Jingle Bells."*

Christmas Day was much quieter when we gathered, sans Harold & Vera, for dinner at noon. Stoney's mother is deathly ill and he left afterward to visit her at his country estate. I went back to the cottage to write to Claire and do my hand washing for the week.

The weather has been so horrible here, Mama— freezing, snowing, thawing, then freezing again. The snow is piled up to four feet in some places. On my walk to work mornings, I've had to wear a wool scarf over my mouth and nose because the air burns like fire and ice. We've been swamped at St Mary's with cases of bronchial pneumonia and several of our older patients died. The wounded are pouring in from the battlefields in Italy, and everyone is rejoicing about the US Marines landing in the Solomons, and the fact that the Russian army has taken back Kiev. I wonder if my pilot friend, Ireni Igorsky, was involved in that? I know you're aware of this news, so while the censors will have field day with my letter, you'll know my intent here.

I read the following recently and found the numbers staggering: 22,750,000 women and men are in service to the British military or Civil Defence worldwide, according to the UK Ministry of Labor. Do you have any idea of what that number might be for the US? I'm sure it's just as mind-boggling as this one. What will all of us do when the war is over? What will happen to all the military and civil defense jobs? How will people earn a living again?

Stoney took several of us out for dinner and dancing last night at the Savoy Hotel to celebrate New Year's Eve. I wore the Nile-green gown I bought when I lived in New York and it was fine. There's not much by way of fashion here these days, because we all live in our uniforms. We danced a lot, as the orchestra was good. So was the food. At midnight we made toasts with French champagne— quite a treat. Then about 150 of us revelers joined hands across the ballroom to sing "Auld Lang Syne" and "God Save the King."

The name on everyone's lips at dinner was Eisenhower, and there was considerable conversation about why Montgomery had not been named Supreme Commander of the Allied Forces instead of Old Ike. Invasion is the most talked about topic here, along with the RAF's continuing raids over Berlin. Did you hear Ed Murrow's broadcast about that on CBS? It has really stirred up a can of worms, all those German civilians being burned to death just like poor people here in London were in 1940.

Perhaps FDR, Stalin, and Churchill came up with the answers to bring an end to all these problems when they were in Cairo. I saw the president on a newsreel and he looks awful, bless him. I don't see how he keeps going. Thank God he has Eleanor and her healthy legs!

I've saved my biggest news for last. Don't faint, but I've cut my hair! I guess you might call it a "bob"—a very popular style here in England with the women who work in the war factories because it's so easy. Wearing my hair so short has been an adjustment, Mama, but I don't miss long hours in front of a heater or fire trying to get it dry. And putting on my nurse's cap is much easier now, too.

Time to close and get some sleep. The last week has been fun, but I'm pooped! I'll work for the next four days and then have three off. We're all praying like mad for a break in the weather. Can't wait to see those little hyacinths and daffodils blowing in the spring breeze. Please write when you can, Mama, and give my love to Aunt Hepsi and Uncle Robert and to Maddie and Fletcher. I miss you, miss you . . . and long for the day when I'll be able to give you a big hug!

Your loving daughter,
Evelyn

CHAPTER 25

Good Night, Sweetheart

London, England • February 14, 1944

My old RC supervisor, Marjorie Reynolds, called two weeks ago and asked if I would sing a couple of songs for the upcoming Valentine's Dance. I agreed and asked if I could bring a couple of friends. Stoney did the same, so we were able to invite the whole Beech Tree Group, as well as Miriam, to go with us.

By the time we made our way into the big reception room at HQ, the place was packed as tight as a tin of sardines. More than two hundred thousand GIs are living in southern England now, a third of them right here in London, and it seemed like most of them were there. I enjoyed singing two numbers with the band—"Sentimental Journey" and "You Belong to Me." Stoney and I danced a dozen times, and I danced with Barney and Rutledge. How that Pole can waltz!

Miriam looked especially pretty in deep red chiffon and Sylvia wore her navy-blue taffeta. Stoney and I were dressed in our RC uniforms, but Rutledge and Barney wore evening clothes to complement Miriam and Sylvia's gowns. I'm so glad my hair is long enough now for me to pin curl it at night. When I brush it out I look sorta like Shirley Temple. Stoney loves it and says it makes me look more the imp I really am. Thank goodness for mirrors and shampoo and lotion and all the things I had to do without when I was living with the sisters. But what a small price to pay for my life! I still have the gray-and-black knit cap I wore the night Rene rescued Ireni and me. I keep it in the drawer of the little desk in my room and I'm sure it will go with me wherever I go for the rest of my life.

All anyone can talk about these days is the upcoming Allied invasion. Several people stopped by our table tonight to say hello and asked if we had any bets going on the date we thought the invasion would begin. Stoney managed to evade them all, laughing as he told them that such information had not been shared by members of the War Ministry with ordinary people like us. But big money is being laid down all over the city, and Miriam and I have half a quid in the hospital pool with our pick being April 30.

At midnight everyone joined arms (getting that done with such a big crowd took time) to sing "Let Me Call You Sweetheart." When we finished, Stoney completely ignored Miriam and Barney, who were standing on either side of us, and pulled me close. "Oh, Evelyn," he whispered, his voice heavy with obvious longing. "I don't know what I'd do without you."

Afterward, we returned to Corrie Cottage where Rutledge put a log on the fire while Barney poured brandies. Rutledge joined Sylvia on the sofa, Barney sat with Miriam, and Stoney and I stretched out on the rug in front of the fire. We talked briefly about how lovely it was to have a clear night for the dance, and Miriam asked Sylvia for the latest on the weather.

"Rain," she said, "starting late tomorrow with highs in the mid-thirties." We groaned at that, but she just laughed. "Quit your grumbling," she admonished. "Things are going to get a lot worse, old things, before they get better. The prime minister has asked me to brief you about another mission. This one's called *Operation Tiger*. Next month, a hundred and fifty thousand GIs will be moved to Slapton Sands, a village on the coast of Devon where they'll be practicing ship-to-shore maneuvers in advance of the upcoming invasion. Because their houses are likely to be blown to pieces, the families who live at Slapton are being moved to new locations." She paused for a moment and looked over at Barney. "Barney will be hopping a Lizzie tomorrow, taking caches of weapons to our friends in France who'll be fighting right alongside the Allies during the invasion. The War Ministry is putting enormous pressure on the weather wizards to come up with three possible dates to ensure a safe Channel crossing for the four thousand ships involved in the invasion, which has been christened *Operation Overlord*. I'll keep you posted as things unfold."

Barney stood up and pulled on his overcoat. "This has been a wonderful evening, my friends, but it's time for me to call it a day. Have to be at the airfield by six in the morning. Come on, Miriam. I'll walk you home."

Stoney and I accompanied the two of them to the door and said good-night. As soon as they'd gone, Stoney closed the door and took me in his arms. "Let me stay," he whispered, his finger tips caressing my cheek. "No one will know if I go upstairs with you." I shook my head and told him that Sylvia would know and so would Jerusha.

Stoney seemed unconcerned about their knowing reminding me that Sylvia and Rutledge were having an affair. I'd known about it for months, but it didn't make it any easier for me. I reminded Stoney that Sylvia was a widow and Rutledge a bachelor, both as free as birds to do as they pleased. "You're married," I said a little more emphatically than I should have. "Please try to understand my feelings."

"I don't," Stoney blurted. "But I'll honor your wishes and go home." After removing his hat and coat from the hall tree, he pecked me on the cheek. "Good night, sweetheart," he said. As he closed the door, a rush of freezing air assaulted my ankles and I wrapped my arms around myself in an effort to ward off the cold. But nothing could assuage the remorse I felt as I slowly climbed the stairs to bed.

CHAPTER 26

The Playground of Mars

London, England • June 6, 1944

Late on the afternoon of June 6, 1944, Miriam and I were making final rounds in the recovery ward when our chief administrator, Dr. Platt-Simpson, appeared in the doorway accompanied by nurse Iris Higgins. He walked quickly down the row of beds where Miriam was working, and I heard him ask if he might speak privately with her and Matron Sanderson. I left my patient's bed on the far side of the room and followed the two of them into Miriam's office. The doctor closed the door and said, "I've had a telegram from Dr. Rankin at Army Medical HQ on Gold Beach." From his pocket, he pulled the beige paper and read us the message: *Request your team depart London as scheduled.* STOP *Transportation arriving 0600 St Mary's Lindo Entrance 6-8-44.* STOP

He stuffed the paper back into his pocket. "Neither of you has had a day off since last Thursday and I know you must report tomorrow to collect all your gear before you leave for France, so Nurse Higgins will finish your rounds and remain here until the new shift arrives at seven. You have a big assignment ahead of you, ladies, so go home now and try to get some rest. Please excuse me while I locate Dr. Atkins and Dr. Brompton." He made a bow, drew his heels together, and said, "Good luck!"

A heavy mist was falling when Miriam and I finally left the hospital at a quarter of six. We were bone-tired, having spent a long day treating two dozen patients who'd suffered third-degree burns in a massive explosion at a munitions factory. As we hurried down Praed and turned onto Spring Street, I commented to Miriam that I'd never seen the streets so quiet at the end of the day. The corner pub, the Grey Heron, was practically empty. Through the windows I saw only two men sitting at the bar, which most evenings was three-deep. But I knew why. Everyone was home beside their radios waiting for news. At nine thirty that morning, Supreme Headquarters of the Allied Expeditionary Force reported that the invasion known as *Operation Overlord* had begun. But very little beyond that simple announcement had been reported. As a result, people remained near radios in their homes, in offices, in shops. Miriam had kept the radio on in her office all day, checking off and on for any piece of information about fighting on the beaches of Normandy. The fact that *Overlord* had been postponed for a day due to high seas and heavy squalls only heightened our anxiety.

When we arrived at Corrie Cottage, Jerusha took our coats and bags and invited us into the lounge where flames from a small fire instantly cheered us. She'd prepared a tea tray and urged us to sit down, take off our shoes, and relax. Sylvia, who was not home, had told me days before that Miriam was to have her bed because the prime minister had asked her to remain at Whitehall for the duration, possibly a week. Miriam and I quietly sipped our tea, mostly hot water with just a hint of mint, while the radio played softly in the background. Jerusha left us alone for a while, but soon returned to tell us that dinner was ready. I insisted she join us, but there was little conversation during the meal, because our ears, hearts, and minds were focused on the Motorola.

After we finished eating, I helped Jerusha stack the dirty dishes on a tray. Then the three of us went into the lounge and sat down near the radio. At exactly eight o'clock, the announcer began with his well-known greeting heard around the world: *This is London calling.* Then he asked that the audience stay tuned for His Majesty, King George. The king began in his usual halting way and it took him a moment or two to get going. *Four years ago,* he said, *Great Britain stood alone. We were tested and we survived. Now we must assume a new resolve. We must win. May we offer up earnest, continuous, widespread prayer to help fortify our soldiers, sailors, and airmen as they go forth to set the captive free.*

At eight thirty, Ed Murrow began his regular broadcast by playing a tape he'd been sent from an American war correspondent aboard a communications ship in the early hours of the invasion. During the first few seconds, all we heard was the sound of muffled voices and shuffling feet. Then we heard the roar of several big guns in the distance. Beyond them a barrage of artillery kept up a steady *rat-tat-tat.* Above this din, an officer barked orders: *Come on, you men! Get to your post!* A series of loud explosions blasted the airwaves and Jerusha grabbed the arms of her chair. The explosions brought harrowing cries from several men who'd been hit. One young voice in the background kept screaming, *Bring the hoses! The hoses, for Christ's sake!* There was a very loud boom and the reporter began to stutter as he tried to describe the chaos that had ensued when a torpedo struck the ship's stern. Suddenly, the voice of this trained radio announcer deteriorated into gushing sobs followed by soft murmurings of *oh, no . . . oh, no.* A shrill piercing cry from a whistle sent the signal to abandon ship and the recording came to an abrupt end. Ed Murrow returned to sign off with his usual closing . . . *And that's how it was today for some of our troops off the coast of Normandy.*

A month before, Miriam had been summoned to a meeting in the Fourth Floor Conference Room at St Mary's— the only room in the hospital with soundproof walls and doors. She was told to bring along her most skilled colleague from Emergency Surgery and insisted that I go with her. "I know you don't want to go to France again, Evelyn," she'd said, "but I don't think I can do this without you." When we arrived at the meeting, Dr. Platt-Simpson was standing at the front of the room chatting with a silver-haired man wearing an Army tunic arrayed with medals, ribbons, and braid.

He called the meeting to order and introduced the man in uniform as Dr. Theodore Rankin, Colonel and Chief Medical Administrator for the Second British Army. Colonel Rankin took the floor and told us that we'd been recommended by Dr. Platt-Simpson for a highly confidential, top-secret mission in which our participation would be strictly voluntary. He went on to say that ten-man teams made up of volunteer doctors, nurses, and orderlies from six London hospitals would be assisting the British Second Army Medical Corps following *Operation Overlord,* the Allied invasion of Normandy, which had been scheduled for Monday, June 5. Those who signed on would be issued a regular army uniform, boots, helmet, dog tags, a duffel bag, and a Browning GP35 which he or she would be required to wear in a hip holster at all times.

In accordance with the Emergency Powers Act, each volunteer would assume a rank corresponding to the position he or she currently held at the hospital. The CCS (Combined Chiefs of Staff) had ruled that non-military personnel would not be allowed on the beaches of Normandy until seventy-two hours after the invasion had begun, so our "tour of duty" would not begin until D-day plus three. Our team would depart Portsmouth late on June 8 and arrive at the British Sector, Gold Beach, at dawn on June 10. We would serve for only one week, beginning with our departure date and ending the day (or night) we arrived back on British soil. Women were to put their full names on all forms but would be listed on army payrolls and departure manifests with last names and initials only to conceal our gender. As one would expect, there had been considerable resistance at the War Office to the idea of having women on the beaches at all. In the end, the higher-ups had decreed that no women serving in any military or non-military branch, including RC nurses, would go ashore before June 10.

Colonel Rankin paused and linked his fingers across his ample girth. He hesitated a moment before speaking again in a quiet voice. "I cannot overemphasize what a dangerous undertaking this is likely to be. And my staff and I will certainly understand if some of you decide you'd rather not be a part of it. Like the invasion itself, your Channel crossing will be extremely hazardous. The Germans will come at us with all they've got. I don't need to tell you what it will be like when our troops go up against the Atlantic Wall. There will be no cover, no shelter, nowhere to run. But we hope that by the time you and your team of medical volunteers arrive, combat on Gold, Utah, and Omaha Beaches will have ended.

"If you sign up to do this, you'll be taken across the Channel at night in an LCL or an LST—or a similar amphibious vessel that has been manufactured in America and specifically designed for this operation. You'll be housed in tents—no running water, no toilets, no heat. And you'll be working in unprotected medical tents nonstop, which means no rotation. Sleep and meals will be catch-as-catch-can. As soon as possible, Army engineering crews will begin assembling metal runways above the beaches so that C-47s will be able to bring in supplies and equipment. Those same planes, once they are unloaded, will be reloaded with the seriously wounded whom you will have treated in tents on the beaches. These men will be returned to airfields here in southern England and taken by ambulance to area hospitals or on to Prestwick, Scotland. Each of those planes is equipped with canvas cots attached to the inside walls of the fuselage. A Chief Flight Nurse will be in charge of loading the wounded and you'll be expected to assist in these operations and follow her orders. While I'm sure most of you are fully aware of how hospital planes operate, let there be no doubt about what the Germans will do to try to bring them down. So keep in mind just how dangerous this mission will be. If you volunteer today you must complete a Next of Kin form so that we have necessary information about you just in case."

Colonel Rankin looked over at Dr. Platt-Simpson and said, "You've assembled a fine-looking group of likely volunteers, sir. I can tell by their faces that they're not only capable, but also dedicated. In closing, I want to reiterate the fact that this is strictly confidential and totally voluntary. And I cannot overstate the gravity of the challenges you'll face and the demands that will be made on you if you sign on for this mission."

Miriam and I rose together, gave each other a brief knowing look, and headed to the table to sign up. Behind us came Dr. Clement Atkins and Dr. John Brompton, two of the most respected surgeons at St Mary's. Six orderlies, whom I knew only by their last names, followed them. After we'd completed the necessary forms, we shook hands with Colonel Rankin, who told us to report to Second Army HQ the week of June 5 to pick up our uniforms, boots, and gear. "I'll see you soldiers in France," he said as he paused to salute us on our way out the door.

* * *

Miriam and I probably had a better understanding of the deadly seriousness of our mission than most of our colleagues from St Mary's because we had the advantage of knowing someone who'd been present at the War Office during planning sessions for *Overlord*. Back in March, Sylvia had briefed us one night at Corrie Cottage with as much information as she could. She talked about possible high tides and blustery seas, and what an important and precarious factor the weather might be for the converted liners, destroyers, and trawlers that would transport troops to locations within a mile of the beach, where they would off-load to LCLs, LSTs, or other amphibious vessels. Then she showed us drawings of the fifteen-foot-high barricades called "hedgehogs" the Germans had built along the shore, the miles of razor wire, and the concrete "pill boxes" jutting from the ridge tops above the beaches. "The beaches themselves are virtual mine fields," she'd said. "We have diagrams showing where the Germans have buried thousands of mines beneath the sand. Even if their bunkers are blown to bits and the soldiers in them are dead, German snipers with high-powered scopes will be everywhere ready to take your heads off." She took a sip of coffee, leaned back into her chair, and continued. "One thing that will give us an edge in this undertaking is the enormous effort being made to fool the Germans into thinking that *Overlord* will be launched via the Pas de Calais. To that end, hundreds of old ships and planes in every size and form imaginable are lined up on the coast of Kent. Naval Intelligence has dubbed this clever ruse *Operation Quicksilver* and General Patton has been named its commander. Let's just hope it works. The prime minister says that the element of surprise is our most vital weapon against the Germans. We must catch them unaware."

* * *

Early on Thursday morning, June 8, Miriam and I arrived at the Lindo entrance of St Mary's and found our colleagues waiting. Within seconds, an army truck rounded the corner and pulled to the curb. A private jumped from the cab and quick stepped to the rear of the truck, rolled back the tarp covering the bed and released the chains on the tailgate. We climbed in, threw our duffels on the floor, and sat down on them. Ten minutes later, we stopped to pick up the ten volunteers from London Central Hospital. As soon as they were settled, we started south. An hour or so into the trip, our truck slowed to a crawl and came to a stop at an intersection on the southwest side of the city where three major highways merged. One of the men from the cab came back and told us that we'd be stopping for a while and were free to get out for some air. We piled out and congregated on the side of the road next to an old wooden gate. And there we stayed for the next two hours while countless trucks, jeeps, tanks, and dozens of regiments of infantry marched by us headed in the direction of the sea. Finally, an Army MP entered the center of the intersection, halted traffic from the main road, and motioned to the drivers of our truck caravan to move forward. We'd been warned that our journey to the Portsmouth Naval Station would be a long one and now we knew why.

About one o'clock, we arrived at a makeshift back entrance to the station grounds. Our credentials were quickly checked before we were ordered to the mess tent for a lunch of potted meat and crackers followed by tins of sliced peaches. The nicest thing was the coffee we were given—real coffee served with real milk and real sugar. For the next two hours we sat on our duffels, teasing one another, singing popular songs, and playing cards, while a kind of organized chaos unfolded around us. Every fifteen minutes, as regular as clockwork, a male voice rose above the din of rumbling truck engines, and hundreds of men merged into perfect formation and marched away. Finally, a soldier appeared and told us that his name was Sergeant Wright, and that he would be in charge of us from now on. "You'd better prepare to move out," he said. "Our LCM is moored close by and you civilian volunteers will be the first to board."

Each of us was given a life belt, told to put it on immediately, and reminded to wear our helmets at all times. Our credentials were checked again just before we stepped onto the dock. There was no ramp or gangway, so we simply stepped across the gunwale into the boat. I asked about its size and was told that it was forty-eight feet long by fourteen feet wide, and built to carry a hundred troops. But on this day it would carry only eighty soldiers, because our medical crew from St Mary's would take up the rest of the space. It was rather like a large bathtub, wider at the front and narrower at the back. Across the stern above the hold was a gun platform about twelve feet long by ten feet wide. A Bren machine gun was bolted to the center of it, surrounded on three sides by a metal apron. Beside it, a young soldier stood quietly with his hands clasped behind his back, his eyes on the sky.

Sergeant Wright looked directly at me and pointed to the area beneath the gun platform, so I dragged my duffel down into a low-walled space where four canvas cots were hanging in pairs from walls on either side. We put our duffels up against the bulkhead on the starboard side and sat down on them. The orderlies ducked in and filled the other side. Dr. Atkins and Dr. Brompton arrived and sat down in front of Miriam and me, providing a sort of shield between us and the open area that soon filled with soldiers. We craned our necks forward to get a look at the men as they came down into the open hold. "So young," I whispered to Miriam. "Hardly any fuzz on their cheeks."

She nodded. "Soon they're gonna be just like the boys in the hospital, aren't they? An arm blown off, an eye missing, crippled for life—if they live. Oh, dear Jesus, why? Why must we send these strong young boys to their deaths?"

I reached over and took Miriam's hand. "Hush, honey. Don't let them hear you. Those boys are trying to do their part just like we're trying to do ours. And there's nothing we can do about how young they are. All we can do is pray, which is something you do very well. So pray. Please." I heard Dr. Atkins clear his throat and I squeezed Miriam's hand. She closed her eyes and her lips began to move.

Heavy scudding clouds banked on the horizon, and before long, darkness was upon us. Sergeant Wright appeared again with a large box of C rations, and Dr. Atkins asked him how long it would be before we got underway. The sergeant told him we would not leave port before midnight. He handed each of us a small carton containing a tin of ham with pineapple chunks, two chocolate bars, and a package of soda crackers. After I'd eaten, I took a sip of water from my canteen, settled back against my duffel, and closed my eyes.

I was startled by the sound of metal grinding against metal and heard someone say, "They're weighing anchor." I checked the luminous dial on my watch and saw that it was quarter of two. Our faithful sergeant appeared once more to remind all of us that there was to be no smoking while we were underway. Several men near us groaned in response. The sea around us soon filled with the sounds of hundreds of ships as they began to move. Amid the hum of smaller engines like ours was the low rumbling of the big ships accompanied by the steady *slap, slap, slap* of the waves as they beat against our metal hull.

An arc of freezing water washed over me and I gasped. The sergeant spoke in his clear resonant voice, telling everyone that our pilot boat was now in position to lead us across the Channel. Soon swells were rising to dizzying heights and we were forced to hunker down and try to hold on as wave after wave of cold water sloshed over the gunwale and ran over the tops of our boots. Once the boat finally gained a steady rhythm, I gave in to an uneasy sleep.

When dawn arrived, it came wrapped in soft gray light on a calm gray sea. Sergeant Wright greeted us with a hearty "Good morning!" and gave each of us a little box that contained a block of white cheese about the width and length of two of my fingers, a half dozen Eton wafers, and a tin of prunes. Dr. Atkins told him he was ready for his morning cup of coffee, but the sergeant just laughed.

From a distance came the unmistakable drone of fighter planes. The sound began to expand, and suddenly a half dozen Stukas filled the horizon. They came straight toward us, broke formation, and swooped away while the *zing, zing, zing* of their artillery fire tore into the port side of our boat. We could hear the answering staccato of the machine gun right above us, hear the *clomp, clomp, clomp* of the gunner's boots as he ran back and forth across the metal apron in an attempt to hit one of those planes. The sergeant kept yelling, "Heads down! Heads down!" Miriam and I crouched in a huddle with Dr. Atkins and Dr. Brompton, our faces so close we could have kissed. Our engine ground to a halt and Sergeant Wright's voice came clear as he radioed our pilot ship for assistance.

No more than a minute passed before the clouds above us parted and the planes came at us again. There was a loud *thump* and we watched in horror as our gunner careened toward us, catching the toe of his boot on the rim of the platform. He hung just above our heads for an instant, before he cartwheeled over the gunwale into the sea.

The boat shuddered to a sudden stop and two soldiers helped Dr. Brompton haul the wounded gunner aboard. Dr. Atkins borrowed a length of rope from the sergeant and laid our duffels side by side to form a square atop the deck's wooden slats. He tied them end to end to make a kind of bed, and Miriam and I helped him position the gunner in the center of it. Dr. Brompton knelt down beside the boy and began examining him while Miriam retrieved our med bags. As soon as we were able to locate the correct instruments, we removed the shrapnel imbedded in his left shoulder. While the boat struggled to mount waves as high as a house and swooped back down again, Dr. Brompton closed the boy's wounds and sewed him up. Miriam fashioned a bandage around his shoulder and I gave him an injection of morphine. The boat was checked for damage by the coxswain who deemed it seaworthy and soon we were underway again. About a half hour later, the sergeant came to tell us that we'd been ordered to stay put for the time being. The anchor was lowered again, the LCL settled itself into a steady roll—up and down, up and down—and, eventually, I slept.

The growl of the engines woke me and I crawled out from beneath the gun platform and peered over the gunwale as we approached the beach. Sergeant Wright was standing amidships barking orders: soldiers were to disembark first, civilians last. Dr. Atkins brought a canvas stretcher from inside the hull, and two of our orderlies helped him put our wounded gunner on it. Once all of the soldiers had safely reached shore, Dr. Brompton and Dr. Atkins helped the orderlies take the gunner down the ramp into the gray light of dawn.

Miriam and I were last off the vessel, stepping into cold water that swirled just above our knees. We struggled against the strong current, trying to keep our heavy duffels out of the drink. Dozens of other medical volunteers and hundreds of soldiers were disembarking from vessels on either side of us. As soon as we reached the shore, Miriam and I paused to catch our breath and take in the scene.

All kinds of wrecked vessels—LSTs, LCLs, DUKWs—lay scattered along the beach, obviously the victims of mines. Blocks of concrete the size of automobiles, held hostage by endless coils of barbed wire, stood in the surf at regular intervals as far as the eye could see. Rifles, life belts, canteens, and helmets lay where they'd been abandoned. I walked past an army boot standing upright in the sand and saw the remains of a maggot-riddled lower leg still in it. While there were no bodies in sight, deep craters perhaps seven feet wide and twelve feet long stretched before us like footprints made by a giant. Curiosity got the best of me and I took a little detour to look over the rim of one. Down inside I could see small pieces of jagged metal that I suspected were the remains of buttons, canteens, and belt buckles. Scattered nearby were shreds of khaki fabric. A little later, I learned why. The Army Corps of Engineers had been ordered to dig huge craters in the sand to bury soldiers killed in the early hours of the invasion, en masse, so the troops who came ashore after them would not see bodies piled up on the beach.

On the ridge above us, hundreds of bodies were stacked one on top of another like logs in a bin. Several men from a graves unit were hard at work putting their charges into clean canvas bags and loading them on a half dozen, jeep-drawn wagons. Beneath the wagons, chickens scratched and pecked in the bloody soil.

Off to the right, a bulldozer was pushing battle debris into a pile while men in blue work shirts, American Seabees, heaved bundles of metal rods onto the bed of a nearby truck. Every twenty yards or so, a gunner stood behind a tripod that held a Thompson submachine gun. His hands gripped the handle while he moved the gun left then right, as his eyes searched for any sign of the enemy. We'd been told that the password of the day was "handle" and the correct response was "with care." The password and response changed every day and all of us had to remember both.

Dr. Atkins and Dr. Brompton led the way up the ridge toward one of a half dozen medical tents. Behind it we could see three makeshift shelters where several medics were working. We left our duffels outside and passed through the tent's wide opening into a waiting area where at least four-dozen wounded were lying on stretchers on a filthy canvas floor. The smells of urine, carbolic, anesthetic, and feces assaulted us as we made our way back into the operating theatre where a single Army doctor was removing shrapnel from a man's back.

"Am I glad to see you," he said to Dr. Atkins before yelling to a medic to set up another table. "Reinforcements at last! I'm Dr. Thornton. Welcome to the Army."

Dr. Atkins introduced Dr. Brompton, Miriam, and me, and asked Dr. Thornton how long he'd been at it.

"Sixteen and a half hours," he replied, stripping off his surgical gloves as he started toward us. "I'm going to grab some sleep now if you don't mind."

As soon as Dr. Thornton left, Miriam and I began sizing up the area where the four of us would be working, moving tables and equipment to accommodate our team. On either end of the operating table were metal buckets filled with various body parts—lengths of grayish intestines, ends of fingers, rib bones, swatches of greasy brown hair, toenails, an eyeball trailing tiny arteries—all floating in bloody slime. Dr. Brompton asked two of the orderlies, Reed and Haskins, to remove the buckets and bring in two clean ones. We'd brought a folding metal table with us from St Mary's and two collapsible sets of shelves. Soon these were in place and we had a system going. Miriam would assist Dr. Atkins and Dr. Brompton with surgeries, while I performed triage with a team of Army medics in the shelters outside.

Medical Corpsman Reggie Stock met me at the edge of a makeshift tent where more than two hundred wounded were waiting to be treated. He made note of the stripes on my collar and sleeves, and my name badge, before giving me a sharp salute. He handed me an open cardboard box filled with manila-colored tags like the ones we used at St Mary's. "As soon as you decide the category of care needed for each of these poor devils, Lieutenant Sanderson," he said, "Corpsman Stratton and I will write their name and company number on their tag and have the orderlies take them away. There's a regular hospital tent just over that hill." He pointed toward the burned-out farmhouse behind us. "Whoever don't go to surgery first, goes there."

I took a deep breath and knelt down beside a man whose head was wrapped with filthy bandages. Thick splotches of blood covered the front of his tunic and continued down his left thigh. I felt for a pulse, found it faint and erratic, and handed Corpsman Stock a tag with a black star on it. This was a man who would not live and I knew it. I moved on to a young boy with sandy-colored hair whose leg had been shot off just below the knee. He was conscious, and when I lifted his wrist to check his pulse, he smiled and whispered, "Mum." I quickly located a tag with a red star indicating a need for blood plasma and attention in the surgical tent.

Three hours later, I ran out of tags with red stars and had to open another box. Most of the men I'd seen were in desperate need of plasma, morphine, and a new drug called penicillin. We'd had limited supplies of it over the past year at St Mary's, but our Dean, Dr. Wilson, had insisted that his personal patient, Winston Churchill, ensure that it would be available for troops during *Operation Overlord*. It would be months before we realized the tremendous effect it had had in saving lives.

Soon two more surgical tents were erected by the Army Corps of Engineers. I stood for a moment watching as orderlies lined up hundreds of stretchers of helpless men, many of whom would die before the tables and equipment could be put in place and operations could begin. Beyond the tents, further down the beach, another line was forming beside a cafeteria wagon. A quick glance at my watch told me it was dinnertime. The afternoon had disappeared in a sea of blood, shattered bones, crushed skulls, and missing limbs. I turned back to my task and pulled a tag with a red star for a man who had a three-inch-long crucifix embedded in his left palm.

At seven, both Corpsmen Stock and Stratton went off duty. They were replaced by Corpsmen Brown and Farrell. Ten minutes after he'd left, Corpsman Stock returned, bringing me a peanut butter and grape jelly sandwich and a tin cup filled with apple juice. I gulped them down in such a hurry that as I kneeled over my next patient, I began to burp.

A little after midnight, Stock came back over the ridge and told me to collect Lieutenant Colonel Broadhurst, bring our duffels, and follow him. He took us to a regular Army tent where other volunteer civilian nurses were settling in for what was left of the night. Four cots were lined up on one side of the tent and four cots were opposite. There was no room in between them, only a narrow passage in the middle. Miriam and I treaded our way through it to the back wall where I saw a covered bucket in one corner that I assumed was our toilet. One of the women pointed to the bucket in the opposite corner and said, "You can get some water for washing from that one, but you'll have to use your helmet for a basin." Neither Miriam nor I had the energy to wash. We didn't even bother to brush our teeth, but stretched out on our cots fully clothed with our boots still on. I knew I reeked with the animal odor of dried blood and the sweet sickening smell of wet clots that clung to my shirtsleeves and hung like Burma rubies from the edge of my tunic. I knew I stank of urine and mud, of salt spray and pus. But I hadn't the energy to care. I closed my eyes and conjured up the scent of the honeysuckle vines that grew behind my mother's garden.

* * *

The following morning I awakened at five to the sound of Corpsman Stock's voice outside our tent. He called to tell us that he'd brought mugs of hot tea and spam rolls, and urged us to come out and get our breakfast before it got cold.

We women sat on our cots eating, talking among ourselves, relishing the heat from the tin cups, trying to decide how best to wash and dry our dirty underwear. All of us were to report for duty at 0600, so time was precious. One of the nurses from London Central had brought a piece of small cording about fifteen feet long, and we strung it from the front pole of the tent to the back. We rinsed our panties out in our helmets and hung them over this improvised line.

Miriam and I met Dr. Atkins and Dr. Brompton just outside the surgical field tent, all of us arriving there about five minutes before six. Inside, the smell of fresh blood and human waste hung in the air, but the stronger scent of carbolic permeated everything. Debris had been removed from the floor and it had been mopped. The buckets that had been filled with body parts over and over the day before were now scrubbed clean and empty.

We made our way to the center area where three operating tables had been set up. Two metal tables, covered with white towels, stood nearby. I pulled one back to find shining sterilized clamps, lancets, retractors, rubber tubing, and syringes—all the tools we would need in the long hours ahead. Steam rose from two Primus stoves sitting off in a corner. On another table were a dozen blood pressure cuffs, a box filled with hypodermics, canisters of oxygen, and a Yankauer mask. Lined along the walls of the tent were dozens and dozens of stretchers of seriously wounded young men.

Dr. Atkins turned to Miriam. "You shall be the operating theatre manager, Matron-in-Chief Broadhurst. Decide where you want to start."

Miriam walked quickly to the far side of the tent and stooped to check the tags on a half dozen men lying there. She rose and pointed to one of the stretchers. "This man's dead," she said addressing Orderly Reed. "We'll start with the two on either side of him."

And we were off. Most of the men brought to us that morning had been treated initially by medical corpsmen during the invasion, and their wounds were covered with the filthy, foul-smelling bandages they'd been wearing for days. These had to be removed carefully and, more often than not, the area beneath them was infected. I had to clean the wound first with peroxide, give the poor man a shot of Novocain to deaden the area, cut away the damaged flesh, and sprinkle sulfonamide powder generously over the wound to kill the infection.

Men whose wounds had been treated by this method were taken by orderlies to the front of the tent where they awaited their turn on the operating table—an area that never cleared. As quickly as I could prepare a man for a surgical procedure, Miriam began to sedate him. She placed the cone-shaped "Yank mask" over the man's nose and poured pentobarbital sodium or sodium pentothal onto the piece of folded gauze she'd fitted over the cone. Once the patient was asleep, she began selecting sterilized instruments and handing them to the doctors.

My sixth patient that morning had suffered severe wounds to his feet. After giving him a shot of Novocain in the left one, I spent ten minutes removing chunks of shrapnel from his sole. He was conscious the entire time, and talked a mile a minute, telling me how anxious he was to get back on his feet so he could go back to the front to fight again. I took one look at his right foot and knew there was no hope. Miriam, who was standing beside me with the mask and gauze, nodded to the orderlies who took the man to the operating table where Dr. Brompton stood with a saw hanging from his hand.

Just before noon, an eighteen-year-old was brought to my table wearing around his left ankle a putrid bandage of dried blood running with pus. It took several minutes to cut it off. The wound was particularly bad because most of the bones in the boy's ankle had been crushed and the major artery running from the ankle to the foot had been severed. While I knew this would require amputation, I tried to reassure the boy, telling him that everything would be okay.

"No, it won't," he said, his voice a seething whisper. "I saw them! I saw all those poor guys get run over by those fucking tanks! I saw them fall in the water right in front of those goddamned monsters. And the fucking sergeant yelling 'Keep going! Keep going!' while those tanks crushed their bodies and buried them beneath the waves. They almost got me, too, but I managed to crawl right over top of one of those poor bastards. Then I finally get to shore and what happens? I get run over by a fucking jeep!"

Miriam brought me a bottle of chloroform. "The doctors are waiting," she said, and nodded to the orderlies who moved the boy to the operating table. The afternoon followed with pretty much the same routine as the morning. More crushed bones, more amputations, shrapnel buried in organs so eviscerated they couldn't be sewn up, brain matter seeping like pink icing from cracks in swollen skulls, ropes of bluish intestines cradled in strong young hands caked with ribbons of dried blood. We used up our supply of gauze and had to send an orderly for more. About four, we ran out of morphine ampoules, and Dr. Atkins gave Corpsman Stock a serious dressing down before he sent him for a new cache.

We'd administered four dozen bags of blood plasma and most of the penicillin on hand.

Soon, we found ourselves dealing with a particularly difficult patient and no supplies. When the orderlies brought the man to the auxiliary table, I checked the triage tag on his wrist because I felt sure he was dead. The star on the tag was red, not black, so I felt for his pulse and after a moment found it. He was barely alive. Both of his legs had been blown off below the knee and the stumps were wrapped in bandages so filthy I couldn't determine where they began or ended. His chest cavity was just that— a hole from which most of his left lung was missing. His eyes were open, so I passed my hand over them. When he didn't respond, I told Miriam I was going to change his tag to one with a black star. As I turned back toward the table to remove the old tag, a soldier burst through the tent opening, a Webley .38 in his right hand.

"Leave him the hell alone!" he cried, pointing the gun at Dr. Atkins. "Listen, you bastard," he yelled. "You leave my baby brother alone. He ain't going home to me mum without no legs. Get back!" He took a step toward Dr. Atkins, then turned back to the table, and whispered, "God forgive me!" before he shot his brother in the head. Orderly Reed grabbed him from behind and began wrestling him to the floor. As Orderly Haskins started toward them, the man turned from his dead brother and fired. And Mr. Haskins went down. Corpsman Stock rushed in, fell on the soldier, and snatched the gun from his hand. He helped Orderly Reed lift the man from the floor, and together, they led him away to a barn on the ridge where a crude brig had been cordoned off in a cow stall. Dr. Brompton and Dr. Atkins worked frantically to try to save Mr. Haskins, but there was nothing they could do. We learned later that the soldier who'd shot him was a member of an elite company of expert marksmen.

* * *

June 12, 1944
Gold Beach
Normandy, France

Dearest Mama,

*It's about five o'clock in the afternoon and I'm sitting
on a scrap of tarp with my back against the warm flat
stones of a wall, trying to free my mind of the horrors
I've seen over the last few days. My colleague, Corpsman
Reggie Stock, from the little town of Bolton in Hampshire,
is sitting about twenty yards away from me with his
harmonica. He's playing "I'll Be Seeing You" and you
cannot know how much I long for the day when I'll be
seeing you. This letter will not arrive in the mail, because
I intend to put it in my duffel for safekeeping and take it
home to you when this stupid damn war is finally over.*

*This past spring, Miriam and I volunteered to be part
of a select civilian medical corps destined for Normandy.
By now, you know all about Operation Overlord and that
our Allied forces have finally pushed the Germans thirty
miles inland from the Channel coast. I'm sure you were
stuck by the radio on June 6 and heard Churchill and Ed
Murrow on the BBC. While the number of lives lost has
been enormous, I will tell you in confidence, that it was
not as great as the War Ministry expected.*

*Miriam and I arrived at the British sector in an LCM,
an amphibious vessel manufactured in the good old US
of A. We went to work immediately in a large field tent
erected by the British Second Army Medical Corps. I'll
not bore you here with too many details about the ghastly
wounds, missing limbs, infections, horrific burns, or
problems we've had to deal with. I've written so much in*

351

my letters over the past three years about my work at St Mary's that you've read more than enough about my life as a nurse. But, Mama, working in a canvas tent on a beach while the fighting rages around you is very different from working in a hospital. We've averaged between 100–110 operations here per day, something that would never happen at St Mary's.

The most amazing thing is how much has been accomplished despite the grueling circumstances. The naked light bulbs that dangle from poles in the med tents sputter off and on all day and all night, and sometimes go out completely. When that happens, the orderlies bring in lanterns—which give virtually no light at all. Two of the major power generators sitting on the ridge above us were strafed yesterday by German planes, leaving us in the dark for hours. Conditions in London are dangerous, but they are nothing compared to this—the constant drone of bombers overhead; the high-pitched shrill of the fighters diving down on us; the ground shaking beneath our feet as rockets explode all around and, worst of all, the wrenching sobs of the dying boys as they beg for water and their mothers. It's almost more than anyone can bear.

Our ability to save lives has hinged on two things: (1) the steady supply of blood plasma and our ability (luck) to get the equipment necessary for a transfusion to a dying man _before_ he dies, and (2) a new drug called penicillin. I was told that large quantities of penicillin had been stockpiled in the US last year and brought to England specifically for use during the invasion. What a monumental difference it has made. I've treated men with it who were at death's door one day, and twenty-four hours later, found them sitting up in bed eating broth. Miriam told me that this drug has been around since the early

'20s, but was so expensive to produce that drug companies refused to take it on. She said that President Roosevelt did a little arm-twisting within the industry to force production. Thank God!

Plasma, penicillin, oxygen, morphine and sulfa drugs have been in good supply here thanks to "The Red Ball Express." Convoys of trucks are ferried across the Channel on large ships every day, bringing a hundred tons of supplies and equipment, food and petrol, to keep this massive operation going. They travel to bases as far as twenty-five miles inland, following a route that is marked by big red balls—hence, the name.

The Army Corps of Royal Engineers spent most of today setting up and stocking a mess tent that will feed three hundred people in a single seating. It will be officially "inaugurated" tomorrow afternoon at 4:00 p.m., and our commanding officer has asked me to sing.

One of the most interesting (and difficult) things about this situation, Mama, has been the treatment of the German prisoners. Some of the doctors and many of our orderlies simply refuse to help them in any way. I was told there are about four hundred prisoners being held here in "G Section," (including several dozen high-ranking officers), and at least half of these men are very sick. They have tapeworms and ringworms, scabies, lice, and rotten teeth and gums. Most are at least twenty pounds underweight and their pallor is the color of a raw biscuit. Besides all this, the Wehrmacht has provided a steady supply of Pervitin to all its soldiers, sailors, and airmen—a stimulant to keep them revved up and full of aggressive energy, which means they have had very little sleep. Men in the British Infantry stationed here told me that thousands of German soldiers had surrendered to them without the slightest *resistance. No wonder!*

*A fascinating feat of engineering occurred day
before yesterday when dozens of corpsmen from the
Royal Engineers started laying hundreds of square feet of
perforated metal sheets over wide gravel paths to make
runways large enough and strong enough to accommodate
big transport planes. Tomorrow morning, planes like
the Douglas C-47 will begin landing on these newly
constructed runways, bringing supplies, equipment, food,
even jeeps! As soon as one of these behemoths is unloaded,
forty of our patients will be carried aboard it on stretchers
and strapped into canvas cots attached to the walls of the
fuselage. A medical evacuation squadron of twenty-five
Navy nurses will arrive today, and it is they who will care
for our patients when these "flying hospital wards" return
to bases in England. The first US Army nurses reported
for duty on Utah Beach on Saturday, and a company of
QAIMNS (Queen Alexandra's Imperial Military Nursing
Service) were put ashore soon after.*

*I must bring this letter to a close and stand in for a
nurse matron working in the triage tent so she can get a
quick bite of supper. But before I do, I want you to know
that despite the long hours and hard work I've put in here,
I'm not blind to the enormous cost of this enterprise, the
incalculable sacrifice made by so many, and I don't mean
just those who've died here. I'm sure the war industries
in England, and at home, have raked in a fortune. But
what else could we have done? Thank God we had the
brains, the skills, and the determination to make this
military operation work. But what a godless waste all of it
is! Yesterday morning, I treated two brothers raised on a
farm in Gloucester. Both died before lunch. What of their
parents? How will they ever get beyond such a crushing loss?*

I love you beyond the stars, the sun, the moon and long for the day when I can cover your sweet face with kisses.

Your faithful daughter, Evelyn

* * *

Four o'clock came early, but I felt rested after a good night's sleep. Miriam, Dr. Atkins, and Dr. Brompton were tying on their aprons when I entered the surgery, and it wasn't long before our first patient was put on the auxiliary table and we got our routine going. The day was pretty much like the others. There were the usual problems with shattered bones, ruptured intestines, and shrapnel wounds.

Our Pharmacist's Mate came in at noon to keep an eye on things while we took a short break for lunch—the inevitable spam rolls, tinned fruit, and chocolate bars. The four of us spent those precious moments away from our duties talking about the real dinner we'd be served in the new mess tent that afternoon. How we longed for something good to eat.

Dr. Atkins released me at a quarter of four, telling me to go wash my face and comb my hair. He knew that Colonel Rankin had asked me to sing for the Corps when we gathered for dinner. The mess tent was a massive thing about half the size of a circus tent. In the center of each side, flaps had been pinned back to help keep the air circulating—which was a good thing as it was a warm, muggy day. I joined the volunteers from St Mary's at one of the side entrances at 4:05 and we went through the serving line together, cafeteria-style, each of us picking up metal trays filled with generous servings of sliced turkey and gravy and all the trimmings. I didn't want to, but after a couple of bites I knew I had to stop eating if I were going to sing.

Colonel Rankin came over to our table to tell me he thought I ought to sing just before dessert was served, because the apple cobbler had significance for the song I'd chosen, "I'll Be With You in Apple Blossom Time." He picked up a wooden box about two feet square, turned it upside down, and gave me a hand up before addressing the group. "We have a very special treat for you today. One of our own, Matron Evelyn Sanderson of the Second Army Medical Volunteers, has agreed to sing a song to commemorate this special occasion."

There was a lot of clapping and whistling before Colonel Rankin told the audience to settle down. "I'm very pleased that Matron Sanderson will be accompanied on the harmonica by Corpsman Reggie Stock." The audience began clapping again and I looked over at Reggie to let him know I was ready to begin. He put the harmonica to his lips and let out a slow, mournful chord in the key of G, and I let it hang suspended while I took a deep breath and imagined myself back on stage in New York. I delivered that song with as much emotion, as much sadness, as I could. We were all so homesick, so desperate for the war to be over. By the time I'd sung the first two measures, I could see tears glistening in the eyes of many.

As I began the line, "What a wonderful wedding there will be," Sergeant Wright came into the tent, a rifle held across his chest. He was followed by six shuffling, shabby Nazi prisoners who lined themselves up against the wall and turned their attention to me. I lost a note when I saw Osterlitz—third from the left—and had to close my eyes to bring the song to an end.

Everyone began clapping and I took a quick bow before I stepped off the wooden box and made my way over to Miriam. "I don't feel well," I whispered. "I'm going to lie down." I didn't wait for her reaction, but fled out the nearest opening, my hand clutched around my pistol as I ran to our tent.

A few minutes later, Miriam found me bent over the waste bucket. "What's the matter, honey?" she asked, kneeling down beside me. "What happened back there?"

"It's him," I whispered into the bucket.

Miriam put her hand under my chin and wiped my dripping mouth with her handkerchief. "Who? Who's him?"

"Osterlitz. The SS officer I told you about. He was one of the prisoners that came into the mess tent." I reached up, grabbed Miriam's wrist, and squeezed. "He's here and he'll kill me if he gets the chance! Didn't you see Sergeant Wright when he brought those prisoners in?"

Miriam was quiet for a moment. "No," she said finally. "I was looking at you."

She put her arm around my waist and walked me over to my cot, insisting I lie down. As soon as I was settled, she touched my forehead. "You're a little warm, Evelyn. You may have a low-grade fever. Just rest for a minute while I speak to Dr. Atkins. He's right outside the tent waiting for me to tell him what happened to you." She turned to go.

"Wait!" I blurted. "You can't tell him. You can't tell anyone outside Beech Tree. You'll have to lie."

And she did. She told Dr. Atkins I'd come down with a sudden chill and blamed it on all the excitement of the new mess tent and the rich food we'd eaten. She found Reggie Stock and asked if he'd keep watch outside our tent that night, assisting the regular guard with that duty. Then she came back in and pulled her cot over beside mine. "I'll be here all night," she said, patting my arm, "right here beside you if you need me." She filled a cup with water, added several drops of ammonia, and handed it to me.

At ten the next morning, Miriam covered me head-to-toe in blankets. "We're not taking any chances," she said as she and Reggie lifted me onto a stretcher. She held my hand and walked alongside as Reggie and another orderly carried me aboard a C-47 where I joined forty wounded soldiers on a flight to a military hospital in Kent.

CHAPTER 27

Bark Lodge

Betws-y-Coed, Wales • October 16, 1944

Oh, what a merry bunch we were that bright fall morning traveling through Oxfordshire and Gloucestershire on our way to Stoney's fish camp in Wales. How wonderful it felt to be out of the city away from the dust and dirt, away from the blood and mud, and the poor mutilated boys in the surgery ward.

Never mind the war. We were on holiday and that meant jokes and funny stories, laughter and song. As we rode along we played silly car games like "I Spy" and "Counting Cows." We lifted our voices in old songs and new songs and songs none of us had thought about in years. As we pulled into the rustic entrance at Bark Lodge, Stoney said, "Remember, lads, we're not here to plan any missions, or gripe about our jobs, or figure out how to solve the problems of this poor benighted world. We're here to relax, fish, and have fun."

Set deep in a wooded glen perched above the River Llugwy, the grounds of the camp reminded me of the Black Mountains of North Carolina. When we arrived late that afternoon, mighty chestnuts, oaks, and elms were surrendering their brilliance to ever-deepening shadows in what the French called *l'heure bleue*. From somewhere in the distance came the mournful cry of a turtledove, reminding me that our care-free day was coming to an end.

Bark Lodge was a two-story house designed in the shape of a V. The outside was made of bark shingles laid one over the other in an ancient pattern typical of that part of the country. The entry hall, which smelled of wood smoke and cigars, was paved with flagstone and hung with dozens of mangy hunting trophies. There was a first floor lounge of comfortable furniture, and off it, a beautiful stone terrace that overlooked the river. The two upstairs wings contained eight bedrooms and four baths. The lodge keepers, Mr. and Mrs. Hind-Farthing, lived in a cottage about thirty yards away. At Stoney's request they'd hired two extra maids to help with the housework and meals while we were there.

That evening, we gathered for drinks in the lounge. Afterward, Stoney invited us into the dining room where he surprised everyone by asking Miriam and me to sit on one side of the table beside each other. I wondered why, but kept quiet because I knew him well enough to know he had a reason. We luxuriated in a fine meal and the kind of lively conversation we usually enjoyed when all of us were together. As one of the maids brought in a tray of coffee, Mrs. Hind-Farthing came in behind her carrying a large white cake, which she set down in front of Miriam and me. On top, written in dark blue icing, was the word *Congratulations*.

"I told Mr. and Mrs. Hind-Farthing about your volunteering last June to work in the medical tents on Gold Beach," Stoney said, "and about the ceremony last month at Buckingham Palace when King George presented both of you The Order of the Golden Oak. They wanted to do something special, so I suggested that Mrs. Hind-Farthing make one of her delicious cakes."

Miriam and I were overcome by Mrs. Hind-Farthing's magnanimous gesture, and she was just as amazed when both of us rose to give her a hug—not the English thing to do. I should probably have told her about Buckingham Palace, about what it was like to meet not only King George and Queen Elizabeth, but also the Princesses Elizabeth and Margaret, who were so kind and gracious to the fifty-seven medical volunteers who'd been presented The Order of the Golden Oak that day. But I felt such remorse sitting there thinking about the three volunteers who hadn't come back—our orderly, Mr. Haskins, a doctor who'd drowned as he tried to save a mine sapper who'd been swept out to sea, and a nurse from London Central who'd suffered extensive head wounds during a bombing—that I couldn't bring myself to talk about the splendors of the palace, nor the thrill of meeting the royals. That had been a heady experience, but the fear I'd felt on Gold Beach still lurked in my gut clawing at me like a hungry beggar. I concentrated instead on the smiling faces around the room which helped me keep the lid on a pot of worrisome memories.

After generous servings of decadent cake and cups of real coffee, we adjourned to the lounge for brandies in front of the fire. Barney had recently returned from France where he'd gone in early August to join the Francs-Tireurs et Partisans ("free shooters") and Free French Troops in their fight to liberate Paris. One of the main reasons for our holiday in Wales was to give him a chance to tell us about this experience.

He began by saying that on the twentieth of August, the French Resistance had staged an uprising, and reminded us that the Francs-Tireurs et Partisans were not only French citizens, but also Algerians, Poles, Hungarians, and veterans of the war in Spain.

"Hundreds of women and children fought alongside us in the streets," he said, "hauling carts filled with rubble and rocks and boards that they used to construct barricades. They turned over Nazi trucks to use as cover, and cut down trees and blew up bridges and dug up pavement. We opened German work camps and prisons all over the city, and gave guns to any former prisoner who was willing to shoot Nazis. Hundreds of British and American fliers came out of hiding to fight with us and we managed to hold onto the inner city for three days and three nights, because the Germans hadn't the manpower to take us. Then Hitler's military governor, Dietrich von Choltitz, ignored the orders of the Führer and surrendered at the Hotel Meurice on the twenty-fifth of August. What a glorious moment that was!"

I interrupted Barney to say that all of us had seen the newsreels of General de Gaulle leading a parade down the Champs-Élysées on August twenty-fifth. "But we want to know more," I urged. "What went on behind the scenes . . . the stuff the cameras didn't capture?"

Barney laughed. "Ah, Evelyn, you little minx. You always want to know the other story, don't you? Well, all right—here it is. Something happened during the liberation that was unthinkable . . . at least as far as the Allies were concerned. On August twenty-fourth, General Leclerc, Commander of the Second Armored Division of the Free French Army, disobeyed the orders of his higher-up—that was none other than US Army Commander General Leonard Gerow—and sent a vanguard of his men into the city to say that he and his battalion were coming in to fight with us whether Gerow and the Allies liked it or not! Then the Free French Ninth Armored Company—mostly veterans of the war in Spain—rolled into the city on Sherman tanks that they'd confiscated from the Americans! Behind them came dozens of US Army trucks hauling Free French soldiers. Choltitz surrendered on the twenty-fifth, so de Gaulle made his victory speech later that day."

Barney stood up and put his index finger across his upper lip, and in a striking parody of the famously obstinate general, he repeated de Gaulle's entire speech in a mocking holier-than-thou fashion, and we all burst into gales of laughter. He laughed along with us until tears streamed from his beautiful eyes. But a moment later, the laughter stopped and he became serious again. "The world may never know, or understand," he murmured, "but it was critical for the citizens of Paris to liberate Paris . . . not the US Army . . . nor the British . . . nor the Russians. Paris did not want to be divided into zones by the Allies. Like all of France, Paris wants to be free to govern herself."

Rutledge rose from his chair and thrust his goblet toward Barney. "Vive la Paris!" he shouted, his voice trembling with emotion. "Vive la France!" We all stood to join him, and Stoney said, "To those who fought and died today and those who lived to fight another day," bringing our lovely day to an end.

* * *

When we women arrived downstairs the next morning, the men were gathered on the terrace smoking their pipes. Stoney was dressed in a fishing vest, waders, and a well-worn hat decorated 'round the crown with a delightful collection of colorful flies. Arrayed on a couple of wooden benches were all manner and size of fishing gear, and he urged us to take whatever we wanted and put it on, as Hind-Farthing would be along any minute to guide us on our expedition. About ten minutes later we followed our leader down to the banks of the river.

As Stoney waded in, he turned and said, "Remember, whatever you catch is dinner, so catch a good one. Come on, Evelyn. I'll help you get started."

He held up a rod. "Slowly," he said, demonstrating. "Pull your arm back slowly and give your wrist a little flick. Throw out the line as if you were a ballerina casting fairy dust . . . gracefully, gracefully." I watched in awe as he pulled back and his line arched in the air just where he intended, hovered for a split second, then dropped onto the water without a sound.

I tried to imitate him by casting ever so slowly, but my line collected on the water like a pile of spaghetti and there it sat. I tried again. Up . . . pause . . . flick. More spaghetti, but this time it landed on a passing limb. "Oh, goodness," I muttered.

"You're reaching too far," Stoney said. "Bring your elbow closer to your body. You'll get it. I don't know a single person, man or woman, who has mastered the art of fly-fishing in a single day. Why don't you just practice casting for a while? Raise the rod to noon, then flick down to ten o'clock."

I cast and cast . . . back and forth, back and forth. Out of the corner of my eye I saw Miriam pull in a large trout. Then Barney caught a pike, and a moment later Stoney was holding a net under a magnificent salmon. Thank goodness, I thought to myself as I reeled in my line. They've caught enough to feed us.

That night we had more fish than we could possibly eat. Mrs. Hind-Farthing spoiled us with her apple-current tarts, and we left the table well satisfied. Stoney, who'd set up the Victrola and rolled up the rug in the lounge, invited us to dance. By eleven, we were danced out and chose partners to play cards. That went on for perhaps an hour. About midnight, the others drifted off to bed, leaving Stoney and me behind.

I plopped down to curl up in a corner of the sofa. "Oh, Stoney, thank you for this glorious day and all you've done to make our time here so grand. I've never been to Wales before and I'm so taken with its beauty . . . the river, the hills, those huge boulders everywhere. This is such a magical place. I can't tell you how I dread leaving here tomorrow and returning to blood and burns and broken bones. Say it isn't so!"

Stoney sat down midway the sofa and handed me a freshly poured brandy. "Evelyn, how I wish I could wave a magic wand and make this time go on forever. But I have that meeting at the War Ministry tomorrow. Sylvia says Hitler is massing tanks and thousands of troops in Belgium. If only Stauffenberg had killed that crazy son of a bitch in July."

"He won't give up, you know. Hitler will never surrender." I leaned toward Stoney. "But let's not talk about that. You haven't mentioned your mother lately. How is she?"

"She's been confined to her rooms by her doctor. He says it just isn't safe for her to be moved up and down the stairs on a litter anymore. I'm sure I've told you it's tuberculosis of the spine—an awful thing. I doubt she'll live to see her rose garden bloom again."

"Oh, Stoney. I'm so sorry. I wish there were something I could do to help." I reached out and took his hand. He moved closer and drew me to him.

"Your being here is enough," he said, giving my shoulder a squeeze. "Just the sight of you lifts my spirits . . . and these days my spirits need lifting. That phone call I took after breakfast this morning was from Lydia's doctor at The Elms. She's tried to kill herself again. She somehow managed to get her hands on a metal spoon and evidently sharpened the end of it on the stone hearth in her room. Yesterday morning they found her at the foot of her bed in a pool of blood. She'd slashed both wrists and stabbed herself in the throat."

I was so shocked by what he said that I pulled away from him. "How awful! How is she? Are you going to see her?"

Stoney sighed. "No," he said, his voice edged with a kind of tedious impatience I'd never known him to use. "I've gone and gone again after these things have happened. And what difference has it made? None! My being there asking questions does nothing but take the doctors and staff away from their duties. Lydia won't know if I'm there or not . . . and she wouldn't care if she knew. I mean nothing to her. And I never have."

I leaned in and touched his left cheek. "How can you say such a thing? You and Lydia had a child together. Surely you cared for her."

"Yes, I cared for her when we were young. But I don't think she cared much for me. Ours was one of those situations . . . a matter of convenience, one might say. We grew up together and we married too young. In 1917, when I was at Eton, I came home for Christmas and saw Lydia at a dance. She was engaged to an officer and seemed very happy, but she had no problem dancing, or flirting with me, while her fiancé was giving his all for King and Country.

"The following June I joined the Falmouth Fusiliers, and my father, at my mother's insistence, intervened with higher-ups to make sure I wasn't sent to France. So I spent the last year of the war working in a supply office in Cornwall. That's where I met Sylvia's father, Dr. Blessington. He was our chaplain and a great comfort to me when my brother was killed.

"When the war ended in November, I went home to Stoneham Feld. That Christmas, I was invited to a holiday party where I saw Lydia again and learned that her fiancé had been killed in France. In January I returned to Eton, and that spring invited Lydia to the Marches . . . it's a spring celebration. She came and that's where our courtship began. A year later we married, and by the time another year had passed, I knew we were not suited. The following year she gave birth to our boy, Lionel. Then she suffered a miscarriage. Over the next three years, she gave birth to two baby girls, both of whom died before they could walk. About four months after we buried our last daughter, Lydia began having an affair with one of my closest friends. But I knew nothing at the time.

"As soon as Lionel was old enough for knee-britches, Lydia acquired the habit of disappearing for the weekend. She had a cousin in Cirencester, Lady Frances Montcriffe, and they were very close. Lydia used Frances as her cover. Word drifted back to me, of course, from people who'd seen Lydia in hotel dining rooms with her lovers.

"Lionel was struck and killed on a Tuesday morning. Lydia had returned to Stoneham Feld the Monday evening before from Thaxton-on Thames, the estate of Lord Richard Thaxton, with whom she was having an affair. Thaxton had lost his wife to cancer two years before. I learned later that Lydia was going to sue me for divorce so they could marry. Thaxton had a cattle ranch in South Africa and he'd already sailed for Cape Town that Tuesday morning. She and Lionel were going to join him there. On the evening following the accident, my groom called me to the stables and showed me the suitcases she'd hidden there among the saddle blankets. I opened all of them and found a letter to my wife from Thaxton that made their plans quite clear."

Stoney pulled me onto his lap and kissed me full on the lips. "That's enough about that depressing saga," he said. "I don't want to think about it anymore. Let's talk of something more pleasant. Let's *do* something more pleasant!" He kissed me again and again until I protested, saying I couldn't breathe. "Good!" he exclaimed, and began kissing me once more. Soon, we were lying on the sofa together, our bodies pressed against one another. Stoney's hand went to my breast and I moved closer.

While Stoney's hands moved over my hips and thighs, a smoldering fire spread through my body all but taking my breath away. As he unbuttoned his trousers, a voice inside me kept whispering *yes, yes, yes.* But it was another voice that cooled me down and brought me back to reality. Millicent's words reverberated like a chant in the dark recesses of my mind . . . *married man, married man, married man* . . . and I pushed Stoney away.

He jumped to his feet and gave me a scowl. "What's wrong, darling?"

"I can't do it," I mumbled. "I just can't. Even if your wife doesn't love you, you're still married. This kind of thing is nothing but heartache," I replied, fighting back tears.

Stoney wandered around the room for a few minutes buttoning up and rearranging his clothes. He took a moment to select a pipe from a rack on a table and brought it back to the sofa where he sat down and lit it. Then he turned to me, and with the tips of his fingers, began pushing tendrils of damp hair away from my face. "I've spoken with a barrister about getting a divorce," he whispered. "He says that if one of the leaders in Parliament were to introduce a bill that would provide more flexibility to the current laws, it might be possible. In a case like mine—like Lydia's—a team of psychiatrists familiar with her case would testify before a judicial panel. And if it is made clear the patient has no chance of recovering, the plaintiff could petition the courts for a special dispensation and our marriage could be annulled."

My temper got the best of me and I lashed out. "How many years would it take, Stoney? Five? Ten? By that time we'd be so old we wouldn't know which end was up!" I pulled away from him and began working on the buttons on my blouse. "I've told you about Larry Christian and why I left New York," I said, turning to look at him "I adore you, Stoney. But I can't stop asking myself why I keep doing this when I know our relationship can never be anything *but this.* And in your heart of hearts, you know that, too."

"No, I don't." he said. "I love you, Evelyn. And I won't give you up."

"That's what Larry said. He wouldn't *give me up.* But the Nazis marched into France and my world collapsed like a deflated balloon. And I was such a fool that I went on singing and dancing thinking it would all work out because I was Eve Sands. Eve Sands—a name that appeared in playbills and on marquees, in newspapers and magazines. There was an autographed picture of Eve Sands on the wall at Sardi's. Eventually, I had to face the fact that no Cole Porter tune, no orchestra warming up, no house lights going down made any difference. It took a long time, Stoney . . . months and months for me to realize that Eve Sands was nothing but a cover. Evelyn Sanderson had gone along for the ride, and in the end, it was *she* who'd been lost. I knew I had to try to find her again and that's what I've been trying to do since the night we met. Don't you see, Stoney? I can't be true to someone else until I'm true to myself."

Stoney stood up, reached for my hand, and pulled me to my feet. "But you're not the problem, darling," he said as he kissed me on the forehead. "I am."

CHAPTER 28

A-hole Buddy

London, England • January 2, 1945

Dearest Mama,

I'm sorry to be so slow with this letter, but we've been overwhelmed at St Mary's with wounded returning from the battlefields in Belgium, plus Miriam and I had to work both Christmas Eve and Christmas Day. We'd heard that US commanders doubted the Germans could mount another major offensive, but gosh, were they wrong! The boys who were brought here from hospital ships in mid-December told us they'd been pinned down in waist-deep snow in the Ardennes Forest with nothing but C rations and a sleeping bag, while temps dropped to zero each night. One man told us that when he awoke in the mornings his overcoat was always frozen to the ground. He went on to explain how he and a buddy dug a hole in the snow down to the dirt, lined it with straw, and spent the daytime hours (as well as night) back-to-back in that hole. He called his partner his "A-hole buddy." I'll let you fill in the missing letters if the censors let that pass. He also told us that during those awful nights, their M1 rifles froze solid and every morning they had to pee on them to warm them up enough to get them to work again. Those poor men had not had any hot food, no toothbrushes, no showers, no baths, no change of clothes for a month. Many came in wearing

German overcoats they'd stolen from corpses, and some had on rings and watches they'd stolen from German POWs. The ultimate prize is a German helmet, and we've seen several of those, too.

The biggest news here has been the Allied victory at Bastogne. Thank God the weather cleared so C-47s could fly in enough supplies and equipment to help the troops hold the line and keep the Germans from crossing the Meuse. In an address before Parliament, Churchill called it the "greatest American battle of the war."

But, Mama, what price glory? Thousands upon thousands of young men died—and not just ours. Many who made it back have lost their fingers and toes to frostbite and gangrene, and their legs and arms to ghastly wounds. We treated three dozen double amputees in our unit on December 24th. Merry Christmas, boys!

I treated one young man, about twenty-three, who was stationed in North Africa for two years, then sent to Italy and later to Belgium. He was on his way home to Staffordshire, having not seen his parents and younger siblings for four years. He was worried about what he'd say to them—what could they possibly talk about, as they had been living in two different worlds for so long? He has no idea how he'll make a living, because he went straight from school to war. But he was looking forward to lots of hot water for shaving, and clotted cream, and his mother's sticky toffee pudding. He was on his way to Horbeck's with his mustering-out pay to buy her a cameo broach, as "she's always fancied a cameo broach."

Dr. Platt-Simpson insisted that Miriam and I leave the hospital at five on Christmas Day and get some rest. I knew Jerusha had a goose in the oven, and told Miriam she wasn't going home to her cold flat and eat canned soup.

So she joined Sylvia, Stoney, Barney, Rutledge, Jerusha, and me. While it was not the feast we'd had last year at Croxdon House, it was fabulous! We had no tree, but enjoyed exchanging small gifts after dinner. No Boxing Day festivities, as all of us had to be at work the next morning!

Surely I'll be in Baker with you next year. I miss you so terribly and love you, love you so much.

OXOXOX, Evelyn

CHAPTER 29

Coldest Winter on Record

London, England • February 22, 1945

A heavy sleet rode in on a mighty wind this afternoon rattling the windows and depositing a treacherous glaze over everything. When my shift ended at six, Stoney picked me up at St Mary's and we went from there to Whitehall to fetch Sylvia. We'd hoped to go to Beech Tree Farm to plan our next mission, but the weather squelched that idea. So Stoney suggested Corrie Cottage instead.

As soon as Sylvia and I changed into sweaters and slacks, Jerusha called us to the table where she joined us for braised tongue and boiled parsnips. Sylvia gave us an update on the blizzard raging in the North Country, which has dumped more than two feet of snow across Yorkshire and Cumbria. "All the telephone lines are down there," she said, "and we haven't heard from our contacts up north for the past two days."

Jerusha changed the subject, telling us that Princess Elizabeth had joined the Women's Auxiliary Territorial Service as a trained mechanic and driver. "Ain't that something," she beamed, "the Princess Royal driving an Army truck! Wonders never cease!" She handed 'round bowls of spotted dick, minus the raisins, which made the name of the pudding ludicrous. It was a bit bland, but the dollop of apricot jam she'd put on top added flavor.

Afterward, Stoney led us into the lounge where we gathered near the fire to enjoy a tot of brandy. "To those who fought and died today," he began, "and those who lived to fight another day." We raised our glasses in unison, and I shuddered as the burning liquid slid down my throat.

Sylvia, who was sitting beside me on the sofa, set her empty glass down on the table. "There's been some interesting chatter on the wires over the last few days," she said, frowning. "It's been a bit spotty, but it seems a company of Russian soldiers stumbled upon one of Hitler's largest camps a couple of weeks ago. It's called Auschwitz and it's in southern Poland. We don't have much information, I suppose because the Soviets don't want it to be known, but evidently thousands of Jews died there. The Russian soldiers reported that they'd found about seven thousand *living skeletons* in the camp. The poor Jews they found told them that the Nazi guards had marched more than sixty thousand prisoners away the day before and had left them there to die. Pravda has been very quiet about it and seems to be focusing instead on news about the conference at Yalta, and Stalin's role in it."

"Dear Lord," Stoney exclaimed as he refilled our glasses. "The Nazi guards marched away sixty thousand? Hard to imagine, isn't it? Please keep us informed on that, Sylvia, as more information comes in."

Sylvia nodded to Stoney, then turned back to me. "I have another bit of news from the Soviets that's more personal, but I'm afraid it's rather *bad* news. Evelyn, I cannot say how much I dread telling you this. Your friend, Ireni Igorsky, is dead. It came over the wires today and I made a copy." She pulled a folded piece of paper from her pocket and handed it to me. I took it, but couldn't bring myself to open it. Finally, Stoney took it from my hand and read it aloud.

Russian Fighter Pilot Dies in Crash

Russian ace, Ireni Igorsky, Major in the 586th Fighter Regiment of the Soviet Women's Air Force, who was known as the beloved White Rose of Stalingrad, died in an explosion over Düsseldorf, Germany on January 29, 1945. Igorsky, one of the most decorated pilots in Soviet air history, and member of

Russia's elite Order of the Hero of the Soviet, was memorialized by Generalissimo Joseph Stalin in a ceremony in Moscow on February 4. Navigator Katrina Nosal and Gunner First-Class Vera Polaza, who were with Igrosky, survived and remain in hospital where they are listed in critical condition.

I excused myself and hurried upstairs to the bathroom where I collapsed on the toilet seat and had myself a good cry. Over the next few minutes both Sylvia and Stoney came up to check on me. Stoney talked to me through the door, asking if I wanted to postpone the meeting for a few days. "Should I tell the others to go home?" he asked. Since it was hard for all of us to get together, and Barney was leaving again, I told him I'd come down.

When I walked back into the lounge, the BBC was reporting on the Pacific, where US Marines had landed on a tiny volcanic island called Iwo Jima—a stronghold of the Japanese and home to a very strategic air runway. Once the Americans raised Old Glory on Mount Suribachi, C-47s had been able to land, bringing weapons, food, and equipment. This victory, which had come at a terrific loss of life, was a major breakthrough, as Allied planes could refuel on that little island and fly their bomb loads all the way to Japan.

The announcer went on to report that British, American, and Canadian troops were approaching the Rouen River where they would join the US Ninth Army and push on to the Rhine. Every effort was being made on the part of the Russians and Anglo-Allies to reach Berlin and bring the war to an end in Europe.

This drive to Berlin by the Allies was the reason our Beech Tree Group had gathered on such a bitter night. Barney had been urging us to mount one last mission for the sake of our colleagues who were blowing bridges and railroads, and cutting telegraph and telephone lines in an effort to help the Allied forces push German troops from the borders of France and Belgium back into the heart of Germany. Stoney and Barney had decided that Barney would make a trip along the back roads of the eastern ranges of the Ardennes to deliver thousands of American dollars to our colleagues there. What remaining diamonds Stoney had, no matter their true worth, would not bring anywhere near what they had earlier. So Barney thought US dollars were the answer. Like chewing gum and chocolate bars, he said, they'd be welcomed anywhere.

Neither Sylvia nor I had any prior knowledge of the plan to secret thousands of US dollars to our colleagues. Until we began talking about it, I'd thought Barney was going on this mission alone. And evidently, so did Stoney. When Barney looked at me and suggested I wear the uniform of the French Red Cross, he caught me off guard. I opened my mouth to ask *why* just as Stoney came out with an emphatic *"No!"* He turned to Barney, eyes like daggers, and said, "Evelyn's not going this time. You're doing this one on your own, my friend. I've got the cash ready and all you need do is pack it in a money belt and hide it under your priest's robes."

Barney shook his head. "Evelyn has to go," he said. "Someone with experience must come along in case something happens to me. I need a first-rate partner and that's Evelyn."

Stoney leaned toward Barney, and through clenched teeth, spat, "Are you mad? Evelyn's been shot. She spent two and a half months in a French convent. She's given her pound of flesh!"

Barney, who was not easily cowed, merely nodded. "Yes," he said. "Evelyn has suffered, as have many." He settled back into his chair. "I suppose I could ask Holmes Jephson or Ian Talbert. But I don't have faith in them the way I do Evelyn. For this kind of work, you need someone with a bag of tricks and that's Evelyn."

When Stoney looked over at me, I saw a storm brewing in his dark eyes. "Please don't do this, Evelyn," he begged. "Please don't put yourself in danger again. I'll get someone else to go with Barney."

Barney got up and began refilling our glasses. "I'm afraid you don't understand, old boy," he said with his back to Stoney. "I've accrued a considerable amount of sweat equity in Evelyn . . . as she has in me. We trust each other completely and that's critical to the success of any mission." He shrugged his shoulders as he turned around to look at Stoney. "If you're not satisfied with my reasoning, why not ask Evelyn? Ask *her* if she wants to do this . . . or not. What do you say, Evelyn?"

A twitch grabbed my side, pinching the place where I'd been shot. It passed quickly, but I needed no reminder of how scared and miserable I'd been in the convent—and the terrifying nights alone in le cache when I feared I'd never get out alive. However, France was free now, and the areas along its borders with Belgium and Luxembourg where Barney and I would be working were overrun with Allied troops. And I knew Osterlitz had been taken prisoner, so I didn't have to worry about him anymore.

I reached out to cover Stoney's hand with mine. "It will be my swan song," I said. "I promise. Remember what you said to me after Johann Claus and Blackstoke were arrested and sent to prison? You said I should never forget that I'd done the right thing . . . that because of me, thousands of lives had been saved. I think I'd better go with Barney."

Stoney gave my hand a quick squeeze and muttered, "Someone should have cut out my tongue." He was quiet for a moment and we all waited, as his word was the *last* word. Finally, he zeroed in on Barney and said, "I don't like it. And I want my concerns understood by everyone here." His eyes flashed as he looked back at me and said, "Especially you, Evelyn."

He rose from his chair, slammed his glass down on the table, and streams of golden liquid sloshed over the rim. "I've been informed that Barney and his partner will sail with the tide tomorrow night. Both of you have made up your minds to do this, so I'm no longer needed here." He left in a huff, rattling the hinges on the door with a bang.

Sylvia followed behind him and started up the stairs. "You'll be on a Red Cross hospital ship that's sailing from Dover tomorrow night at two thirty," she called back to us. "I think Barney has taken care of the details, Evelyn, so I'll see you when you get back. Good luck!"

Left alone, Barney and I sat down together on the sofa to go over the plan. "I'm ready to go," I said, "but I have one condition. I won't dye my hair brown. It's finally long enough to pull back into a bun. And I'll cover it with something so it won't show beneath the Red Cross cap."

Barney nodded. "I'm not as concerned about your hair as I once was. I don't think the fact that you're a redhead will matter much in the areas where we're going." He paused to clear his throat. "Don't worry about Stoney, Evelyn. It's not only you he's fretting about. He had a call this afternoon from Lydia's doctor in Cumbria. They haven't been able to get her to eat anything. The doctors wanted to start feeding her through a tube, but Stoney absolutely refused. He's planning to drive up to Cumbria to meet with the doctors as soon as the roads are passable. Lydia Beeton-Howard is a wretched soul, Evelyn. And she's hell-bent on being with her boy . . . and the only way she can do that is by leaving this earth. I'm just glad she's not my responsibility."

With that, he took another sip of brandy. "Now, let me tell you about our mission. Remember Marcel Guillion's brother, Rene? He's meeting us at the docks in Calais with his truck, which he'll load with goods packed in Red Cross cartons that we'll be delivering along our route. You and I will carry the money. Maybe you could get five medical envelopes to put it in." He paused to remove a packet from inside his jacket pocket. "Here's ten thousand US dollars in five-hundred-dollar bills," he said, handing it to me. "Put two thousand into each of the five envelopes . . . one envelope for each of our contacts. You'll be taking your medical bag, right?"

I nodded.

Barney downed the last of his drink. "Perhaps you can put the envelopes of money down in the bottom under some bandages and underwear or something. After we board the ship, I'll transfer half of it to the money belt I'll be wearing under my priest's robes." He looked toward the front door. "I'd better go now and see if I can smooth the old rooster's ruffled feathers."

CHAPTER 30

Haus Kreble

Merzig, Germany • February 23, 1945

When we awoke the next morning, a quarter-inch of ice lay like a mirror on the streets making early morning travel impossible. But the temperature soon rose to the mid-thirties, and by eleven, I was able to get to St Mary's. Miriam was there, but the rest of our staff hadn't shown up.

Hundreds of medics had recently been released from the British Army Medical Corps and Dr. Platt-Simpson had requested assistance from their commander, Colonel Rankin. Miriam called me into her office to tell me that six former medics would be under my supervision in our unit until eight that evening. I hated to tell her that I was leaving on another mission and would be gone for the next four days, but I had no choice. I promised to stay until eight and asked if she could spare five sulfonamide envelopes.

"Sure," she said, "I have plenty. And don't worry about these medics. They have lots of experience. And besides, more staff should be able to get in tomorrow. Let's see . . . what's today? Oh, yes, it's Tuesday. You'd have had the next three days off anyway, Evelyn."

She turned toward the door. "Here come the boys now. Get them started in pre-op and meet me back here at noon and I'll help you get your bag ready for the mission. Thank goodness we have plenty of penicillin."

I was late getting to Miriam's office for lunch, arriving there about a quarter after twelve to find her pouring tea into cups. "Come on in, partner," she said. "I took the liberty of grabbing some pea soup and crackers in the cafeteria. I hope that's okay."

"Oh, Miriam, you're an angel—so thoughtful. One of these days, all of this will come to an end and you and I will be separated by the Atlantic Ocean. I can't bear the thought of that."

"We'll figure it out when it happens, honey. Now take a load off and sit down while I open your soup. What's all this about a mission? I thought the Beech Tree missions were finished."

I told Miriam why Barney needed the envelopes, where we were going, and how Stoney had gotten his hackles up because he didn't want me to go.

"Stoney has a point," she said, handing me the soup and a mug filled with hot tea. "You've been shot, Evelyn. And even though our boys have pushed the Germans way back, it's still very dangerous on the continent. I think you should take something along for protection, just in case."

I gulped down a spoonful of warm green mush. "Barney will have his pistol and I'm sure Rene will take one, too. That ought to be enough."

"What if you're separated from them? What if something happens to Barney?"

"Oh, Miriam," I sighed. "We'll only be gone three days."

"Look what happened when you and Barney went to Roscoff. Barney was arrested by the Nazis and beaten within an inch of his life. And you had to run to save yours. And the two of you were separated and never got back together . . . remember?"

"Of course, I do. But the war is almost over and this mission's a lot less complicated than that one was. I could take something to be on the safe side, but it'll have to be something small enough to fit in my bag. I know a cyanide capsule is small, but I'm not doing that."

"I know you won't," Miriam replied, "and I don't blame you. But I'm not talking about how you'd kill *yourself*, Evelyn. I'm talking about how you'd kill someone else. I think your best bet is 10ccs of potassium chloride."

I bit down so hard on the metal spoon in my mouth that a chill went up my spine. "Good lord, Miriam! That's crazy! Just the thought of that makes me cringe."

The idea of killing someone scared me so badly that I fled to the sink where I quickly emptied tea dregs from my mug and began washing it. "I don't want to do that," I murmured, scouring the mug with the kind of ferocity I used on bedpans. "I don't have the kind of nerve it takes to kill someone."

Miriam came over, took the dishrag from me, and threw it down in the sink. She gathered my soapy hands inside hers, and I watched as her green eyes darkened to slate. "So, you'd rather die than try to save yourself?"

A long empty moment passed between us as her hands tightened around mine. "Just do this for me," she said. Five little words uttered in perfect cadence that went, like a train on a track, from her mouth to my brain. "I'll feel better knowing you have a hypodermic of potassium chloride with you. Okay?"

I nodded. Miriam released my hands and went straight to the supply cabinet. "I'll prepare it with a 15-gauge needle and put it in your bag right in that big pocket down on the end where you usually store hypodermics," she said as she began pulling things from shelves. "And along with it, I'll add a half dozen hypos of penicillin and a half dozen of morphine."

"But they'll all look alike. How will I know the difference? I wouldn't want to give someone who's supposed to get an injection of penicillin something as dangerous as 10ccs of potassium chloride."

Miriam opened a box, drew out a glass ampoule of colorless liquid, and studied it for a moment, turning it 'round and 'round in her fingers. "Why don't I label all the penicillin hypos with a capital *P* and all the morphine hypos with a capital M? I'll make the labels on the typing machine so you'll be able to see them clearly. I won't label the hypo of potassium chloride. It'll be the plain one with no label. Okay?" She gave me a quick glance. "Hurry up, honey. We've got to be back in the ward in five minutes. Now, where'd I put that big roll of gauze?"

* * *

I left home wearing long silk underwear, two pairs of wool stockings, the winter uniform of the French Red Cross, a wool overcoat, cap, scarf and gloves, and still I was freezing! The wind cut right through me as I made the short walk down the gangway of the ship to the dock in Calais. Barney was just ahead of me, trying desperately to keep his fancy hat from blowing off. He was dressed in the heavy black robes of a French curate, and I assumed he was wearing several layers of clothing beneath them. He looked about five pounds heavier, but that could have been the bulky money belt he was wearing.

Rene and his gray truck with the large red crosses were a welcome sight. It was snowing, but the truck's heater was working and soon the three of us were comfortably riding the back streets away from the city. Rene took us to an inn where we had a hearty breakfast that included precious eggs. Afterward, we slept there for a couple of hours.

When I got up, I fastened my hair in a bun on the back of my head with Kirby Grips and covered all of it with a dark brown, tightly knit snood. Then I used brown mascara to darken my brows. My carte d'identité said I was a brunette named Claudine Morisette, and I needed to look the part.

By lunchtime, we'd crossed the border into Belgium and reached our first destination—the village of Leuze where we took a table in a small out-of-the-way café, ordered coffees, and waited. A bearded man came from out of a room behind us and sat down. Barney carefully passed him an envelope of bills. He whispered, "Merci, Father Barney," and disappeared.

That night, we met another man in a wooded area off the road near Palisent. As we stood together shivering in the blowing snow, he said, "Beware, comrades. There are cells of Boche hiding in these woods waiting to slit your throats." We spent that night in a safe house with friends of Rene's who'd operated it for the past five years.

On Saturday morning, Rene filled the truck's gas tank, along with an extra gallon container, which he put in the back among the Red Cross cartons. We continued south, staying just inside the French border with Luxembourg, to Bouzonville. The roads were rough but passable, and the snow wasn't falling as heavily as it had been, so we were making good time. We stopped for lunch at a picturesque hotel outside Creutzwald, about two miles from the German border, where Barney gave the owner one of the envelopes. Three officers wearing uniforms of the Free French Army were seated at a table nearby. As we got up to leave, they came over, shook our hands, and thanked us for our help.

Late that afternoon, we entered the vast forests of the Vosges Mountains and headed north into a world blanketed by deep snow. "We just passed into Alsace," Barney commented. And Rene grunted before responding, "The Boche are angrier than ever about their sacred Alsace region, but it will soon belong to France once more."

The road narrowed and we found ourselves in a canyon walled on both sides by rocky cliffs dotted with majestic fir trees, their branches drooping with the weight of the snow. I remember I had just commented about how silent the woods were when the truck lurched to the left and we heard a crunching sound as it crashed into something. "Merde," Rene grumbled under his breath. "Qui est ce?"

When we got out we discovered that several rocks, the size of basketballs, had been evenly placed in a line across the road. "Huh," Rene said, scratching his chin. "It looks as if someone deliberately put these here." Barney squatted down to help him remove the rock from under the truck's fender. Just as they dragged it clear, we heard an engine grind into low gear and turned to watch as a green Dodge truck with US Army painted on the bonnet came slowly around the curve toward us.

"Oh, good," Barney said, standing up. "Now I can get some American cigarettes." Those words were hardly out of his mouth when a soldier in a US Army uniform jumped from the cab of the Dodge, raised a pistol, and shot Rene. A second man, also dressed in a US Army uniform, took a step toward us. Barney snatched the Webley from inside his robe and got off a shot that grazed the man's left temple. Two soldiers, who were standing behind the roof of the cab, raised high-powered rifles, and fired. Before I could duck, a bullet zinged past me and hit Barney. I watched in horror as his skull burst like a melon sending shimmering fragments of bone and teeth into the air amid a swirling vortex of quivering pink flesh. Blood, in great gobs, catapulted skyward with the force of a volcano, then rained down like rose petals onto the snow.

I fell to my knees and buried my hands in the steaming gore strewn across the front of Barney's robe, trying to get a hold so I could lift him up. His beautiful eyes were gone, but he kept gurgling, so I ran my thumb inside what remained of his mouth hoping he could speak.

"Get up, whore, so I can knock you down again," a deep voice demanded in singsong French.

I managed to get up on one knee before the voice backhanded me on the side of my head. He reached down, grabbed my wrist and hauled me, like a deer carcass, across a blood-drenched stretch of snow to the open door of the green truck. There he stopped and there I remained with my face down. I heard a *thud* as he threw something onto the cab's floor. Then he leaned over me, and using the barrel of his pistol, pushed the skirt of my coat, and my uniform, up to my waist. "What a glorious ass!" he boomed in a voice that sounded familiar. Then he began to chuckle and I heard another voice say, "Nice, Oberst Osterlitz."

Osterlitz! The sound of the name made my heart jump. But Osterlitz is in prison, I reminded myself. It can't be him!

The Dodge came to life and he jerked me to my feet and shoved me onto the seat between him and the driver. As we began moving into the shelter of the forest, he turned to look at me and I pulled as far away from him as I could. "You French think you've got your country back, don't you?" he sneered. "Well, think again! Alsace belongs to Germany, to the Third Reich!"

He thrust his hand inside my coat, savagely grabbing my right breast. "But in the meantime, you and I will have some fun, won't we?" The dimple in his left cheek deepened as he leered at me—a ludicrous anomaly to what I knew was his true nature. He continued to paw me, rubbing one of his big hands over both my breasts, then pushing it down between my legs as he and his driver passed a bottle of schnapps back and forth.

A miserable hour passed before the driver veered off onto a side road and stopped in front of a dilapidated two-story building with a marquee that read Haus Kreble. Osterlitz got out and peeled off the US Army uniform and cap he'd been wearing, revealing the black uniform of the SS. On each shoulder was a silver-braided epaulet. Since I'd last seen him he'd been promoted to the rank of colonel.

As soon as he'd straightened the hem of his jacket, he grabbed my medical bag from the floor and dragged me out of the truck. "Ferme la bouche!" he ordered. "If you utter one sound, I'll cut your throat."

I kept my eyes on the frozen gray ruts beneath my boots, my ears on the hard crunching sounds that split the air as I was dragged forward. We walked across a porch and into a small lobby dominated by a wide ornate desk. Standing behind it was a tall black-haired woman with deep-set smoky eyes. Osterlitz gave her a curt nod and she hesitated a moment before she looked at me and said, "Welcome to Merzig."

Osterlitz led me up a set of carpeted stairs and down a hallway to a room where he unlocked the door and relocked it as soon as he'd pushed me inside. There was only one window, and what light was coming through it was fading. But it was enough for me to get my bearings. Sitting beneath the window were a ratty upholstered chair and a small table that held a candle in a chipped cruet. On the wall opposite was an old wooden bed with four high posts crowned by large Empire-style finials. A beat-up dresser, empty except for a single candle in a stand, stood just inches from its footboard. I took a step toward the window hoping to see how far it was to the ground. But Osterlitz jerked me back and sank his fingers into my right shoulder with such force that I went down on my knees. "Swine," he whispered. "You French whores are nothing but swine."

Then he yanked me by the hair and the snood I was wearing came away in his hand. "You," he screamed as his eyes widened in surprise.. "The English bitch! What luck!" Grabbing the lapels of my coat, he snatched me up lifting me off the floor. "Get your clothes off, bitch," he ordered, his face so close I could smell the schnapps on his breath.

I undressed as slowly as possible, watching over my shoulder as Osterlitz set my medical bag on top of the dresser and began rifling through it. He removed a roll of gauze and a bottle of carbolic and turned back to me.

I was completely undressed, shivering from the cold, hugging my arms across my chest trying to get warm. I took a step back as he unbuckled his belt and drew it from around his ample girth. He held the buckle end with his hand while he grabbed my left arm and struck me three times across the shoulders. "Get down," he ordered, and I sank to my knees once more.

He wrapped the buckle end of the belt around my left wrist, tied it off, and looped the center section of the belt around the bedpost at the foot of the bed. Then he grabbed my right wrist and wrapped the other end of the belt around it, tying the end in a knot. He pulled a box of matches from inside his jacket and stepped to the window to light the candle on the little table sitting beneath it. Then he went back to the dresser, lit the candle in the stand, and plunged into my bag again.

I heard a clinking sound and knew he'd removed the scissors—a pair of regulation issue that I'd sharpened just the week before. He began cutting something and I glanced up to see him drenching a piece of gauze with carbolic. He cursed again as he dabbed at the bloody scrape at his temple. He paid no attention to me for a while, but sat down in the chair and poured himself a glass of dark liquid. As he put the glass to his lips, a faint humming, like that made by a squadron of bombers, reverberated in the distance. He sprang from the chair to look out the window. "Goddam fucking Americans and their shit for planes," he hissed. He turned, crossed the room in two steps, and jerked me by the hair. "Farmers and cowboys and money-grubbing Jews—the scum of the earth!" he railed, as he began swaying back and forth. He thrust his hips toward me, and as he unbuttoned his trousers, a stench like rotting horse flesh made me gag. I began to cough, but he paid no attention, so intent was he with his conquest.

I've never been as degraded as I was at that moment, never felt more helpless, nor worthless. He put a hand on either side of my head and held it like a vise while he banged the back of my skull, over and over, against the dresser all the while ramming himself in and out like a jack hammer. After he'd spewed his filth into my mouth, he climbed up on the bed and fell into a deep sleep.

Somewhere a clock struck nine, and soon after, I heard light footsteps coming down the hall. But whoever it was went past the door. Men's voices were coming from the room below, and there was a sound like silverware makes when it hits the side of a plate, so I assumed they were having dinner.

Soon they were singing, their voices slurred. They started with "The Horst Wessel Song," moved on to "Deutschland Über Alles," and ended with "Die Wacht am Rhein." When I heard chair legs scraping the floor, I knew they were done with their merrymaking and would soon be coming up the stairs. I drew my legs in, hoping I might be able to slide under the bed, but the rails were too low.

I dozed, but came fully awake when Osterlitz sat up suddenly and began talking. "I must eat," he said before staggering from the side of the bed down to the dresser, where he leaned into the mirror to study the scrape on the left side of his head.

"Mein Gott," he mumbled. "I'll have a scar there for sure." He turned around and began yelling, "It's all your fault, cunt! If it weren't for you, this never would have happened." He gave me a vicious kick before he untied the ends of the belt from around my wrists. "On the bed, whore. I'm going to fuck your ass until you die." He bent down, scooped up one of his socks, and crammed it in my mouth.

I fell against the bed, but regained my balance and scrambled toward the headboard to try to get away. But he hauled me back and punched me in the mouth. Then he crawled on top of me, pinning me down. "Do you realize," he said as he began rutting like a hog, pushing deeper and deeper into my anus, "that hundreds—perhaps thousands—of good Germans have died because of you!"

He sank his teeth into my right shoulder and buried his fingernails in the flesh of my hips. Then he turned me over and viciously bit my nipples and I all but passed out from the pain. When he was done, he lurched his way to a chamber pot at the far end of the dresser and stood there, hands on hips, while he peed a loud stream, most of which went on the floor. Then he crawled on top of me again.

Just after the clock struck midnight, Osterlitz rose from the bed and poured himself another drink. He sank into the chair with a grunt and pressed his fingertips to his forehead.

"Schiest," he moaned, "my fucking head hurts!" Suddenly, he lurched from the chair and wrenched my arm. "You have morphine," he screamed. "Get it!"

Fearing he would hit me again, I moved as quickly to the dresser as my poor battered body would go and lifted the candle to search the end of my bag where Miriam had placed the hypodermics. I rifled through them until I located one labeled with a capital M, set the candle back down on the end of the dresser, and turned toward him.

"Give it to me, stupid whore!" he said. "Put the needle in my fucking arm."

After I'd finished, he dragged me to the foot of the bed, and knotting the ends of his belt around my wrists, he tied me to the post. Then he crawled up on the bed and was soon asleep.

That's when I went to work on the belt. Using the index finger and thumb of my right hand, I pushed and pulled, trying to free the knot tied around my left wrist. It wasn't long before my fingers seized and I had to stop. Then I started again, but my hand was trembling so badly that I couldn't get my fingers to work. It was then that I remembered the scissors. If I could get to them, I might be able to cut the belt. I got up on my knees and peered over the end of the bed. Osterlitz was on his back, sleeping the undisturbed sleep my patients experienced after I'd injected them with morphine. It was now or never.

Every muscle in my shoulders, back, and legs screamed in protest as I slowly rose to my feet, dragging the slack in the belt up the post as I went. The candle was still burning in the stand and the scissors were lying where he'd left them in the center of the dresser. My right shoulder burned as I stretched it just far enough for my elbow to make contact with the dresser's edge. Now, I thought, if I can just get my hands that close. Oh, God, I prayed, help me get those scissors.

I lowered myself back down the bedpost and eased my bloody bottom to the floor to look around. The skirt from my uniform was lying about two feet away. I stretched my legs out in front of me and, using my toes, grabbed the hem and dragged it across the floor until it was lying beneath the edge of the dresser.

It seemed to take forever, but I sidled up the bedpost again. Then I blew out the candle and waited for it to stop smoking. Stretching the slack in the belt as far as possible, I thrust my elbow at an angle and knocked the candle from the stand onto the top of the dresser. Bloody saliva dripped steadily from my lips, but I sucked it back while I thrust my head forward like a turtle, clamping down with my teeth on the wick end of that little wax projectile so I could drag it toward the scissors. When I finally reached them, I eased off on my bite so the base end of the candle would slide down inside the rim of the nearest finger loop. Then I began to pull. Slowly, I kept saying to myself as I buried my teeth in the soft flesh of the candle, pressing down to hold it in place. A second later the scissors slipped off the edge of the dresser and fell onto the soft folds of my skirt.

I let go the candle, sank down the bedpost again, and sat on the floor to catch my breath. Then I used my toes to pull the skirt, and its precious cargo, toward me. I tried to pick the scissors up with my toes, but couldn't get a grip. So I got up on my knees and twisted my body around so I could kneel over them. I grabbed one of the finger loops with my teeth and pulled. It was nothing short of a miracle that the slack in the belt was just long enough for me to get my right thumb down into that loop. I jerked it upright, separating the two blades, and using my knees as a vise, I held the scissors in place and began sawing on the leather belt.

My hands swelled so badly that every few minutes I had to stop. About an hour later, the belt finally came apart, and I swallowed and swallowed as lump after burning lump rose in my throat. I held onto the bedpost trying to stand, but my legs had turned to jelly. I lifted one, then the other, over and over, until circulation brought them back. While I worked my legs, I kept my eyes on Osterlitz. He appeared completely inert, but I knew he'd put up a fight and I began thinking about how to deal with that.

After freeing my wrists from the ends of the belt, I rubbed them until I was able to flex my fingers. I re-lit the candle and began rummaging around in my bag until I located the two extra pairs of stockings Miriam had insisted I take. Then I hobbled to the head of the bed where I lifted Osterlitz's left wrist and wrapped one of the stockings tightly around it. Using a double knot, I tied it to the post above his head. Then I did the same with his right. With the second pair, I tied each of his ankles to each of the posts at the foot of the bed.

I went back to my bag, found a roll of gauze, and searched the pockets until I located a wooden tongue depressor. I stuck the end of the depressor deep into the center of the roll of gauze and wrapped the two together with adhesive tape. My fingers trembled as I fished out the hypodermic with no label and removed the cap from the long needle. After slipping my left hand into a leather glove, I picked up the "fat lollipop" I'd fashioned from the roll of gauze and tongue depressor.

When I climbed up on the bed beside Osterlitz, the springs creaked, giving me an awful fright. I waited a moment, then lifted myself over him and settled down on my knees. I took a deep breath, bent down, and put my ear to his naked chest. While I could hear the slow, steady beat of his heart, I knew I needed to be closer to the source of that sound. I raised up and moved forward on my knees about an inch, then carefully bent down to listen to his chest again. His heartbeat sounded much stronger and I knew I'd found the aorta, the place where I could do the most damage. Using my left hand, I steadied the gauze lollipop directly in front of his open mouth. With my right, I took aim and plunged the needle into the top of his heart.

His eyes flew open and I was somehow satisfied knowing he'd seen me. His teeth clamped down over the wad of taped gauze and I crammed it as far back into his throat as I could while he spit and gagged and gasped for breath. When he began to heave and buck his death dance, I ground the needle in, rotating it 'round and 'round, until he finally went limp.

I wasted no time getting dressed and quickly gathered up all my things. Just as I cut the last stocking from Osterlitz's ankle, the clock struck five. I put the remains of the stockings and his belt inside my bag, took the key from his trouser pocket, and unlocked the door.

With boots in hand, I crept out in stocking feet and locked the door behind me. I was afraid to go down the carpeted stairs to the front door, afraid I'd be seen. So I tiptoed down the hall and all the way 'round to the other side of the building, where I found a handwritten exit sign on a door. I opened it to falling snow and made my way down a set of crude stairs. When I reached the bottom, I slipped into my boots and hurried toward the woods behind the inn.

I'm sure it was nothing but adrenaline that kept me going in those frightening moments, that and my need to get as far away as possible. But whatever it was didn't last long. I'd not gotten more than three hundred feet when my head started swimming. Suddenly the ground beneath me shifted sending me reeling into the trunk of a tree. When I came to, I found myself lying in the snow. Oh, God, I thought, pulling myself up to a sitting position, what happened? For a few minutes I sat there wringing my swollen hands trying to get my mind to work. My first clear thought was of my mother. What would she think when she learned I'd been killed in Germany? Then I did the only thing I could think of. I whistled. But the three notes Lily Suchette had taught me died on the frigid air. I ran the tip of my tongue over my lips, gasping as the salty saliva stung the broken places in my skin, and tried again. A response came so quickly that I scampered away from the base of the tree to burrow down under the snow-covered branches of a bush.

A moment later, the woman with long black hair I'd seen at the desk was standing over me. "You must let me help you," she said, bending down to look at me. "I'm Babette." She offered her hand and helped me get up. "You cannot hide in these woods," she said. "Osterlitz will find you. You must come with me, mademoiselle." She put her arm around my waist and held on to me while we walked back to a door that led into a kitchen. Once inside, she pointed across the room to another door. "In there," she said, "you must stay in the pantry."

I felt I had no choice. But as soon as I stepped into the pantry, she closed the door and locked it. I'm done for, I thought. She'll go upstairs and tell the Nazis and they'll drag me off to prison. I sank down onto a wooden stool to wait for them.

A few minutes later, Babette returned, bringing a man with her whom she introduced as her brother, Paul. Paul pushed his sister out of the way, frowning as he looked at me. "Who is this? What's she doing in here?" he demanded in a low angry voice.

"She's a night bird," Babette whispered. "She was hiding in the woods. I was coming from the shed a few minutes ago and heard her call. I was at the desk yesterday when Osterlitz brought her in."

Paul came closer to get a better look. "Who did this to you, mam'selle?"

When I told him that Osterlitz had beaten me but I'd gotten away, his mouth dropped open. "Mon Dieu!" he cried. "But he'll kill us all!"

"No," I said, "he won't. He's dead."

Out of the corner of my eye, I saw Babette cross herself before babbling, "A German colonel dead in my hotel. God help us!"

Paul turned to her. "Hush up. Give me moment to think. First of all, he can't be found here. We'll have to get rid of him—and say we never saw him. We'll come up with something. How did you kill him, mam'selle? Did you stab him?"

"He . . . he did it," I stammered. "He got into my bag." I pointed to my medical bag sitting on the floor beside me. "He had a head wound, you see, and was in a lot of pain. And he got into my bag and took out what he thought was a hypodermic of morphine. But it wasn't. It was poison." I paused, trying to think of a way to make my story more plausible. "He injected the poison in his thigh."

Paul looked over at his sister. "We have about fifteen minutes—maybe twenty—before that pack of bastards will want their morning coffee. The two of you go up there and wrap Osterlitz's body in a blanket and gather up all of his things. I'll be back in a few minutes."

The thought of returning to that room sent a chill down my spine that all but paralyzed me. But I knew Paul was right. It was just a matter of time before the soldiers would be up and expecting their leader to meet them for breakfast. I left my medical bag and boots in the pantry and followed Babette up the stairs. She stopped in her tracks when she saw Osterlitz lying dead on the bed. I hurried past her to the dresser where I opened the bottom drawer and pulled out a blanket. I stumbled back to the bed and grabbed his trousers, thinking I'd put them on. But I found that I was too weak and sat down in the chair instead. Babette told me to rest, and after a few minutes she had the body dressed and rolled up in the blanket.

"There's never been a nastier bastard than that one," she said. "Oh, how we hated him." She crossed her arms, threw back her head, and spat. "He and his thugs did nothing but roam the countryside killing and stealing and raping. His brother was taken prisoner by the British during the invasion and he's been on a rampage ever since."

I kept my eyes on the floor while my mind returned to the mess tent on Gold Beach. The man I saw there was his brother, I thought, not him. Then Babette started talking again. "You know the Boche think our country, *our* Alsace, belongs to them. When they came here in 1940, they conscripted more than a hundred thousand Alsatian men into their army. They sent Paul east in '42 and when the Nazis were driven out of Russia, he was taken prisoner. But the Russians freed all the French nationals and Paul came home and joined Francs-Tireurs et Partisans."

She paused for a moment and gently ran her fingertips along the edge of the dresser. "My aunt and uncle owned this old hotel. It was The Forest Inn for a hundred years. When I finished school, they hired me as receptionist and part-time cook. Then the Nazis came and arrested my aunt and uncle and sent them to work in a labor camp. They changed the name of the inn and forced me to operate it as a barracks for their officers. I know what happened to you last night, mam'selle. I know it only too well. And I'm glad that monster is dead. I'll be glad when all of them are dead!" She clenched her right fist and spewed, "Vive la France!"

The door opened and Paul stepped in. "Shush," he whispered, "I could hear you from outside the door! I've borrowed Flaubert's truck to haul him out of here. We can throw the body in that ravine behind the logging camp. It's snowing again, and if it keeps up, he won't be found for days." He looked around the room, then turned to his sister and asked, "Are you sure you got everything?" Babette and I took a moment to check the table, the bed, and the top of the dresser. Then the two of them lifted Osterlitz's body off the bed and I opened the door.

When we reached the kitchen, they laid the body on the table and waited while I retrieved my bag and put on my boots. Babette grabbed a jar of water and a bag of crackers and handed them to me. "I don't know where he'll take you after you leave the logging camp," she said, looking over at Paul, "but you'll need something."

"I want to go to Paris."

Paul frowned. "That's too far. I haven't enough petrol. I'll take you to a safe house across the border."

I reached into my bag and pulled out a sulfonamide envelope. "Inside this envelope," I said, nodding at Paul, "is two thousand dollars American. It's yours if you'll take me to Paris."

I took a quick look at the shabby environs—the smoke-stained hearth, the sooty walls, the scarred furniture. "If you take me to Paris, you'll never have to do this again," I said, cutting my eyes at Babette. Without another word, she stripped off the apron she was wearing and lifted a shabby gray coat and battered purse from a hook on the wall. "Just where is it you want to go in Paris, mademoiselle?" she asked as she started to the door. And I smiled as I answered," To the Convent of the Sisters of Saint Lorraine."

CHAPTER 31

Safe and Sound

London, England • March 16, 1945

Crossing the Channel on the deck of an open ferry buffeted by high winds was an unsettling experience, and I could not have done it without the help of Reverend Mother and the sisters. Over the last three weeks, they'd nursed me, fed me, bathed me, and nurtured me back to health, just as they had two years before. As soon as I was able to give voice to the horrors of Haus Kreble, I'd taken Reverend Mother into my confidence. Afterward, she went to the Hotel Albert and told Marcel Guillion about his brother Rene, and how he and Barney had been killed by Osterlitz. Then she sent a cable to Stoney, relaying the awful news about Barney and Rene, and telling him that I'd escaped and was recovering at the convent. As soon as that cable was on its way, she wrote Stoney a letter saying that he must not come for me, as I was down with a nasty cold and sprained ankle. "Your friends in London must not see you like this," she'd said as she slid the letter into an envelope.

As soon as I was strong enough to sit up, Reverend Mother told an anxious Marcel he could come visit, but for only ten minutes. She propped me up against some pillows and when Marcel arrived and took a look at me, he burst into tears. I told him that Rene and Barney had died instantly in an ambush just over the German border. I explained that I'd been captured and held hostage overnight, but with the help of Babette and Paul, had managed to get away. Reverend

Mother poured cups of hot cider for us, and when we finished drinking them, she told Marcel I needed to rest. "You can see what she's been through," she said as she led him away. "I'm afraid it will be weeks before those awful bruises fade, and it will take even longer than that for all the internal injuries to her back and chest to heal. She has dreadful cuts on the insides of her knees like someone sliced her, over and over, with a knife."

When I'd arrived at the convent, melon-sized bruises the color of eggplant, covered my face, neck, shoulders, and back. Eventually, they faded to violet, then lavender, and finally to a rather putrid shade of yellow. I had a gash over my right eye that required five stitches and numerous open sores on my back, buttocks, and knees. But I knew nothing of this because Reverend Mother had spooned warm soup between my broken lips each night, and after I'd eaten, held a cup of water to them she'd laced with ammonia to help me forget.

As soon as I could stand, Marie Francine and Marie Louise got me up each day and helped me walk the hallways, just as they'd done before. They fed me stews and fresh bread they'd made in their kitchen, and fresh fruits they'd begged from GIs stationed around the city. They laundered my underwear, stockings, and uniform. They polished my boots, brushed my cap, and washed my hair. I'd been with them almost three weeks when I wrote Stoney to tell him I'd be arriving on the afternoon ferry at the Southampton docks on March 16.

The ferry docked on time, and as I made my way down the gangplank, I thought surely I'd find Stoney. But it was Mrs. Cargill who was waiting.

"I cannot tell you how happy I am to see you, Evelyn," she said as water welled in her olive-green eyes giving them a shine like marbles in a pool. "But losing our precious Barney . . ." She tried to speak again, but shook her head. "I'm just so stricken by what happened that I don't know what to say. Please forgive me, but I haven't any words."

She took me by the hand and led me to the parking lot where she opened the passenger door to a Morris Minor. After settling behind the wheel, she turned to me and said, "The Countess died yesterday."

"Lady Lydia?" I asked, as I tried to suck back the obvious lilt in my voice.

"No. I should have said the Dowager Countess, Lady Millicent. Tuberculosis of the spine is a long, painful battle and I'm glad she's well out of it. Stoney called late yesterday to ask if I'd meet you this afternoon and take you to Beech Tree for the night. He's not sure when he'll get back to London, but I assume from what he told me that he won't return until after the service and burial at Stoneham Feld on Saturday."

Gunning the engine, she pulled into traffic. "You don't mind staying with me at the farm tonight, do you? I've some lovely lamb shanks stewing in the pot for dinner. And tomorrow morning, I'll take you into Basingstoke so you can catch the ten-ten to London."

* * *

When the cab turned into the lane at Corrie Cottage the following afternoon, I broke into tears. I was so happy to see that it hadn't changed and couldn't wait to be with Sylvia and Jerusha in our cozy little abode. After paying the cabbie, I removed the key from under the mat and opened the front door. "I'm home," I called. But there was no answer. I walked into the lounge and found a note sitting on the mantle.

Dearest Miss Sands,

Mrs. Kendall and I are taking the train to Stone this morning (Friday) to attend Lady Millicent's funeral and help milord with the reception afterwards. We will return to London with him late Saturday afternoon. There's fresh bread and potato soup in the larder. We have missed you

terribly and pray you are feeling much better. All love,
Jerusha Tuttle

I went up to my room where I took off my uniform and put on a robe. I'd not been able to write to my mother for weeks and I sat down and hurriedly dashed off a short letter telling her a big lie about how I'd had the flu, but had finally recovered. Then I went down to the lounge, lit the fire, and poured myself a glass of sherry. Please, God, I thought, let things be as normal as possible. Even if I'm alone, I'm *here.* Later, I ate a bowl of soup, and by eight was snuggled down in my own little bed in my own little room with one of the books Stoney had put on the little desk.

On Saturday I awoke about noon, took a shower, and dressed. Then I went to the green grocer's and the butcher's to buy some special things for dinner. I found fresh oranges and bananas and enough precious white flour to make a cake. I knew the reunion with my friends would be hard and I wanted to do something to try to lighten the burden of Barney's not being there. I spent the afternoon making mutton stew, fruit salad, and banana cake.

By four I was feeling a bit weary and lay down on the sofa in the lounge to rest. I must have fallen asleep, because I had no idea that a car had turned into the driveway. I heard someone knocking and hurried to open the front door. There stood Stoney, still dressed in the formal attire he'd worn to his mother's funeral. He threw his arms around me and rocked me back and forth as tears filled his eyes. "Evelyn, darling," he whispered. "God help me, I've all but lost my mind worrying about you." Then he lifted my chin and kissed me full on the lips while Jerusha, Sylvia, and Rutledge stood watching.

The four of us stood in a circle and hugged each other over and over through tears, and I all but passed out from the sheer exuberance I felt at being with them again. Finally, I excused myself and went down to the kitchen to warm up the stew and slice the bread. Soon, we were gathered around the table in the alcove for dinner. No one was hungry, nor talkative, and I suspected that each of us was trying, in our own personal way, to deal with the empty chair on one end where Barney usually sat. Rutledge commented on the music at Lady Millicent's service and the beautiful anthem sung by the chapel choir. Then Sylvia remarked on the size of the crowd, saying that the old church had been overflowing with mourners. Jerusha jumped in at that point. "Seeing all them lords and ladies in their finery was something to behold," she exclaimed as she reached over to pat Stoney on his arm. "But it was him they come for, not her."

When I served the banana cake, everyone suddenly found their appetite, and all of it disappeared. As soon as we'd finished our coffee, four pairs of eyes settled on me. They wanted to know the details of what had happened and, like it or not, I was the only one who could tell them.

Stoney went to the sideboard, picked up the coffee pot, and began re-filling cups. "We don't have to talk about it tonight, Evelyn."

Hoping to maintain my composure, I said a little prayer asking God to give me the strength to face those terrifying moments again. I started by telling them about the nice people who'd fed Barney and Rene and me along our route and given us a bed that first night. I talked about how strangers had gone out of their way to thank us. Then I got to the hard part and stumbled around and found I couldn't go on. I started again, telling them how we'd hit a rock, how we'd gotten out of Rene's truck to assess the damage, how the green Dodge truck had come around the curve behind us with four men dressed in US Army uniforms. I told them how Rene had died instantly from a bullet to his chest and how Barney had drawn his Webley and fired a shot that grazed Osterlitz's temple. Then I tried to tell them about the soldiers who were standing behind the cab in the back of the truck . . . about the scopes on their high-powered rifles. I faltered then as watery bile rose in my throat. I looked at Rutledge, because

I could not bear to look at Stoney—especially not Stoney. I wiped my nose on the back of my hand and began again.

"A soldier in the back of the truck shot Barney in the head." I stopped and took a couple of short breaths and tried to go on but found I couldn't say anything more about Barney. "Then Osterlitz took me to a room in an inn and tied me to the bedpost with his belt. The place where Barney had grazed his temple was bleeding pretty badly, and he opened my medical bag and found some gauze and carbolic and bathed it. Then he saw the hypodermics I had and forced me to give him an injection of morphine. He tied me to the bedpost with his belt and stretched out on the bed and went to sleep. It took me a while, but I finally managed to get free of the belt. About five o'clock that morning, I left there and sought shelter in the woods. That's where I met the woman who ran the inn. I was hiding under a bush when she found me. She called her brother and he borrowed a truck and the two of them took me to Paris."

I looked at Stoney. "I gave them two thousand dollars to take me to the Sisters of Saint Lorraine. I hope that's okay. I gave two thousand dollars to Marcel for our contacts working on the border . . . and the remaining money to the Reverend Mother."

When I said *Reverend Mother*, I broke down completely. I sat there as helpless as a newborn sobbing, sobbing, until my nose was running like glaze on a doughnut. Stoney came and knelt down in front of me and handed me his handkerchief. He tried to put his arm around me, but I wouldn't let him. I jumped up, blew my nose, and apologized for losing my composure. Then I fled upstairs to my room to be alone with the nightmare that had haunted me for weeks—the forest so dark and still, the snow so clean and white, and the piercing sound . . . the keening wail of an animal caught in a trap . . . that had reverberated through the rocky hills when Barney's head exploded. I'd no idea I'd made that sound until I saw Stoney.

CHAPTER 32

The Calendar

London, England • April 12, 1945

On Thursday, April 12, President Roosevelt died at the Little White House in Warm Springs, Georgia. Miriam happened to be in her office late that evening and heard it on the radio. She hunted me down in the supply room and the two of us had a good cry.

We were off the following Saturday, so I invited Miriam to dinner at Corrie Cottage. Roosevelt had been elected for an unprecedented four terms, and Miriam and I could hardly remember a time when he hadn't been our president. Stoney made a touching toast calling FDR the most courageous of leaders—a man who had no use of his legs, but walked on water all the same.

Jerusha joined us in the alcove for a dinner of carrot and leek soup followed by dishes of School Boy's Pudding. Just before we adjourned to the lounge to listen to the latest news from the BBC, Sylvia reported that German troops were surrendering in the thousands to General Bradley's Ninth Army on the southern banks of the Ruhr River. "And the Soviets are moving north to meet them," she said. "The wires in my office hummed nonstop today with constant updates about the advance of Allied forces into the heartland of Germany."

As Stoney passed around glasses of sherry, he smiled at Sylvia and said, "That's the best news we've had in years. Please, God, give our boys all the strength—and all the ammunition—they need to stop the damn Nazis once and for all." He raised his glass, "To those who fought and died today, and those who lived to fight another day."

On Sunday afternoon, I sat down at the little desk in my bedroom to write to my mother, but got no further than the date, which was April 15. At that moment it dawned on me I'd not had a period in April—nor had I had one in March. My hands went cold and I laid the pen down and stared at the wall in front of me for perhaps ten seconds. I pulled open the drawer of the desk, removed my calendar, and turned to February. In the little square marked "February 12," I'd written War Bond Concert. Sylvia, Miriam, and I had attended that fund-raiser. At intermission, I'd gone to the WC and found that I'd started my period. I remembered rolling some toilet paper and putting it in my underpants, hoping it wouldn't leak before I got home. That had happened on the twelfth of February. March had come and gone while I was recovering in the convent. Now April 12 was a thing of the past—like my period. During the last couple of weeks, I'd felt a little queasy early in the morning, but had thought nothing of it because my system had been out of whack since I'd returned from France.

I picked up the pen again and got busy with my letter, telling my mother about the dinner we'd had to honor FDR and what a somber occasion it had been. I included details about several none-too-savory incidents at St Mary's, and how much I'd enjoyed Easter services with Jerusha and Sylvia at St Martin-in-the-Fields. I struggled as I wrote the last paragraph relating the sad news that we'd lost our dear friend Barney Fogelman. I did not tell her how or where he'd been killed, and I certainly didn't mention that I'd been with him. But I went into some detail as I described the memorial service we'd held for him at Beech Tree Farm two weeks earlier.

I closed with my usual words of longing and love, and after folding and sealing the letter, I walked down to the bathroom and weighed myself. I'd gained four pounds.

* * *

On Monday, my shift ended at six, but I stayed in the ward waiting for Miriam to return from a meeting. The moment she walked in, she looked at me and said, "What is it, honey? Why are you still here?"

"Could we talk for a minute?"

"Sure. Let's go in my office."

She closed the door behind us and invited me to sit in the chair in front of her desk. "What's up?" she asked, her voice bright with anticipation.

To avoid her eyes, I looked down at my stomach. "I'm pregnant."

As quick as a rabbit, Miriam came from behind the desk to put her hand on my shoulder. "Are you sure, Evelyn?"

I nodded, but didn't raise my head.

"Stoney?" she whispered.

That surprised me and I looked up at her. "No . . . not Stoney."

I watched as her eyes grew wide. "Oh, no! It happened on your mission, didn't it? Osterlitz raped you, didn't he? Of course. Now it all makes sense. No wonder you were gone so long."

She was quiet for a moment and her face took on a distant look. "I kept wondering why you didn't come home when you were supposed to. You couldn't because . . . because you . . ." She gave my shoulder a squeeze. "Oh, Lord, this is awful. What are you going to do?"

I shook my head trying to decide what to say. Finally, I found the courage to tell her I wanted to get rid of it.

"No, Evelyn," she said, shaking her head. "You can't do that."

I reached up and squeezed her hand. "You've got to help me, Miriam."

She surprised me by pulling her hand out from under mine. Then, in her most professional voice, she said, "The first thing we need to do is be sure you *are* pregnant. We'll do a blood test. That would be the quickest and most reliable method."

I stood up. "Fine, let's do it right now."

Miriam went to the supply closet and brought out a syringe and a length of rubber tubing. She pulled the tubing tight around my bicep and tied it off. Her fingers were warm and steady as they located a vein in my lower arm where she inserted the needle.

* * *

The next morning I went to work a half hour early and found Miriam in her office. "Well?" I asked, removing my coat and gloves.

She looked up and I knew from the expression on her face.

"You've got to help me, Miriam," I begged as I took a step toward her.

She shook her head. "I can't. I'll go straight to Hell if I do."

I threw my gloves on her desk and sat down. "Then I guess I'll have to do it myself. I'll find a coat hanger and straighten it out and . . ."

She reached across the desk and grabbed me by the wrist. "Hush, Evelyn!" she warned, tightening her grip. "No more of that talk. Do you want to die?"

I shivered as an image of curly black hair and alabaster skin smeared with blotches of bright red blood flashed through my brain. "No," I cried. "I want to *live*! But having this baby would ruin my life. Please help me, Miriam. Please tell me what I have to do. Can't you do something right here in your office? Can't you give me something?"

"Are you crazy? I'd lose my license. Not to mention ten to fifteen years."

"But how, Miriam? How can we do this? And if not here, then where?"

"I don't know, but I'll think about it tonight. Tomorrow we'll get out of here at lunchtime so we can talk."

When we left the hospital the next day at noon, it was raining cats and dogs so we had to slog our way through puddles to a little tea shop. As we nibbled buttered toast, I told Miriam that over the coming weekend both Sylvia and Jerusha would be away—Jerusha to visit her cousin in Milford and Sylvia to see her in-laws in Delbridge. It would be the perfect time, and probably the only time, we'd have such an opportunity.

"If you don't help me, Miriam," I said, "I'll have to try to do it myself. I don't want to because I won't be able to see what I'm doing. But what scares me more than anything is being alone. I don't want to die—especially in such a way that would leave nothing to the imagination."

Miriam gave me a hard look. "I've thought about this for hours and I'm not going to let you die. But this is serious, Evelyn, *as you know*. And it's painful. And if something goes wrong, you could bleed to death. You can't be alone. Somebody has to be with you."

I'm sure Miriam heard hope in my voice when I said, "You could spend the night in Sylvia's room in case there's a problem. She won't mind. Please tell me what you have to do to make this happen."

Miriam turned away from me and stared out the window at the falling rain while she twisted a napkin in her hands over and over until it became a lumpy rope. "I'll have to inject a solution into your uterus—a saline solution. Over the course of several hours, it will cause the lining to pull away from the wall. Eventually, it will collapse on itself, and if there are no complications, your body will expel it and you'll experience a preterm miscarriage."

I nodded. "Is there anything I should do to prepare?"

"Pray," Miriam said, her voice as hard as steel. "Pray that nothing goes wrong. And keep lots of aspirin handy. You'll need it." She got up and threw the twisted napkin on her empty plate. I could almost see steam coming out of her ears when she looked down at me and hissed, "I don't like this, Evelyn. I don't like it one bit. And if it were anyone but you, I'd . . ."

We walked out into the rain together, sharing an umbrella, while cold water washed over our ankles. As we started up the steps at St Mary's, Miriam turned to me and said, "After our shifts end on Friday, I'll go to Corrie Cottage with you and take my med bag and nightgown."

I squeezed her arm. "God bless you, honey."

"No," she said, her voice flat. "God help me."

* * *

I removed my underpants, crawled onto the bed in nothing but a short nightgown, and pulled the sheet over me. Miriam settled her medical bag on the little desk, opened it, and began removing the things she would need: cotton wool, a roll of gauze, carbolic, and a large syringe. She brought out the scissors and cut a long strip of gauze on which she laid a nine-inch needle. "It's a bit cool in here, Evelyn," she said, "I think I'd better light the fire." She removed a match from a box on the mantel, struck it, and carefully inserted the little flame into the pile of coals stacked in the grate. Then she turned to me. "I need to go down to the kitchen and boil some water. I'll be back in a moment."

A few minutes later she returned, bringing Stoney with her. He stumbled as he came quickly toward me, his face flushed, his breathing labored. It was obvious he'd come running from Croxdon House the moment she'd called.

He went down on his knees beside the bed and grabbed my hand. "Evelyn, please don't do this," he begged. "Please take some time to think this through." The same words my mother had said to me just before I'd left New York in 1941.

I looked over his shoulder at Miriam. "*Why* did you tell him?"

"Because I . . . I can't do it. And I don't think you should either. This isn't like you, Evelyn. You're better than this."

"Miriam's right," Stoney said. "You are better than this, Evelyn. You're not only better, you're stronger . . . the strongest woman I know . . . and a hell of a lot stronger than most men. Just think what you've been through and what you've accomplished over the last few years. Surely having a baby is easier than being hunted down, *and shot*, by the Gestapo."

I tried to pull away. "You don't understand, Stoney. I'm pregnant because . . ." I took a deep breath. "The baby is the result of . . ." I stopped again.

"Osterlitz," Stoney said. He got up from his knees and sat down on the bed beside me. "Osterlitz raped you, didn't he?"

I glanced quickly away from him, but he persisted. "Do you want to tell me about it?"

"No!" I shouted jerking my hand from his. "I'm trying to forget about it! I . . . I thought he was going to kill me. I *knew* he was going to kill me."

I closed my eyes and leaned into the pillows behind me. I tried not to cry, but tears oozed from under my lids as the disgusting smell of Osterlitz's body returned. I shuddered and drew back, trying to hide myself from that memory.

Stoney squeezed my hand. "Just try to relax, Evelyn, and rest for a while. I'll come back in a bit."

"No," I whispered. "No, I have to deal with this sooner or later. And you have to know the truth. I killed Osterlitz."

Stoney stood up and Miriam came to stand beside him. "Good lord!" she blurted. "You used that potassium chloride, didn't you?"

I nodded to her, then looked back at Stoney. "When Miriam and I packed my medical bag for the mission, she insisted I take a hypodermic filled with potassium chloride as a precaution. It saved my life. Osterlitz was passed-out drunk and full of morphine. So I tied his wrists and ankles to the bedposts and got up on the bed and put the needle in his heart."

Stoney grinned. "Good," he said. "Just what the goddam bastard deserved."

"We were in a hotel—an old inn way back in the woods just inside the German border. Babette, the woman who ran the inn, hated Osterlitz. And so did her brother, Paul. They were the ones who carried his body out of the hotel. Babette wrapped it in a blanket and they put it in the back of a truck. Paul drove down several back roads until we came to a deserted logging camp. He and Babette dragged the body out of the back and propped it against a rock. Then Babette covered my front with the blanket to protect my uniform and I used Osterlitz's pistol to shoot him in the head. I put the bullet into his temple right where Barney had grazed him, hoping it would look like a suicide because I was worried that when a dead SS colonel was found, there would be reprisals. We pushed his body over the side of a ravine. I rolled the bloody blanket we'd used around a couple of large rocks, and when we crossed the bridge over the Marne, I threw it in. Babette and Paul took me on to the convent."

I drew a long breath. "Now I'm in a mess. I can't have the child of a monster like Osterlitz. I know every time I look at it, I'll see him . . ." I buried my face in my hands. "I don't want it," I sobbed, "but I'm terrified of what might happen if I try to get rid of it."

Stoney pulled my hands away from my face and gave me a stern look. "Your baby is innocent, Evelyn, and it deserves to live. Why don't you go ahead and have it," he said, pausing for a moment to cock his head to one side, "and I'll raise it."

I almost laughed. "Stoney," I said, shaking my head, "you can't be serious. What would you do with a baby?"

"The same things I did for the babies I had. I'll feed it and rock it to sleep and love it. I'll do the things you do for a baby. I've had three, remember? It's not like I don't know what to do. Let's try to find a way to do this, Evelyn. You don't want the baby. But I do. You can go to Beech Tree Farm and live there with Mrs. Cargill until the baby comes. Rest assured you'll get the best possible care. And after the baby is born, I'll bring it home to Croxdon House and raise it as my own."

At that point, Miriam began to back away. "I can see I'm not needed now, so I'll go downstairs and make us some tea," she said before she left the room.

Stoney moved closer, and with his fingertips, gently lifted my chin. The look he gave me bored right through to my brain. "Do you love me, Evelyn Sanderson?"

I nodded. "Yes," I whispered. "I love you, Stoney Beeton-Howard. I've loved you since that day in the Dower House at Stoneham Feld when you told me that you knew who I was when we met on the train."

"Then let me do this for you."

"You're so good, Stoney," I mumbled, "and I sincerely appreciate the offer. But it wouldn't be fair."

"*Fair!* Who said anything about fair? This is not a cricket match, Evelyn. It has nothing to do with fair. Let me tell you something, pretty lady. There's no issue worthy of consideration in this argument more important than the simple fact that I love you. And right now, for the first time, I'm going to tell you just how much you mean to me. Back in the winter of 1941 before we met, I was just a man who was going along—going along with the death of my son, going along with a deranged wife, going along with a sick mother, going along with my job. My life could have been summed up on my breakfast plate—two poached eggs, two pieces of bacon, and toast with marmalade . . . every day . . . every single day. But the morning after you and I met on the train from Southampton, I threw my breakfast plate across the room. And I told Hatch I never wanted to eat another poached egg as long as I lived. I didn't know it then, but that was my first awakening to the realization that there was still something I wanted out of life. That cold December night when you stepped into that train carriage in your fancy new shoes and funny little hat, you turned my world upside down. It was as if a heavy fog had miraculously lifted and the air was suddenly clean and new and full of promise. Remember the night of your first Red Cross Christmas party when we danced to 'Beat Me Daddy, Eight to the Bar'? Whirling around with you, I felt as if I were sixteen again. That was a heady feeling and I didn't want to let it go. When you came into my life, darling, my whole perspective changed. Now I find myself laughing out loud when I'm alone—and whistling—something I haven't done in years. I smile more. I'm much happier and at ease with myself. And in spite of all the daunting situations we've found ourselves in—including this last one—I still have hope. I have hope because of *you*."

By then I was sniffling. Stoney pulled a handkerchief from his jacket pocket and I wiped my eyes and blew my nose while he smiled at me. "Oh, Evelyn," he said, "you look like hell. Please stop crying and let's find our way through this."

There was a knock on the door and Miriam poked her head in. "Are you all doing okay?" she asked. "I've got the tea pot on and Jerusha left a tin of cookies on the sideboard."

"Go on," I said to Stoney. "I'll put on some slacks and join you just as soon as I dress and wash my face."

Stoney started toward the door, but turned around and came back to stand beside the bed. "My offer still stands. You can live at Beech Tree, if you want, until the baby is born. Then I'll adopt it. I can't abide the thought of you doing harm to yourself, Evelyn, or to any part of you. And that baby is definitely a part of you. Please don't do anything rash."

"I know having the baby is the right thing to do, Stoney. But what am I going to tell my mother? And Sylvia and

Jerusha? What am I going to tell them? They'll want to know why I'm leaving and they deserve to know the truth."

Stoney appeared lost in thought for a moment. "You may not need to tell your mother anything," he said. "If the war were to end in the next few weeks . . . perhaps by June . . . no civilian would be given permission to board a ship and cross the Atlantic for months. You could just write your mother and tell her about your work at the hospital, as you've always done. When the war ends, all the hospitals in London will surely be swamped with sick soldiers from all around the globe. So, dealing with that will be easy. As for Jerusha and Sylvia, I'll be glad to tell them if you want me to."

My hands grew cold at the thought of having to talk about Osterlitz again, but I knew I had to tell my housemates what happened. "No. I'll talk to them after they get back home. Go on down now and have your tea with Miriam. I'll be there in just a moment."

Stoney gave me a smile as he closed the door, leaving me alone in the little room that had been my private haven for the past four years. Oh, how I shall miss you, I thought, gazing at the old wardrobe where Jerusha had carefully arranged my things when I'd moved in. And there beside it was the desk where I'd written my mother so often. On it sat the collection of books Stoney had left for me that first day. My eyes traveled to the little fireplace where I paused to focus on the bright orange glow of the coals as they radiated warmth into the room and stirred up memories of the times my friends and I had shared at Corrie Cottage—the pleasant meals around the table in the alcove, the deeply personal moments when we'd bared our souls giving voice to our deepest fears and secret longings, the laughter, the tears, the heartfelt devotion we'd felt for one another. I'd never been a member of a more intimate caring group. And while it was clear that over the past few years these dear people had become my family, I'd been so preoccupied with work at St Mary's, with the Beech Tree missions, with Red Cross events, that until now I hadn't fully appreciated what all of that meant. How would I ever adjust to life without them?

The sound of footsteps outside the door startled me. I grabbed my robe from the end of the bed and slipped it on just as Stoney came in.

"Are you all right, dearest?" he asked. "Miriam sent me to tell you the tea is getting cold. You're not worrying about the baby, are you? I thought that was settled."

"No," I replied. "I was thinking about something else entirely . . . something I should have realized long ago."

Stoney crossed the room and put his arms around me. As he pulled me close, he said, "Promise me you won't do anything foolish, darling. I've lost my daughters and my son, my father, my brother, my mother, and my dearest friend. I can't lose you, too. Nor any part of you." He released me for a moment, and when I looked up, I saw tears in his eyes. "We'll work this out together, won't we?" he whispered. "Promise me, Evelyn."

As I gently wiped a drop of water from his cheek, I promised. "You have my word, dear Stoney. Now go away and let me dress. I'll join you shortly."

EPILOGUE

The Times, London; 18 August, 1995 *Lady Evelyn Beeton-Howard, Countess Croxdon, passed away at her Hyde Park home on Thursday last following a brief illness. She was preceded in death by her husband, Lord Charles Edmund Stoneham Beeton-Howard, Sixth Earl Croxdon. The daughter of the late Carl and Anna Sanderson of Baker, North Carolina, USA, Lady Beeton-Howard came to England in 1941 to join the Red Cross. After serving briefly in a RC Hospitality Unit, she worked as a nurse at St Mary's Hospital where she received the Bronze Award for meritorious service as Assistant Matron of Emergency Surgery from 1942-45.*

Prior to coming to England, Lady Beeton-Howard achieved fame as Eve Sands, a well-known performer on the Broadway stage. She appeared in such musicals as Gay Divorce; Anything Goes; Very Warm for May; Red, Hot and Blue; and, DuBarry Was a Lady. In 1932, she won the Fresh Face Award presented by the Broadway Theatre Producers' Association.

During World War II, Countess Croxdon was a member of the Beech Tree Group, a non-military underground organization that provided resources to Resistance forces on the Continent. In 1942, she was deemed Most Honorable Servant of the Realm by Prime Minister Winston Churchill. In 1944, she was made a Chevalier of the Legion of Honor and awarded the Cross of Saint Lorraine by General Charles de Gaulle. In September of 1944, King George VI conferred upon her the Order of the Golden Oak for courageous work during Operation Overlord; and in 1945, His Majesty awarded Lady Beeton-Howard the esteemed King George Medal for valor during The Ardennes Campaign.

Lord and Lady Beeton-Howard are survived by their daughter, Lady Anna Claire Beeton-Howard, who is President and CEO of Beeton Consolidated Industries, London.

SOURCES

Adams, Helene Deschamps. *Spyglass: The Autobiography of Helene Deschamps Adams.* New York: Henry Holt & Company, 1995.

Albright, Madeleine. *Prague Winter: A Personal Story of Remembrance and War, 1937-48.* New York: HarperCollins, 2012.

Adler, H.G. *The Journey.* New York: Random House, 2008.

Anthony, Evelyn. *Voices on the Wind.* New York: Putnam & Sons, 1985.

Banning, Margaret C. *Letters from England, 1942.* Philadelphia: Harper & Brothers, 1943.

Belfoure, Charles, *The Paris Architect.* Naperville, IL: Sourcebooks Landmark, 2013.

Binney, Marcus. *The Women Who Lived for Danger.* New York: William Morrow, 2002.

Cavanaugh, Jack. *The Victors.* Colorado Springs, Co: Chariot Victor Publishing, 1998.

Chiaverini, Jennifer. *The Spymistress.* New York: Dutton, 2013.

Craig, Phil, Producer. *Finest Hour: The Battle of Britain.* Boston, MA: PBS Home Video, WGBH, 2003.

Davies, Peter Ho. *The Welsh Girl*. New York: Houghton-Mifflin, 2007.

Devereaux-Rochester, Elizabeth. *Full Moon to France*. New York: Harper & Row, 1977.

Faulks, Sebastian. *Charlotte Gray*. New York: Random House, 1998.

Fraser, David. *BLITZ: A Novel of Wartime London*. New York: Doubleday & Company, 1979.

Furst, Alan. *Night Soldiers*. New York: Houghton-Mifflin, 1988.

Gilbo, Patrick F. *The American Red Cross: The First Century*. New York: Harper & Row 1981.

Gluyas, Constance. *Bridge to Yesterday*. New York: Signet Books, 1981.

Griner, Paul. *The German Woman*. New York: Houghton-Mifflin, 2009.

Harris, Robert. *Enigma*. London: Random House, 1995.

Jopling, Lucy Wilson. *Warrior in White*. San Antonio, TX: The Watercress Press, 1990.

Keneally, Thomas. *The Daughters of Mars*. New York: Atria Books, 2012.

Lerner, Alan. *The Musical Theatre*. New York: McGraw Hill, 1986.

Litoff, Judy B. & Smith, David, Eds. *American Women in a World at War: Contemporary Accounts From World War II*. Wilmington, DE: Schelary Resources, Inc., 1986.

Lukacs, John. *Five Days in London May 1940*. London: Yale University Press, 1999.

MacIntyre, Ben. *Operation Mincemeat: The True Spy Story That Changed the Course of World War II.* London: Bloomsbury Publishing Plc, 2010.

McBrien, William. *Cole Porter*. New York: Vintage Books, 1998.

Milburn, Clara. *Mrs. Milburn's Diaries: An Englishwoman's Day-to-Day Reflections, 1939-45*. New York: Schocken Books, 1980.

Miller, Grace Porter. *Call of Duty: A Montana Girl in World War II*. Baton Rouge, LA: Louisiana State University Press, 1999.

Monahan, Evelyn M. and Neidel-Greenlee, Rosemary. *And If I Perish: Frontline US Army Nurses in World War II*. New York: Knopf, 2003.

Moorehead, Caroline. *A Train in Winter*. New York: Harper-Collins, 2011.

    Village of Secrets: Defying the Nazis in Vichy France. New York: Harper-Collins, 2014.

Morton, H. V. *In Search of London*. New York: Dodd, Mead, & Company, 1951.

Mosely, Leonard. *London Under Fire*. London: Pan Books, 1972.

Moynahan, Brian. *The Russian Century: A Photographic History of Russia's 100 Years.* New York: Random House, 1994.

Myles, Bruce. *Night Witches: The Amazing Story of Russia's Women Pilots in World War II.* Chicago: Academy Chicago Publishers, 1990.

Nemirovsky, Irene. *Suite Francais*. New York: Knopf, 2006.

Nichols, David, Ed. *Ernie's War: The Best of Ernie Pyle's World War II Dispatches*. New York: Random House, 1986.

Norwalk, Rosemary. *Dearest Ones*. New York: John Wiley & Sons, 1999.

Olson, Lynne. *Citizens of London: The Americans Who Stood With Britain in Its Darkest, Finest Hour*. New York: Random House, 2010.

Last Hope Island. New York: Random House, 2017.

Orringer, Julie. *The Invisible Bridge*. New York: Knopf, 2010.

Pargeter, Edith. *Warfare Accomplished*. London: Headline, 1947.

Pearson, Judith. *Wolves at the Door: The True Story of America's Greatest Female Spy.* London: Lyons Press, 2005.

Pennington, Reina. *Wings, Women, and War: Soviet Air Women in World War II Combat.*, Lawrence, KS: University Press of Kansas, 2001.

Rosbottom, Ronald C. *When Paris Went Dark: The City of Lights Under German Occupation, 1940-44.* New York: Little, Brown & Company, 2014.

Ryan, Cornelias. *The Last Battle.* New York: Simon & Schuster, 1966.

The Longest Day. New York: Simon & Schuster, 1955.

Reynolds, David. *Rich Relations: The American Occupation of Britain, 1942-1945.* New York: Random House, 1995.

Sorel, Nancy C. *The Women Who Wrote the War.* New York: Arcade Publishing, 1999.

Sperber, A.M. *Murrow: His Life and Times.* New York: Bantam Books, 1986.

Stafford, David. *Ten Days to D-Day.* New York: Little, Brown & Company, 2003.

Stelzer, Cita. *Dinner with Churchill.* New York: Pegasus Books, 2012.

Strebe, Amy Goodpaster. *Flying For Her Country: The American and Soviet Women Military Pilots of World War II.* Westport, CN: Praeger Security International, 2007.

Thoene, Bodie. *Vienna Prelude.* Minneapolis, MN: Bethany House Press, 1989.

Wandrey, Jean. *Bedpan Commando: The Story of a Combat Nurse During World War II.* Elmore, OH: Elmore Publishing, 1991.

Ward, Geoffrey C. and Burns, Ken. *The War: An Intimate History 1941-45.* New York: Knopf, 2007.

Wynne, Barry. *The Scarlet Countess: The Incredible Story of Mary Lindell.* Kindle Edition.

CPSIA information can be obtained
at www.ICGtesting.com
Printed in the USA
LVHW02s2021280818
588400LV00003B/168/P

9 781986 277396